PRAISE FOR
Lucie Yi Is Not a Romantic

"*Lucie Yi Is Not a Romantic* kept me gripped from the very first page. It's full of humor and heart." —Beth O'Leary, author of *The Flatshare*

"A sharp, fresh story of finding yourself, and letting love follow. I AM a romantic—and I was rooting for Lucie Yi!" —KJ Dell'Antonia, author of *The Chicken Sisters*

"Fresh, funny, and thought-provoking—Lucie Yi is a romantic heroine for the twenty-first century." —Sophie Cousens, author of *Just Haven't Met You Yet*

"A captivating and original take on modern love, family, and friendship, written with sparkling voice and humor." —Helen Hoang, author of *The Heart Principle*

"My expectations were unreasonably high, but Lauren Ho somehow managed to exceed them. Prepare for a heroine who is laugh-out-loud funny and incredibly savvy." —Jesse Q. Sutanto, author of *Dial A for Aunties*

"Thoroughly modern and witty . . . With a great cast of characters, unexpected plot twists, and complex family relationships, *Lucie Yi Is Not a Romantic* is fun, compelling, and a charming love story." —Farah Heron, author of *Accidentally Engaged* and *Tahira in Bloom*

"A reassuring and tender look at modern motherhood, families born and found, and the breadth of parent-child relationships. *Lucie Yi Is Not a Romantic* exists in that wonderful, terrifying gap between what we think motherhood looks like and what it *actually* is." —Lillie Vale, author of *The Shaadi Set-Up*

"Lauren Ho has a knack for creating stories with a compelling blend of humor and honesty. *Lucie Yi Is Not a Romantic* is a sharp, refreshing novel that explores parenthood, love, and identity. This delightful novel will win over readers everywhere!"

—Saumya Dave, author of *Well-Behaved Indian Women*

"Laugh-out-loud funny and unflinchingly honest, *Lucie Yi Is Not a Romantic* is a love letter to friendship and found family that manages to be head-spinningly romantic while simultaneously burning down the patriarchy."

—Madi Sinha, author of *At Least You Have Your Health*

"Smart, fresh, and incredibly funny. Lauren Ho's voice is so distinct and witty, and she nails the impressive balancing act of writing a book that feels light and effortless while still offering a thoughtful look at friendship, family, and the sometimes-winding path to finding love."

—Martha Waters, author of *To Love and to Loathe*

PRAISE FOR
Last Tang Standing

"Andrea is a relatable, laugh-out-loud protagonist, a high achiever who also gives in to her weaker instincts on occasion. *Last Tang Standing* is a near-perfect blend of *Crazy Rich Asians* and *Bridget Jones's Diary*, yet it still feels wholly original."

—*BookPage* (starred review)

"The combination of an appealing lead, a glamorous setting, and relatable, funny portrayals of relationships and workplace politics make this debut one of the must-read escapist pleasures of the summer. Fans of Kevin Kwan's *Crazy Rich Asians* and Sally Thorne's *The Hating Game* will be dazzled."

—*Library Journal* (starred review)

"A lush portrayal of Singapore life filled with vibrant characters and a lovable leading lady readers will root for."

—*Kirkus Reviews*

"Witty . . . Ho's cute, quippy love story is sure to captivate rom-com fans."
—*Publishers Weekly*

"Charming and witty . . . It's a good match for fans of *The Hating Game*, *Crazy Rich Asians*, and young professional women who feel at a crossroads."
—*Booklist*

"The funniest rom-com I've read in a very long time. . . . The writing is so slick, the characters are so real, the pacing is so perfect! Andrea stole my heart."
—Beth O'Leary, author of *The Flatshare*

"A hilarious transcontinental romp filled with characters that crackle off the page. Lauren Ho's incisive, sharp voice lays bare one of the central questions in many professional women's lives: Is everything we give up to live a 'good life' worth it?"
—Andie J. Christopher, *USA Today* bestselling author of *Not That Kind of Guy*

"Your new favorite singleton is here and her name is Andrea Tang! Lauren Ho's irresistible *Last Tang Standing* sparkles with that perfect match of hilarity and heart on every page. Smart, successful, driven lawyer-on-the-partner-track Andrea is the most endearing of heroines: trying to be a boss in her love life as she stumbles—uproariously!—through Singapore's dating world in search of Mr. Right. You'll fall in love with this warm, witty, and winning tale of a woman learning to follow her heart—not her head—for the first time in her life!"
—Aimee Agresti, author of *Campaign Widows*

"Joyful, exuberant, and very funny. An absolute treat."
—Nicola Gill, author of *The Neighbours*

"A smart and witty depiction of navigating the world of dating, coupled with the messy (but amusing) dynamics of family life."
—Jennifer Joyce, author of *The Accidental Life Swap*

ALSO BY LAUREN HO

Last Tang Standing

LUCIE YI IS *Not* A ROMANTIC

~~~

A NOVEL

Lauren Ho

G. P. PUTNAM'S SONS
New York

PUTNAM
— EST. 1838 —

G. P. PUTNAM'S SONS
Publishers Since 1838
An imprint of Penguin Random House LLC
penguinrandomhouse.com

Library of Congress Cataloging-in-Publication Data

Names: Ho, Lauren, author.
Title: Lucie Yi is not a romantic : a novel / Lauren Ho.
Description: New York : G. P. Putnam's Sons, 2022.
Identifiers: LCCN 2022011446 (print) | LCCN 2022011447 (ebook) |
ISBN 9780593422267 (trade paperback) | ISBN 9780593422274 (ebook)
Classification: LCC PR9530.9.H6 L83 2022 (print) |
LCC PR9530.9.H6 (ebook) | DDC 823/.92—dc23
LC record available at https://lccn.loc.gov/2022011446
LC ebook record available at https://lccn.loc.gov/2022011447
p.   cm.

Printed in the United States of America
1st Printing

For my parents

LUCIE YI
IS *Not*
A ROMANTIC

Chapter 1

～～～

THAT SATURDAY, LUCIE Yi headed to the pastel world of So Bébé, fully intending to purchase just a pair of lightweight summer booties and maybe a matching bobble hat for each of her best friend Weina Ling's newly minted triplets. She was not extravagant.

Fall had arrived, bringing bone-stinging rain. Although it was still early, in this cobblestoned stretch of Tribeca the doors were already open, the shops warm with money. Lucie, wearing worn running sneakers, her hair in her usual low ponytail, swept past the cafés touting seasonal lattes and hot buttery things. She had a mission—So Bébé, which didn't do anything as tacky as sales, ever, was having a special Fall-in-Love Fair. Fifteen percent off everything, *no fine print*. Hence the excitable queue even before the store had opened, and by the time Lucie hurried inside, So Bébé heaved with bargain hunters in designer dresses scything through packed aisles, elbows out like knives. The air stank of credit cards and cold ambition.

Lucie hugged the sides of her puffer jacket close. Truth be told, she had considered buying everything online, but the pull of a leisurely walk with a spiced latte after shopping proved too difficult to resist. So here she was in this foreign land, and here was the saleswoman, Erin, a ponytailed strawberry blonde, who had somehow steered her from a rack of baby wear to a display of high-tech fabric body cocoons that would "totally displace traditional swaddling blankets one day" and "would you believe how soft the de-stressed organic cotton fibers feel," *having never seen the inside of an office?*

Lucie shook her head to clear her thoughts and regarded the MamaOneWrap, basically a Velcro-fastened straitjacket for babies. Had the saleswoman really said "de-stressed" or "distressed"? And where could you get an adult size? She could use a swaddle. Her last stretch of unbroken sleep was two nights ago. "I'm just here for booties," she mumbled.

Erin leaned close, conspiratorial advice forthcoming. "But if you sign up as a So Bébé member today, everything is twenty percent off," she said. "That means the MamaOneWrap, which never goes on sale, *would be a steal.*"

Lucie didn't have the heart to tell Erin that she could probably buy something similar on Taobao at a quarter of the price. "But what does it do?"

"What does it do!" Erin exclaimed. "What doesn't it do? Hold on." Erin groped the arms of the cocoon, and alarmingly, the wrap started to vibrate, and a melancholic tune that Lucie would never have picked for a lullaby played. Erin smiled. "That's Tchaikovsky."

Lucie's brow started to sweat. It didn't happen often, but sometimes she got triggered by piano music and words that sounded like "Kumon." "That's . . . nice."

"It's revolutionary. Babies can't resist dreamland. And—voilà!"

Erin, sensing weakness, was now detailing the removable padding, the windproof, Oeko-Tex-certified stain-resistant outer fabric with sparkly eyed enthusiasm. Lucie rubbed her temples. She had a call in—she checked her watch—ninety-five minutes. "The contraption looks really uncomfortable. Too restrictive."

Consternation at Lucie's use of the word "contraption," a hard, unlovely word for such a cuddly store. Erin blinked, recovered. "Oh, babies love it. It's like being back inside the womb," Erin said, with the privilege of one who had been loved without conditions.

Lucie—claustrophobic and seasonably matricidal—shuddered. They'd just escaped, after all.

Erin would not be dissuaded. "The MamaOneWrap is like a mother's embrace, only better, because it will always be there, no matter what."

Lucie peered at the price tag and was glad for her poker face. The RoboCop swaddle was close to $120 a pop. Didn't cloth swaddles cost a tenth of that? But this one simulated a mother's hug! And—Erin's sales pitch was subtext heavy—if it would prevent the kids from needing therapy in the future . . . She sighed. Now that she'd seen the MamaOneWrap, heard the spiel, the booties and hats seemed so basic—even the oatmeal cashmere pixie hats by the window, which were from a "proudly child-labor-free co-op." (*As opposed to what?*) "I'll take six," she said.

"Six!" Erin said, joyous. Her smile could have warmed the sun. "Oh, then you'll have to get them in different colors. They have such a pretty selection. There're even limited-edition prints! I'll bring the swatches so you can see it on a doll." She took out a large, startled doll with a headful of wheatish hair and blue eyes. "This is Ri, one of our gender-neutral, life-sized dolls approximating a three-month-old." Gender-neutral, sure, but still very white. "We also have Avi, which is more, ah, pigmented." Erin's face was flushed.

"Ri is fine," Lucie said, distracted by the bland smoothness between the doll's legs and the weird, flickering eyelids.

Erin exhaled. "OK, let me get the sample swaddles!" Then she was gone. The lone MamaOneWrap lay, a puffy shell, on the counter.

A passing shopper in her seventies stopped to check out the MamaOneWrap. "I've heard of these." She wrinkled her nose. "Bit of overkill, isn't it?"

"It vibrates," Lucie said tiredly.

"There's just so much overengineered nonsense out there," the shopper said. "In my day we just stuck the kid in a diaper, and if it made it through the day, it was a keeper."

She pointedly picked up a swaddle pack from a nearby rack. Lucie dropped her gaze. She wasn't going to argue with someone who thought Panic! at the Disco was a breaking news story.

Erin was back. She fanned all the designs out on the counter. The baby straitjackets came in the usual white, pink, blue, pastels, gray, with a selection of cute animal and fruit prints. Lucie picked out two prints (hippo and pineapples) and a plain, dove-gray one. "Two of each please." Lucie handed her credit card over to Erin.

Erin nodded. "Brilliant choice. Let me get Frieda"—signaling to a lurking staffer with close-cropped bronze curls, also smiling—"to ring these up for you while I put one on. You're going to see how cute the baby will look when it's swaddled." You knew the place was fancy when customer service reassured you on the validity of your choices, even after you'd paid.

Lucie let Erin put the doll into the pineapple-printed one and press the swaddled doll into Lucie's arms. "Hold it. It's about the right weight, too."

Lucie held Ri close to her chest. Its almost cobalt-blue eyes were fixed on her, the blinking stilled. She closed her eyes and breathed. The swaddle or the doll had been scented with something milky and soothing, chamomile and talc and bergamot.

"This isn't too bad," she said, wondering how Weina was coping, breast-feeding three of these at a go. She was always saying that she was too old for her surprise triplets and she had only that one pair of boobs and the babies were sweet but so, so needy; they were always hungry and she was so, so bone tired; she sometimes confused the babies and had to write their names on their fists, their soft, dimpled baby-fatted fists. . . .

Lucie started to shake.

"Are you all right?" Erin said from far away, because Lucie was laughing—and weeping. Loud sobs rattled from her chest without hope of concealment.

"Yes," Lucie replied when she finally could. Snuffling hard, wiping stray tears away with the back of her hand, she struggled to speak in her normal voice. "I-I just had Lasik done and my eyes are s-so . . . so *dry*."

Erin whisked Ri out of Lucie's arms, ducked behind the counter, and started pulling tissues out of a box so fast she could have been a magician's assistant. If she didn't buy the Lasik excuse, she did not show it. "Here," she said, pressing them into Lucie's hand. "Take them."

Lucie blew her nose in a series of honks. "Thanks. I'm sorry."

"Don't be," Erin said, as though (a grown woman) sobbing in a high-end store for children was a quotidian occurrence. "It happens more often than you think." Maybe it did. She reached out to give Lucie a hug, which the latter folded into with an uncharacteristic lack of resistance. "And considering everything that's happened in the last two years—perfectly normal behavior."

Normal. *What is normal these days?* Lucie thought, as Erin rubbed her back and made shushing noises. She was thirty-seven, and she had no idea.

Chapter 2

L UCIE WOUND HER way toward her apartment in a daze, her haul from So Bébé in two cotton tote bags, spiced latte forgotten. She was mortified. What had prompted that meltdown? That was so unlike her. She was always in control, or appeared to be, anyway. Hey, *she* was RoboCop.

She stopped by the park to watch her favorite dance collective practice in the Bosque Fountain area of Battery Park. The instructor, Sangwany, always waved her over to join them, and she always declined. It was almost a tradition now. Lucie sat by the sidelines as the dancers spun and warped their bodies into shapes that were both familiar and not. Watching them always soothed her; today, it did nothing. She got up after a few minutes and headed home.

She made it back with thirteen minutes to spare before her Zoom call, one of only two on that Saturday. The client, CEO of a buzzy polymer company, was interested in optimizing their European structure's tax compliance in light of new legislation. Her firm had secured the client because Lucie had deep experience in international tax restructuring. It was all her. Repeating this fact to herself as she set up for the call, she tried to psych herself up. *You're number one. You're number one.* She even did a few jumping jacks to get energized. But they didn't help; she felt dull, uninspired. She pressed her knuckles into her temples and massaged them, wincing. At least the case was straightforward and the structure familiar, requiring little more than her face time for today's call. She could go on autopilot. Still, she was being paid a lot per hour to project a certain kind of impression. She pulled off the hoodie and put on a pearl-white Chloé ruffled silk shirt and a sharp blazer, and gathered her hair into a neat knot secured by a silver chopstick. A quick dab of tinted lip balm and some mascara, and she was ready.

Clearing her throat, she dialed in absently a couple of minutes before the call, trying to center herself. He was late, and despite her irritation, she schooled her features into a pleasant mask when he finally joined the call.

"Thomas. Perfect timing, as usual. How are you?"

"Brilliant, love, and you?" Thomas Katz, originally from Yorkshire, had invented a type of biodegradable plastic polymer and was now—like so many "tax optimizers"—a resident in the principality of Monaco.

"Tip-top," she said, smiling. Her teeth had just been whitened a week ago, her nails perfectly manicured. You wouldn't have guessed she was the crying kind.

She spoke with Thomas Katz for an hour and thirty-two minutes, though she would bill his company for the full two hours, since he had kept her waiting for twelve minutes. When she was done it was almost two; she was almost tempted to skip lunch but had another call—a much more complicated, triparty one— and needed the sustenance. She opened the fridge, grimacing at the contents or lack thereof. It was a tough decision between a giant tub of Greek yogurt (which had recently expired), a bag of browning apples, condiments, crisps, and something that could have been a burrito but smelled like fish. She threw the mutant burrito out, grabbed the bag of crisps and an apple, and began feeding herself mechanically, chewing while practicing her smile.

When her second call was done, she poured herself a large glass of wine, threw herself onto the couch, turned on the TV— a *Friends* marathon—and tried not think about how she had lost it in a baby store. It had to be an aberration. She was Lucie Yi. Rising star of her management consultancy firm. She had her health. She had friends, family, parents who raised her with all the privileges she needed to succeed. Lucie knew she had a life that most people coveted. Smooth as churned butter. Yet ten minutes into her third episode of *Friends*, she was crying over Phoebe's triplets (she'd always been partial to Phoebe, who was as antithetical to her as it was possible to be). She cried through three glasses of 2015 Châteauneuf-du-Pape, which, quite frankly, was a bad way to treat good wine.

It was eight o'clock at night in New York when she called Weina Ling and Sushila ("Suzie") Mahmood, her best friends since university and primary school, respectively, for their biweekly intercontinental catch-up, a sacrosanct pillar of their friendship.

The Fab Trio, as the women called themselves, were formed, like many good things, under the full moon of a particularly louche freshers' party at their university in Manchester. One-pound shots were involved. Suzie had been abstaining on the grounds of her faith, though she never did need alcohol to have fun, whereas Lucie—who wasn't shy, just humming with self-consciousness—did. Suzie and Lucie, who had been sticking together by virtue of their long history, were drawn to Weina's very bad and very loud rendition of Alanis Morissette's "Ironic" in the middle of the dance floor, where she spun, grinning, before throwing up on Suzie's favorite burgundy Doc Martens. Weina had, it would later turn out, had a few sips of cider. A friendship soon formed, albeit only after Weina offered Suzie triple what the Doc Martens had cost. She had not, to date, paid Suzie.

"Nice to see you," Suzie shouted, on-the-dot punctual. Lucie winced and drew back from the laptop. "Oh, sorry. I've had a couple of these." She held up a takeaway coffee cup with a scowl. "This place calls its lattes 'handcrafted' lattes. Er, as opposed to what?"

"There *are* vending machine lattes," Lucie said reasonably.

"Yes, but I was at a café. Of course the coffees are handcrafted!" Suzie sneered. It was Suzie's new crusade: anti-hipster language-ism. "Why stick the superfluous adjective in front of everything? If I see one more sign that says 'handcrafted,' I tell you . . ." She made a stabbing movement. "Honestly!" Having ranted, she settled down and drank her seven-dollar latte in quiet contentment.

Lucie had to laugh. "Thanks, I needed that. Lemme guess, office again?"

"Where else?" Suzie said. Suzie was a shipbroker—she called it "the wheeling and dealing of ship stuff"—and a partner at her firm. It was Sunday morning in Singapore, and she was wearing a white T-shirt, barefaced, skin shining, her thick wavy hair scraped back into a messy bun, making her look much younger than thirty-eight. "Isn't it ten past nine? Is Weina actually on the call?" Weina was muted, and her camera feed was off. "Honestly, if I can make it on time, she should make it on time, too. It doesn't matter that she has four kids; it's about respecting—"

"I'm here," Weina said in a whisper. Her camera turned on to show a dark room with the blackout blinds drawn, whereupon a hazy gray image—her face—floated into view, jolting the others. "Sorry, I just had to put Aster down for a nap, and do it in a way that doesn't set off Annabel and Aaron, you understand." The triplets, at two months old, were not surprisingly uncooperative with all attempts to sleep-train them two months ahead of schedule.

"Of course, *sayang*, you take all the time you need," said the hypocrite.

"So how are you guys?" Weina whispered. Even in the dark, you could see that her eyes were ringed with circles. One eye was puffed shut. Bucking the trend in many affluent Singaporean households, Weina was handling the triplets on her own without help, while her husband, Simon Hahn, made money in dark, dexterous ways (officially, he ran a cryptocurrency exchange). Arwin, their eldest at five, lived in a parallel universe of kindergarten followed by as many extracurricular classes as was possible to pack into a day before Weina picked him up at six in the evening.

"I brokered an extremely important deal on Friday," Suzie said, beaming. "It's going to be in all the papers next week, so you'll see all the details. I'm celebrating by taking my parents out to that new Michelin-starred Peranakan place Beelan's Kitchen tonight."

"Congrats, love," Weina said, sounding envious. Weina used to be an investment banker until she stopped working after Arwin came along; now she discussed her friends' work with the intensity of a pining ex.

"What about you, Weina?"

"Well, since the triplets are going through colic, which is where they scream and scream and scream for no reason for hours, and I want to scream and run away but I can't because I *love them SO MUCH*—" Weina was no longer whispering.

"Colic! Loud! Sleep!" Suzie whispered urgently, at which Weina got a hold of herself and mouthed, *thank you.*

"Your children are so cute, though," Suzie said. "They almost make me want to have kids." Both Weina and Lucie knew that Suzie was lying through her teeth—she was very happily child-free. The Instagram-friendly Hahn children were indeed adorable, though.

Lucie's chest constricted again. It had been doing that lately, around puppies and children. And she was no longer able to pretend it was food allergies, since she had exorcized a host of allergenic foods from her diet, after she had done an eye-wateringly expensive immune profiling a few years ago the results of which her parents laughed at and said, "Science!" in the same way one said "Witchcraft!"

"Then you can have Arwin over for the weekend, how's that?"

"You mean, like, for a day? Not the entire weekend, surely . . . You'd miss Arwin, wouldn't you? He's your firstborn."

Weina didn't even pause to consider this. "I really won't. I have so many children, you see."

Nervous laughter. "Oh, I can take Arwin, sure. Maybe just half a day though, to ease into it. Or an hour, really."

"As long as you want," Weina said earnestly.

Suzie ripped open a bag of beef jerky and started shoveling panicky fistfuls into her mouth. Through a mouthful of food, she said, "So, how are you, Lucie? How's New York treating you?"

Lucie wondered how much she should say about her little episode. "It's—Weina, don't you think you need to get some help? Professional childcare? Neither you nor Simon have family in Singapore," she said, buying time.

"Professional childcare!" Weina repeated, as though Lucie had suggested she brand her children. "I can handle my own children. My grandparents didn't flee communist China so I can be a weakling."

"Er, OK," Suzie said. None of them were privy to the details of how the Ling family escaped Mainland China to Hong Kong in the early 1970s. Weina had only said that her parents told her it was "cinematic."

"Look"—Weina's voice was dangerously chipper—"if my great-grandmother could raise eleven children, on her own, while her husband worked the fields until he died, age fifty-four, which is like one hundred years old today, not of exhaustion *but from cholera*, I think I can handle three babies and one child."

Just then one of the babies started making chuffing noises over the baby monitor. Weina's face froze. Everyone collectively held their breath until the danger was over.

Weina's lip trembled as she smiled. "They're such light sleepers! But it's just a phase, I'm sure."

"Oh my God, you need help," Suzie said. "Just admit it. Why are you two so freaking stubborn?"

"I used to manage a few hundred million AUM in my portfolio, for clients that used to treat me like shit—so even if my flesh and blood are a *little* difficult right now, I've got it under control," Weina said. "Also, I might have trust issues."

Something inside Lucie's chest broke wide open, but she fought it. She fought hard. She said, brightly, as she stretched in a nonchalant fashion, "So, ladies, something weird happened today. I was shopping for something awesome for the babies, which I bought and am going to ship to you over the week, Weina—"

"Aww, Luce, you don't have to. Just pass me whatever you bought when you're back for a visit next, and make sure you get them a couple of sizes up, you know how babies are, they just take and take and grow and grow, leeching—"

"Yoo-hoo, Weina! You're spiraling," Suzie reminded her. "It's Lucie's turn now."

"Sorry, sorry. You were saying?"

"I cried in a baby store today," Lucie said conversationally.

Her friends froze. "What?" Weina said, forgetting to whisper.

"So I was at this baby store, and for some reason, I just, I don't know, maybe it was stress or whatever, I just started crying. Isn't that insane? Stress, huh."

Suzie said, "Oh, Luce." Then, to Weina, "It's almost October, isn't it?"

"I almost forgot. I'm so sorry, Luce," Weina said, not meeting her eyes.

"It's OK. I don't even think about it anymore."

They were all thinking of it now, even though no one would say it out loud. "You need counseling," Suzie said. "Maybe you're not as over the whole . . . situation as you think."

Weina nodded. "You should see someone about Mark and . . . y'know."

Mark. Just the mention of his name, and what happened, was an icicle that made Lucie's insides clench. "It doesn't matter. Maybe being a parent isn't in my cards. That's fine. I'm good. Life's great. Things are fine." It had been more than two years—she had to move on.

Weina said, in her gentle, steel-laced way, the voice of a woman with four children and no help, "Lucie."

"Yeah."

"I know we haven't really talked about it since Markgate. But . . . do you still *want* kids?"

Silence. Suzie was just pretending to chew now.

Lucie forced herself to think about this. She'd never been particularly maternal. She used to think that children—even the ones that had sprung from the loins of people she loved, like Weina, and her elder brother, Anthony, and younger sister, Hannah—were, at best, viewed from a distance. Like beautiful but possibly poisonous plants. Or rabid wildlife. And then there had been Mark's condition, which they'd been told meant that spontaneous pregnancies were highly unlikely. So, when she and Mark found out that she was pregnant, and she started trembling in that doctor's office with anxiety, sure, but also the wildest of joy, it was a revelation to her. She hadn't guessed that she was pregnant; she'd been on birth control for the longest time and she thought the unusual cramping was something more sinister. Cancer, maybe—she had always been a glass-half-empty kind of person. But a baby! Looking at that tiny grayscale blob, the shock of recognition, of want, hit her full force before she could gather herself. She started to bawl. "I thought I had cancer," she blurted to the doctor, "but this is so much better!"

When it was taken from her a couple of months later, the loss had almost obliterated her. It certainly destroyed them. The New York secondment made perfect sense in the wake of all that. She couldn't wait to leave. To forget.

"Lucie?" Weina prompted delicately.

Lucie stared at her nails. Even among her closest friends, this discussion was loaded, difficult. Admitting that you wanted something that was drifting farther from your reach with every moment, not because of your own ability but because of reasons that were biological, was not easy. "I can't . . . I haven't found . . . you know. It's going to be a moot discussion soon."

She could tell that Weina was picking her words carefully, speaking slower to avoid using filler words. "I wasn't going to suggest the traditional route of romance, marriage, then babies. That's so 2010."

"I wasn't aware that romance and marriage were no longer on trend," Lucie said dryly. "I'll have to let my parents know. And TLC. Where're we at now, *Say Yes to the Dress: Antarctica*?"

Weina stuck her tongue out. "Listen. I'm talking about the heart of the matter: kids. Frankly, the whole 'being in love before getting married then having kids' part is *so* recent in the history of matrimony. I'm pretty sure 'love marriages' weren't a thing back in our grandparents' day—even our parents', for that matter. Marriage used to be about ensuring the family line. Forget marriage: We need to take it back to the basics. What if we just cut to the baby-making chase?"

"Says the woman who married her college sweetheart and cried so hard during her vows we were afraid she would pass out," Suzie said, rolling her eyes. *"J'accuse!"*

"Touché," Weina said wryly. "But I mean—what does marriage mean in this day and age of divorce?" She rapped on the surface of her wooden table. "What's stopping us from procreating just for the sake of it, the way our ancestors did, *Free Willy*–style?"

"I'm not sure that's an appropriate reference," Suzie said. *"Free Willy* is about the bonds between a boy and a rescue orca—"

"I have never watched *Free Willy*. I have no interest—"

Suzie's eyes had an all-too-familiar bulge. "But *Free Willy* is more than a movie about a whale and a boy, it's about—"

Lucie interrupted before the debate spiraled out of control. "Look, I'm not about to sleep with some rando just so I can fall pregnant on purpose. It's not me. Plus, you're forgetting something: it can't be that easy or one-touch at our age."

"It happened to me and Simon," Weina said. "All it took was an episode of *Game of Thrones*—you know the Khal Drogo and the Khaleesi-on-top one—"

"Weina!" Suzie and Lucie chorused in unison. They had

known each other, including Simon, for far too long. If they let Weina run her mouth, Lucie would no longer be able to stomach playing golf with Simon once she was back in Singapore, and she really enjoyed golfing.

"Sorry. TMI."

"You can just get sperm off the shelf, you know," Suzie said reasonably, as though they had been discussing cherry tomatoes.

"I really don't think going at it alone with stranger sperm is for me," Lucie said. "Also, I've read too many sensational news stories about one-man sperm banks."

"No, you dopes, listen. We all know Lucie doesn't do 'unplanned' or 'risky,' so what I have in mind is very Lucie appropriate. I'm talking about elective co-parenting. The other day a friend in Hong Kong—you remember Ali?—told me about this platform called Co-Family.com that she's been using to make connections with other potential co-parents. There's a lot of people on it, and VIP packages if you need help whittling down the numbers."

Co-parenting. Wasn't that basically what Hannah did, with her ex-husband, Gerald, most acrimoniously? "Sorry, maybe I've had too much wine, but I don't understand. What kind of platform is this exactly?"

"It's Tinder for would-be parents, essentially."

Those did not sound like words you should group together— "Tinder" and "parents."

Lucie pulled out her phone to search; she could see Suzie doing the same. "Whoa, this is next level," she heard Suzie say.

"It's so . . . so . . . unconventional," Lucie said, scrunching her nose. "I can just imagine what kind of comments people"—by which she meant her parents and possibly most people in her circles—"might have if they found out I did that."

"Who cares," Weina said. "It's no one's business. It's a brilliant, techy solution to beat a biological system that's rigged against us."

Suzie nodded. "Yeah. I would imagine we'd be having a very different conversation if you were a man. We'd be saying 'good on you, mate,' taking control of your reproductive destiny. Why can't we apply the same standards to women?"

"Why are you adopting an Aussie accent?" Lucie wanted to know.

Weina snapped her fingers in front of the screen. "Don't get sidetracked. Think about it: instead of wasting time dating, you can define what matters to you, and theoretically you should be matched with someone who shares your worldview, or at least wants the same things you do for your future offspring. This way you'd be creating life with a like-minded person. Some of these VIP packages even screen against people with a criminal record!"

Imagine that! Lucie thought. It was a step up from not pre-screening, of course . . . unless of course you're a criminal, but you've never been caught, like Dexter. Hmmm.

"And don't worry, everyone has to be registered with their ID and credit card details in order to access the other members' profiles, and you don't see the full name until you ask to be connected. It's all very discreet," Weina said, sensing her hesitation.

"How do you know all this?"

"I did some research."

"Ah."

"So, all in all, it's a very, very calculated risk to be taking."

"So sexy," Lucie murmured.

"Well, a major advantage you have entering such co-parenting arrangements is how all the big issues should've been worked out before you even sprog up, which is more than what I can say for most of us in 'traditional' relationships, since we're usually confronted with such issues only after the kids have arrived. Like, did you know Simon absolutely wants the kids to go to public schools, and he doesn't want the boys circumcised, like him?"

"Weina!" Lucie and Suzie chorused. "TMI!"

"Sorry, sorry." Weina grinned. Sometimes Lucie believed she said such things on purpose to creep out her friends—actually, she was sure of it. "Look, if you like the concept of co-parenting but don't want to go it with a stranger, then, I don't know, get one of your friends to do it with you."

Lucie ran through her roster—a handful, really—of single, male friends who might be interested, and she shuddered. No way.

"Well, since you're single, and you have the resources, and friends to support your decision, you have nothing to lose by checking it out. I'd imagine the rewards outweigh the risks."

"This isn't the same as getting a date or even a partner. This has lifelong consequences. And it's just so—so untested." It was also exactly the kind of endeavor that her politically ambitious family would strenuously disapprove of, if not disown her over.

Weina gave one of her barky laughs. "Well, that's what people used to say about online dating, and it's not going away anytime soon. This is the future, and it's here to stay. Just promise me you'll keep an open mind and—" A bloodcurdling shriek issued from the baby monitor, and Weina's mom-game face slipped back on. "Oh dear, I think one of the sweethearts is up and . . . ah fuck, it's all of them." Weina never used to swear before she had triplets. "Gotta run and be a milk dispenser to my darlings! Just do the research before you nix it, Luce!" she said in a chipper way, even as a large wet spot was spreading across her chest. Then her screen went blank.

Suzie took a deep breath and exhaled. "Phe-ew. It's tough

being so soft-spoken." She was speaking and masticating in what was her default, normal volume now, that is, with enough vigor to grind bone to dust. "Seriously though, that platonic parenting site sounds like it could be a cool option."

Lucie, ominously, said, "Anything that you have to use the adjective 'cool' to sell is never a good option."

"Just check it out," Suzie said with an eye roll. "I'm sure you'll do a SWOT analysis once I'm off this call anyway."

"Suzie," Lucie said, pleased. That was exactly what she had planned on doing.

They exchanged a couple of updates and gossip about their families until Suzie pleaded work call—she might have been a junior partner, but with times being tough, she didn't want to take her chances since she hoped to be an equity partner. No one was more married to her job than Suzie—it was quite inspirational.

Lucie sat back and considered her options. The rest of her Saturday night stretched before her without promise or surprise. There was no one she wanted to call, no one she wanted to see. The uncomfortable truth was she hadn't made many real friends in the twenty months she'd been in New York—her secondment had a clear expiration date: end of February. Barring any extensions, she would be on her way home, and she hadn't cared enough to make the effort to network. She'd been in mourning, and then she'd thrown herself straight into work, allowing herself the numbing drug of perpetual motion. If her mind was occupied, she didn't have to think; she wouldn't have to feel.

What next, Lucie?

She could jog. She could open another bottle and watch Netflix. Or—she could look up this platonic parenting site.

This is the future, Lucie's Inner Weina said. *Embrace it.*

Skynet is from the future, y'know, Inner Suzie piped up. *Just saying.*

They were both right.

She reflected on this and, with some trepidation, visited Co-Family.com. What could possibly go wrong?

Chapter 3

~~~~~~

Co-Family.com had a distinctly "Match.com for would-be parents" vibe, which was probably better than "Tinder for would-be procreators." The models on the website banner were of real-life, un-airbrushed clients, across the gender and race spectrum, who looked earnest and happy. Even the founder, Ben Carminsky, a fortysomething salt-and-pepper dead ringer for Paul Rudd, gave out wholesome, gentle-guy vibes.

So far, so interesting. As she navigated the site, she ran a desktop search on elective co-parenting. What had always been informally embraced in the queer community was now seeing wider acceptance in the heterosexual community. Co-Family.com's stats showed that up to two-thirds of its users identified as cishet, of which the majority sought platonic arrangements, while others, romance and a co-parent.

She found articles on heterosexual couples that had used the service and found themselves in a kid-first-then-love-blossomed situation, which they saw as an unexpected bonus. This confounded her. Surely any romantic feelings that arose from such an arrangement should be viewed with suspicion—what if they were a result of convenience, of resignation? There was a warning anecdote of a couple where one party's feelings became romantic, while the other's didn't, and how their arrangement devolved from a no-fuss pact to a messy disaster. If, *if* she did indeed choose this path, she would take care to avoid romantic entanglements and choose someone who didn't want anything more than a co-parent. This, she decided, would be purely transactional.

Other than that, the articles she found gave her hope. There were many successful stories in actual newspapers, not just Reddit forums. So, despite her initial hesitancy, an hour later Lucie was setting up a trial account—that is, after she had:

- Checked out the Trustpilot score of the company
- Google-stalked the founder, Ben Carminsky (taken, sadly)
- Considered the different tiers of membership, from Basic (free) to Triple Platinum Elite (very not free)
- Read through the fine print of the terms and conditions of the membership agreement

Then came the technical part: setting up her profile.

Step 1: Describe yourself in a paragraph, for example: your likes, dislikes, strengths, and weaknesses—anything that shouts "you"!

If we ever descend into a post-apocalyptic hellscape or find ourselves in a *Squid Game*-like situation, make no mistake, you want me on your team. I'm fast, ambidextrous, and can calculate risk at the drop of . . .

She deleted this and asked Suzie and Weina over the group chat to write something on her behalf, because she couldn't find the words to market herself on this platform.

Suzie: I'm very likable and surprisingly funny for someone who reads a ton of boring political commentary pieces. I love puns and horror movies. You won't know it just by looking at my rigid posture, but I'm also very generous and kind and, bonus, pro-science. (Do not put "fiscally responsible" in your goddamn bio.)

Weina: As you can tell from my very symmetrical features and high-quality education and achievements, I am both healthy and very good at adulting. I pay my taxes on time and do not have a criminal record. Also, I like jogging and nature walks.

She uploaded:

I'm an independent, fiscally responsible career woman who enjoys documentaries, quirky humor, and jogging.

Step 2: Upload at least one recent photo that shows you being you.

Nice euphemism for "don't airbrush a decade off your face," Lucie thought wryly. But which pic to use?

Lucie scrolled through her private Instagram profile and her smartphone camera's gallery. There was nothing in her meager arsenal of selfies that caught the right essence: serious, dependable, intellectual but full of quirks. If anything, her LinkedIn profile was worse. No one would click on the stern specter she used for her LinkedIn image, where her posture, so ramrod straight it would have scared a ruler, had been paired with hair so coiffed and precisely highlighted it made her wince remembering the five hours she'd sat in the salon, or even the slightly friendlier one they used in her company's marketing literature— no one would want to procreate with such a humorless paper cut.

In desperation, she scrolled though her album of Facebook profile pictures, which, though extensive, came up short. Some of the shots dated five years or more, not because of vanity but just from inactivity. A lot of them had been taken when she was out with Mark.

I was so happy.

She shook her head to clear it. In the end she settled for a close-up shot that Suzie had sent over, cropped from a group pic on a girl's night out three years ago, where Lucie was wearing her favorite V-neck taupe silk tank top, her hair down and her eyes sparkling and easy, trusting, her skin glowing.

The questionnaire got even more nerve-racking, especially once she cleared the multiple-choice ones and came to revealing ones like this:

> Step 7: Rank what matters to you, in order of importance, the following: looks, intelligence, compatible values, religious beliefs, income bracket . . .

There are no right or wrong answers, the prompt to this question said. Being as upfront as possible will help us match you as best as we can! In other words: *Don't try to sugar-coat your base instincts.*

Lucie was deeply private and mistrustful of most attempts to data collect, having grown up in the '90s on a diet of *The X-Files,*

Terminator, and the hysteria of Y2K apocalypse, but she powered through. "The things I do to find a baby-maker," she told Keanu Reeves, circa *John Wick*, who watched over her from her desktop wallpaper—she particularly identified with this version of Keanu, who did not take loss lying down, literally. John Wick's father would never tell John Wick to go back to her—*his* ex—and stop being so calculating. She gave a final once-over to this window to her innermost self, clicked "submit," and waited, wondering if she would get a handful of hits even in a city as large as New York. *God, I hope I don't see my favorite barista on this site. That would make her mornings very awkward.*

The results came as a shock. The database of eligible possible dads in the tristate area was larger than she had anticipated, especially when she didn't check "heterosexual male" as a filtering option. There were at least 50-plus matches within a hundred-mile radius of her, a wall of men hugging furry companions while grinning at the camera. If she was cynical—and she was 100 percent a cynic—she figured the animals were being used as props.

Lucie didn't enjoy shopping, not if she didn't know exactly what she was after. Her forehead was glazed with sweat by the time she read the eleventh profile. "I'm a fun person. I just don't like smiling in photos," she read out loud, scrolling through a series of blank-faced photos of a securities trader, Dan V., in various fluorescent-lit settings. *No thanks, Mr. Serial Killer.*

Would you like to try our VIP concierge? a pop-up cunningly suggested. Lucie threw herself with relief at the message and bought herself access to the Diamond Sapphire tier—the sensible, medium-tier paid option—only to react with dismay when she was given another set of questions, ones that also demanded actual writing. "Seriously?" she muttered, before answering all twenty of them conscientiously (she couldn't help

herself—a blank field was an affront to her). In "Other Consider-
ations," she made sure to highlight that the father had to be either
based in Singapore or able to relocate to Singapore should she get
pregnant. Singapore was her home, and she wanted to raise her
child there, with someone who either shared her culture or at
least understood it.

When she was done, she pulled out her phone. She'd barely
had time to doomscroll Twitter when a few minutes later her message box blinked red. You have sixteen matches!

Let's see who technology thinks I should be procreating with, she
thought sardonically.

She scrolled through her list of matches, in order of descending
percentile. All in their mid-thirties to late forties (her narrowed-
down age range helped), all university grads at managerial level
or higher, a Pantone palette of skin tones.

Carl S., forty-nine, was an Asian American petroleum engineer currently based in Singapore. He was tall, robust-looking,
had gone to HARVARD BUSINESS SCHOOL (all caps), and
appeared to enjoy collecting cigars and watches. He put an inspirational quote as one of his profile pictures, not a good one either
("Shoot for the moon—even if you miss, you'll land among the
stars"). He was her highest-ranked match.

Having always put stock in the safety of numbers, she messaged him.

Hey Carl, how's it fracking. (She was immediately ashamed of
that opening line.)

Hey gurl *syringe emoji* (All right, OK, she deserved a nonsen-
sical emoji.) Sup sup! Good vibrationz, you?

OK, maybe he hadn't left the '90s yet, but the '90s had a lot
of good things going for it, including Backstreet Boys, Carolyn
Bessette-Kennedy's wedding gown, and trans fat.

After they had exchanged some pleasantries, Carl let her know whassup:

> Just so we clear, I know many are fine with IVF or turkey baster, however if you choose me, I only want to go the old-fashioned way. For religious reasons.

She deleted the chat and fought the urge to squirt sanitizer into her eyes.

Taking a couple of cleansing breaths, she proceeded with her next match, George P.

George P., forty-three, Greek Australian, handsome, was a physiotherapist also based in Singapore. She liked that he had a way with words on his bio ("I'm a cricketer who deals with rickets!") and a sailor's tan. He had completed three marathons. A runner! Lucie was intrigued.

Hey there, she typed.

> Hey there, Lucie Y. How's life in NYC?

> Not too bad. Wish it wasn't so cold in winters though.

> I miss the cold! It's fun having four seasons. Australia's great like that. You ever been?

> Quite a few times. I love Australia. Spent a couple of months backpacking across the country with a friend on a working holiday visa. Which part of Australia are you from?

> I'm a Sydneysider. You're cute. How old are your parents btw.

What a weird question to ask, Lucie thought. Er, in their 60s, why?

You've pics of them to share?

What? Maybe he just wanted to see who she resembled.

I don't feel comfortable at this stage sending those, to be honest.

OK fine, does your dad still have a full head of hair? I want to avoid passing down a genetic predisposition for male pattern baldness.

Lucie deleted him and shuddered. *See, I told you this was a pointless endeavor.* But now that she'd actually paid for a package, she'd be damned if she gave up so easily. Her next match was Ming K., thirty-five, Singaporean, and a real estate agent. All his profile photos showed him with a red Lamborghini in the background. His hobbies were "snow and water boarding." He might have missed out on a few English lessons.

K you got any sibling or not, he wanted to know, after Lucie had ascertained that it had been a genuine mistake and he had meant to say "wakeboarding."

Two, why?

Then can, he replied in Singlish.

I don't understand why it matters.

Coz I dowan start anything with a mom who's a single child.

Lucie wondered why, again.

A single child got to take on financial burden of caring for
both parents later when they're old, so not the best kind.

She sat back, drained. What was going on? Were *all* her
matches trash people? Was the algorithm out of whack?

She was about to give up when she skimmed down the list
(for his profile pic, one of the matches used a photo of him at a
wedding—and, at this rate, she couldn't be sure it wasn't his)
and saw:

COLLIN R., 39 (he/him)
Hobbies: hiking, yoga, dancing (*Everyone says that*, she thought cyni-
cally), rock-climbing, reading, traveling (*And that!*), cooking, sudoku
and puzzles (*Well, well, well*, thought Lucie, completely turned-on.)
Profession: Software engineer
Kryptonite: Lactose and nuts

Ah well, no one was perfect. "You had me at 'sudoku,' anyway," Lucie said, clicking on his profile. Collin R. was not holding
any animals. He was on a hiking trail, alone, though she supposed his six-pack was practically a companion unto itself. His
floppy dark brown hair had warm golden highlights under the
sun, and he was very tanned. Big friendly amber eyes that crinkled in a (slightly crooked) smile, a dimple in the left cheek, a
jawline of a model. Something gentle in his demeanor. There was
another photo of him hanging off the face of a cliff, some climb-
ing gear tacking him to life as he faced the camera above him,
making an undignified face for someone so close to death; and

another smiley photo of him, wearing a suit, taken with a couple of friends in a well-lit restaurant. He looked even better clothed. *Well, thank my stars I'm only here to select a potential mate, not a romantic partner,* she thought sardonically, before she started chatting with Collin R., not seriously thinking he'd be compatible. He was too perfect on paper; there must be a catch. Like liking dubstep, or overemphasizing consonants.

How are you single? was her first question. Tell me the truth, cyborg.

Nice to meet you too, he replied, after a few minutes. You don't beat around the bush much, do you?

Right. Lucie's mouth twitched. Sorry. My bad. IRL I have a much better filter when it comes to small talk.

Collin: Nah, it's OK. Don't apologize for being direct. It's refreshing, and the whole point of sites like this, really. I prefer to get right to the heart of the matter anyway. So, Lucie Y., why are you doing this?

Lucie: Talking to you?

Collin: No, silly. Trying this service.

Lucie: I'm getting old and my knight in shining armor died in the last pandemic.

Collin: *😄* Seriously though. What gives? You sound amazing.

Flattery always works, Lucie thought wryly.

Lucie: Well, Collin, I've hit a wall in my dating life, and now I'm thinking, maybe I just cut the crap, skip to what I want, which is to have a child. Or twins. That's the limit though. I'm not greedy. And you?

Collin: I've always wanted to be a dad, and I've . . . well, I've not met anyone I wanted to have kids with.

Same here, she replied, though she was lying. And as a woman, well, you know. It doesn't get easier with age. Biologically.

Collin: Urgh. Tell me about it! A few years ago I never cared about my joints, now I'm popping glucosamine and chondroitin. And I even know how they're pronounced and spelled without spell-check.

Lucie: Preach! Aging sucks.

Collin: Agreed. So how are your parents dealing with this childless state of yours, if you don't mind my asking? I'm assuming they are like most Asian parents I know, desperate for (your) issue.

Lucie: "Desperate for issue"? Who are you, the queen?

Collin: Why thank you for remarking on my verbal prowess.

Lucie: JK. My parents already have grandchildren, thank goodness, so they aren't exactly harassing me. Or maybe they think I'm a lost cause.

Collin: Well, it's early days, but just off the five minutes we've been chatting, and your, erm, long list of qualifications and achievements on your bio, if you're a lost cause just because you're unmarried, then your parents don't know how lucky they are.

Lucie: Thanks. How long have you been on this site? Are you talking to anyone else?

Collin: Well I've been using Co-Family for 5 months, but the 3 matches that I'd been speaking with didn't work out for one reason or another. It's rough out there, even on these platforms.

Lucie: These?

Collin: Yeah, I'm also on GetTwoGather.com, which is bigger and not as curated. You?

Lucie: I see. I just joined. I'm glad we matched up, then.

Collin: I'll thank the algorithm gods later, sacrifice a mouse or something.

Lucie: I was just thinking Co-Family's algorithm sucked before I met you. It really threw me for a loop. My faith has always been in numbers.

Collin: Algorithms only work well when people are honest with the data they give. I'm guessing some of your matches were gaming the system. Happens on all platforms, even real life.

Lucie: Wise words. So, why elective co-parenting?

Collin: I want a two-parent household. More stability.

Lucie: Same. I'm not doing this if I don't have a hands-on partner. I wouldn't be able to work at the same pace, for one. And Singapore is sooo effing expensive. That's why I won't even consider using a sperm donor, in case you were wondering.

She was shaking her head as she typed this out. Barely ten minutes in and they were talking about sperm, easily. Incredible.

Collin: I get it. It just makes sense to give elective co-parenting a chance. Btw thanks for not asking why I wouldn't consider adoption "if all else fails," the way some people throw it out there like it's an easy fix, or an interchangeable substitute.

Lucie: I know. I don't know about you, but I can't imagine my parents supporting me if I choose to adopt, especially as a singleton. Though I'm not sure they would even support THIS idea, quite frankly, but for once, I'm taking a punt and putting my wants first. Of course, my being in New York and thousands of miles away from home is 100% conducive to such boldness.

Collin: LOL. I have mad respect for people who choose to adopt. Maybe I'll do that one day, I don't know. Are you close to your parents?

Lucie: I don't know if we're close, now that I'm an adult and I have my own opinions, but I love them. I have to? I owe everything to them. And I'm oddly invested in getting their approval, even now. There's something Pavlovian about it. It's hard to explain.

Collin: I get it. Confucianism/filial piety. Obey your parents and honor their wishes, it's a virtue; fail to do so and be deemed a shithead by society. Oh, I remember it well. I was raised by a second-gen American mom and spent most of my life in America, but some of it still filters through.

Lucie: I figured you'd understand. Says on your bio you're part Malaysian? I'm Singaporean.

Collin: Oh, yeah. I didn't see that. I guess this is the end, then. Ciao.

She smiled at him ribbing her.

We can't all be perfect, she typed. As in, I won't hold you being Malaysian against you.

He LOLed. Nice. Anyway, because it comes up a lot, at least in the States, I'll just cut to the chase and spell out my ancestry for you. I'm hapa. My mom was Japanese Scottish American, although most people thought she was white. Dad's Malaysian but is now a permanent resident in Singapore; he's Peranakan: mostly Chinese, a dash of Malay and Portuguese. I'm a salad bowl of genes. I grew up in Singapore, left for the States when I was 12. Been here ever since.

Well, I'm mostly Chinese, with some Malay blood from my Peranakan mom's side, Lucie typed. She's Malaysian. My dad's Singaporean.

And because she felt it needed to be clarified: I didn't just contact you because you're part-Malaysian Chinese, although I do like the fact that you mentioned it. Is it an important facet of your identity?

> **Collin:** I don't know. I've always felt, as a hapa and third culture kid, that I straddle so many worlds and identities. But I still felt the need to put it out there that I'm part Malaysian, so that my fellow Americans are exposed to Malaysians who aren't corrupt politicians and swindlers with super yachts. Sometimes we're emo software engineers who hike and read fantasy.

And look like you, she didn't say. She grinned. She liked this guy.

They exchanged a few more factoids, including medical history. It was reckless how much personal information she was giving away to this Collin R. This wasn't even a face-to-face date.

> **Lucie:** Death penalty?

Anti, he wrote. I just don't see any justification, especially when there's no reversal if someone makes a mistake.

> **Lucie:** Euthanasia?

Can I call you? he asked suddenly.

Sure, Lucie typed, startled. Call me. She gave him her number, something she hadn't thought of doing so early in the process, in case he was a creeper or straight-up insane. And then she spent the next few minutes fretting over her uncharacteristically snap decision until the phone rang.

"Hey," he said when she answered. A warm, husky voice. "Sorry to be so direct. It's just"—he laughed, a little self-consciously—"I get migraines from reading text. I'm old; I think I'm going to need reading glasses soon."

"It's all right," Lucie said, smiling at this candid admission. "So, what are your thoughts on euthanasia?"

He laughed, before launching into a diatribe that was earnest and unrehearsed. Lucie leaned back in her chair and listened to him. She thought, *This is nothing like Tinder.*

IT WAS ALMOST two in the morning before Lucie noticed how much time had passed.

"I'm sorry, Collin, but it's a been a long day and. . . ."

"Sorry. I got carried away again. My great-aunt tells me I can yak the ear off any auntie."

"Not at all, it was fun debating about the existence of ghosts, and whether fifty Romero or ten Rage zombies would prevail over a group of ten humans with machetes, but I do have to work tomorrow."

"On a Sunday?"

"Yes." Usually she would never admit to being so uncool, but she felt like she should be honest.

"Wait, I feel like we haven't really looked at the sample size of the ten humans though, and what kind of apocalypse they find themselves in? Are we talking the 'total desolation' kind experienced by the father and son in Cormac McCarthy's *The Road* or a time of implausible abundance, like in *Zombieland*?"

"Good night, Collin," Lucie said firmly, before hanging up with a smile. Suddenly, for the first time in a long, long time, she was ravenous. *Strange.* She decided to make herself a midnight snack: a bowl of instant noodles with fried egg and a side of

Spam—in her opinion, all the best trimmings. She'd balance it all out with a cold-press juice from the twenty-four-hour bodega later.

She was pleasantly surprised by Collin, although the bar, admittedly, had been set very low. It had been such a good chat. The paranormal aside, they'd covered one important issue after another, dissecting and holding each other's positions up to the light. Lucie was pleased to know he had a considered opinion on most matters, not ready-prepared sound bites. And thankfully, on many of the hot-topic issues they were largely aligned. But even when he held different opinions, he listened first. Or he gave the impression that he was listening, at least. After almost two years of keeping mostly to herself except for work and superficial socializing at attendant events, she had almost forgotten the pleasure of having a proper discussion with someone new to her—probing, sparring, building on a thread of connection that grows when you discuss something real.

I know where he stands on so many issues, much more than some of my family . . . or even my oldest friends, Lucie thought, somewhat disconcerted, after listening to his thoughts on mandatory vaccination programs, after they had just discussed their respective stance on raising children with religion.

Surely these were the kinds of questions one should ask of romantic partners, potential or current (*Well, maybe not the "Which zombie is superior in close combat?" question*, she thought)—and the kinds of questions one should answer in all honesty, without coyness. Yet she'd never, in her history of dating, ever asked these questions, instead finding out her partner's position on them months, and in two cases, years after they'd gotten together, and she wasn't exactly apathetic about these issues. But why was it so difficult to be so open about real issues; why did we cling to faux mystery, when we wanted to seduce?

On this platform, she was eliminating risk and increasing efficiency by cutting the bullshit. *This is me. I like X and Y. I want you, and our kid(s) to be fine with X and Y. And if you don't like it, fine, we won't speak again and your opinions won't matter, but if it does work out . . . pay dirt.* And then she got it. She suddenly understood what George P., Carl S., and Ming K. were doing. Maybe they had indeed been good matches with her based on the answers given to the questions raised in the questionnaire, but understanding the value of time the way many on other platforms didn't, they hadn't hesitated in making their deal breakers known (Carl S. could just be a straight-up creep, since there was a bad egg in every basket).

What are my *deal breakers?*

That was a good question. She'd never thought about it before. She'd always just skipped along from one serious relationship to the other (all five of them), like a monkey reaching for another branch as it traveled over treetops. By the time she was in the relationship, it was too late to think about deal breakers, aside from the ones everyone joked about.

Scrolling through their text messages and recalling their conversation, she felt giddy at the simplicity and efficiency of the system. If only real-life dating were so uncomplicated. Could finding a co-parent really be this easy?

Chapter 4

~~~

By mid-October, Lucie knew that when Collin wanted to get off the phone, he would say "it's late," and she would agree and say "Cashew later," which was always good for a groan, and they would hang up, even though he was a night owl and continued posting on his social media—they were mutuals—long after they'd ended the call. He worried about getting prostate cancer (his uncle had it) and would not want to be kept on life support if he ended up in a persistent vegetative state. He promised to support his child whatever their sexual orientation or gender identity. Zero shop talk between them. She understood Collin in a way she hadn't expected after only three weeks of chatting daily. And yet, she couldn't be sure what his favorite color was or if he liked durians—not that those things mattered in the grand scheme of things, especially given the power she would have to pull the plug (he wanted his co-parent to have that power). "I should be able to trust you with my kid *and* my life," he'd said, utterly serious. She spent a couple of nights gripped by insomnia after that call.

And then there was that other thing. If she liked Collin

enough, and he liked her enough, sooner or later they would have to decide if they would move ahead with the whole reason they started talking in the first place: creating a life together, and all that would follow, or not. She couldn't just idly chat with Collin forever, even if their conversations were enjoyable. "If this elective co-parenting thing works out," she said, over the girls' last chat, "I'll never have . . . I'll never have *it*, will I?" Too superstitious to say what she meant by "it."

"Oh, you mean the De Beers fantasy?" Suzie said. She'd been married once, too young, and her marriage had shattered at a rumor of infidelity that was proven to be untrue two years ago. Her family had taken the divorce harder than Suzie and her ex-husband, Hafiz, had.

"I don't just mean marriage." She meant missing out on a Great Romance. What if she met her Someone after she got pregnant? How many men would be fine with that arrangement?

"Now I don't believe in 'the One,' but the way I see it, that person wouldn't be the One if he didn't have the balls to be with a woman who'd had another man's child," Suzie reasoned.

But Suzie and Weina understood why she hesitated. The idea of romance, culminating in marriage or a civil partnership before kids, was so ingrained in modern culture that the thought of someone skipping straight to the making of progeny was alienating to most. Even Weina was having second thoughts. Now that the plan was in motion, she kept asking Lucie to call up Collin's work references, his friends. ("Do you need Simon's uncle in Korea to run some surveillance on him?" she'd suggested, without giving details as to how said surveillance would take place, except she just needed his phone number and his email login, *preferably*.)

"Anyway, enough dilly-dallying, when are you going to let us 'meet' him?" Weina asked. So far, Lucie had been parent-dating him without sharing his profile with her friends. She hadn't wanted their opinions to taint her assessment. In her professional and personal life—with the hard-hitting exception that Mark had turned out to be—she had always prided herself as being a shrewd judge of character. "It's been a few weeks; also, how can we offer solid, unsolicited advice if we don't know more about the man?"

"Fair enough." Somewhat reluctantly, she sent screenshots of his profile over to the group chat. Of course, as soon as they saw those, they were Camp Collin or at least in the gnarly woods Camp Collin adjacent.

"Hello, hello, Mommy like," Weina said, making grotesque lip-smacking noises.

Lucie mimed barfing.

"What, a mom can't express her sexuality? What kind of patriarchal bull—"

"Weina, you *know* that is entirely not what my reaction is about."

"Well, well, well," Suzie said. "He does sudoku and puzzles for fun?"

"Among other things, yes," said Lucie, thinking of the shirtless workout video he'd posted four months ago on his IG that she might or might not have been playing on loop.

"He's clearly into elf porn," Suzie decided on the spot. "You have got to get Weina's uncle-in-law to hack into his laptop. ASAP."

"Uncle Hahn's not a hacker," Weina said automatically.

"Lucie, don't you want to know if the guy whose DNA you are infusing into your egg—" Suzie began.

Weina interrupted, "Do you know how procreation works, Suzie?"

"Of-fucking-course, Weina, I was just being *poetic*. You don't own the monopoly on science just because you made four children. Anyway, as I was saying"—Suzie was shouting now—"would you want the DNA of a man who might be into elf porn?"

Lucie hung up. Their expertise didn't extend to this uncharted territory. She would just have to rely on her own instincts, even if her confidence in that respect had taken a beating.

A while later, she was jotting down her notes on a client file when she heard Collin's specific message notification tone.

I know it's early days, but maybe you'd like to meet up? IRL? If you want, that is. No pressure. I'm free tomorrow. Or next Saturday. Most Saturdays actually. I think it would be fun.

Lucie's heart sped up. Meet up? Already? It had only been three weeks.

Why is he so eager? Inner Weina's suspicious voice spoke up. *What's his deal? What's the catch?*

He's definitely into elf porn, her Inner Suzie chirped. *No, it's worse.*

There's worse? Inner Weina challenged.

He's in elf porn!

She dismissed Inner Weina and Suzie with a shake of her head and set the phone aside without replying. She wasn't putting the brakes on this, but she needed to give herself some space to breathe before she took the next step.

ON TUESDAY, SHE went to a house party of an old friend, Belinda, who had threatened to drag Lucie bodily to her condo on the Upper West Side if she refused. "We never see each other anymore," she'd said; they'd met up twice in the early days of Lucie's secondment in New York and not since. Lucie, who'd engineered it thus, sighed and caved, even though the pair had nothing to say to each other aside from reminiscing.

Belinda's sheer luck in life, in spite of her general blandness—she was the beige underwear of people—made it hard for Lucie to be around her. Take Belinda's fiancé, Adama, and how they met, for example. A rainy afternoon at the Danish Architecture Center, strolling through an exhibition of Bjarke Ingels Group's architecture and philosophy. Belinda hadn't even meant to go to Copenhagen, but she had to represent her audit firm at a conference. They'd reached for the same brochure. Hands grazed and eyes locked. It was love at first sight. He was older, but appropriately so, a teacher of philosophy, Danish Senegalese, shockingly handsome. He didn't even mind that Belinda was cheerfully plain, which somehow made it harder for Lucie to bear. Lucie wanted a Danish meet-cute. And now they were getting married. Belinda had asked if Lucie would come to their wedding in Copenhagen next summer, and Lucie was already planning on improvising a work-related excuse not to attend.

Or, Lucie thought with growing excitement, *maybe I'll be pregnant by then.* Pregnant *and* single? Nobody would expect her to travel to destination weddings, *ever.*

By the time she arrived at the ground-floor apartment where Belinda was shacking up with Adama, an icy downpour had begun and she found herself huddled under the awning, shivering in spite of her padded parka, waiting for Belinda to answer her doorbell.

"Need help?" someone asked beside her, a man in a raincoat who had just arrived. She nodded, the rain making her squint up at him. "You going to Belinda and Adama's? The doorbell doesn't work. Let me call Adama; he always picks up."

He got Adama on the second ring, and the latter buzzed them in. They entered, teeth chattering, and hung their wet outerwear on a rail that had become an impromptu coat rack. They straightened their clothes in the large mirror in the hallway, the light flickery and harsh. Lucie had eye bags that she tried to ignore and a small stain from the rain on her metallic gray silk top. "Thanks."

"I'm not sure what for, but you're welcome. I'm Bryan."

"Lucie." They shook hands.

"Adama's or Belinda's?"

"Belinda's," she said, wondering why he asked.

"Good," he said, smiling down at her. "In case you run out and forget to give me your number."

"Whoa, give it a minute before you hit on a lady," she said. "I just got here."

"So did I."

"Why can't you ask for my number now?"

"Would you give it to a stranger at the start of the evening?" He nodded at the crowd. "Also, I want to give the rest of them a chance to disappoint you first."

Lucie laughed. As they made their way through the living room, cutting their way through a throng of people in search of the hosts, she took him in. He was tall, had dark blond hair, good teeth, and a confident smile. She liked the way he dressed, an olive sweater over a collared shirt, chinos, leather sneakers. He seemed very popular—people kept stopping him, breaking into smiles. Eventually they separated. She hoped he wouldn't leave before she could give him her number.

She found Belinda and was introduced to Adama. "The famous Lucie, Belinda's best friend in primary school," Adama said.

Lucie smiled back. "The very one," she concurred. "It's such a long time ago, though."

"Not really," Belinda chirped. "Well, it feels just like yesterday, every time we catch up. Twin souls, we are."

"You know what," Adama said, cocking his head, "you and Belinda even dress alike."

It was true: she and Belinda were wearing similar cap-sleeved silk tops (Belinda's in a pale shell pink) and black cigarette trousers, shoulder-length hair styled in a side part, and diamond studs. *Oh no. Oh no.*

"I met one of your friends, Bryan," she changed the subject.

"Oh, he's my friend," Belinda cut in. "Or a colleague, really. From my firm. He's also an auditor." Then casually, "He's divorced. His ex-wife, Maura, is a good friend. An artist." Something about the way she said "artist" made Lucie wince on behalf of Maura.

They glanced around the room for Bryan. Almost as though he sensed them, he looked up and gave them a wave from across the room. "Nice guy," Adama said.

"Why did they split?" she asked. "Do you know?"

"Maura intimated that there was a 'misalignment of expectations.' But nothing scandalous, don't worry." She shrugged. "He's not my type, but don't let that stop you!"

"Hmm," Lucie said, warming to Bryan.

She did her time in the party and left, but not without giving Bryan her number. They agreed to meet for dinner that Friday. Lucie did not tell Collin about the date, and she did not tell Bryan about Collin.

On Friday, she left work early (5:40 p.m.) and took the subway to Midtown. It was her first date in a long time. And they had met on the stoop of a mutual friend's! So serendipitous. It felt very promising.

Give it a chance, OK? she told herself as she poured her body into foundation undergarments. *Don't compare every guy you meet with Mark. Unless it's the version of Mark who fucked up. And relax. But also how cool would it be if we fall in love and get married and it was all because of Beige Belinda's house party?*

She entered the steakhouse she had proposed for the meetup (he'd asked her for suggestions in Midtown) and found him already waiting for her in a low-lit booth. He was in his work clothes (a suit), as was she (also a suit with a V-neck magenta silk-blend top), although she had made the effort to apply makeup and put her hair in a loose chignon. They fit right in with the steakhouse's minimalist upscale decor, with its dove-gray suede banquettes, sleek lighting, and wooden accents.

"Only five minutes late," he remarked.

Lucie, unsure if he was teasing or annoyed, gave him a double thumbs-up. "The food is supposed to be good."

"You've never been before?" He sounded a little accusatory.

Lucie never brought a date to a place she liked because she was a creature of habit and she didn't want to lose a place if she didn't like the memories created in it, but she didn't feel comfortable telling him that. "I like to be surprised," she said instead.

When the waiter came, Bryan ordered a bottle of champagne to start, then the house specialty, rib-eye steak and fries for the both of them, and a bottle of chinon red to share. He ordered his well done; Lucie, cringing internally, ordered hers medium rare.

"Dessert?" the waiter—Sean, according to his name tag— asked. "We have Jack Daniels pecan pie and a peach rhubarb tart with vanilla ice cream."

"She decides," Bryan said. It wasn't clear to Lucie if he meant Lucie should decide whether they would be having desserts at all or what type of dessert. She gave him the double thumbs-up again.

"I'll circle back," Sean said wisely.

After he was gone, Lucie and Bryan smiled at each other and said inane things about the restaurant.

Bryan: "Love the lighting!"

Lucie: "These suede seats are so plush. I wonder how they get stains out."

Bryan: "Did you know that restaurants make most of their profit on drinks?"

The champagne arrived, and Lucie took a deep swallow to calm her nerves and loosen her tongue. Date chat was terrifying. It was hard to be clever and funny and careful, all at the same time.

"So," Bryan said, "how long have you been in New York?"

"What, I don't scream 'native' to you?" she teased.

"Nope." They laughed.

"I'm crushed. I've been here for almost two years. You?"

"I'm from Baltimore," he said. "Moved to New York twelve years ago. Where're you from? You're not American, judging from your accent."

"I'm Singaporean. I'm on secondment here."

"Oh, are you here temporarily?"

"Four more months, ten if I extend my secondment."

"You're breaking my heart," he said coyly, reaching across the table and taking her palm. He began stroking it softly while looking deep into her eyes. He'd obviously been practicing this move. "Anything I can do to make you stay?"

"I suppose you could marry me, if push comes to shove," she joked.

His fingers stilled before powering on. "Oh, you're funny," he said, in a "How dare you!" tone.

"Not *too* funny, I hope," she said sardonically.

"I like funny women," he said.

"Do you like them frank, too?"

"Sure, who doesn't?"

He said that now, but it probably wasn't the right moment to tell him she wanted kids—too soon. Men got precious about their sperm when you said that. Suddenly they couldn't put on a condom fast enough.

They started eating. Bryan was talking about food as an aphrodisiac, asking what food she found sexy.

"None," said Lucie. "And for the record, I'm very much against the term 'food porn' and the objectification of phallic vegetables."

Bryan gave an awkward laugh, unsure if she was joking or not. He changed the subject and started talking about hobbies.

This stinks.

Lucie remembered all the reasons why she hated small talk in dating, and how much of it there was. Especially now that she had gorged herself from the buffet of Real Talk.

There were four main so-called taboo subjects on dates: money, politics, religion, and exes. Suddenly Lucie was determined to broach all of them.

She pulled out the big guns. "Are you happy where you are right now?"

"Right now?" If he was startled by that question, he recovered quickly. "Yes, very much so. I'm in a gorgeous restaurant on a date with—"

"I meant with your life."

"Wow, OK," Bryan said. He took a bite of his steak. "Life's great. I'm making good money. I'm, ah, relatively easy on the eyes, single in NYC, so yeah, I'm living the dream. I wouldn't mind finding someone special though." He winked again, but it felt hollow. He was going through the motions.

"You are divorced, right?"

"Belinda told you?"

"Yup. We don't have to go there if you don't want to."

"Feels like you do, though."

"I totally don't mind, if you want to. Let me go first. I was engaged, he showed his true colors, and we broke up. It was bad."

He considered her with a thoughtful expression. "I figured you had a skeleton or two in your closet." He jittered his fingers on the tabletop as he contemplated her before nodding. "OK, let's do this. I got divorced last year. Her decision. No one's fault."

"Then why?"

He swigged his wine and grimaced. "She wanted children. I didn't."

"Now we're talking," Lucie cried. She refilled their glasses merrily. "I suppose we can talk about religion now."

He laughed. "I suppose we could."

The date ended amicably an hour and a half later, both of them tipsy and too disillusioned to even bang desultorily. Turns out that the truth wasn't an aphrodisiac in this case.

Far from it being a bad date, Lucie thought the date had been *amazing*. She hadn't wasted time, the most precious commodity of all, by dating a man who didn't want children. This evening brought home the fact that most people beat around the bush—even straight-up lied—when they first started dating, and she could play the game only to in fact end up with nothing.

Elective co-parenting made sense. Sure, it was risky; it certainly wasn't ideal, but wasn't it better than ending up with nothing? Shouldn't she take the leap at least when it came to having a child?

All right, let's do this.

She opened a message to Collin, typing quickly before she could change her mind. Hey. Sounds good. I'll meet you at 1pm at Elsie's Cake Shop, on Duane Street next Saturday? It's a nut-free establishment.

Great, he said. Looking forward.

No pressure, she told herself. *This is about a baby, not about love.*

Chapter 5

~~~~~~

LUCIE GLANCED AT her phone again. Collin was four minutes late. She bit her lip. That's it, he was definitely going to be a no-show. She had grossly miscalculated how much they'd connected.

She caught herself shifting her weight from one foot to the other and stopped, tugging at the super-scratchy turtleneck of her yellow sweater. It was too chunky and poufy to be figure flattering, which was probably why she had chosen it. And she wore no makeup. Almost as though, subconsciously, she'd wanted to prove a point—that she wasn't trying to impress him, looks-wise. Now, glancing at her boyfriend jeans and scuffed white Keds in Elsie's glossed windows, she wondered if she had pushed it too far. Had she always been so washed-out? What if he turned up wearing a blazer and trousers?

Her forehead filmed with sudden sweat. Was it too late to run into Elsie's bathroom and put on some makeup?

"Lucie?"

Lucie stopped, one foot in the shop, and turned around.

"Collin?" Lucie blinked back the sunlight and stepped toward him, smiling. Thank God—he was just as casually dressed as she was, in a black pair of Under Armour running tights and an indecently filmy running shirt, black suede sneakers, and a light gray fleece hoodie draped over his shoulder along with a small backpack. But instead of giving off the impression he hadn't bothered, something about the way he carried himself pulled the entire look together. Lucie's confidence faltered.

"I'm so, so sorry I'm late," Collin said, engulfing her in a hug instead of taking the hand she'd proffered. He smelled like a fresh bar of soap, underscored with an almost marine note of new sweat. "I got lost, even with Maps."

"It's OK," Lucie said, relaxing. "I'm just glad you're here." *Be cool, Lucie.*

"I hate being late," Collin said. Lucie realized he was reddening and a little out of breath. "I took every precaution to get here ten minutes early, but—" He choked back his words, blinking rapidly.

Oh God, is he going to . . . is he going to cry because he was four minutes late?

Collin stumbled a little, wheezing as he started to break out in the ugliest hives she'd ever seen. Big, pink welts blotted the tan brown of his skin. His face was swelling. Maybe he wasn't about to cry. "Did you eat something with nuts before meeting me?" he gasped.

Collin, it appeared, was more allergic to nuts than she'd realized.

"Oh shit! I had an almond croissant this morning," she said, frantically fanning him with her notebook as he slumped onto the bench outside the café, wheezing as he groped around in his backpack. "But that was a few hours ago. What are you looking for? Can I help?" His neck, even his fingers, looked like they were swelling. Or was that her imagination?

"Just . . . my EpiPen," he said. He found it and injected his thigh in a panicky move before slumping, eyes closed.

"Shit! Shit!" All thoughts of being cool and composed flew out of the window. Lucie was close to tears herself, wringing her hands. "I'm so, so sorry! Oh my God! I didn't know it was so bad. Do you need to go see a doctor?"

"In a bit," he said, pale, breathing heavily through his mouth. "But no worries. Sit down."

No worries? She'd almost killed him!

A bald, harried-looking man in his forties in jeans and a black T-shirt came out of the coffee shop and passed them a cup of water. "Are you all right?"

"I think this lady just ruined my tights," Collin said hoarsely, smiling up at her to show he was not serious. "I'm good. I just need to let the EpiPen work. Then we're going to the ER."

"All right." The man looked hesitant. "Well . . . just give me a holler if you need anything," he said before disappearing back inside.

Lucie looked down at her feet, her cheeks flaming. She was sure he would leave as soon as he could walk, and she wouldn't blame him. Forget the weeks of camaraderie—he'd barely escaped with his life. "Honestly, I can't tell you how sorry I am." She gave a shuddery laugh. "I've never nearly killed someone on a first meetup before. If you hadn't had an EpiPen on you . . ." She swallowed.

"Someone in the half-mile radius would have had one; it's New York. And I'm always packing at least two." He took her hand and gave it a quick squeeze. "Seriously, don't beat yourself up over an innocent mistake. I guess I should have re-emphasized the four-hour no-nut rule." A hiccup. "Thank goodness these yoga tights are pretty resilient."

Her eyes slid down involuntarily. Yep, they were resilient. And tight. She jumped up to her feet. "Let's get you in front of a doctor ASAP. I cannot ruin my perfect no-deaths-on-a-first-date track record, not now."

They took a cab to the nearest ER and waited for someone to see him, Lucie feeling sick to her stomach with fear and finding it hard to breathe. She hated hospitals, after what had happened two years ago.

Luckily, Collin's reaction was deemed non-life-threatening, and after a couple of hours of monitoring, they discharged him. As they stood outside on the sidewalk, Lucie thought sadly, *This is it. Forget about us fusing DNA. He'll never want to see me again.*

Instead, he said, "Shall we go back to Elsie's?"

"Really?"

"You would laugh, but this isn't the first time this has happened to me."

"Stop trying to make me feel better."

"Seriously, you won't believe how many first dates end up with me on my back, dying. The first time at age thirteen, my second kiss, the culprit: my crush's walnut carrot cake snack bar." He waggled his finger. "It'll take more than anaphylaxis to get rid of me. That's my motto in life: whoever doesn't kill me at first deserves a second date."

She laughed. Much harder and longer than was necessary. She had to rein herself in because she could sense another So Bébé–level outburst coming. "Honestly, this is not what I would call an Ideal First Meetup."

He offered her an arm. "Forget 'ideal,' aim for 'fun.' I'm having fun. Now how about some breakfast for dinner? Elsie's has an amazing all-day breakfast."

"I'm buying. Don't even try to go dutch."

"Woman, I'm going to be mailed a giant bill from the hospital in a few weeks. Of course you're buying."

She laughed again and took his arm.

They chose a table by the window and ordered the house special all-day breakfast and two kale shakes. Now that the drama of him almost dying had passed, she felt a strange shyness descend on her. She found it difficult to meet his eye, so she focused on his carefully unshaven chin. It wasn't that he was so physically overwhelming or attractive—her last date, Bryan, was more conventionally handsome—it was how she felt around the entire arrangement. Seeing him brought home the reality, the magnitude of what they were thinking of doing together.

Not that he was a bad choice for the job—far from it. Sporty, smart, a decent human being. And good-looking to boot.

But still not Mr. Right.

Her expression must have clouded over; he hesitated before saying, "A penny for your thoughts?"

"I'm still conflicted about taking this path to parenthood," she admitted. "And you." She and Collin were beyond the smoke and mirrors of regular first dates.

"Oh. And here I was thinking you're my butter half."

She cocked her head, not sure she'd heard right. *Did he just pun?* "Did. . . . did you just say 'butter half'?"

"Yeah."

"I don't have thyme for this. And by 'thyme' I mean *T-H-Y—*"

"I got it." He laughed. "By the way, full disclosure: I'm not a pun person," he said. "But I remember from our chats that you liked them." He made a face. "You sent me so many punny texts. So, so many."

"I'll stop."

"No, don't, don't change who you are. Pun away."

She smiled back. "OK."

No, he's not Mr. Right, but he's Mr. Right Enough, right now. And that, she decided, was good enough for her.

Chapter 6

~~~~~~

THEY SPENT AN hour at Elsie's before heading to a bar Collin was sure did not serve nuts, a small hole-in-the-wall. His favorite drink was Guinness; she drank a couple of IPAs. She bought all the drinks. He joked that he was in love.

With Collin's phones-away policy, she barely noticed how much time had passed until the bartender kicked them out.

"Would you like some company on your way home?" He laughed when he saw her hesitate. "Tell you what, you can stop me at any point on the route."

"OK." She liked how perceptive he was.

It was a surprisingly warm night. She was glad for it; they were underdressed for nighttime in autumn.

"Tell me again, why are you doing this?"

He stuck his hands in his pockets. "Haven't I answered this?"

"You have, but I want the long answer."

He shrugged, keeping his eyes fixed on the pavement as they walked. "Remember when I told you I hadn't met someone I wanted to have kids with?"

"Yeah." Of course she remembered, because she'd fudged her answer to that.

"I wasn't really truthful about that. I did think, with my last serious partner, Nina, that she could be the one. I've always wanted to be a dad, but she claimed she didn't want kids, so . . . so I compromised. Maybe I hoped she'd change her mind one day. We were a good fit on so many fronts . . . and with time, I told myself that was enough."

"How long were you together for?"

"Three years. My longest relationship."

"What happened?"

"I don't know. One day she just ended it, out of the blue. That was about two years ago. Then this Easter, I found out she had married a mutual friend last year and just had a baby." He shrugged in faux nonchalance. "Guess she just didn't want to have a baby with me."

She touched his arm. "I'm sorry, Collin."

"Don't be. I kind of expected it." He said this last part under his breath. He gave a wry laugh. "I mean, I'm not exactly a catch. My nut allergies, my lactose intolerance, my height."

"That's ridiculous, you're a catch," Lucie blurted. He wasn't being falsely modest or ironic—he really meant it.

"Thanks." He laughed self-consciously. "Anyway, I just wished Nina'd told me earlier. Since our breakup, I haven't found anyone I want to commit to, and I thought, why wait? I want to be able to carry my child and not throw my back out. Maybe play a little catch."

"Men are so lucky to not have real biological clocks," she said.

"Agreed. But it's not great to be the old dad, trust me. My dad is one. Plus he was always so busy at work when I was young. I barely knew him as a child, and the divorce didn't help. But I'm getting close to the age he was when he had me, and I think I see him better now."

Would she ever reach that stage of understanding her parents? Their relationship was so distant. But blood was thicker than water, in theory. "That makes sense. I doubt my age is what's holding me back from having a close relationship with my parents. They're just so fundamentally different from me. We get along fine enough . . . so long as I'm telling them what they want to hear. I call it the Asian Parent Filter."

Collin nodded. He hunched his shoulders just a bit when he walked, a trait Lucie found endearing. "I get it. I have secrets from my family, too."

"Oh?"

He nodded. "We all do. But I think with age, I'm slower to rush to unfavorable conclusions when it comes to my parents . . . well, my dad anyway, since he's my sole surviving parent. If we get pregnant, your perspective might change. I've heard that being a parent helps you understand your parents better."

"Maybe. Speaking of, does your dad know you're thinking of doing this? I will be withholding a few key details, let me tell you up front, should we go through with it—just for my sanity and peace of mind. It's kind of fucked up but necessary."

Collin hesitated before speaking. "Yes, my dad knows. I told him over WhatsApp. He's so excited; he's going to the temple every day to pray for a miracle. I should tell him it was effective." He chuckled. "You know, I have so few memories of my dad, having spent most of life after my parents' divorce in the States. And since my mother passed away eight years ago, if things work out . . . Well, my dad is a major reason why I would be happy to move to Singapore, if you choose me. I would love to reconnect with my Southeast Asian and Chinese heritage. And I have a good friend who has his own tech consultancy in Singapore, and I could always work for him. He owes me a favor."

They stopped at a red light. He turned to her. "I guess I should ask, what happened to the dead knight? Is he definitely out of the picture?"

"We are definitely over," she said lightly. She didn't say that her heart had been so dashed by the loss of Mark, that and the other big loss, that before her date with Bryan she'd only been on one other date since, an unmitigated Tinder disaster.

The light changed and they crossed the street. They were approaching her place, she realized with a start. She slowed down, not wanting the evening to end. "You know, when I signed up for the custom matching package, I put all kinds of improbable criteria on there, like—"

"Agonizingly adorable?"

"Don't kid yourself."

He wagged his finger at her. "I'd never. I kid others."

"Anyway, as I was saying, my wish list of criteria in the second round of the survey included 'mobile worker' and 'willing to move with me to Singapore once I'm pregnant,' since my secondment ends early next year. I didn't expect to get any matches, much less one with such high compatibility. I guess I was trying to . . . strike out before the game began in earnest. Unless . . ."

"You wanted a sign that this was the right path to take."

"Exactly."

"I guess I'm your divine sign."

"Urgh, stop flexing your arm muscles. Be serious."

"Sorry."

She stopped a block from her apartment, as he'd suggested. "Well, this is close enough. Good night."

He gave her a quick hug. "Good night, Lucie."

He walked a few steps away before turning around and calling, "Hey, Lucie?"

"Yeah?"

He scrunched his nose. "Please don't consume tree nuts before the next time we meet."

"Right."

He was almost halfway down the block when she called out, "Hey, Collin?"

"What?" he called, half over his shoulder.

"Cashew later," she shouted, before she could stop herself.

He froze mid-stride, almost tripping. He should have run. She would not have blamed him—clearly, she was the architect of her own destruction. Instead, he turned back and locked eyes with her. He was smiling. He doffed an imaginary cap at her, then he left. She watched him till he had rounded a corner before jogging the rest of the way home, not even taking the elevator to the third floor. She was buzzing: despite a less-than-ideal first act, she'd really enjoyed herself. Collin was exactly as advertised, if a little shorter than he had made himself out to be (he couldn't be five feet eleven if they were almost eye to eye when hugging). Incredibly, her punt might just work out after all. She flopped on her bed with a contented smile, recalling the easy, intimate way they'd chatted like old friends.

She busied herself with her nightly ablutions. Now that the adrenaline was leaving her system, all she wanted to do was curl up and watch a documentary, as soon as she was done with work, of course.

She turned on her computer and began checking her work and personal emails, humming, and stifled a cry when a name flashed in her personal inbox—one she hadn't seen in a while, since she'd blocked him on all her inboxes and social media and scrubbed him from her life.

Mark Thum.

She could see a preview of the contents of his email, and before she knew it, she was already reading the damn thing.

> **Lucie. I know you're coming back late next February. Khong told me. Would you please let me know when you're in town? There's som—**

She blocked this latest email address of his, sent the email to oblivion. The pleasant buzz she'd been holding on to evaporated, and she hurled all her pillows onto the floor, red in her eyes. How dare he contact her and presume—*presume*—she would be willing to meet him after everything that had happened?

Grief and fear can mess with your sanity, he'd said in one of his emails last year, as though it was enough to justify what he'd done.

What about my grief? My fears? My sanity? Shaking, she paced around the living room, trying to drown out the images flooding her head, the jumble of emotions that she'd been successful in suppressing for the longest time.

And worst of all, underscoring all of it: a sharp pang of longing for Mark. In spite of everything.

Chapter 7

~~~

Collin: Hey Lucie. You've disappeared on me for the last few days. What's up?

Lucie: I've been busy working. Project deadline.

Collin: I was getting worried. You're rarely so busy you couldn't say "hey" back. I thought our first meet went well—right?

Lucie: Yes, yes it did. I promise I'm not ghosting you.

Collin: Then what's up?

Lucie put the phone down, unsure of what to say. Their first face-to-face meeting had gone so well that she'd finally accepted that she would go ahead with what she was beginning to term, euphemistically, "the Arrangement."

And then Mark had happened. Mark and what he had represented: the Grand Love of her Life. The One. Seven years of life intertwined, until it was all shot to pieces. To save herself, she thought she would put him—them—away. But ever since Mark had messaged her, despite all she had done to suppress the memory of him, bombing the fields of her memory with industrial pesticide, and—surveying the barren land and thinking she had won—stepping away, the weeds of Mark sprang forth with a vengeance. This was how she ended up, for the past week or so, playing a horrible, familiar game with herself called My Ex Would Never! Little pieces of Collin held up, unfavorably measured, against little pieces of Mark.

My Ex Would Never call insect protein "an exciting innovation"! He thought veganism was inconvenient—and he wasn't wrong.

My Ex Would Never wear tights that tight! He favored classic, well-tailored styles and cuts. He dressed his age.

My Ex Would Never encourage my puns! He didn't like them, found them annoying, and pleaded with her to cut them out. And he was probably right about that—it wasn't dignified.

And even when she deliberately subjected herself to the memory of his betrayal, she couldn't stop reliving the good parts, almost obsessively. It was as though a dormant portal had been opened and now all the ghosts of their relationship, the happy and the ruinous, were tumbling out before they could be sorted and banished.

We really should talk through next steps, if we're going ahead. Especially if you're/we're going to move back to Singapore in the spring, Collin texted her a couple of days after Mark's email had detonated her life.

Sure, she replied, filled with dread. She had always been a planner, but now, looking at her calendar, she was overwhelmed.

You're sabotaging a perfectly good opportunity with Collin, she chided herself.

Something's wrong, isn't it? he said, after another day of silence passed.

No, she replied. I'm just working on some stuff.

I'll give you some time to figure out what's bothering you (and I know something's up), but please—don't string me along.

My Ex Would Never let himself be strung along.

I'm not, she said, hating what she was doing. Just give me a week, a couple of weeks tops, to sort some stuff out.

OK, he said.

Weina and Suzie both wanted to know how the whole process was going, after the glowing report from Lucie.

What's next? they asked.

We're figuring it out, she lied.

My Ex Would Never wait around for an answer. Mark was a doer.

THEN THE GAME began to morph alarmingly into Our Children Might Be!, the Deluxe Psycho Edition.

The obvious issue was Collin's nut allergy. Were nut allergies hereditary? Yes, apparently. But the environment also played a part. Collin had mentioned that his nut allergies were never that severe until he moved to the States. Still, nut allergies were definitely not a fun thing for one's children to inherit. Nuts were used liberally in many Southeast Asian cuisines, and nut allergies weren't as common in that part of the world.

And his eyelashes were practically fans. Could they be—too thick?

And hadn't he admitted to her that he didn't know what an em dash was? And said "between you and I" and "me either," instead of—

Oh God.

She was spiraling. Who cared about perfect grammar and punctuation? You couldn't feed anyone with diction or hide behind Oxford commas.

Yet the waves of doubt and fear were relentless. After all, look at how well she thought she'd known Mark, before he'd gone and done something so destructive and callous. Was she kidding herself, thinking that just a month of chatting could be enough to get to know someone, even if they were allegedly baring all?

I was a fool to think it'd be this simple.

She called Suzie six days after the email, on a listless afternoon. "Suzie, we need to talk."

"Hello to you, too," her best friend replied blearily, before Lucie realized it was 5:15 a.m. on a weekday in Singapore. Suzie slunk off to work at 8:00 a.m., after getting up at 7:35 a.m. sharp. She lived in the condo right across from her office for a reason.

"Sorry about the hour. I'm not doing well."

"Hey, no worries," Suzie said. "I'll listen. I might fall asleep at some point. Such is the risk when you panic-call at this hour."

"I love you."

Suzie grunted.

"The thing is, Collin and I should be combining gametes soon."

"How do you manage to make it sound *so unsexy*?" Suzie complained. "It's so wrong!"

"Reproducing this way isn't *supposed* to be sexy—that's the whole point. I'm putting the 'mate' in 'gamete,'" Lucie couldn't resist adding.

Over the phone Suzie let out a tiny scream of disgust and frustration. "Why are we even friends? Why? You are shortening my life span!"

She was awake now, though.

"I know I want to go ahead with him, but lately I'm all over the place, freaking out over the smallest things," Lucie said.

"That sounds like a normal reaction. It's a big decision, of course you can still have doubts. Life isn't, like, a fixed medium, right? You get new information and the mix, the recipe changes. Great, now I'm hungry. URGH! I hate you!" There was some background rummaging and a slow, ripping noise as Suzie tore open a—based on the crunching—bag of crisps.

"OK, listen, you dope, we've been treating you with kid gloves for the longest time because of YOU KNOW WHAT, but enough is enough! Let me tell you what's what!"

Lucie held the phone away from her ear.

"You want a kid. I mean, I don't get it, but sure. You're not in any serious relationship, and you're worried about your bio age. So, being resourceful, you find a workable solution that isn't conventional, but could serve your needs. You even find a perfectly nice co-parent who ticks all the major boxes. Also, independently he checks out, background-wise, as well. No red flags."

"What?" Lucie asked, startled.

"The less you know the better," Suzie said. "And now you're going to let the ghost of your douchey ex waste more of your time? How long are you going to live in the past, Lucie Yi May Ling?"

ıcie massaged her ears gingerly.

e love of all that is good, make a
ınt to proceed with the arrange-
Listen to your gut and trust it."

ught that far ahead. It's 5:30 a.m.!"
."

"Honey, ｙ w what you want to do; you don't
need me to validate your decisions. Now go get him."

So Lucie made plans to meet up with Collin at Elsie's later that
afternoon for tea. They had a lot of ground to cover.

This time, Lucie wore a black wool-blend long-sleeved zip
dress, black knee-high boots, and a beautiful leather-trimmed
shearling coat in dove gray, an outfit that, she told Collin when
he'd complimented her, she'd "thrown on, literally," instead of
"agonized over for ages and chosen for maximum understated
hotness." She wanted a do-over. Whereas Collin was quite likely
wearing the exact outfit as before, except with jeans.

They paid for their food and drinks and sat down with iced
lattes at a table by the window. A server came by with a tray of
scones, clotted cream, and jam, and a large double chocolate-chip
cookie that they intended to split. "I think we need to set out
everything in a co-parenting agreement," Lucie said.

Collin put down his scone. "Hang on, what, like with clauses
and lawyers? I doubt such an agreement would even be recognized in Singapore."

"Well, we don't need lawyers, but we should write one out,

like the site recommends. Even if it's not recognized in Singapore, it's important to codify our co-parenting arrangement in a formal document. It simplifies and clarifies things. And gives us something to ground us in case things go south."

Collin considered her. "It's not a path I normally would have taken, but I see your point. If it'll help ease your mind, then sure. Let's do it. How do we start?"

Lucie released a breath and brought out her iPad. "I guess we should just nail down big-picture stuff, save the nitty-gritty for later. First up: let's start with where we will raise the child. We'd talked about us moving to Singapore once I'm pregnant. That's still the case, right? We're raising them in Singapore?"

Collin nodded. "Yup. At least for the first five years. It'll be good to have familial support. And financially, logically, it makes the most sense since you're the one in the higher earning bracket and with a permanent contract. When does your secondment end?"

"End of February, but I can easily extend it for another six months if we need more time. It should give us some buffer, in case we—I—don't fall pregnant as fast as we'd like whether because of age or because of . . . because of possible complications from the miscarriage." She flushed. Lucie had only told Collin the barest details. "I have an appointment with my gyno scheduled to check things out."

Collin reached out and placed a hand on hers. "Let me know if you need me to come with you."

Lucie shook her head. "No need."

"I know you're tough, given all that you've been through, but if you want me there, I'll be there." He gave her hand a squeeze. "As a friend."

As a friend. Lucie took a moment to marvel at the transition in their relationship. They weren't just two acquaintances discussing zombies and their thoughts on corporal punishment anymore. Collin meant something to her and vice versa. Even if this experiment should fail, she had found a real friend in this experience. The sad truth was that as one got older, life got in the way and it got harder and harder to make new, lifelong friends, so she knew that their friendship was a gift.

"Thank you, I really appreciate that. But it should be fine. And by the end of August next year, if nothing happens, we'll cease all . . . er . . . reproductive efforts."

"Reproductive efforts," he echoed.

"Yup," she said, flushing a little. "Look, I don't know how else to call it. Anyway, if it . . . doesn't work out, no harm, no foul. We'll move on. You start looking for a new match. And I'll send you a postcard from Singapore." Her tone was light, but if this didn't work out, there was no plan B for her if she moved back to Singapore, where a woman couldn't get access to IVF or other types of assisted reproductive technologies, including social egg freezing, if she wasn't married.

This was it for her. This was all her plans, in one basket. She was in the right place, and she had the time, the resources, and the man. It was now or perhaps never.

No pressure, she thought, biting the inside of her cheek.

"That's . . . harsh," he said lightly. "You could at least write me a letter—I deserve more than a postcard."

Lucie smiled. Collin always knew how to lighten the mood. "So, it's settled: if all goes well, we'll move to Singapore as soon as my secondment ends."

"Sounds good."

"And your friend is fine with hiring you, right?"

"Yup, I just need to give him the go-ahead to start applying for my employment pass. It's a start-up salary though, so I have to be frugal. But I insist on splitting all expenses down the middle. I want us to be equal contributors, financially."

Lucie toyed with her napkin. "Is that really fair? I mean, I'm happy to contribute more, proportionally." That seemed like the feminist, fair thing to do. Although she had to admit, a treacherous part of her whispered, *But the man is supposed to be the breadwinner.* Culturally, that's the way it's always been. She silenced it immediately. *We have to work to fight internalized gender biases,* she reminded herself.

"I want to. It makes sense in an equal vote, equal share way." His tone brooked no argument.

Lucie shrugged. "Fine by me."

Now it was Collin's turn to let out a breath. Clearly, the subject had been weighing on his mind.

"Next rule. We can date other people, if we want, during this arrangement. No need to be monks."

Collin said, almost immediately, "No worries there."

"Well, that was quick. Were you already thinking of dating?"

"Well, no. But I just assumed that we'd both agreed from the beginning, in principle, that this is all about making a kid, and if we find romantic love outside the arrangement, that's fine, although we can wait till—"

"Yeah, no worries, I was just yanking your chain. I'm not imposing a waiting period. Do whatever you want."

A long pause. Collin finally said, "What else is on your list?"

Lucie scrolled down her list of topics. "Let's see. There's a whole list. For example"—she squinted at her screen—"we should figure out our position on screen time, our religious intentions for our child, what style of discipline we will use, and things that involve our personal capacities as parents: like if either one of us loses our jobs or our capacity to earn money. Or what happens if either of us falls in love and decides to have other children. Or if we have disagreements, change our minds about the conditions . . ."

He had a pensive expression on his face. "All that is important, but you know what I think matters most?"

"What?"

"That *you* know all the reasons why you're doing this, because almost everyone you know will have an opinion on this and will want to discuss it with you, and some of them will be very firm and very in-your-face on why it is wrong. And you don't strike me as someone who's used to being told they've gotten things wrong."

Lucie folded her arms across her chest. "I can take criticism," she said hotly.

"There you go, proving my point," he said. "Look, I'm just prepping you. I think you care a lot about what people think about you."

"And you don't?" she said, rankled.

He laughed. "Try being the short Asian-looking kid with the severe nut allergies in the heart of Texas. I care, of course—but I also have really, really tough skin. And I'm used to sticking out like a sore thumb." He took a few sips of his coffee before saying, in a voice she identified as his "being diplomatic" voice, "And most of all, you and I both know Singapore has very different cultural norms and value systems from America, especially in the circles we move in, here in New York."

She bit her lip as she tried to ignore the doubt that gnawed at the edges of her thoughts after his remark. He was right— Singapore was more conservative. She knew of acquaintances who'd hidden their IVF treatments from friends because they didn't want the scrutiny; she'd heard stories of couples whose own parents didn't know the grandchildren they doted on were conceived with donor sperm or egg. What would people think about their unconventional arrangement? And he'd gotten an accurate read on her—she was a perfectionist and not particularly daring, but if she could make up her mind to take an unorthodox step for once in her life, then surely she could work on the rest of it.

She looked around the café and caught the eye of a wide-eyed toddler with her natural hair in two lemony ribboned puffs; the child lifted her chubby arms and gave Lucie a hearty wave. Lucie's heart squeezed and expanded till it was fit to burst. She would do anything for a chance at that. What did it matter if people she didn't care about whispered about her behind her back? She would prove them wrong.

"I'm ready," she said, squaring her shoulders. "For all of it."

THEY HAD DISCUSSED starting IVF in two to three months, so that they would have enough time to optimize their chances for conception—Lucie wanted to do a full-body cleanse, abstain from alcohol, exercise more regularly, and so on. And just so they'd have more time, she planned to ask her work to extend her secondment by six more months; she didn't foresee them rejecting her request, considering the volume of business she was bringing in. As for her apartment, the landlord, a family friend, would extend her lease without issue. No problem.

She went for her physical and the requisite scans and bloodwork, while Collin went to get his own tests done. She started tracking her cycle with an app and a basal body thermometer. Then they met with Farid, Collin's nutritionist and good friend, who advised them on nutrition and lifestyle changes they could make to maximize their chances ("More sleep" was his advice to Lucie, once he heard of her typical weekday schedule). Collin had even gotten them both a subscription to a juice shack near her office as—he joked—a fertility optimization gift. On good days, they sometimes went for jogs together.

It was a short walk from Lucie's office to that of Dr. Fisk, her ob-gyn, where she was headed to discuss her results, but Lucie quickly wished that she had switched from heels to ballerinas. Still, the three-inch pointed burgundy leather pumps always gave her a boost of confidence. She needed it today.

Dr. Fisk's office in the Financial District had celadon and eggshell walls hung with elegant silver frames of inoffensive watercolor seascapes. Shallow stone bowls of white orchids dotted the reception table and the side tables, alongside cream leather couches. Though the decor was soothing, it did not help Lucie's nerves. The low buzzing sound in her ears signaled an oncoming stress migraine.

Dr. Fisk smiled as she entered his office, and they exchanged quick pleasantries. "I feel like I'm in school again, at the headmaster's office," she said, nodding to the folder with her name on it. "Anyway, how does everything look?"

His smile faltered a little. "Physically, everything looks fine, but I thought I should talk you through the results of the ovarian screening test. I'm not going to sugarcoat it—the results show that you have lower egg reserves than expected."

Her stomach plummeted. "Wh-what? Can I still . . . can I still have children?"

"You could conceive naturally, but the window of opportunity to conceive may be shorter than you'd initially calculated. There's a lower chance of successful fertilization and implantation, should you choose to pursue IVF. If you do wish to conceive using your own eggs, and if you aren't currently with a partner"—a delicate clearing of his throat—"you should, for prudence's sake, consider egg freezing ASAP. Just to boost your chances if you are still interested in getting pregnant in the future." He had a kindly face, but his words left her cold.

"I-I wasn't expecting this."

"I'm sorry, Miss Yi," he said. "I know it sounds grim, but the good news is at least you know now, and there is just so much more we can do these days to help." He hesitated before he put a gentle palm on her right hand, which was lying limply on the desk. "I know it's not great news, but it doesn't mean all is lost. You do, however, need to take rather decisive action soon. Would you like me to refer you to a fertility specialist to advise you on all your options?"

"Yes please," she said, in a daze.

She started texting Collin as soon as she had left the doctor's office, blinking back tears as she tried to compose herself. Her limbs felt too long, too heavy. Several times she crashed into other pedestrians. She hadn't expected to be confronted with yet another stark biological reminder of how high the stakes were, even though she knew the theoretical odds; she had looked them up.

We should get right to it, if we want a child. We need to schedule IVF ASAP.

What do you mean? Collin replied.

I've got low egg reserves. Isn't that just perfect?

Where are you? Do you want me to come over?

It's Tuesday, she said, as though it mattered what day it was.

I work from home. Don't worry about it.

Yes please, come over. I need a friend.

Chapter 8

~~~~~~

AN HOUR LATER, Collin was at her door with a bag of pastries and two bottles of wine.

"Cupcakes from that bakery you like. I went in without googling their nut policy and risked anaphylactic shock for them."

She hugged him and let him in wordlessly. He removed his shoes and put them on the shoe rack, which she appreciated. "You OK?"

She shrugged. "As good as I can be, under the circumstances."

He gave the apartment a once-over. "Nice place. Empty, though."

"What do you mean?" she said, bemused. Sure, the apartment was sparsely furnished: the high-ceiling living room held a two-seater blond leather couch on a large, oval sisal rug; a tiny copper-legged side table; a tall wooden shelf that held a few (formerly succulent) succulents; and a large, cluttered beechwood desk, which doubled as her dining table, and the only piece of art was a large black-and-white print of the city in the 1950s, which she had inherited from the last owner. But she liked the uncluttered look of the space.

"I'm here temporarily," she said, a little defensively.

"What I mean is, where are the pictures of your family? The books? A lounge chair? The quirky bronze umbrella stand you fell in love with at a flea market with the red stain that you told yourself was just dried beetroot juice?"

"You weirdo." She cocked her head. "Anyway, why would I need all that clutter?"

He sighed. "A lounge chair would hardly be considered clutter. This is actually a pretty spacious two-bedder, I mean, you can Lindy Hop here."

From the slight bounce in his step and his nodding, he seemed poised to do just that. She had to stem the threat. "We have a strict no-dance policy in this building. On account of the bad soundproofing. You'll wake the rats."

"That's ageist," he chided. "You can't call old people that."

Was it possible to choke and snort simultaneously? Apparently it was. She caught the mischief in his eyes and swatted his arm. "Sit. I'll get us some wine glasses."

"Oh, so you do have wine glasses here?" He regarded her with a mock stern expression.

"Yes, what kind of wine did you get?"

"I don't know. Real middle-shelf stuff."

"Right." She returned with white wine glasses. They sat down on the couch and he served her some wine, the pastries forgotten on the rug at their feet.

"I'm sorry if I'm being a jerk. I still can't get over how . . . empty your apartment is." He peered at her bookshelf. "No books. Do you even own an e-book reader?"

"I used to. No time these days."

"You should always make time to read," he said. "Just like you should always make time to dance." He shook his head. "Man, we're really from different worlds."

She told him about the diagnosis. "This doesn't change anything," he told her. "Not for me, anyway."

"We'll have to get started with IVF right away. I'll need to follow up with my insurance, but I'm positive they offer capped coverage for fertility treatments."

"And I'm good for out-of-pocket expenses up to the amount we discussed. Although . . . there's also . . . the other time-honored alternative that we discussed." He cleared his throat.

"Oh, that." Her face was heating up.

"Yeah. I mean, if you want to."

She was sure the tips of her hair were on fire.

"You've seen my STD test results."

"And I have mine from just now. All clear."

"When are you ovulating?" Zero segue.

"The next day or so, I guess." Striving for nonchalance. She doubted she'd ever discussed her cycle with Mark. To preserve the mystery of the relationship or something she'd read in some *Cosmo* article. Well, that worked out for the seven years they were together. So much mystery preserved that she didn't even know—

"Well, in that case, we could do it today if you wanted to." He grinned, looking around the apartment. "Although I'll be frank: I think this"—gesturing around the place—"could be a deal breaker."

"I doubt your place is much better," she said, a little petulantly. "I mean, if I dropped in unannounced, I'll bet. If we did it today."

"I never did believe in putting off until tomorrow what we can do today." He stood up and held his hand out. "Let's go."

THEY DISEMBARKED AT Myrtle–Wyckoff, walking to Collin's studio in the Bushwick neighborhood of Brooklyn, which he had been renting for the past eight years.

"I can't wait till you see my stemware."

"Collin, don't tease."

"I'm not. They are crystal and amazing. And you should see the awesome cocktail cart I have, as well as the other unnecessary accoutrements you clearly have missed out on in life."

"So I'm not a hoarder."

"Sure, but we're talking next-level austerity. A pathological aversion to nesting."

"I'm spartan. Minimalist. Haven't you heard of Marie Kondo?"

He cocked an eyebrow at her. "She did say you need things around you that spark joy. I didn't see a single joy-sparking thing in your apartment. Everything was so functional. Get a vase. Embroidered hand towels. A calendar of puppies."

Collin's apartment was not minimalist. Sunlit, cozy, small, it had exposed-brick walls decorated in warm jewel tones with lots of charm. Hand-knotted throws, knobbly woolen rugs, oil paintings, and pictures framed in gold. The leather sofa was large enough for a lie-in, a great buttery brown. Bric-a-brac littered his shelves and cupboards, clearly not purchased from a fancy store. He even had books—mostly fiction, too many to really get an idea of his taste, grouped not in alphabetical order but according to the color of their spines, which boggled Lucie's mind—and a shelf of CDs. She peered at nooks and crannies and was satisfied that there were no dust (or Playboy) bunnies. The shelves, the glass-topped coffee table—the surfaces of which she surreptitiously traced—were also very recently dusted.

"Everything to your liking?" he drawled, as she was running her fingers over the mantelpiece.

She grinned, a little embarrassed. So much for surreptitious. "Yes."

"Please, don't be shy," he said laconically as she zoomed in on his CDs, fingers outstretched, eager for a glimpse of Collin of the Old.

"REM, Smashing Pumpkins, Nirvana, Metallica, Soundgarden." She nodded in approval. "Good stuff good stuff." She continued flicking through his CDs and wrinkled her nose at the next CD. "Puddle of Mudd?"

"I was young," he said. "This was before Spotify, remember?"

"Dark days."

"Yeah. I wonder how we survived."

She continued thumbing through his CDs before recoiling theatrically. "Urgh, Nickelback? OK, fuck it, deal's off."

He laughed when he saw her moue of distaste. He stepped closer and reached for a Nickelback CD. "I was eighteen! Give me a break. What were you expecting? Chopin? Phil Collins?"

She squinted up at him. "I don't know. You look like you'd be into Enya and Backstreet Boys. I didn't expect Nickelback. And"—she thumbed through his CDs—"almost all of their studio albums, too."

He grinned. "You know, for someone who claims to hate Nickelback, you seem awfully familiar with their body of work."

Dammit, he had a point. But the truth of the matter was, now that he was this close to her, radiating body heat and smelling like salt and citrus, she was disturbingly unperturbed by the fact that he had such bad taste in music and, what's more, was not afraid to display it. Lucie Yi was suddenly staring at Collin Read like he was bacon and she'd just come out of a vegan fast.

Snap out of it.

They stood there, neither moving.

"Erm, so . . . what happens next?" she said lightly, not quite meeting his eyes.

"Has it been that long?" he exclaimed. "You know how insemination happens, right?"

She smacked his hand. "Of course I know how it's done."

"Well, first, I have something that I think we need." He went to the kitchen and returned with a bag. "You're lucky I recently went shopping for Thanksgiving."

She peeked at the contents. "Lovely."

"Do you need more wine? To help get you in the mood? Oooh, I know"—he leaned close and stage-whispered—"we can do it on top of the Nickelback CDs, if you want. We can even—break them." He winked.

"Don't worry, I think I can manage without wine or your help," Lucie said with a weak grin. She picked up a long brown paper package and took out what she assumed had to be a turkey baster (she'd never cooked turkey before). She squinted at the clear tube. "So we've got the turkey baster. What next?"

"I'll take the bathroom. Give me ten minutes."

"Only ten?"

"Plenty long, ten is," he said, looking a little affronted. "I'll come over to pass the sample to you"—he waggled an egg cup, which she hoped he would never again be using to hold actual eggs, in front of her—"and you can, y'know, do your thing."

"This is so sexy," Lucie grumbled.

He put his hands on her shoulders and gave them a shake. "Lucie, if everything goes well we'll be making life. Imagine it. *That* is sexy."

That was true. She took a deep breath and looked him straight in the eye. "Then you go in there and do your baste."

He groaned. "Why?"

"I like puns, you know that."

"You didn't quantify how much. No fair."

"You're shorter than five eleven, mister, not 'tall' as you put in your bio."

"Fair enough." He cleared his throat. "Just you wait. I'll get the baste of you."

Now she groaned.

"How do you like me now?" he crowed, before leaving the room.

A lot, Lucie thought suddenly, her face heating up. And—if she was honest—not all of it was entirely platonic.

Chapter 9

~~~~~~

HALF AN HOUR later Collin came out of the bathroom, red-faced. When she lifted an eyebrow and said, "Well?" He shook his head.

"Maybe it's the pressure; maybe it's the egg cup. I don't know, but I've tried everything." He sat down next to her on the couch, bouncing his legs, and cleared his throat. "I just want to state for the record that this has never happened before."

"Noted. Not that there's anything to be ashamed of."

He ran his hand through his hair. "So what now? Do we wait for your next cycle, plan for the IVF?"

We're wasting time. "There, um, is one more option. The obvious one. The, ah, old-fashioned way."

His hand stilled; he brought it to his lap. "Lucie Yi, I'm going to need you to spell it out, because I don't want to end up saying something that scares you off."

"We could have sex," Lucie said, affecting nonchalance by staring at the ceiling.

Collin looked at his egg bowl. "Hmm," he said, also casual.

"While that is logical, are you sure? Would we be crossing some kind of professional line?"

"You know, I don't think that this is a traditional, purely business partnership in any way, so we can't box ourselves in by being too stickler about boundaries. We must pivot and . . . innovate."

"Clearly," Collin said. "Innovation is always good. It's how our species adapted. Evolved."

"Exactly. We can, erm, innovate, then go back to the way things were, after the innovation. We just need to set some rules to protect both parties and to abide by the original spirit of the arrangement, which is platonic."

"Sure."

"First and foremost, we need a neutral ground. Neither of our homes would be appropriate. Too intimate. For maximum romance inhibition, it has to be in a Ramada-like setting, efficient and comfortable but nothing extra. No claw-footed bathtub, no recessed lighting, no twenty-four/seven room service. What do you think?"

Collin rubbed his chin thoughtfully. "I guess if we're doing this, we should be saving money from the moment of conception. Quite frankly, I never did see the point of splurging on fancy hotels anyway. When I travel, I sleeping bag or couch-surf it, all the way."

Lucie cringed inwardly—his poor future back. *It's OK, you're not dating him.* "Right. So. Ground rules. Strictly business. We're doing it *Pretty Woman*–style. No kissing. No romantic eye contact. No calling out my name."

Collin raised his hand. "Question: What if you're hurting me? Can I say your name then?"

She pondered this. "Sure. That seems fair. And I guess we should set a timer. One hour?"

"Two," he said, cheeks reddening. "Just in case."

She replied in an equally nonchalant way, "All right. Two."

Some googling later, they found a Ramada midway between hers and his.

Lucie looked at Collin and said wryly, "If this works, there will be no risk of us naming our child after the place where it was conceived."

"I think people usually use the city name, Lucie."

"No risk there, either."

They hammered out the timing (two o'clock, harsh sunlight) and agreed to meet the next day. Collin, it seemed, needed to rest up.

AT THEIR ROOM in the Ramada, both of them dressed in athleisure (Lucie had no work calls that day, and Collin was working from home), Collin brought out a hip flask. "Whiskey," he said. "For the nerves."

He took a swig and offered it to her. She glugged it and gagged. "It's bourbon," she protested.

"Yeah. Whiskey."

"That's—forget it. I thought it would be Scotch."

"So, what now?"

Collin cleared his throat. "I'll take the bathroom, and you can undress here."

"Right." She gestured at the curtains. "Permission to draw them? I thought a lunch-hour rendezvous would be more, er, utilitarian, but I'm not comfortable doing this with you in the daylight, on second thought. You're too buff next to me." Looking at Collin's honed body, clearly outlined in his running gear, Lucie worried that she looked soft and wobbly in comparison.

Collin held her gaze and said, "Draw them if you want, but for the record . . . I think you look"—his voice was gruff—"amazing."

"Right," she said, smoothing the flyaways in her hair.

They proceeded, dutifully avoiding eye contact. With the blackout curtains drawn, the room was dark, except for the emergency light in the hallway. Lucie undressed down to her plain, seamless white bra and underwear, slipped under the sheets and turned off the lights. He closed the bathroom door behind him and got into the bed. From the corner of her eye, she saw that he was wearing black boxers just before he yanked the duvet up to his chin.

They seemed to be holding their breaths. The room was very quiet, except for the occasional rustle of the bed linens. She could hear the hum of the heating system. It rattled like the disapproval in her mother's throat.

"You have to come closer," she told Collin finally. "You know. There needs to be actual contact. We're not making history here."

He edged closer to her, inch by slow inch, till they were lying side by side. They were still not touching. But she could feel the warmth radiating off his skin.

She cleared her throat and gestured in the vague direction of his legs. "Do you . . . do I?"

"I, er, took care of that," he said gruffly. She let her eyes slide down the length of his body and saw what he meant. *Whoa.*

"So. What position?" he said. He wasn't looking at her; she knew this because she was looking at him and wondering if they were mad. His jaw was very finely stubbled and his profile elegant.

"Just . . . come here," she said quietly.

He clambered over her without touching and then he was

holding himself on top of her like he was planking. He was breathing irregularly. No one was moving, still.

"What do you want me to do next?"

"It's biology; let's not overthink it," she whispered, lacing her arms around his neck. She suppressed an involuntary shudder at the sensation of his skin, the silk of his boxers brushing her thigh. "But maybe stop planking."

He stopped, gently, and now the length of him was pressed against her thighs. It was lucky he couldn't see her blush. "All right."

"All right. OK."

He kissed her neck with a tender, velvet kiss, and she guided his wandering hand down from its tentative perch on her shoulder. Down, down.

"There," she said, her voice hitching.

It was awkward, and then the awkwardness was forgotten.

WHEN IT WAS over and they were catching their breaths, he said, "Maybe we should have used the turkey baster," and she smacked him on the head, laughing.

"Do you think it worked?" he asked, placing a hand on her belly a little gingerly.

"I hope so. I'm just going to lie here for a bit." She stuck a pillow under her hips, trying to act businesslike after the way she had fallen apart for him. While both of them had agreed there would not be seconds unless there was a failure to launch, there was a moment after—when they were breathing hard in each other's arms, his lips in her hair, every part of her tingling as though gentle flames were dancing across her skin—when she thought that there would be room for discussion because it had been so good. But after some time had passed, he let go of her and got up, eyes averted again, and said, "You take the bathroom, and I take the room this time?" She nodded, pulling the sheet around her as she left the bed, not sure why she did so, not sure why they even had to go, but then the timer rang and she jolted to her senses, and the entire thing was done.

Chapter 10

~~~~~~

Lucie sat on the toilet, holding the stick in her hands. *All right, Lucie, you can do this.* Her hands were shaking. And then, involuntarily—*You've done this before.*

She successfully followed the instructions. She tried not to think of another morning just like this one.

The timer on her phone rang. Lucie closed her eyes and steeled herself. *Whatever happens, you'll be OK*, she told herself, even though it was a flimsy lie that did not convince her in the least. Her stomach roiled. She wanted it so much her hands shook as she held the stick up. She had to double-check the results with the directions.

Then she called Collin. He didn't answer, so she started texting him, too excited to wait.

Lucie: Hey stranger.

Collin: What's up.

Lucie: Remember what happened last month?

Collin: You mean, the day you came over to mine, discovered my secret stash of Nickelback CDs and still wanted to have my baby?

There was a long pause between the last two texts. Even though they had met up a couple of times after the Ramada Affair and chatted regularly, they had not talked about what actually happened in the hotel room, as per their agreement. The flashbacks to that interlude were giving Lucie heartburn. Or something like it.

There was something else that surfaced, recently. She hadn't dwelled on it until now. A moment when their eyes had met, when she was close, and so was he, and their eyes had locked and she thought they would hold until the end, but he turned, closed his eyes, and shattered, and then she had.

Lucie: So. *It* happened.

Collin: ?

Lucie: I'm pregnant, you spermy dolt! I'm pregnant! We did it! WE DID IT! *confetti emoji*

Collin: WHY ARE YOU TYPING OUT CONFETTI EMOJI YOU PSYCHO

[incoming call]

OVER THE NEXT few weeks, to celebrate, Collin brought Lucie to the following places, where—to his horror—she had never been: the Brooklyn Flea; the Bronx Zoo, where he quoted lines from *Madagascar*; the Comedy Cellar, Birdland Jazz Club, and the Village Vanguard; and a string of speakeasies, where they sipped mocktails. They laughed a lot.

"What have you been up to in the past twenty-two months?" he wondered out loud, after each place.

"You know," she said. She'd been sleepwalking.

A few days before Christmas, Collin brought her out for a seafood dinner on City Island. "The best lobster joint, if that's your thing," he said of the place, once they were seated at the cheerfully checkered tablecloth. "They have steak and non-seafood dishes, but people come here for the lobster."

"I don't eat lobsters, just like I don't eat shark fin. On principle."

"Oh, why's that? I mean, I get why you don't eat shark fin—people really need to stop eating sharks—but lobsters?"

Lucie was earnest. "Lobsters mate for life."

Collin cocked his head. "Says who?"

"Phoebe mentioned it on *Friends*."

Collin took a deep breath. "Phoebe. Phoebe Buffay is your reference point."

"Well, yes. People don't give Phoebe enough credit, but she *knows* things."

"OK. So you're telling me that the reason why you don't eat lobster is because they mate for life."

"Yes. What if the lobster catcher takes one mate and leaves the other hanging forever in a sexless, companionless existence for the rest of its days?"

Collin leaned his chin on his cupped palm and regarded her. "Good heavens. I don't believe this: Lucie Yi is a romantic."

She blushed. "You say it like I'm a flat-earther or something."

"I think it's admirable," he said. "I'm not. I'm a skeptic. But hey, to each their own. Although—" He took out his phone and googled it. "I do want to disabuse you of this fanciful notion of lobster fidelity. Lobsters are pretty much nautical horndogs." He passed the phone to her.

She read the article and tossed the phone back at Collin with a groan. "You mean I stopped eating lobsters for over a decade because. . . . because of something I watched on TV?"

"Yup," he said, deadpan. "You got conned out of an overpriced cockr—"

She placed a finger on his lips. "Hush right now, before you put me off co—I mean, lobsters. I'm going to eat lobsters all night long. Waiter!" she said, raising her arm, and Collin laughed as she ordered lobster three ways.

She smiled at him, a tingle shooting down her spine when her eyes caught his.

"What's up, stranger?" he said, nudging her playfully.

"I was just thinking I'm glad I—we're doing this together."

"Me, too," he said, taking her hand and giving it a quick kiss. "We're going to have a baby."

Just then someone squealed, and Lucie looked over to see a dark-haired man on his knees, his eyes starry with unshed tears, holding a ring out and proposing to his date, who sobbed, nodding, joyous, and then the both of them were kissing exuberantly while the other dinners cheered.

That should have been me, she thought, before she could dismiss it. She wanted what that shining couple had. She wanted the whole package.

Stop living in a fantasy, she chided herself. She shouldn't be too greedy, otherwise she'd be waiting around forever. The only thing that mattered, right there and then, was this: she was finally going to be a mother. That was good enough.

Chapter 11

~~~~~~

PREDICTABLY, THE EIGHTEEN-HOUR direct flight from New York to Singapore—in coach even though Lucie had offered to upgrade them—saw Collin and her seated in the same row as a couple and their very new baby, who had chosen this flight to debut its newest skill: operatic screaming. One hour after take-off, it had still been in mid-aria. *They weren't kidding when they sold this as a red-eye,* Lucie thought.

The landing was bumpy; she looked out of the window and saw that it was hailing. "I've never seen it hail so hard in Singapore," Lucie overheard a flight attendant say as the plane nosed to a stop at Changi Airport. *Great, this bodes well,* she thought, biting her lip and surreptitiously crossing herself. She turned on her phone and saw that her parents had already left her five messages, asking her which date she was arriving exactly. Lucie had deliberately left it vague, not wanting to deal with her parents' questions as to why she wasn't staying at theirs. Instead, she had fixed a date to dine with her family at the weekly Yi family dinner, next Wednesday. *I'll text them to say I've landed . . . next Monday.*

They didn't lose any luggage at the bustling Changi Airport, despite having checked in eleven pieces; she'd even made a bet with Collin about it on the long flight. "This is Singapore," Lucie said smugly, holding out her hand for payment, "we don't lose luggage. Ten Singaporean dollars, please. None of that Malaysian ringgit."

"Man, you really know how to sell your country," he grumbled, forking over the cash. "Singapore: Your Luggage Is Safe with Us. So catchy. You guys should make it the next tourism slogan." They were wandering in the new terminal of Changi and he slowed down to admire one of the indoor gardens. "Have they given the airport a facelift or something?"

"New terminal. Come on, I don't want to be late to meet your dad." Collin's father, Peter Read, had offered to see them before he had to fly off to visit a new F&B project of his in Penang, Malaysia.

"Don't worry about it; he runs on Malaysian time. He's always fifteen to twenty minutes late for everything."

"Well, I don't, and I have to make a good impression," Lucie said.

Peter was on time. He met them at the arrivals lounge, a smiling, trim, silver-haired man in his late seventies in a saffron-and-black batik shirt and linen pants. It was a good thing Collin had spotted him from a mile away, because they looked nothing alike, except for the deeply tanned skin. Lucie had been nervous about meeting him, but just as Collin had predicted, he was very relaxed about the arrangement. They had a quick coffee and kaya toast (Lucie was hungry) in a casual eatery in the swanky mall next to the terminal, over which Lucie observed father and son.

Collin, Lucie, and Peter pulled some pretty slick moves in the obligatory check dance when the bill came, but surprisingly, Peter, whom she thought would be allowed to "win," gave up and let Collin take the bill. Collin took the opportunity to go to the counter to pick up extra tins of pineapple tarts (for the baby, she'd claimed) and left Lucie alone with his father.

Peter turned to her and said, in a low, slightly strained voice, "Forgive me if I'm overstepping, but ah, were you in charge of booking the flights?" He caught her by surprise.

"No, Uncle Peter," she said. "Collin insisted on handling the booking."

"I see." He was quiet, then he asked, "If you don't mind my asking, was this the earliest you could have flown in?"

"Well . . . I mean. Collin is pretty much a digital nomad, and I've been packed and ready to leave for about six days. I mean, we did do the touristy things I should have done when I first arrived in New York, y'know, as a last hurrah, but—"

"I knew it," he said.

"What's bothering you, if you can share?" Lucie squirmed, unused to being so direct with someone much older than her, and a stranger at that.

"It's just . . . he booked the flights knowing today is when I have to leave for my project inspection. I just—I'd been looking forward to spending more time with you and Collin." He sighed, rubbed his chin with a rueful expression. "Oh well, I suppose I should just be glad that he's going to be in the same country. I'll have more opportunity to see you all when I'm back, I suppose."

"Yes," Lucie said, a little thrown. "I mean, he did say he's moving back to Asia so he could spend more time with you."

"Did he?" Peter said, surprised.

OK, what's going on?

But then Collin was back, and they resumed polite chatter. Peter and Collin were smiling at each other like Peter hadn't just revealed that his son had orchestrated their meeting times to coincide with his leaving. *Should I be worried that Collin had stretched the truth?* she wondered.

Peter escorted them to the taxi and private-vehicle-for-hire queue. "I was hoping to meet your parents today, Lucie," Peter said to Lucie, after he'd helped load everything onto a six-seater Toyota Vellfire.

"Oh, you'll meet them soon enough." She had to bite back a grimace at this lie; her parents didn't even know she was landing today.

Turns out she and Collin had another point in common. *We all have bodies to hide, eh?*

During the cab ride to their service apartment, Lucie pointed out the sights and doled out trivia, while Collin made the obligatory oohs and ahhs. This version of Singapore was new to him; since the last time he had visited in the early 2000s, the entire skyline had changed, especially where they were driving. "See that? The boat-shaped building? That's the Marina Bay Sands. It's built on land that before 2007 didn't even exist. And that lotus-flower building? That's the ArtScience Museum, my personal favorite. Recognize anything?"

"Not really. I definitely don't remember Fullerton Hotel surrounded by so many buildings," he murmured, when the cab made a detour so he could have a peek at the Central Business District, where Lucie worked. "But I guess twenty years will do that to any place."

They arrived at their service apartment, jet-lagged. Lucie was more nervous about this than she had let on. This next step—living together, sharing belongings, in such close proximity—this was a massive commitment in itself. Aside from Mark, Lucie had never lived with anyone, one-on-one, although Collin had even less experience, having never lived with any of his exes, even the one that he was with for three years, *when they were both in their thirties*. (This, Lucie thought, might have been one of the reasons why Nina broke up with him.) Living together would be a test.

Tactfully, she thought, Lucie had asked Collin to book their accommodation. She liked that he had chosen one in Bugis, which was central even if it wasn't splashy, and the apartment was supposed to be highly rated in its price range.

Until she saw the space.

"Isn't this a tad . . . small?" Lucie asked, after they'd had a tour of the space.

"It's only for a week, two, max, right?"

"Yes, but . . ." Lucie made a face when she saw the shared toilet, with its desultory shower stall. "Only one toilet for the both of us? We could have paid a little more for two; I'm pregnant."

"You get priority status in case of a tiebreaker," he said, grinning. Lucie sighed. She didn't ask what he thought would happen in case of dual emergencies. "No tub?"

"Do you need a tub?"

"No, but it would be nice to have a warm soak. I'm preg—"

"Pregnant. Yes, I'm aware, but we need to start saving. Singapore is expensive. That's one of the reasons you wanted to co-parent, right?"

"Hmmm." She regarded the cramped dining room table, the flickering lights, and sighed when she thought of what Suzie and Weina would think when they came over for dinner that Saturday.

"Look at the balcony. Natural ventilation and tropical sunlight!" he said, stripping down to his linen pants and stretching bare-chested, catlike, on their tiny balcony.

She intervened when he started to pull off his pants. "It's illegal to be naked if you're exposed to public view, even in your own home," she said, pointing to a gawking man in the glass-fronted office tower facing their apartment.

"Seriously? There's a law against that?"

"Yup."

"Underwear isn't naked though."

Lucie made a non-committal noise. She wasn't sure if the kind of underwear Collin wore counted as "visible from a distance."

Collin buttoned his pants with great reluctance. "I'll bet I could walk around naked in our apartment if we were in Malaysia," he said slyly.

"But you'd probably have to because you'd lost your luggage, so."

They grinned.

"OK, pal. First house rule: no walking around naked in common areas."

He opened his mouth to protest, but she held up a finger. "It's not appropriate. Considering our . . . platonic status."

He gave her a thumbs-up. "Noted. Permission for boxers, though?"

She pretended to consider this. "Yes, OK, fine. But nothing sheer or cheekless."

"Why would there be cheekless . . ." He shook his head. "OK, noted. Anyway, Lucie?"

"Yeah?"

He met her gaze squarely. "I'd like it on the record that I have no issue if *you* choose to walk around in your underwear in the common areas of our dwelling."

"I will most assuredly not be," Lucie replied, not flinching as she stared back. He was trying to goad her.

"I know you won't—but I won't be sorry if you do," he said in a husky voice that made Lucie's stomach somersault.

He helped her drag her luggage to her room and they spent the next hour unpacking before taking a break for lunch at the Golden Mile Food Centre, the open-air hawker center nearby.

Unable to be sure of the nut-free status of the food preparation, Collin had brought a supply of EpiPens, and he declined to eat at the hawker center, saying he would make a sandwich once they got back. He sat at a table while Lucie went from stall to stall, ordering food.

"Is that all for you?" he said when she plonked down her tray with chicken rice with a portion of roast pork, fried banana fritters, glutinous rice dumplings, and avocado juice.

"Yup! The baby demands it. For, er"—Lucie racked her brains—"its growth spurts."

He did not look convinced. "How is eating all that oily food healthy?"

"Allow me to introduce you to the Lucie Diet, based on the System of Offsetting, the principles of which can be applied to other facets of your life as well, really."

"Kindly elaborate."

"So, if you eat something that's not as good for you, you have to supplement with so-called good, healthful ingredients or food groups. Take ramen, for example. When I make ramen, I make sure I add organic vegetables, an egg, and some lean chicken to offset all the MSG and artificial flavorings. And if I eat, say, three donuts for breakfast, I just drink water laced with apple cider vinegar and eat a fruit to balance the equation."

He was flabbergasted, possibly by her brilliance. "That's . . . your system?"

"Sure it is. It's pretty much how I view everything and run my life. Not enough exercise over a week? Take a day off and work out till you drop. Same for work. Like I spent two years put out 'to pasture'"—she put the phrase in air quotes but it was how she, and no doubt her office, viewed her secondment—"in New York, and now I need to compensate for that, double down, work super-duper hard, so that I can be partner. Anyway, look how healthy I am!" She eyed a dessert stall. She could use a bowl of cendol. The baby deserved, nay, *demanded*, cendol. Plus this version of cendol had red beans, which—being legumes and part of the vegetable food group—was good for you, never mind the palm sugar syrup they swam in. "I'm thinking of getting cendol. You want some?"

"No thanks. Back to our discussion. I won't even get into how not sustainable a system that is. And by the way, being lean doesn't mean you're healthy. And now that you're pregnant, you have to be even more careful with your sugar intake. And the shaved ice!" He gestured at the exposed block of ice in the machine used for making cendol and made a face. "Repository of listeria and worse. But you know, your choice."

"Why are you such a killjoy?" she grumbled.

"I'm sorry, I'm not trying to control you. I'm merely giving you my opinion. You have free will. If there's something you're craving, go for it. But maybe not the cendol."

"Don't worry, you'll killed my craving completely," she said. She tucked into her chicken rice, wistfully contemplating the cendol from a distance. Funny how once you're told you can't have something, you want it even more.

Chapter 12

~~~~~

On Saturday, Lucie woke up with a smile on her face. She couldn't believe she'd be seeing her friends in the flesh that evening after such a long separation, and she was eager to introduce Collin to them and to see if they would get along. After a couple of days of sleeping off their jet lag, ordering in, and surfing real estate listings, she couldn't wait to let loose with her friends. She went out to buy flowers, and Collin began food prep.

Lucie wasn't expecting much in terms of food, since Collin had said he was only an OK cook—the last person who told her he was an OK cook was Mark, and all he could make was what he claimed was an omelet—but Collin was full of surprises. She came home to the rich aroma of cheese baking in the oven and saw Collin bopping his head to pop music from a small Bluetooth speaker as he pan-fried potatoes. "Would the lady like to dance?" he said, reaching a spatula out to her and giving an exaggerated shimmy.

"Maybe later," she said, laughing while she deflected. She put the flowers—a simple green bouquet of succulents, ferns, and white roses—in a vase and went to take a shower.

Lucie was prepping the place settings when the doorbell rang. When she opened the door, Weina swept in wearing a sleeveless, multicolored pleated dress and citrusy perfume.

"You're half an hour early!" Lucie exclaimed. She engulfed the more petite Weina in a bear hug.

"And I would have arrived even earlier if not for my handover to Simon," Weina said. It was the first time in the triplets' seven months that Simon was going to solo parent them. Apparently, she'd given him a folder full of instructions. She disengaged from Lucie and gave her a once-over. "May I say how glowing you look, my dear!"

"Thanks," Lucie said. "Conversely, I've never been more constipated in my life."

Weina gave her shoulder a sympathetic squeeze. "Just wait till the last trimester. That's when you get *really* vascular piles."

"Oh, the Things They Don't Tell You Before You Get Pregnant," Lucie intoned.

"If they did, no one would procreate," Weina said. "Now lemme see the belly." She sank to her knees and made low crooning noises at the general direction of Lucie's crotch, along the lines of "Auntie Weina is here! Auntie Weina is here!"

"Urm, do you mind not scaring off my co-parent?"

"Am I interrupting something?" Collin said, laughing as he entered the room. He offered a hand to Weina a little bashfully. "I'm Collin, father of the baby, as you might have heard."

"Of course." Weina grinned and pulled him into a bear hug.

Soon they sat in the living room with mocktails on a tray ready for both Lucie and Suzie, while Collin sipped on a stout. Weina was still gloating because she had arrived ahead of Suzie.

"Suzie isn't technically late, you know," Lucie said. "You're just early."

"It doesn't matter, I win!" she crowed. "And it's pump-and-dump night. My first since the triplets. Give me all the alcohol."

"Don't give her *all* the alcohol," Lucie muttered to Collin in the kitchenette. "She was never good at holding her drink, that one."

"Gotcha."

They came back in the living room with lime-flavored soda water "with a measure of gin"—a soupçon of gin, really. Weina guzzled it happily.

"Where are the children?" Collin asked before Lucie could shush him.

"With the father," Weina said, her smile wobbling just a little. "All—four—of them."

The room considered the mathematics and wisely refrained from pursuing that line of questioning.

The doorbell rang at eight sharp. It was Suzie, dressed in skinny jeans and a boxy navy cotton tee. Squealing, Lucie threw herself at her best friend. The women did a hug-dance.

Weina turned to Collin and said, conversationally, "Did you know that the first time those two met, Suzie tried to kill Lucie?"

"I . . . can't imagine," Collin said. He exchanged an amused look with Lucie—both flashing back on their first meetup.

"An exaggeration, and a complete misunderstanding," Suzie said, breaking apart from Lucie. Suzie, then a stranger, had intentionally held Lucie's head down under water "for a couple of seconds" in a public pool to teach her a lesson when Lucie—not maliciously—had commented on the odd fit of Suzie's home-made, full-length swimming costume. Their swim coach had had to intervene and fish Lucie out. Once their swim coach understood what had set Suzie off and asked her to apologize for hurting Lucie, he had pulled them aside and helped Suzie find the words to explain why she had to wear such an outfit, and

Lucie had unreservedly apologized for her ignorance; she continued to feel a twinge of guilt to this day whenever this incident was brought up, even though it had been the catalyst for their friendship.

Suzie hugged Collin, murmuring her congrats, and looked disappointed to see that Weina was on time. She gave Collin a once-over before proclaiming, "You look normal."

"Was I not supposed to?"

"I don't know. I was hoping you'd look more nervous. You are meeting the most important people in Lucie's life."

Collin laughed. He excused himself to continue plating the food.

"What's she on?" Suzie nodded at Weina, who was aggressively bopping her head to no music.

"Gin."

Suzie nodded sagely. "Anyway, you look well. Lighter, somehow."

"I don't *feel* lighter, but thanks. I'll be right back." She went to the kitchen to get Suzie's drink: ice lemon tea, maximum sugar.

Since Weina had to be home by eleven, otherwise Simon might "accidentally kill the children" (in all fairness, Simon was actually pretty adept at handling the children, although Weina often acted like she was the only one who could parent), they started dinner at 8:15 sharp. Collin had made a magnificent meal—roasted black cod with morel mushrooms and asparagus, and mini jacket potatoes, with baked cheese tarts for dessert (none for him)—everything halal for Suzie, even if she was not too fussed about that, so long as there wasn't pork. The food, as always, was delicious, and everyone did not speak for a while, eating energetically—except for Lucie, who was too nervous and a little nauseous. She picked at her cod.

"How are you adjusting to Singapore, Collin?" Suzie asked. "Since you've been away for, what, two decades?"

"Yup, thereabouts. Most of the time, my dad flies to the States or Europe. He likes to travel." Collin made a face. "I haven't really done or seen anything since I got here, aside from cruising real estate listings."

"I was keeping a low profile with Collin, since my parents don't know we're back," Lucie said. "I told them to expect us next Wednesday. Work starts the week after."

"What about you, Collin, what's the plan in terms of work?"

"I start at my friend's tech company about a week after Lucie starts. We should hopefully be done with apartment-hunting and moving in by then."

"What do you do?" Weina asked.

"I'm a software engineer."

"Really?" Suzie said in an overtly surprised tone that didn't match her face. "That is *so* fascinating."

"Hmm," Collin said, his mouth twitching. "I wish my job elicited this kind of response elsewhere."

"My uncle-in-law is a hacker!" Weina chirped.

"There, there," Suzie said, patting her arm while carefully maneuvering Weina's drink out of her reach. "Have some water." She turned her attention back to Collin. "What are you going to do when Lucie's away at work?"

Collin grinned. "I'm thinking I'll join a couple of meetup groups. And when my dad's back next week, I'll catch up with him, too."

"Interesting," Weina said. Her eyes were trained on Collin, not so drunk suddenly. "What kind of groups?"

"I wanted to see if there were some outdoor gym groups, get a fitness thing going."

Weina's eyes lingered on his arms. "Oh no, we won't want your fitness levels to drop."

". . . and maybe date," Collin added. You could practically hear the whipping of their necks as they turned to stare at him, raptors Suzie and Weina.

"What's your type?" Suzie said, in what she clearly assumed was a casual tone but actually sounded like she was interrogating a murder suspect.

Weina leaned forward. "Lucie's type is Tall Mean Bunker."

Lucie spat out a mouthful of potato in surprise.

"I think she means 'Banker,'" Suzie said.

"Noted," Collin said.

Lucie made a mental note to not offer Weina anything with alcohol ever again.

"I like you," Weina said. "You'd be great for Lucie. If only you were tall."

Lucie's face heated. Collin raised his eyebrows. "I'm tall."

"No, you're not," Suzie muttered.

"I'm five eleven," Collin told Suzie.

"*Are* you, though?" Suzie said, sitting up straighter. "I think I'm as tall as you are."

"Why do you want to date other people? Don't you find Lucie attractive?" Weina was like a dog with a bone.

"Because Collin and I are strictly platonic," Lucie said, sinking down in her seat. She wished the earth would swallow her. It was good to know she was not too old to be embarrassed by her friends. "Anyway, I'm going to date, too."

"How are you guys going to openly date other people once Lucie's family finds out it's Collin's baby?" Weina wanted to know.

"Collin and I will tell them we 'made a mistake,' but we're

going to raise the kid together," Lucie said. Her parents' reaction to an illegitimate pregnancy was likely to be negative, but she figured given her age, they would be too ecstatic about the pregnancy to care about the legitimacy. Right?

"I think your parents will force you two to marry. They will kill you if you don't," Weina told Collin.

"Interesting how Lucie failed to mention that her parents are prepared to murder," Collin said dryly.

"Her parents are scary," Weina said.

"I don't scare easy," Collin said.

"I'll bet you don't," Weina said, staring at his chest.

"Anyway," Collin said, folding his arms uncomfortably, "I really don't believe in marriage. I mean—and Lucie knows this—if I absolutely had to, I'd do it. But I'd hate if I was cornered to do it. Why do we as a society still pretend to believe in the fantasy of the One and forever love?"

A couple of seconds later, Lucie's phone vibrated with a chat notification from Weina, saying EMOTIONALLYU STUNTEF? (She had texted Lucie under the table.) Collin, of course, caught everything.

"You're just saying that because your last girlfriend ran off with your friend," Weina said.

Lucie and Collin froze. Not that Weina noticed. There was a couple of terse seconds before Collin got out of his seat and left the table with a curt "Excuse me." His face was pale.

Suzie groaned. "Weina. You are a gremlin when you drink."

"That reminds me—I think I need another cocktail."

Lucie turned to Weina and said, "Doesn't one of the triplets have a rash that needs a special salve? Are you certain Simon knows which triplet is which?"

Weina stood up. "I have to go."

Suzie rolled her eyes. "Subtle, Lucie."

Collin came back with a platter of baked cheese tarts and a fixed smile. "Dessert before you leave?"

They agreed to have one each, because it was the polite thing to do. They finished the entire tray of twelve tarts between the three of them. Ten minutes later they were exchanging air kisses, Weina's aim particularly airy. "Come over to mine next!" she said to Collin. "I'll host a lovely soiree!"

"Just how much gin was in that cocktail?" Lucie asked, once they were alone again and clearing the table. She was eager to postmortem the event.

Collin's voice was stiff. "You told your friends about Nina?"

It took her a couple of seconds to figure out who Nina was. She blinked. "I'm sorry. I thought you knew I spoke to them about stuff. They're my closest friends."

"That was shared in private. It's not a punch line."

"We weren't . . ."

"Didn't sound like it."

The atmosphere between them crackled. Lucie scrambled to make it right, to explain that the trio's decades of history translated into verbal shorthand, whose familiarity could be cutting to an outsider. Surely he got that? And that because he was her soon-to-be co-parent, he was being fast-tracked into that intimacy, with its jokes and barbs.

But it's not fair for you to assume that; he doesn't know you, or your friends, well enough, yet. He doesn't share your history.

He was, in some ways, a stranger, still.

Lucie reached out and put her hand, hesitantly, on his arm. "Collin, I didn't mean to share something out of bounds. I'm really, really sorry. I'll do better, I promise."

The tension in his carriage resolved somewhat at her words.

He shrugged, affecting nonchalance. "Hey, I'm over it. Let's move on." He started washing up; over the roar of the faucet, Lucie almost missed what he said next. Maybe it was deliberate. "I did mean what I said earlier, though. I don't believe in marriage, the whole pretense of forever."

Lucie looked at him, perplexed. "Yet you're willing to commit to having a child?"

He turned the faucet off. "That's completely different. Your bond to a child, that love survives breakups. It's forever. Romantic love isn't. Look at my parents; me and Nina; look at you and Mark." Lucie flinched; even now, his name was a violence. "That's why this arrangement makes sense. It would never be clouded by bad feelings when love turns sour. We're in it for the child's future."

Everything he said was logical, sensible. It was what appealed to her in the first place about Co-Family.com. Yet his phrasing was defeatist; the stark lines he drew in the sand saddened her. Unlike Collin, Lucie *did* believe in the One, in forever loves— call it Disney indoctrination, call it a quirk of her nature in spite of her pragmatism. She thought she'd found it with Mark, before it all went south. To Lucie, forever love wasn't a fairy tale. She had always yearned for it.

But maybe he's right, and I'm just the one clinging to a false ideal. I'm the silly one who believed in lobster monogamy.

They dried the dishes in silence. Lucie felt like she was being buffeted on all sides by strong wind. She thought she'd done enough due diligence to prepare for all eventualities, all practical complications. But now she realized she was naive in believing that just because there was no romance involved in this setup, everything would proceed without hitches.

"I do like your friends, though," he said after a while.

"I'm sorry Weina was so direct."

"I prefer when people are. I know where I stand with folks like that."

"Oh, then you're going to enjoy my parents."

"Are they direct?"

She nodded. "Especially when they dislike you. They aren't *passive* aggressive, unlike most Asian parents—they're straight-up aggressive. You'll see on Wednesday."

Collin contemplated her with a small smile. "Well, as long as their daughter likes me, I can deal with them."

Chapter 13

~~~~~

SINCE HANNAH WASN'T attending the Yi family dinner, even though technically she had been invited, Lucie went over to her sister's on Sunday for a long-overdue catch-up.

Gerald, Hannah's ex-husband, was at the door when she came, struggling with two bags of groceries. He started when he saw her. "You're back," he said. He put the bags down and she saw him debating internally as to whether to shake her hand. He didn't.

"Yup, over a week ago." She would have asked how he was, but the divorce had been acrimonious.

He nodded. "The kids are in there with Hannah." He rang the bell, and moments later, Hannah was ushering the both of them in. She gave Lucie a quick hug, as Gerald hurried to the kitchen to unload the groceries and the children, Ying Wei, six, and Yi Na, four, circled, bashful around an aunt they hadn't seen for two years. Lucie gave them their Christmas and birthday gifts, both scampering off as soon as they got Hannah's assent. They were more interested in unwrapping the gifts than hanging around the adults.

Gerald came out and conferred in low tones with Hannah.

Their body language was tense, and Lucie gave them as much space as she could by squirreling herself in Hannah's bedroom/ study. Then Gerald was gone, and Hannah broke into a big smile and hugged her sister anew, glancing down at Lucie's belly as she did. "Lucie, my goodness!" She'd heard all about "the Arrangement."

Growing up, the sisters had not been close, in part because Hannah was six years younger than Lucie; she was also much more reserved than her sister. Maybe there'd been a little jealousy on Lucie's side, because Hannah had always been known as "the beautiful sister," while Lucie was "the smart one," although the division wasn't as clear-cut as her parents led them to believe. Until her divorce, Lucie had always found it difficult to connect with her younger sister, growing up as they had in a household where they'd been somewhat pitted against each other, but they had built up a steady friendship over the past five or so years, since Hannah had first come to Lucie's door, pregnant, telling her that it was over with Gerald.

Hannah brought out a pot of rooibos tea and a tray of biscuits, and the sisters settled down in the cramped dining alcove. Lucie caught Hannah up about the pregnancy and how they were settling in, Hannah nodding and fielding questions in her serious, quiet manner.

"I can't wait to meet Collin. He sounds so nice."

"Yeah, he is," Lucie said. "I think as far as co-parents go, I made a sound pick."

Hannah opened her mouth but closed it with a shake of her head. "I'm sure you did. Have you guys nailed down all the nitty-gritty?"

They had not; they had gone down the model checklist and discussed the items, intending to draw up a co-parenting agreement at the end of it, but the document ended up being so long that they tore it up and agreed to just always put the child's best interests first. After all, they knew each other's position on the important issues; they reasoned that since any agreement they made wouldn't likely be recognized in Singapore, it didn't make sense to make their arrangement so legalistic. Not that Hannah, who'd fought tooth-and-nail in family court for just that kind of certainty, would understand. So Lucie fibbed. "Yup, we have a document."

Her sister nodded in approval. "That's smart. How's house-hunting going?"

"Not good," Lucie conceded. She was a little stressed about that. Their agent, Derek, had shown them seventeen properties in total; they'd short-listed three, made a list in descending order before submitting their formal expressions of interest. All three were rejected. They tried for the next two and were rejected for those, too. "My agent says that as a single tenant, I keep getting passed over for couples and dual-income households. Doesn't even matter that I offered above the asking rate. The rental market's hot."

"Why isn't Collin on the lease?"

"His employment pass is still being processed; until then, he has no official status here."

Hannah frowned. "Is there anything I can do?"

"Nah, don't worry about it. Thanks, love." Hannah had enough worries and financial commitments of her own. Weina and Simon had offered to co-sign the lease, but Lucie declined. She wanted to do this on her own.

"How are things with Gerald?"

Hannah sighed; she lowered her voice. "They are what they are. Civil. He's helping, at least. But his new wife wants the boys over more often. They get along so well with her daughter, who's five. It's great that she loves the boys, but . . ." Hannah's lips trembled. "I never wanted to split custody. Now I'm living in fear she's going to persuade him to renegotiate the current arrangement."

"Is there anything *I* can do?"

"No," Hannah said. She forced a smile. "It's fine. Let's talk about other things." She checked the teapot. "Want more tea?"

"Sure."

Lucie bit her lip as she watched her sister get up to boil the kettle, noticing how her sister's mouth was etched with new worry lines and her fine skin had a feverish, high color she'd never seen before, and even though Lucie knew it was irrational to want to turn back time, she wished she could go back and vaporize the day her sister met Gerald Lim.

It was Tuesday by the time Derek finally found a great option— a split-level three-bedder loft unit—with an understanding land-lord. The hitch was the money—they wanted much more than the budgeted $4,600. By now Lucie was getting desperate; a service apartment wasn't a long-term, economical solution. She wondered if Collin would play ball.

"Collin, we might have an apartment."

Collin looked up from the steak he was pulverizing—he rarely ate red meat anymore, but Lucie did, so he was cooking for her— with his new toy, a meat mallet. "Oh? What's wrong with it? It's haunted? Asbestos in the walls?"

"Choi, don't be so cavalier about ghosts," she said, crossing herself.

"Choi?"

"It's this thing my mom says in Cantonese. It's a catch-all word to ward off curses or prevent bad things from happening."

He nodded. "Very useful, you being a tax adviser and all. You must be used to people cursing you."

"That's . . ." She took a deep breath; they didn't have time for a spiel on how useful her work was. To society. "Anyway, we're in a desperate situation."

He rolled his eyes. "No, you just want something that everyone wants: three-bedder, close enough to public transport, in a nice area, not too expensive." He swung the meat mallet like he was Thor. "You don't want to compromise."

Her head began to throb. "Let's see—by 'compromising,' do you mean taking the place that had an actual termite infestation? Or the one with a damp patch on the wall that the agent called 'seasonal,' as in every time it rains?"

"We have a budget. Maybe we'll have to get a smaller place. Somewhere farther, less trendy."

"I'm not doing a one-hour commute in my condition. And I've to go to my office in Raffles every day, once my maternity leave is done." She tried to reason with him. "Look, Collin, everything we liked is out of our price range. This apartment is in the same development we fell in love with, same layout, three floors up. Only it's nine hundred dollars more per month! I think if we each just put in more—"

Collin stiffened. "Lucie, when we got into this, I made it very clear that I wanted to contribute equally to all our child-related expenses. But four hundred and fifty dollars more per month is not a small sum to me."

"I think y—we should be contributing in proportion to our earnings."

"No, I just don't think that's fair. That would put you in a higher bargaining power than me, which I am not fine with. What I mean is, I'm fine with you earning more. But I'm not fine with us being unequal contributors."

Lucie decided to change tack. "This is the twenty-first century. If I am earning more and am comfortable paying more, my share should proportionally increase."

He swung the mallet into the meat. "I have absolutely no problem with you paying more if you earn more—but only in terms of non-child-related expenses. Not when it comes to our child."

"And why not?"

"Maybe think of it like having voting shares in a company. It's just about having equal say, represented by an equal economic stake in this endeavor."

Lucie made a face. "In our baby. In something I'm carrying in my body."

Collin frowned. "Yes, and you don't have to phrase it that way. You know that what I'm saying is fair. And the other thing is, if we set a budget, we should stick to it. We decided on forty-six hundred dollars per month for rent. Split equally between us. So let's stick to it."

Lucie could feel the pressure building in her temples. *Why was he being so hard-line about this?* "Fine. We'll wait till something suitable comes up."

"Thank you." He turned away from her and resumed pounding the steak with even more vigor.

Lucie watched him for a few moments, rooted to the ground, unsure if she should leave or stay. She wished he wasn't so stubbornly against them contributing in proportion to their salary—it made sense and she was quite happy to do so, especially when she didn't think it was because he was insecure about her being the primary breadwinner in this relationship. But just talking about money brought out an unusual tetchiness in him that made her reluctant to broach the subject. There was something else to it, she knew that. If she wanted to get to the bottom of this, she needed to tread carefully.

Thumph! She was jerked back to the present at the loud, slightly wet sound of the mallet hitting meat. Good God, was he working out or tenderizing meat?

She was seized with a powerful urge to put her hands around Collin's neck and strangle him. Really pressing her fingers into his thick neck, whipping him around to face her, and—and—

She had a sudden flashback involving Mark, one of those times when he had done something to really irritate her (or was it the opposite?) and they had been shouting at each other until he had scooped her up, dunked her on his bed, and proceeded to hash out the disagreement with her until they reached a very agreeable compromise, which is to say nothing more was said about the subject matter, and they both moved on and watched TV, satisfied with their superior conflict-resolution skills.

She gave herself a mental shake, aware that her heart was racing. She went into her room and took out her own purple conflict-resolution wand. It was stressful living with another adult under any circumstances—she needed to massage the kinks out, yes.

She lay on the bed and yawned.

But first, maybe a nice nap.

SHE WOKE UP to a knock.

"Dinner's ready," Collin said through the door. "Wanna eat?"

She followed him into their tiny living room/dining room, where he'd laid out a table for two. He'd made her steak, roasted vegetables, and proper fries, none of that air-fried nonsense. She groaned as she bit into a fry. Perfection.

"And we're having ice cream for dessert. The perfect Lucie Diet dinner," he said, grinning. "Lots of unhealthy stuff balanced by the good stuff. I'm all on board now."

"You see," Lucie said through a mouthful of potato. "It's sensible."

"Only in certain areas of life. I mean, you can't murder a bunch of people while making your fortune, and then build a hospital for the poor and a couple of universities, you know?"

"Mmm." The fries were fried in duck fat.

"OK," he said, after she'd polished off the plate.

"OK?"

He shrugged, affecting nonchalance. "OK, yeah, I'll put in more money."

"Really?" she said, surprised. She put her fork down. "Is that—is that something you are comfortable doing?" She was suddenly embarrassed by the conversation.

"No, it's not, if I'm being honest. But I don't want you to be stressed about something I can work with. You're pregnant, I should take this off your mind. I'll . . . dig into my savings if I need to." He cleared his throat. "I'll send you the balance in a week, after a couple of things clear."

"Oh." She shifted in her seat, her eyes lowered at the cringe factor involved in money discussions. "No, I can't let you do that. We had fixed a budget."

"Hey, that can be renegotiated, right? Plus, if we live here any longer, we'll be bleeding money. I'm sorry I haven't been more accommodating, given the circumstances. I understand how stressful it can be, not knowing where we'll be living next. I've lived through it."

"What do you mean?"

Collin looked embarrassed and hesitant. "When I first moved back to the States with my mom, we stayed in a bunch of, er, short-term rentals."

Lucie realized he was opening up to her about his past and held herself very still, not wanting to make any sudden moves in case she startled him away. "Mm-hmm," she said, meaning *Go on, I'm here.*

"My mom and dad split under pretty acrimonious circumstances. When they met, he was a line chef in a fancy Singaporean hotel; my mom was a lounge singer in the bar, so they didn't have much money to begin with. When it all fell apart, she decided to pack up with me and go. He wasn't exactly paying child support—a combination of him being angry at my mom and my mom not wanting him to be involved in our lives—and we had to live in motels, crummy apartments, a trailer park for a bit." He studied his palms. "I was almost sixteen when we finally moved into a house in this dodgy neighborhood in East Austin that she held two jobs to pay for. When he contacted me to reestablish a relationship when I was seventeen, one of the first things he said was he was going to make up for lost time by giving me the child support he owed my mom in a lump sum and that I could use it however I want, as a down payment or whatever. Wish he'd done it when we really needed it." His voice roughened. "It just made me feel . . . like he thought he could buy my forgiveness and erase his mistakes just by handing over a bunch of money." He grimaced.

Lucie tried for tact. "Maybe . . . maybe he's just trying to make up for it the only way he can, now."

"Maybe." His expression was grim. "Maybe the truth is he'd offered to help out when they split up, but my mom just didn't want him to have that power over us . . . who knows. I never got to ask my mom. Whatever it is, I want to avoid their mistakes. I'm in it, fifty-fifty with you, from the beginning."

"OK. I hear you." She reached out and held his hand. "I'm sorry about how things went down between your parents, Collin."

"Don't. I wasn't looking for sympathy. It wasn't that tough for me. It sucked for my mom, though. Single at thirty-three, saddled with a frail kid. Always worried about medical bills." He said all this very matter-of-factly, but his hunched posture gave him away.

Lucie rubbed her forehead, the guilt at making him relive his difficult childhood eating at her insides. Suddenly she couldn't stomach the idea of him forking out more money to go through with this. "Just hold on. I'll talk to Derek and try to find new options. Let's just give it a couple more days, OK?"

"OK."

She called Derek later that night and told him to negotiate with the landlord. She would top up the difference when she transferred the rent to the landlord, if he would keep it off the books and put S$4,600 on the lease agreement.

It was settled. On Friday they would move into their new place, Collin none the wiser.

Chapter 14

~~~~~~

AFTER HER AFTERNOON nap, they were on the way to her parents'. Lucie was on edge the entire cab ride. She had told her parents that she was bringing a friend to dinner, but her parents had to see through that and would be preparing to gather intel. And once they discovered that Lucie and Collin were expecting a child and were not married—much less in some kind of newfangled elective co-parenting arrangement—they were going to freak. The question was: how much?

They arrived at the three-story bungalow in Serangoon, where her parents and Anthony's family now lived. Anthony's household occupied the top two floors.

"Remember," she growled, once she'd rung the doorbell. "Don't veer from the script. And be confident. My parents can sense hesitation and weakness, like rottweilers."

He raised an eyebrow. "These are your *parents* you're talking about, right?"

"Yes. No distractions. Give me your phone!"

"You already have it!"

"I was testing you," she said; she'd forgotten, thanks to

Pregnancy Brain. "Now stand straight. Slouching is a sign of weakness!"

"Lord have mercy," he muttered. He did, however, do as he was told.

After a brief wait at the front door, they were ushered into the Yis' large, modern living room, with its crisp catalog feel of Everything Just Right, All in Its Rightful Place.

"Lucie!"

Ivy Chen, very tall, came toward her dressed in a silk-and-cotton kimono jacket over a cream silk blouse and black trousers. She wore large, cat-eyed tortoiseshell frames that cleverly hid the tell-tale refreshment work she'd done on her cheeks. She looked like an elegant paper crane.

"Hi, Ma," Lucie said, steeling herself mentally.

"Waaaaaah, look at this ham chim peng face," said her mother, who claimed to love her, raking her eyes over Lucie's face and figure. "What happened to you, Lucie? Too many burgers in America?"

Lucie grunted. "Good to see you too, Ma. This is my friend, Collin."

"Collin!" Ivy Chen said, a mysterious British inflection appearing in her accent. "How lovely of you to join us!" She smiled and patted Collin's arm. "Huh," Lucie heard her mother mutter. "Solid." Then she left.

"What's har chee beng?" Collin whispered, as they trailed after her.

"Ham *chim* peng," Lucie corrected him. "It's Cantonese for 'salty fried pastry.' It's a type of Chinese donut.'"

"Wow," Collin said, eyes wide. "That's harsh!"

Lucie chortled. "Well, joke's on her, because people tell us we look exactly alike." Although—her face fell as she realized that people had stopped telling her that some time ago, since Ivy Chen had started going to see an aesthetic doctor. Now they told her she looked like her mother's younger sister.

Dinner was six adults and three children. The Yis had a large round extendable dining table meant to accommodate twelve, or fourteen in a pinch—all the Yis, essentially, but Hannah and her children no longer joined the intimate weekly dinners.

Lucie and Collin moved to sit next to each other, but before they could, Ivy beckoned for Collin to sit next to her at one end of the table and directed Lucie to her father's end of the table, with Anthony and his family between them. "It's easier for them to feed and monitor the children," Ivy explained. Lucie rolled her eyes at her plate—the fighting spirit had been drained out of Anthony's children a long time ago. There they sat, eating with monkish precision, food going into the right orifice each time. It was bloody annoying.

Divide and conquer. This was going exactly as she had predicted. "Remember to read my cues!" she whispered before they took their seats. Naive Collin didn't know what kind of danger he was in. He just smiled at her.

Anthony and his wife, Su Mei, and three perfectly spaced boys—Damien, Justin, and Jason, ten, eight, and six, respectively—sat down with polite smiles and wrinkle-free clothes. "So good to see you back, sis," Anthony said, as he took a seat next to Collin, facing his wife. "You look wonderful."

"Thanks, this is Collin, my . . . friend; Collin, this is my elder brother, Anthony, and his wife, Su Mei," Lucie said. The men shook hands, and Su Mei and Collin nodded at each other across the table. The kids were introduced by name but, with no distinguishing features or personalities, were doomed to be immediately forgotten by Collin.

There was another round of introductions when Yi Wei Liang entered the room. Lucie sat up straight and nodded at her father, and he nodded at her. They weren't a physically affectionate family.

Jen, one of the live-in maids, brought out the dishes she had prepared for dinner: steamed grouper heaped with fragrant fried ginger and soy sauce, braised abalone with sea cucumber, garlic bok choy and fried asparagus with shrimp paste, and a beautifully roasted whole duck, head still on, the dish placed in front of Collin as their honored guest.

Collin stared at the duck. Lucie had to stifle a giggle. He looked a little green. "Pass the duck along. Collin's not used to having whole animals served at the table," she said.

"My apologies," Ivy Chen said. "Should we pass the fish over, too?"

"Oh, I'm fine with whole fish," Collin said, trying to smile as the duck was taken away.

"This is the best duck. We ordered it from Spring Imperial. You must try some," Yi Wei Liang said, gesturing to Jen to take the duck back to Collin.

"Mmmm," Collin said as the duck made its way back. "I sure will." Gingerly, eyes averted from the duck's head, Collin made the tiniest incision into the back of the duck and lifted the smallest scrap of meat off the body. Then he passed the duck to Anthony, who, after a moment's hesitation, took a helping for his youngest and himself, before passing the dish to Lucie and her father's end of the table.

"I haven't had any duck," Ivy called out. And then the duck was passed up the table and placed in front of Collin once more, Ivy taking her time with it, before it was finally taken away again.

It was very good duck.

The Yis were in a chipper mood: Anthony had just been promoted, hence the special dishes (it wasn't all for Lucie, as her mother explained). Lucie noticed when Collin asked the boys by (correct) name if they would like anything else from his side of the table and carefully retrieved each order with a genuine smile; he chatted easily with the boys about school and their hobbies. The adults circled around generic topics, work and the Singaporean economic landscape and sports talk, before Ivy Chen seized upon an opening and said, nonchalantly, "So how did you two lovebirds meet?"

"I'm sorry?" Collin said.

"Come on, you're not telling me you are just friends," Ivy Chen said impatiently. "I can sense these things. I'm no spring chicken, and you're not teenagers! Tell me everything, Collin."

"Well, ah," Collin said, darting a look at Lucie. "I'll let Lucie explain the situation."

Lucie had been waiting for this moment. She decided to cut to the chase. "So here's the thing, Ma and Ba, Collin and I are"—she took a deep breath to calm her nerves—"expecting a child together."

Everyone, except the children, stopped eating. Lucie saw her brother's jaw drop.

"Oh, God," Ivy Chen said. Her eyes were reddening, and not in a "tears of joy" way. "What do you mean?"

"You're going to be a grandmother again! Yay!" Lucie said.

"Grandmother!" her mother said, gripping her glass of water with white knuckles. "Anthony, please ask the children to finish their meal in the kitchen and ask the maids to close the kitchen door behind them!"

Shit, Lucie thought, gripping her fork tight. *She's dismissing the help!*

After the children (and potentially gossip-leaking maids) were safely bundled away, Ivy turned her attention to Lucie. Her face was a mixture of disappointment and fury. "Explain yourself."

"I-I don't know what you mean. I just told you, I'm pregnant."

"With his child?" her father said, pointing at Collin while glaring at Lucie, his genial sample-the-duck voice gone.

"Yes," Collin said. "That's my child."

"How many months?" Ivy Chen said.

"Th-three. Well, thereabouts."

"Three!" her father thundered. "You waited till you were *three months pregnant* to let us know?"

Anthony attempted to defuse the situation. "Technically, Ba, that's the recommended—"

"Shut up, boy," her father snapped in Hokkien. He never reprimanded Anthony, and he only switched to Hokkien when he was very, very angry. Lucie reflexively ducked her head. "We're family. They should have told us as soon as they knew for sure."

"We wanted to tell you in person," Lucie said in a small voice. She turned to her mother and said, "I thought you'd be pleased to be a grandmother again."

Her mother snapped, "I'm already a grandmother *five* times over. What makes you think having an illegitimate grandchild is going to make me happy? Oh, my poor heart! After what happened with Hannah." She meant the Divorce.

"To say nothing of the distress you have caused your parents, the shame, now your actions will also be affecting Anthony. Anthony has political ambition, and having a sibling with an illegitimate child is not going to be a good look for the family, especially if Anthony's going around talking about upholding family values and launching initiatives to support traditional nuclear families in Singapore." Her father spoke quietly, but the fury behind his words was palpable. He could barely look in her direction. Instead, he directed this entire stream of words at Anthony, who fidgeted. Su Mei snuck a glance of pity at Lucie but otherwise directed her gaze at her plate of food, studying its textures with scientific intent.

Lucie's heart was racing. She'd hoped that her parents would be happy for her, since she was going to have a baby in the last years of her thirties, while she had already reached, more or less, the pinnacle of her career. But no one had even asked how she was doing, how she—and Collin, for that matter—felt about the pregnancy. Or even what their plans were. Not that abortion would ever be mentioned, as her parents were Catholic.

Sweating with discomfort, Lucie heard herself say the most incredible thing: "But don't worry, Collin and I are going to get married, so the child won't be illegitimate." A new silence greeted this announcement. Lucie swiveled her head and looked at Collin, pleadingly. "I mean, that's our plan for now."

Collin shot a look at her, and without betraying any of his own feelings about this surprising announcement, nodded at the parents. "Yes, that's the plan. I'm sorry we didn't lead with that, but we wanted to announce it at the right moment."

The codicil had had its intended effect. Ivy Chen's face relaxed. "Oh, so there will be a wedding? You should have led with *that*!" She exhaled and managed a half smile. "I suppose we shouldn't have reacted so harshly. This is after all the twenty-first century. And Wei Liang and I were also young once. Although— I won't exactly say you and Lucie are that young, anymore, and really, you should have known better."

The words stung Lucie.

"I have the very best intentions to make your daughter happy and to raise our child together," Collin said quietly. "We are very happy."

"Then it is fine, all is settled," Ivy Chen said, almost warm. Yi Wei Liang, notably, had said nothing still.

Anthony cleared his throat and smiled. "Well, congratulations, sis. I'm happy that you're happy. This is exciting news."

"Thank you, Anthony."

"And welcome to the family, Collin," Anthony said, nudging Collin with an elbow.

Her father remained resolutely silent the rest of the meal, while Ivy Chen kept shooting Collin quizzical looks. Meanwhile, Anthony chitchatted easily with Collin about international tourism, cryptocurrency, the lingering cultural heritage of the Portuguese in Malaysia, and the American economy. *He was going to be a great politician*, Lucie thought, observing her brother. *I can't be like him. I can't pretend when my own father can't even look at me.*

Finally, an hour later, after a dessert of tang yuan in ginger syrup, dinner was over. Her father uttered a terse "Excuse me" and left the table with a loud scrape of his chair.

Lucie and Collin stood up, but her mother stopped them. "I haven't given you a tour of the house, come."

Lucie knew that she wanted them alone so she could discuss other matters in private, away from the moderating influence of Anthony and Su Mei.

"Oh, we don't have to do this tonight," Lucie said, emotionally and physically drained.

"Nonsense, it'll take a few minutes. You can get a taxi after."

Her parents occupied the first floor and had a study on the second floor that served as a guest room; half of the second floor had been segmented into Anthony's family's living quarters with a separate entrance, for privacy.

With some trepidation, Lucie followed her mother around as she showed Collin the kitchen (wet and dry), the TV room and lounge, the door to their private suite, and the maids' quarters, before exiting to admire the garden with its small greenhouse full of prized orchids that she had tended over the years.

"What a lovely garden, Mrs. Yi," Collin said.

"Oh, call me Auntie Ivy. It's much more friendly this way. We're almost family now."

Lucie braced herself.

"Anyway"—faux casual, still vaguely British, she stroked a nodding sunflower—"since you're going to get married, until you get your own place, why don't you cancel your hotel and stay with us?"

"Oh, Mrs. Yi, we're already ren—*oof!*"

Lucie had stepped on his foot, casually. "Thanks, but no thanks, Ma. We're staying in my friend's apartment, rent-free, so it's fine! We have lots of space!"

"OK, but if you wanted to, you can move in and stay here. Together. In the same room," her mother said.

Lucie stared at the shape-shifter who had replaced her mother. A shape-shifting demon, certainly.

"We're quite enlightened," Ivy Chen said. "Since you're engaged, we don't want you to waste money renting. Right, Collin? Don't you think Lucie, being a much, *much* older first-time mom, needs family support?"

"Er," Collin said, his eyes darting from Ivy to Lucie. "She's very capable."

Her mother made a tut-tutting noise. "My daughter is indeed

strong when it comes to her career, but she is also weak in many aspects. She is too impulsive."

Lucie grimaced.

"We are your family, and we can host you as long as you need, until you get married and have the baby. Then it might get a little crowded."

A subtle hint of how things must unfold, chronologically.

Ivy Chen reached out and put her hand on Collin's right biceps. "We would love to see you around more often, Collin. You are part of the family now."

"How delightful," Collin murmured, adopting a strange British inflection himself. "I assure you that Lucie and I will give this the due consideration it deserves."

"Good," her mother said, squeezing his biceps again. "Wah," she muttered under her breath. And then the evening was over.

"I'm so, so sorry," Lucie said later, when they were finally home and could speak freely.

"Don't be. I had an excellent time. And that roasted duck? Once you get over the dead, staring eyes? Amazing." He made a chef's kiss. "I'll have to not eat any meat for the rest of the week, according to your system. I am really trying to eat mostly vegetarian meals this year, anyway."

"You're starting to incorporate my system," Lucie said, touched before she recalled the more pressing matter at hand. "Look, I didn't mean to put you on the spot. About getting married."

Collin shrugged. "We did talk about that eventuality. If I have to, I'll do it. You know my thoughts on romance and marriage, but what are yours? I know you believe in love, but do you believe in marriage?"

"I—" She faltered. "I actually never really asked myself that question. I always just accepted it as something expected of me." She allowed herself a small, sly smile. "However, unbeknownst to them—and I guess to you, sorry—I have a plan so you don't have to marry me."

Collin made a face. "Wow, you really know how to keep me in the dark."

"We talked about it in a rudimentary form when the girls were over, I was just hoping I wouldn't have to deploy it. See, we won't get married. I mean, in the end. Right now they already think you're my fiancé, but they still need us to commit to a date, which we won't because we'll drag our feet forever—well, not forever, more like three more months, enough for them to let everyone know we're getting married. And then we'll have an epic, absolutely monstrous fight and break up. We'll need to find something truly horrible about you that will make it impossible for them to accept you, but not so horrible they won't want you to stick around as the father and help out."

Collin's jaw dropped. "What the . . . that's . . . that's your *plan*?"

"I really don't appreciate your tone, but yes. It helps them save face vis-à-vis their friends and family, and most of all, their business network."

"Oh. My. God. That's barely a plan. And it's unnecessary."

"Trust me, that's the way it has to go down."

"Can't you just tell your parents the truth and let them yell at you until they get over it?"

Quelle naïveté! "I prefer you don't see what they will subject us to, if we don't do this. This is the way I've always been with my parents."

"You mean, you don't tell them the truth."

"I spare them the details that they don't want to hear, let's just say. A little truth bonsaification."

He was quiet for a while. "I don't want to have this kind of relationship with my children," he said at last.

"Me neither. We'll raise ours different. They can tell us anything."

"Shouldn't it start with your own family?"

He was right, of course. She should lead by example. But it wasn't that simple, and the fact that he thought it was showed her how divergent their upbringings were. She had come up in an environment where if your parents asked you to jump, you asked how high, when, and how often—and if it were in a competitive arena, you made sure to come in first. "It's too late for me and my family," she said. "Please just go with this."

He sighed and held up his hands in surrender. "Fine. So what happens next?"

"Not much. They probably took our announcement over dinner as a 'go' and are consulting some astrology expert on auspicious wedding dates as we speak."

"Even though they're Catholic?"

"Auspiciousness trumps religion."

"Don't they need my date of birth to calculate that?"

"What makes you think they don't have it?"

"Come to think of it, I left my wallet on a sideboard the entire dinner."

"You see," Lucie said. She wouldn't put it past her parents. There had been a period of time in high school she was sure someone had been through her diaries; some pages had tiny dog ears and the smell of disapproval, especially the ones that contained— in retrospect, badly written—erotic *X-Files* fan fiction. "Now we just need to let it play out, pretend to agree with whatever date they pick, and then blow it up later, but not too close to the date that they lose the deposit for the vendors."

He made a *tsk-tsk* sound. "Can I suggest something radical?"

"Sure."

Collin gave her hand a squeeze. "Look, if it matters so much to your parents, and if you want me to, I am prepared to marry you. As a last resort."

"Aw, really?"

"Well, you *are* in possession of a very valuable citizenship."

Their shared laughter broke the tension. "Come here," he said, holding his arms out to her.

She walked into his embrace after a moment's hesitation, nestling close and breathing in the soapy scent of him and listening to the soothing beat of his heart. She wound her arms around his waist as he did the same.

Maybe it was because this was their first hug since the Ramada Affair, maybe it was the excellent duck, but the friendly hug suddenly became . . . more. Closer. Quieter. She turned to look at him, just as he did, and his lips grazed hers just so, light as breath, the electric snap of contact shocking the both of them still and lighting a trail of heat that snaked down her body, a want that grew and grew till it was all she could do not to close the distance between them with a tip of her toes, almost as though she were dancing. His fingers tensed against her flesh, like hers did on his. She willed herself to look up, and her breath hitched when she met his gaze, intent on her. Unwavering. He wanted her, too.

"Collin?" she whispered, her voice catching, seeking permission for more. So certain that she almost moved first.

She'd misjudged everything. At the sound of his name, he released her as though she'd burned him and stepped back in a single, cutting movement, an inscrutable expression replacing the want she thought she'd seen on his face. He folded his arms across his chest, but there might as well have been a physical wall between them. Or a ring of fire.

"Whatever we decide to do, so long as we know what we are to each other, we'll be fine."

For all his jokey banter, Collin could be remarkably no-nonsense when he wanted to be.

"Right," she said, reality reasserting itself. "Right." She took a couple of deep breaths. *Stay in your lane, Lucie.* Because, for a moment, she'd found herself forgetting her place, wanting something that she had no business even thinking about. They had an understanding, and it was time she reminded herself why she'd chosen this path. And the consequences if she—they—messed up.

Chapter 15

～～～～～

THEY SPENT THE next weekend at IKEA buying furniture for their new place. Maybe it was the nesting instinct kicking in, or plain IKEA FOMO (a thing, truly), but they ended up buying more items than their carefully curated list had allowed for.

"I thought you were a minimalist," Collin complained as they left the IKEA.

"Hush, duckie," Lucie said, adrenaline singing through her veins as Collin hauled fairy lights and other important baby room implements into the trunk of a waiting taxi.

Lucie imagined that Collin was looking at *her* with a version of ABR (acute buyer's remorse), but it was clearly too late. There was no turning back now. "Why 'duckie'?"

"The duck is the totem of the Yi family dinner, symbolizing courage in the face of getting picked apart, literally," she replied.

"Uh-huh."

"Plus, it sounds cute."

When the furniture was delivered the next day, Suzie and Anthony came over to help out with the assembly of furniture and the decoration, while Lucie hung out at Weina's, since she wasn't technically supposed to be involved with the moving-in process or home renovation while pregnant, according to local superstition (hammering nails and painting with a pregnant woman present were big no-no's). It was just as well; lately the smallest tasks fatigued her and she forgot her train of thought easily. It was disconcerting to her, as someone who'd always prided herself on being on top of things, physically and mentally, and she had gotten used to living alone and doing everything herself the past two years. Having Collin in her life, working together and splitting what needed to be done between them as they saw fit, was a welcome change.

Between the three of them, they were done in a day, after which Weina and Lucie arrived with takeaway pizzas and inaugurated the balcony with evening drinks.

When everyone was gone, Collin led her to the nursery and flipped on the light to reveal the rectangular IKEA cot that they had bought, now painted a striking olive-green and adorned with a white satin bow.

"Surprise," he said. "You like?"

Lucie nodded. Her throat grew tight with unshed tears as she recalled another cot from another life. She cleared her throat, a little embarrassed. "I *love* it. Wow, Collin. Thank you."

"You're welcome. Anthony helped, too," he said, bouncing a little on the balls of his feet; he did that when he was pleased. "Do you ever wonder if it's a boy or girl?"

"It doesn't matter," Lucie said. "As long as the baby's healthy and here."

Collin gave her hand a gentle squeeze. "You're right, partner."

Partner. Lucie ducked her head and excused herself, saying she wanted to get ready for bed since it would be her first day back at work, but what she really wanted to do was to have a private cry.

On the one hand, she couldn't believe she was here, a mother-to-be, and she was grateful—yet the way it had all come together was so different from how she'd envisaged it happening that sometimes just thinking about what they'd done rendered her breathless. Now she knew it was possible to be toe-curlingly happy, hopeful, excited—but also torn, in a million tiny ways, every single day.

LUCIE WOKE UP after a fitful night of sleep at six o'clock, way before her alarm was scheduled to go off, and dressed herself carefully. She had picked out a pearl silk shirt with a little more give in the waist and threw on a slouchy gray double-breasted plaid blazer that she hoped would hide her new curves. "Hello, elastic waistband," she said, pulling on a maternity-ready pair of black wool trousers. She patted her belly absentmindedly through her clothes, then gave herself a critical once-over. At the boutique management consultancy firm where she worked, especially in the upper echelon, tailoring and accessories were subtle. Pregnancy and its clothing were not subtle.

Lucie threaded diamond studs through her ears, secured the clasp on her vintage Breguet wristwatch, and appraised her look. Her hair was smoothed back in a low bun and her makeup was flawless. They were so particular about image at her firm, and as a woman and a candidate for partnership in a firm with only one female partner, the pressure to conform was strong.

She got to the office by 7:45 a.m., by no means unusually early, but she wanted a few moments to center herself, reorient herself with her surroundings (and admire the view she had paid for with many, many nights of work). The office itself was decorated in gray and black, with a large Martex glass-topped desk in its center; through the glass walls was an unbroken panorama of the crystalline Marina Bay skyline and the sea. This was her safe space, and it felt good to be back. Vanessa Gan, her PA, had prepped the office. On her desk were the latest editions of the newspapers and magazines she liked, a box of Ladurée macarons, and a lush bouquet of fresh white calla lilies in a cut-crystal vase, along with a card holding several impressively scrawled signatures, including that of the managing partner, Samuel Crawford.

"I'm so happy you're back," Vanessa said, after the women had hugged—she had been working solely with Zahid Bashir, one of the busier project leaders, in Lucie's absence. "It's not the same without you here."

"Well, I've missed you and this place. Working alone is boring."

They caught up quickly, and Lucie gave Vanessa a list of to-dos before settling down to triage her emails. She didn't look up when Vanessa let herself in and placed a tray of coffee and biscuits on her desk before excusing herself. Lucie thanked her absently, engrossed in her thoughts, when the smell of the coffee hit her full force. She ran to the wastebasket, barely making it in time before throwing up her morning croissant.

This was new.

"Is everything OK?" Vanessa said, after she had knocked on the door, which had been left ajar. She waited discreetly outside, since Lucie hadn't requested her presence.

"Fine," Lucie said curtly, after she had wrested control over her breathing and cleared her throat. She liked Vanessa, but she was not ready to let her colleagues, even Vanessa, know she was pregnant. Ana Becker, a German woman who used to work as a project leader, had fallen pregnant a few years ago, and she'd gradually been taken off or edged out of all the interesting projects, till all that was left in her portfolio was dud work. The firm had a reputation for hiring the best and the brightest to staff its complex and interesting projects—if you were in Discovery Asia Consulting, you were there because you were hungry for a challenge and you had the brains and drive for it. Ana had quit a few months after her maternity leave was up, sick of being iced out. She hadn't been a principal like Lucie was, but still, she'd been senior enough. Diana Fong, the one female partner, did have a child, but Diana was also married to one of the founding partners, so that helped.

"Let me know if you need anything," Vanessa said, fading away back to her desk.

"OK," Lucie managed before she bent over the trash again.

When everything was done, she knotted up the trash bag, opened the windows as far as they would open, and rang Vanessa to remove the offending drink. If Vanessa found the untouched coffee to be an aberration, she didn't say anything.

Lucie spent the rest of the day answering emails and making calls. When Diana Fong came by to catch up, entering the room after just a single courtesy knock, Lucie was gratified that Diana overheard her thanking the investment manager for one of the wealthiest families in Thailand for choosing their firm for an upcoming restructuring.

"I see our hardest-working principal is back in the saddle," Diana said, shaking her hand. "Welcome back." Diana had been her direct supervising partner, ever since she'd been made principal, just before her move to New York, but they'd had minimal interaction or even contact.

"Thanks, Diana. It's great to be back." Despite being in her late sixties, Diana Fong had a whole head of black hair and the kind of immaculate skin that spoke of a good skincare regime and an excellent aesthetic doctor.

"And we can't wait to see how you'll perform this year, so that we can hopefully have another woman in the Circle."

Lucie mirrored Diane's confident posture and agreed to do her best. Diana was well-known as a brilliant strategist and notorious for being difficult to please, though Lucie had often wondered if the reputation had been perpetuated by threatened men. Regardless, Lucie would have to raise her game now that she was directly under Diana's supervision and seeking partnership.

While Lucie had always wanted to be partner, ever since she'd fallen pregnant she was more motivated than ever to claw her way into that exclusive tier. Weina had added her to a couple of mommy group chats recently, which Lucie found to be even more intense than Slack chats at work. There was a lot of debate about Things. The discourse veered from women asking for recommendations on the best extracurricular classes to how to secure entry to so-called elite public schools, but underlying all the discussions was a constant hum of how expensive raising a child in Singapore was. While this wasn't news—she had grown up here, had seen Hannah and some of her relatives struggle—these chats brought that point home in sharp relief. Lucie knew that in spite of her privilege, she—and her family—weren't wealthy, and solo parenting was not a realistic option if she wanted the best, which is to say a truly limitless future where no option—private schooling, sought-after enrichment courses, or epiphany-inducing gap years—was off the table. She had to make sure she could provide for her child, whatever the cost.

AT EIGHT O'CLOCK, she decided to call it a day. Her stomach grumbled—ever since she'd thrown up, she had not been able to keep anything down, yet she was hungry. She felt a little dizzy and vowed to stock up on snacks, especially flavored popcorn (the baby demanded it). A steady drizzle was falling, and the lobby heaved with office workers hemmed in by the rain. She got into the taxi queue and was just about to hop into a waiting taxi when a familiar face in the crowded lobby before her swam into focus.

Mark Thum. Staring right at her.

She let out an involuntary sound and had to steady herself by grabbing onto the open car door, bile rising in her throat, bitter and thick, choking her. *No. Not yet.* She wasn't ready for him. She had to run, to hide.

But why? her Inner Collin said. *This is just as much your home as it is his. You can't hide from him forever.*

He's right. Lucie straightened up, drawing strength from imaginary Collin's words, and steeled herself to face Mark. *I will run into him sooner or later.* He was the one who had broken them, not her. It was time she stopped running from her past.

She squared her shoulders and lifted her chin, doing all she could to project calm, to show him he was nothing to her, when inside she was glass, she was hollow, she was a ruin, she was the nothing, whose fingers trembled behind her back. But when she glanced back up, Mark was gone—if he had even been there in the first place. The rain stung her eyes and cheeks, blurring her vision.

"Miss?" the taxi driver called out, breaking the spell. "Are you OK?"

"Yes," she lied. "Sorry."

She got into the taxi, hugging her bag to her chest. Shaken and wishing she was as strong as Collin made her out to be.

Chapter 16

~~~~~~

M ark's appearance, whether real or imagined, threw everything out of kilter. Emotions, memories that she had been trying to suppress welled up in her, wreaking havoc with her equilibrium and exposing this new household, Collin, the pregnancy, for the house of cards it really was.

When am I ever going to be done with him? Will it always be this way?

Days after Lucie thought she saw Mark, Hannah came by to drop off some of her recommended pregnancy prep books to supplement those that Lucie had already obsessively read and reread. After being introduced to Hannah, Collin left to get the sisters the brown sugar bubble tea "that the baby was craving," so Lucie spilled her guts to her sister. "I've been freaking out since I thought I saw Mark."

Hannah started. "Where?"

"The lobby of my office building. I'm not sure it was him, but I've been having trouble sleeping and concentrating since."

Hannah was the only one in their family who knew the real

reason why she and Mark broke up. Even till the bitter end, Lucie had protected Mark's reputation.

"Oh, Lucie." Hannah hugged her. "It sucks to hear that he still has power over you like this."

"I don't know what to do. When I saw him, or thought I saw him, it was as though two years hadn't passed since . . . since the miscarriage"—she closed her eyes, not wanting to cry in front of her sister—"and what happened next. I *hurt*."

Hannah hugged her again. "Lucie, you should see a mental health professional. This isn't healthy."

"No shit. But I don't know if I'm ready. To talk about it one-on-one, I mean. I'm not sure I'd be able to withstand that kind of scrutiny."

Hannah bit her lip. "Well, there is one option. A group therapy–lite session, if you wish."

Lucie was immediately skeptical. "What are we talking about?"

"It's unorthodox, but online reviews seem to rave about the concept."

"Dear God. Online reviews?" Lucie didn't think she could handle more unorthodoxy in her life. "What is it?"

"A grief dinner party."

"A what?"

"A gathering where people just talk about their grief while eating together. I know someone who hosts them in Singapore. She's a psychiatrist"—Hannah held a finger up when Lucie made a face—"but she doesn't actually counsel anyone during these dinners. She just sort of directs the flow of conversation and lets the guests talk."

"Sounds super fun," Lucie said sarcastically. "I'll bet the tears enhance the flavor of the dishes."

"Maybe when it comes to mental health, the key consideration shouldn't be whether you're 'having fun,'"—soft-spoken Hannah could be so biting when she wanted to be, throwing out those killer air quotes—"but whether you are getting better?"

Hannah had a point.

Collin was encouraging when she went to him for advice regarding the grief party that night. "Why are you hesitating?" he asked. They were reading side by side on the couch, dipping in and out of conversation.

"I . . . I just—" Her voice trembled; she took a deep breath. "I don't know if I can talk about loss in front of a group of strangers." What could she possibly learn from this exercise? She was a private person. "I'm not . . . I'm not as tough as I appear."

The corners of his eyes crinkled with a gentle smile and he cupped her restless hand, tapping away on a knee. "And yet you were brave enough to do this with me."

She ducked her head and picked at a dog-ear of the novel that Collin had recommended—a Colson Whitehead, his favorite novelist—on her lap. "Brave" was not an adjective she would have associated with herself. "This was a one-off, I think."

He regarded her with that slight quirk of his mouth that always made her smile in return. "I think you're tougher than you give yourself permission to believe."

"Thank you."

"Tell you what, why don't you text me if you want me to call with an out. I could say I ate a peanut."

She laughed. "Sure."

"You can do this, Lucie."

So she agreed. Hannah connected her with the facilitator, Inge Klein, and the following Saturday, Lucie put on her brightest dress (a lemon-yellow sleeveless cotton dress with a teal pineapple print), and with her heart in her throat and wishing she had not said yes, she went to her first group counseling session.

◆ ◆ ◆

Hannah: KEEP AN OPEN MIND!

◆ ◆ ◆

Weina: Don't be afraid to cry.

◆ ◆ ◆

Suzie: Make someone else cry. And take photos.

DESPITE LUCIE'S POKER face, she was more nervous than she cared to admit. Mostly because she'd buried it deep down and done all she could to move on. And she'd succeeded in a way. For quite a while, she had been able to convince herself she was fine by applying the System of Offsetting. Her career was on the upswing, so her personal life could afford to stagnate. The fact that she was busy meant she didn't need a deeper connection with anyone else. She wasn't lonely. She didn't need to have children. These were the mantras that had held her together for the longest time, and she would have continued letting herself believe them if not for her breakdown at So Bébé.

Maybe Hannah was right; maybe she had to confront the past to move on.

The taxi dropped her in front of a three-story townhouse in a quiet gated community near the MacRitchie Reservoir Park.

Hannah had told her that the dinner parties were usually limited to eight persons, including the host, and that the host usually tried to ensure that the group was composed of those with some common points to their grief ("You've lost a sibling? What do you know, so did this guy!"). Lucie figured that the other guests were like her, with the same hurt. But she was sure she would be the only one dressed in ridiculously cheery garb, her way of thumbing her nose at the proceedings.

Lucie was skeptical about the whole setup. She had never been someone easy to get to know, and the idea of opening up to a group of strangers seemed ridiculous.

"Hello," she said to the intercom, after buzzing the doorbell. "I'm Salad Girl Lucie." Everyone was supposed to bring a dish for the potluck. Lucie had—or rather Collin had—made a kale-and-lettuce salad with avocado, crumbled feta, and heirloom cherry tomatoes.

"Hey, Lucie," the voice said, an accent that was both British and Germanic. "You're bang on time. Come in. We're waiting for a couple more folks to arrive."

Lucie was greeted at the door by Inge, in her late forties, tall, blond, and wearing a batik-print robe that was so bold and colorful it made Lucie annoyed. She leaned forward, expecting to press cheeks but was enveloped in a warm hug.

"Welcome, Lucie," Inge said, "to our safe space. I hope you enjoy your time with us."

Lucie pasted on a smile as they pulled apart. "Hello," she said. "Thanks for having me. I'm new to . . . this." She made a twirling motion with her fingers.

Inge beamed. Her green eyes were almost too bright. "I wouldn't worry about it. Normally we'd be eight, but tonight the group is smaller, just six of us including me. One couple had to drop out because their eldest child is down with a cold."

Lucie made suitable noises of commiseration. Runny noses were the paper cuts of diseases.

Inge's home was Scandi-boho chic. The light-wood furniture looked expensive and custom-made, the upholstery done in cream and off-white tones, with abstract art in grays and pops of orange dotting the walls. Lucie was introduced to Desmond, Seetha, and Min Lee, all in their thirties or forties. Desmond and Min Lee were divorced, but on friendly terms—they were fish farmers, tilapia and carp and other freshwater species; both were sleek-haired, short, broad shouldered. Seetha, short-haired curls, tall, new like Lucie to the group, was funny, a chiropractor by day and an amateur stand-up comic by night. Inge handed out goblets of white wine that only Lucie refused, choosing instead to have chilled soda water, as they stood around the kitchen island, chatting and eating homemade crisps and little hummus-filled pastry squares. Lucie found herself intrigued by her fellow diners' normalcy. Where was the sobbing?

Too early, she decided. *Inge is saving that for dessert.*

"Hmm," Inge said, as she scrolled through some texts. "Looks like the last guest might not turn up after all. He sends his apologies. Let's be seated."

Lucie was seated between Seetha and the empty chair for the no-show. "Doesn't matter that it's only five of us today, I'm sure it will be an intimate and productive conversation."

The guests were asked to talk about what brought them to the table. Inge—and to some extent Desmond, through his eager nods and yesses—issued assurances that it was a safe space to discuss their losses.

It would take more than an assurance that this was a safe space from a fellow named Desmond to convince her to let her guard down.

"Hello, everyone, I'm Inge, your host, as you can see." Awkward laughter broke out. "I've been hosting this chapter of grief dinner parties since 2017, a year after I moved to Singapore. It used to be a quarterly thing, but we now meet every other month. My son, Jan, died in a ski accident in 2014. He was seven. I was living then in Switzerland, with my partner, Boris. We have an elder son, Gregor, sixteen, who is at boarding school in Switzerland now."

Lucie was struck by the quiet strength in her voice. Inge looked each person in the eye as she spoke, held their gaze one by one, accepting and giving something primal in each exchange.

Beside her, Desmond took a deep breath and began. "Hi, everyone. I'm Desmond; this is my ex-wife, Min Lee. . . . We've been attending these grief parties since 2018, not long after Inge here started the chapter here." He cleared his throat. "We've found the community to be welcoming, something we really needed after Min and I . . . Min and I lost our firstborn, Ting Jin, aged two, in a car accident in 2016. It *broke* us. . . ." His voice faltered; Min Lee reached over and gave his shoulder a squeeze. He closed his eyes, took a beat, before continuing, "And it'll never stop breaking us, I suppose . . . But we pulled together with the help of Inge and the community, and now we want to . . . to pay it forward."

Min nodded, her eyes wet. Desmond reached out and rubbed her back. Lucie looked away. She tried to control her breathing.

"I'm Seetha, new to this group. I . . ." She inhaled and exhaled sharply, looking down at her lap. "I . . ."

"It's OK," Inge said softly.

Seetha was clenching her jaw. "S-stillborn, seventh month, two years ago, a girl."

And then it was her turn.

"I'm Lucie. I-I'm also new here." Lucie turned toward Seetha and said softly, voice catching, "Mine was miscarriage, at e-eleven weeks, over two years ago. A girl, too."

The women embraced. Lucie realized that she was sobbing. She was sobbing so hard that she didn't even realize that someone else was hugging her from behind. It was Inge.

"It's OK," Inge said. "Let it all out. This is a safe space."

Surprisingly, the urge to punch Inge in the face did not come. Lucie sat there, sandwiched between two women, and let out the poison that had been lodged in the pit of her stomach.

WHEN SHE WAS cried out, Lucie excused herself and tried to address her face in the guest powder room. She felt her phone vibrating in her pocket and knew it was Collin checking in.

Are you OK, need me to break you out?

No, she texted back. I'm good 😃. Then she turned off her phone.

She opened her bag to rummage through her makeup kit but gave up when she saw how blotchy her complexion was, and how swollen her eyes had become. Her eyeliner and mascara were smeared extravagantly over her lids and under her eyes, even the tops of her cheeks. *So much for tear-proof formula*, she thought. All in all, she looked like a train wreck. No amount of makeup could help that, not immediately. The worst had passed, and trying to look like nothing had happened, when a fundamental shift had, seemed ridiculous. She blew her nose again, removed the smudged makeup as best she could, reapplied some tinted lip balm, and returned to the table and sat down.

"T-thank you," she mumbled to the group; what for, she wasn't sure. But she felt at ease now.

"Hey, no worries. It's happened to all of us," Min said gently. Seetha smiled; she hadn't left the table. Despite her tears, she was one of those women who didn't ugly cry. She was red-eyed but immaculate.

"What do we talk about now?"

"Anything, everything," Inge said. "Whatever you can't say to your family and friends who've never experienced loss."

It turns out there was much to say. Inge was right—these were people who understood what she had been through with the miscarriage, in ways even her best friends didn't.

Inge was just serving the main—a cheesy lamb mince lasagna that smelled heavenly and made Lucie's stomach rumble—when the doorbell rang.

"Who could it be?" Inge mused, opening the door. It was almost nine. "Our missing guest?"

The group tittered. Lucie turned her head, smiling.

"Hello," said Mark Thum. "Sorry I'm late."

Chapter 17

THE FIRST TIME Lucie met Mark Thum, she'd been twenty-eight and on secondment in Hong Kong with the management consulting group where they worked. Mark had been a senior, five years older, working in another department. He had a loud, brash personality and a reputation for being a hard partier and one of the best consultants in his line of work. She had bumped into Mark at the Friday interdepartmental drinks. She knew him from sight, of course—who didn't? He was the brilliant, charismatic, if somewhat private, and very attractive star of their firm—and she'd been surprised when he'd singled her out for small talk. He had an easy, ingratiating way about him, helped by his lively dark eyes and laugh lines bracketing a perfect set of teeth, and despite her initial reserve, two hours of small talk and a bottle of wine later they found themselves in a tiny copy room, having very disorganized, cramped, and what she thought would be inconsequential sex. She remembered walking out of that copy room with a paper clip embedded in her back that she discovered only when she changed later that night, her body euphoric. She felt like she'd been drugged, and there was no turning back.

They slept together for five months, and then one brunch late in July, Mark asked her if she would move in with him. There hadn't even been any real interstitial, transitional dating between them. "I'm turning thirty-three," he said. "And you're perfect. You're everything I've ever wanted in a woman."

It all progressed pretty quickly from there, on the career and love fronts. They moved back to Singapore, and she moved into Mark's place. Lucie resigned from the company when she was offered an interesting opportunity at Discovery Asia Consulting, he stayed in the same company and became a managing partner, and they started talking about marriage.

He appeared to be wholly devoted to her and their future. After he met her, he'd stopped partying as hard (Lucie had never really enjoyed that aspect of the work, viewing it as necessary solely for networking and career advancement); they made a home together.

So when he proposed a couple of nights after she'd been made principal, she accepted without hesitation or doubt. She knew that they were good together, he was everything she'd ever imagined in a mate, and she liked that as a couple they were complementary. They were both type As. He was encouraging of her ambition, she of his, and when they were together the pieces just seemed to fit.

And then she fell pregnant, ten months before their wedding. That's when Mark showed his true colors.

"LUCIE," MARK SAID, having the good grace to blush.

"I'm out of here," Lucie said, standing up so fast she felt the room spin.

"I'm sorry," Inge said. "What's happening?"

"We know each other," Mark said warily.

"We used to be engaged," Lucie said.

Inge raised her hand. "OK, but we're not done with the session yet. Would you at least give me the opportunity to lead you all through some guided—"

"There's nothing to discuss, not with him around," Lucie said. She was nauseous. If she did not leave soon, she would retch. She would faint.

Mark took a couple of hesitant steps to her. "Lucie, I am so, so sorry."

"Sorry?" she repeated. "That's laughable."

"Discussion is encouraged here," Desmond said, uncertainly. "We don't need to fear the truth. Nothing said here is repeated outside the circle."

"Oh, Desmond," Lucie said. "I don't have a problem with the Truth. But Mr. Big Shot over here, do you really want me to tell these people why we broke up?"

Mark's face blanched. "I can't stop you," he said. "That's what this group is for."

That was unexpected, coming from Mr. Save Face. Mr. Appearances Matter.

Alrighty then. "We'd been together for about six years; he'd proposed. We went for a fertility checkup because we were both in our thirties and we found out"—her eyes met Mark's, hesitant, and he nodded—"he had a very low sperm count."

Mark was standing very still. Until that day, nobody, aside from the doctor and them, knew about this.

"We were told it was unlikely we'd get pregnant spontaneously, but there were options. Obviously, we were disappointed to hear this. We got a little lax with contraceptives, and somehow, somehow, I got pregnant. Our little miracle baby."

"Lucie . . . ," Mark whispered.

She trembled but powered on. "We were elated. We got one of those really expensive screening tests. And when we found out it would be a girl, Mark got so . . . so excited." She closed her eyes to prevent herself from crying. "Unfortunately, as you all know . . . I lost her."

They'd gone to dinner and an '80s-themed birthday party of a mutual friend's the night before. The next day, driving to work, it happened. Was it spontaneous, or was it the dancing? She would never know.

Seetha reached out and gave her shoulder a reassuring squeeze. Lucie opened her eyes and looked at the table.

"The miscarriage wrecked us. The first two weeks we were barely functioning. But then a month passed, and another. We got better. I reasoned, a child could still be in the cards for us, with time—it happened once, right? And our wedding was still coming up. So almost three months after it'd happened, I went to the office to pick him up for a surprise dinner, the door to his office was ajar, and there he was, you know"—she dug her nails into her lap under the table—"*with* his boss."

The room was silent.

"You know what kills me? He never did come home that night. He didn't realize I'd stopped by. Then he came home in the morning and lied to my face about what he'd been doing. Said he had been 'handling a closing.' Imagine having to deal with that when I'd just fucking *lost* my baby."

"It was a one-time mistake," Mark said, his voice shaking. "I had never done anything like that before."

"Well, you certainly did so with style," Lucie said.

Mark made an anguished noise and clenched his fists. No one spoke.

Lucie said to Inge, "I'm sorry, but I have to leave."

"Please," Inge said. She stood up. "And I'm really sorry this turned out this way."

Lucie nodded at everyone except Mark and walked out of the house.

"Wait." Behind her, she could hear Mark following her. "Lucie," he said, urgently. "Lucie. Please listen. That was the only time. I was going through some stuff, Lucie."

"What, second puberty?" Lucie said, keeping her voice low, aware that they were on the street.

"No. What I did was unforgiveable, I know. I didn't even like Sandra, Lucie. Believe me."

Lucie laughed bitterly. "If that's how you treat people you don't like, then I'm glad I got out while I could."

"Lucie, there's more to it. Please let me explain."

"Oh, can it. You never wanted to be tied down. As soon as I was pregnant, you completely changed."

"No, I *wanted* to be married." His face was twisted. "I didn't want to disappoint you—"

Lucie let out a bark of incredulous laughter.

She turned to walk away when he grabbed her by her shoulders, pulling her close. Lucie flinched and tried to pull away. He held on tight.

"I'm going to scream, you psycho," Lucie hissed, struggling.

"No, you won't," he said in that authoritative voice of his. "You're going to listen to me." He softened his tone. "I mean, please. Please let me explain."

Lucie went limp in his arms. She stopped struggling. He might hold her and force her to listen to him, but she would refuse to acknowledge him otherwise. Although being this close to him was affecting her more than she cared to admit.

"Lucie, I fucked up. I behaved horribly. There is no excuse, but I now understand why I detonated things." He took a deep breath and released it quickly. Lucie averted her eyes. "Y-you never knew this, but when I was five, my one-year-old sister passed away. When the meningitis took her, my parents lost the plot for a few years. My dad checked out, my mother had a very public affair. It was . . . a difficult time. A lot of anguish, shouting, strict disciplinarian action." He was breathing hard. "They only got their act together when I was eight or nine. I-I was too young to remember a lot of this, but the memories surfaced when I went for therapy. Proper one-on-one therapy. I-I've been seeing a therapist for the past two years."

Lucie tried to hide her surprise. *Mark, in therapy?*

"Lucie, I have loved you since Hong Kong, even before I knew it. I was so devoted to you, don't you remember?" She heard his voice break. "Whether or not you believe me, I have done a lot of reflection and I know now that I-I cheated, not just because I was dealing with the loss of our baby, but because I was afraid. I was afraid I'd hurt you and disappoint you as a husband. I knew you wanted kids. My infertility felt like the first sign. And then the miscarriage . . . God, Lucie. I felt like the universe was conspiring against us."

"You don't believe in fate," Lucie said harshly, despite her resolve to say nothing.

"I do now, Lucie. You coming back and meeting me here is fate."

"This doesn't change a thing. You tore up my world once. People can't change."

"I think people can change, Lucie."

He let go of her gently. She heard a muffled *whumph.*

"I'm sorry." *Whumph.* "I'm sorry." *Whumph.*

Lucie opened her eyes. He had knelt, and he was bowing to her. The proud, immaculate Mark Thum was bowing on Inge Klein's brightly lit front lawn, his forehead making that blunt sound as it hit the sunbaked grass.

I'm sorry.

I'm sorry.

I'm sorry.

Lucie stared.

He kept bowing to her, saying sorry, sorry, sorry.

"I WANT TO see you again," Mark had said, when he walked her to the entrance of the condo that she and Collin now called home, his car idling by the curb.

She should say no. But she turned to him, saw the hunger in his solemn face, and instead she said, "Let's see." She hadn't forgotten everything in one evening, not by a long shot, even if she had forgiven him today. This was the best she could do now.

He lit up as though she'd given more. "Thank you. I'll call you."

Almost reflexively, she curled her fingers around the hand he offered to her in goodbye, biting her lip at the old jolt of electricity. He put his other hand around her fingers and held them tight.

"I've missed you so much," he said in a rough voice. Lucie sensed that he was waiting for an answer, a reassurance of some sort, with this statement. She wanted to give it to him, but it was too soon. When she said nothing, he nodded and lifted a hand to her face wordlessly. He pressed a hot palm to her cheek. "Lucie," he said, again. Then he walked away.

Lucie went straight to her room without calling out to Collin, who was in his room with his reading light on, having texted her to say he was waiting for her to reach home safely; she couldn't muster the energy to tell him why she'd been out till midnight. She texted to let him know she was back and called the only person she knew would be up and willing to chat, and the only person she wanted to talk with, anyway. She video-called Suzie.

"He did what?" Suzie said, when Lucie was done. "He stalked you?"

"I never said that," Lucie said.

"What are the chances of meeting in a grief dinner party? It's not exactly a supermarket."

"He's been doing the work for two years, apparently. Going to a therapist. Maybe the therapist mentioned the grief dinner party."

"You're doing it again. You're finding excuses for his controlling behavior."

Lucie laughed out loud. "C'mon. Mark's not like that. He's got some issues—"

"You think?"

"But I just don't think he's the stalking type."

"I wouldn't put it past him. Gaslighting jerkface. And what would Weina say?" she chided. If anything, Weina hated Mark even more than Suzie did. In the aftermath of their breakup, she kept suggesting they contact Simon's uncle's "business partner" in Korea to "teach him a lesson he would never forget."

"Let's not say anything to her," Lucie said quickly. Weina, they agreed, was honey-badger-level scary.

"Well, we'll have to find you a new grief dinner party, won't we? We can't have that rat bastard back in your life."

Lucie dared not admit to her oldest friend that she had already given Mark her number. On Inge's lawn, after she'd pulled him up, her heart thudding dully, he'd taken the opportunity to embrace her, weeping, still apologizing, and she'd said the only thing she could: *I forgive you, Mark.* A weight lifted off her at her words, and she realized she had meant it. Giving him her number after that release between them felt like a done deal, inevitable.

But try explaining that to the woman who'd christened him Mark MacGaslighter.

She studied her fingernails and pulled a Weina move. "Have you heard that BTS might be going on a world tour next year?"

Suzie flipped open her laptop and started typing furiously. "No, wait. What? What? How did I miss . . . I'm on the mailing list of *all* the. . . ." Then Suzie stilled and narrowed her eyes at Lucie. "That's not cool."

Lucie shrugged, a small smile on her lips. "I really don't want to talk about Mark."

Suzie studied her for a long moment. Lucie met her gaze without flinching, then Suzie gave a curt nod. "You're right, BTS is so much more fun. Do you need my help finding another group counseling session, though?"

"I'll find another alternative; don't worry," Lucie said. Only later did she realize she'd been careful to leave Mark out of her promise—and for good reason: She wanted to see him again.

Chapter 18

~~~~~~

THE NEXT MORNING, Lucie woke up earlier than usual and left for the office instead of having breakfast with Collin. Yet another shift had occurred in her world and she needed space to parse through her emotions and thoughts.

Hey sis, just checking in on you. How did it go? Hannah wrote.

It went well, she replied, not getting into the details.

At noon, while she was having lunch at her desk, she received a text: I'm so glad we bumped into each other. Maybe we can meet for dinner? Lunch? Drinks?

She didn't reply. She ignored his texts and continued working on her latest file. But her thoughts kept circling like carrion birds.

I'll even settle for a coffee, at this rate, he wrote, a couple of hours later.

"Go away," she muttered, fighting back a smile.

She turned off all notifications and buried the phone in the deepest recesses of her bag, determined not to reply to his texts until she could be certain of her intentions. She didn't need another friend in Mark; she didn't need another complication, either.

She left the office after seven, having been caught up in a conference call with a client in Jersey. Again, she caught herself scanning the crush of people in the lobby for Mark, even though she knew she shouldn't.

Still, she looked, and she was disappointed when she did not see him.

◆ ◆ ◆

Mom: Hi dear. It's been a while since our dinner and I haven't heard back about your wedding plans. You need to set a date! Preferably in the next 2, maximum 3 months otherwise you can't wear a nice dress anymore, you'll look more like a papaya or worse, a pumpkin in a white dress.

Mom: I mean, you're almost 40. What will people say if you have a child and you're not even married at this age?

Mom: Your father and I will pay for everything, of course. If we want the politicians to come, Anthony needs to send out invites VERY soon.

Mom: Lucie?

Mom: Link: <u>How to plan an elegant wedding for 500 people in under 3 months!</u>

"I can't deal with this bullshit," Lucie muttered, throwing the phone into her dirty laundry hamper. "I mean, I'm thirty-seven, not 'almost forty!'"

She was starfished on her bed, bloated and gassy in her duvet cocoon, Billie Eilish mumble-singing in the background. She was quietly mourning her discovery earlier that evening that vagina farts were a thing, and what's worse, now *her* thing, and that on the off chance that she would have sex again before the baby came, she would need to *manage* that, when she heard a knock on the door. "Yes?"

"I made veggie tacos, homemade nachos, and guacamole for dinner, my liege. Would you like?"

She struggled to her feet and opened the door with a dramatic bang. "You had me at 'tacos.'"

"I'm pleased," he said, bowing. Lucie stifled a laugh when she saw what he was wearing: a T-shirt with the legend "Nuts for You" and—her gaze fluttered down and her mouth went dry, no small feat these days—boxers. "I had to lure you out. You were sulking so hard I could feel it through the walls."

"I wasn't sulking," she said as he put a hand on the small of her back and ushered her to the living room. The contact made her heartbeat race and color rise in her cheeks. *Cool your jets, lady.*

"Tough day at work?" he asked.

"Pregnancy body blues. Everything either works too well, or not well enough, or is starting to look completely different. It's very unsettling." They settled down on the couch. She bit into a taco and groaned with pleasure. "I *love* you."

He laughed his amused-and-surprised laugh. "Your love is cheap. But I'll take it." Now he was blushing, or at least his ears were. He busied himself picking at his own taco, then asked, "How was the grief dinner party?"

She didn't want to think about Mark when she was with him. It muddied the waters. "It went well. You start at Dave's on Wednesday, right?" she asked.

He got the hint. "Yup. The name of the start-up is BofBofGo, in case you forgot."

"You never mentioned it. BofBofGo? Good God, what is that?"

"It's an express logistics company."

"Clearly." She stifled a giggle.

"What's so funny about BofBofGo?" he said with mock outrage.

She shook her head in amusement as his phone vibrated.

He glanced at it. "It's my dad," he said; his face was carefully neutral. "He's back in town and wants to meet up."

She stretched and kept her tone light. "Do you even want to?"

He started. "Of course. Why do you ask?"

"Because you didn't exactly try to make time to meet him when we first got in."

He studied the phone in his hand and stayed silent for so long Lucie worried she had been too frank. When he spoke, his voice was so low Lucie had to lean forward to catch his words. "It's . . . complicated. I want to meet up with him, I know I *should* meet up with him, but I don't want to *spend time* with him. Does that make sense?"

Lucie laughed; he'd perfectly encapsulated the conflicted way she felt about her parents. "One hundred percent."

He fiddled with the buttons on his phone. "When I was young and they divorced, I hated . . . I blamed and resented him for the way things went down, I guess because my mother did. Yet, with the pregnancy and his advancing age . . ." Collin raked his hand through his hair, grimacing.

Lucie hesitated, sucking on her lower lip, before asking, "Was he a . . . a *bad* dad?"

Collin's mouth pulled down in a half grimace. "No. But he was not a *good* dad, either. He was absent, uninterested, never wanted a kid, probably. And I was always so sickly, even besides the nut allergy." He gave a small, harsh laugh. "Probably not what he wanted, since he was really into soccer and stuff."

Lucie put her hand over his and said nothing.

"When I was in my late teens, he reached out to me and asked for a relationship. Since then he's shown more initiative, flown to see me, even if it's for short bursts of time. And he's definitely a big reason for my move to Singapore. Yet I find it so fucking hard to meet him halfway, the weight of all the history between us . . . even though logically I know I *must*, or I'll regret it one day. Do you understand?"

She gave a short bark of laughter. "Friend-o, more than you'll ever know. I mean, you've met my family. How I interact with them could fill a manual on how to navigate dueling impulses. But my sister will be the first to tell you that in these cases, sometimes you have to be the bigger person and just say, 'Hey, I'm here. Do with it what you will, sir.'"

He watched her under the thick curve of his lashes as he weighed her words. Then a small smile broke on his face as he nodded. "You're right. I'll go to his and meet up with him one of these weekends."

"I'm glad." She caught his eye and said, "Thank you for sharing this with me. And let me know if you need me to come with you for moral support."

Collin held her gaze for a few beats longer than necessary and said, "I will."

I would fight anyone who hurts this man, Lucie thought, squeezing his hand, the ferocity surprising her. She pulled back, affecting nonchalance and waving the air. "So, what do you want to watch?"

"You choose."

She scrolled through Netflix and found a promising one: a creepy-looking manor that just screamed "I'm haunted with dead little girls to the rafters, and that's not all!" "This one!" she crowed.

"Sure, looks fun."

"You don't mind?"

"Nope, I *love* horror movies."

Mark would have grabbed the remote and thrown it down the garbage chute. Lucie clapped her hands in excitement. "Ooh, could it be that Collin Read is a man after my own horror film–loving heart? Kiss me!" she said, and then cringed inwardly. She'd been joking, but—sliding a glance at him—it had been a long time since she'd been kissed, and Collin had the best shaped lips she had ever seen. Lips that had been off-limits in their Ramada Affair for reasons that seemed rather arbitrary and ridiculous in hindsight.

Maybe some of what she was thinking showed in her face. Collin's voice was unsteady as he said, "Don't joke. And don't think I won't do it."

"You wouldn't dare," she said, intensely aware of his proximity on the couch.

"I don't think you would be able to handle it," he said. There was a tautness in the way he was holding himself.

"Then do it," she said, her voice low, her heart thudding in her ears. "I dare you."

A kiss dare! How mature! How—

He took a deep breath and reached over in slow motion; Lucie, blinking, hardly dared to move, to breathe, and—

He took a nacho from the bowl on the armrest next to her. He tossed it into his mouth and, not looking at her, said, "We really should stop clowning around and get started on the movie, or you'll be asleep before the end of act one."

"You're right," she said, embarrassed and more than a little stung.

What were you trying to achieve? Don't mess this up, she chided herself. *Keep everything profesh, woman. Private parts, indeed* all *body parts, must not meet again.*

She gave herself a mental shake, got up with the bowl of nachos, and placed it on the coffee table, glad to have an excuse to readjust her position. When she sat down, she feigned a yawn and rested her head on the armrest, as far away from him as physically possible on the two-seater. Not that he realized. He was scrolling through a political news website and scoffing at the headlines. Disgruntled, she pushed "play" without asking if he was ready. Dense, moody instrumental music filtered tinnily from the speakers. Collin looked up from his phone and put it away as the protagonist burst onto screen (as in *literally* burst—she had died in an explosion of gore as a grave VO explained her tragic backstory.

"You know, it's strange—I've never actually verbalized how I feel about my dad with anyone before."

"Mm-hmm," Lucie said, her thoughts still hooked on the "clowning around" remark.

He was looking at her; she could feel it. "You're a good friend," he said.

Lucie ignored him, a knot forming in the pit in her stomach. *Yeah, Collin, I got it. Loud and clear.*

Her phone buzzed. A text from Mark flashed. Lucie unlocked the phone and read, Drive-by this week? I won't even wave if you don't want me to. I just want to see you. Please. She shook her head, a smile on her face. *My Ex Would Never take silence for an answer.*

"A ringgit for your thoughts," Collin said. She sensed his eyes on her, curious about the text.

"I'm thinking let's watch the movie," she said and, with a crisp flick of her wrist, turned up the volume till she could no longer hear herself think.

Chapter 19

~~~~~

Suzie: Wanna check out that BTS pop-up store in that new mall this Saturday, say around 3pm?

Lucie: Sorry Suze, I have our first appointment with my new ob-gyn Sat morn. I'm pretty sure I'll be napping after.

Suzie: Sunday?

Lucie: We've got to check out some prenatal courses. Rain check?

Suzie: Sure. No worries.

◆ ◆ ◆

Anthony: Have you decided on the wedding date? Because the parents are legit freaking out.

◆ ◆ ◆

Mom: The other day I was talking to Auntie Bernice—you know Bernice, her son is the oncologist that went to Johns Hopkins University and married that underwear model—and she said that she saw on Instagram that if you want to hide a baby bump in a wedding dress, you have to get an empire line dress and a REALLY big bouquet. But once you're past your sixth month it's Game Over. In your case maybe fifth month.

◆ ◆ ◆

Dad DO NOT PICK UP: Have you decided on the wedding date?

◆ ◆ ◆

Collin: I bought pineapples and prunes for your bowels.

Lucie: Collin, pineapples are a NO-NO!

Collin: Huh? Why?

Lucie: Didn't you read the link I sent you for foods to avoid according to traditional Chinese medicine principles? So let's just play safe.

Collin: Old wives' tales, surely.

Lucie: TCM is one of the oldest forms of medicine and has THOUSANDS of years of history, so don't be dismissive!

Collin: OK, OK, I'll eat the pineapple. Sorry.

Lucie: Read the article.

LUCIE FIDGETED IN her seat as they waited to be registered at the ob-gyn, Dr. Joyce Shivanathan, who Weina had recommended. Her last visit to the doctor had been in New York just before they'd left, almost two months ago. They could have visited the doctor's sooner and Collin had been asking since they first arrived, but Lucie had dragged her feet a little. It was, in a way, a case of Schrödinger's cat—without confirmation, the baby was and was not fine, in her womb; although she knew that she was still pregnant (having taken two pregnancy tests since her last appointment). But there were so many permutations bad news could take, many ways a baby could be hurting, even in the womb. And now she was opening the box.

She tried to distract herself by focusing on her breaths and the notches in the beige wood of the chair in front of hers. *In, out, in, out.*

Collin had gone to get a takeaway coffee when it came to Lucie's turn to register them. The nurse—in her sixties, tightly pinned bun of graying hair—smiled kindly at her. "Hello. First visit?" she said.

"Yes, for Dr. Joyce please. Ten thirty. Lucie Yi."

The nurse consulted the printed schedule by her desk and nodded. "Found you. You here alone?"

Lucie glanced around, looking for Collin. "My partner will be joining me."

The nurse handed her an iPad. "Come fill out the registration form. Make sure you put your husband's mobile number. Sometimes the baby come early, we need to call him, OK?"

"Oh." Lucie laughed nervously. "That's . . . um, he's not my husband."

The nurse stopped typing and peered over her tortoiseshell bifocals. "Eh, how can?"

"How can what?" Lucie said, replying in Singlish.

"Got baby together. Why not married?"

Lucie blinked, taken aback by the line of questioning. Having been away for two years, she'd forgotten how direct and meddlesome elders, even strangers, could be in this part of the world. "I . . . I don't know?" she stammered.

"Better marry quick. Good for the child and you. Otherwise people talk."

Lucie stared at the nurse. "I . . . I will think about it."

Then Collin was back and they were ushered into the doctor's examination room. Dr. Joyce, who appeared to be in her early forties, exuded a quiet confidence and warmth. Lucie liked her instantly. They chatted about the pregnancy, and she answered their many questions without rushing them, plus she didn't seem perturbed when Lucie used the term "partner" when referring to Collin. Yet Lucie couldn't help thinking about the nurse's advice even when she was lifting her top and lying down on the examination table, clear goo being spread on her belly.

The screen lit up with a flash, and there it was, flailing on the screen. Their baby. Lucie drew in a shaky breath. This time, it was more than just a pulsing bean. It had a head and a body and it was *waving* at them.

"Wow," Collin whispered. Lucie felt as though her heart was too large for her chest. She reached out for Collin's hand just as he did for hers, and he squeezed it. They looked at each other; her eyes, and Collin's, were damp.

She had a sudden vision of them sitting at a dinner table, Collin serving them his Famous Cajun Fried Chicken (he called everything good he made "famous"), regaling them with a story, while she stroked the back of a child's smooth head. She could almost smell the sweet, strawberry scent of its shampoo, hear the child's giggle as Collin made a face. Lucie ached with anticipation.

"Baby looks good," Dr. Joyce said. She swiped the wand around and showed them different angles of the baby, explaining what the numbers on the screen meant. She turned on the sound so they could hear the thumping of the heartbeat, a beautiful regular rhythm. Dr. Joyce nodded, satisfied, murmuring, "Everything sounds good, too."

Lucie sagged with relief at the doctor's words; she hadn't been aware up till then how tense she'd been. *You're OK, baby*, she thought, giddy with hope. It was the first time she directly addressed the child in her belly.

"Do you want to know the sex?" the doctor asked as she whirled the transducer over Lucie's belly.

"You can already tell?" Collin said.

"Well, I have a good idea."

"No, thank you," Lucie said. "We want it to be a surprise."

"Hang on," Collin said, his eyes tracking the baby's movements. "Should we reconsider? I won't mind finding out."

"But we discussed this," Lucie said. "I thought we'd agreed that it's more fun to be surprised."

"We did, but our agreement is a living document, isn't it? We've changed our minds on things before," he pointed out.

If he was referring to their renegotiated rental budget . . . Lucie bristled.

"It's your choice," Dr. Joyce said. "Just let me know if you change your mind, because I've seen it happen a lot."

"I don't want to know," Lucie stressed.

"She doesn't seem to want to know a lot about the baby," Collin said, not entirely under his breath. "I mean, it is the first time we're seeing an ob-gyn together, and we're thirteen weeks in already. Instead of confronting concrete facts about the baby, she's worried about things like me moving furniture when she's in the house and eating pineapples."

Lucie stiffened. Even though she understood his frustration, Collin should know why she hesitated. Could he blame her for clutching onto superstitions, even as she feared being confronted with medical facts?

"I wouldn't worry about that," Dr. Joyce said smoothly. "We get all kinds of parents: those who prefer to take a more relaxed approach to visits, and those who are—shall we say—more regimented. There's no one single right approach. Everyone approaches parenthood differently."

After the appointment, they slowly made their way to the taxi stand at the far end of an outdoor parking lot in silence. The afternoon sun beaded Collin's toned arms with sweat; Lucie caught herself in the act of reaching over to flick them off his skin. She made herself count to ten and think of the sharp ends of pencils.

"I'm sorry for what I said in there," Collin spoke up after a while. "I didn't mean anything malicious by it. I was just a little bit frustrated. Eager and anxious, too."

Lucie bit her lip. She hadn't considered how the wait must

have been for him. "It's OK. I should also be apologizing," Lucie said. She clasped his hand. "I'm sorry I made you wait so long to meet the baby. You were right; I was avoiding it."

He gave her this look, a lopsided smile with a slight squint. "I get it. I don't love it, but I get it." Lucie knew that she was forgiven. She brushed the hair off her shoulders and wrestled it into a knot at the base of her neck, Collin's eyes still on her.

"You were worried in there, weren't you?"

She nodded. "I hadn't realized until then how much I'd been trying not to think about the baby. Just in case." She examined a loose thread in her sleeve. "And I didn't want you to freak out at all the thoughts I was having *around* the pregnancy." *Or the weird sex dreams*, she thought.

"So who do you sound out pregnancy stuff with? Weina?"

"Yeah," she admitted.

Collin shook his head. "Lucie, you can *always* talk to me. About anything."

"You say that, but then you make fun of my beliefs. Like on TCM."

He groaned, dragging a hand over his face. "Lucie, I'm not. I'm questioning them because I want to understand the logic behind it. It doesn't mean I'm making fun of them. I swear."

"OK, fine," she conceded. "Truce?"

"Truce."

They stopped in the middle of the parking lot under the shade of a large rain tree, and shook hands. Collin clasped her hand for a beat longer than she would have liked—or maybe not long enough. Lucie sucked on her bottom lip. She didn't understand why his touch confused her these days.

"Here," she said finally, pressing one of the printouts of the scan in his hand. "I want you to have one."

"Thank you." He took the photo and scrutinized it. "That's a handsome, perfect little baby. The best."

"Not perfect, not the best," Lucie said quickly. "Just average, like any other baby." In her childhood, an older auntie had scolded Ivy Chen when she had praised then-newborn Hannah's looks. "Don't attract bad spirits by praising a baby's looks too highly. Don't you know what happened . . ." And then a detailed anecdote about someone's son and his too-fortunate name, which caused him no end of bad luck.

"*Haiyah*, correlation does not imply causation," her mother, newly Catholic, had laughed, eager to dismiss old wives' tales.

Hannah did turn out to be a beauty, and even though Lucie knew, *knew*, it was illogical to think any misfortune in her sister's life was brought about by her mother's compliment, she would not take that risk—not when it came to her own, and possibly, only child.

Collin was scrolling through a note. "Anyway, shouldn't we start discussing names for the baby? I love the name Finn for a boy, and Lynn for a girl. Or we can look at unisex names, Alex or Da—"

"No names," she said abruptly.

"What do you mean?" He was astonished. "You don't want to name our child? I mean I'm progressive, but I'm not giving it a bunch of symbols in place of a name."

Lucie crossed herself. "What I mean is we can short-list a few names we would *potentially* give the child. But nothing firm. Until the child is actually born."

"Why not?"

Lucie could feel that lump in her chest forming again, a tight ball of emotion that jangled with nerves. "Just—that's just how I want it to be."

Collin frowned. "Is this another one of your superstitious beliefs?"

"Yes, and so what? It's part of our—my culture. Why can't you just accept that there are some norms I want to adhere to?"

"But superstitions are just silly, outdated beliefs and practices. *You* don't even understand why you adhere to them."

His words stung. "So what if I want to err on the side of caution?" Lucie said, raising her voice. "To be safe? What's so wrong with not wanting to take any risks when it comes to *our child*?"

They faced each other in the parking lot of the hospital, arms akimbo and glaring, until a car backed out of an adjacent spot and Collin reached out automatically, pulling her into his arms for safety, so swiftly she bumped her nose into his neck.

In his arms, things quietened, stilled. She could see the sweat starting to bead on his brow and the fresh stubble on his jaw, and she caught the salt in his scent. Their eyes met and for a dizzying moment Lucie forgot that they'd been squabbling, or the conflicting emotions of guilt and anger brought on by the nurse's comment.

She wanted only to weave her fingers through his sweaty hair and kiss him.

Then the car honked, and the spell was broken. She pulled away, a little shaken by the intensity of the moment. *Don't give in. Keep cool*, she told herself. Except "cool" was not the word she was feeling—especially when he was close to her. She didn't understand this confusing new hold he had over her. Was it an organic evolution, or just a reaction to all the pressures to fit a specific mold of what a family looked like? Whatever it was, she had to break it. Put things back in order again. Collin didn't want a romance—he said so, several times. Plus they weren't even right for each other, that way. She would be breathtakingly deluded to push for something more.

Absolutely deluded.

So why did kissing him seem like a logical thing to do?

"You know what? You're right," he said, holding up his hands in surrender as he regarded her with a half smile on his face. "If it's important to you, I should not be dismissing it. I'm sorry. I'll stop."

Lucie blinked, thrown by this volte-face and his sincerity. But even if he apologized to her, did it solve the fundamental issues at hand? They had such different worldviews, in practice. "Apology accepted."

"Let's go home," he said, taking her hand. "I think the baby deserves pancakes."

Pancakes might be what the baby wanted, Lucie thought with increasing unease, *but maybe what it really deserved was a real family, not a simulacrum of one.*

AITA? SHE ASKED her friends later that evening. About wanting to adhere to some cultural norms, to respect old wives' tales or superstitions?

I don't think you're being unreasonable, Suzie replied. You're just trying to cover all your bases. But you should try to make some allowance for differences in opinion.

Weina, what do you think?

It will get easier, with time and communication, Weina wrote. She'd had some cultural-related misunderstandings and clashes with Simon, who was deeply, traditionally South Korean, despite his decade in the UK for graduate school and work. They eventually figured out a way to compromise and work together. Lucie wanted the same for Collin and her; she had thought that having some shared ethnic and cultural background with Collin meant they would have similar cultural touchstones, but he was much more American than she had accounted for.

Case in point: Collin had whipped out a hammer and was going to knock in some nails in the walls *while she, a pregnant woman, was home*, and was actually bemused when she had yelled "NO NAILS!" and wrenched the hammer out of his hand. She then made him promise that he would get those 3M strips that *normal renters* used to put frames up on the walls. I feel like we keep knocking heads these days and all the talking doesn't seem to get us anywhere.

You know what the problem is, don't you? Weina replied.

What?

Where Simon and I can hash things out in a more INTIMATE manner, you and Collin can't. Or won't.

There was a pause between texts. And why not? You've already gone there, she added slyly.

Lucie: We went there with a specific intention and purpose. If we did so again without these guidelines . . . What do you think, Suzie?

Suzie: Look, I get the angst, but if I can be honest, I don't think I can contribute much to this chat. You know where I stand on premarital sex. Also I feel like crap and I want to talk about non-baby or romantic stuff, just this once, if that's OK?

Lucie: Sorry, Suzie. We got carried away again, didn't we?

Weina: Oops.

Suzie: It's fine. So, anyone watch anything good on TV? I'd love some suggestions on bingeable shows. And where are we going to have our next girls' lunch?

Lucie: Can we have dim sum? It's a pregnancy craving. We'll make it halal, of course.

Weina: Of course! Speaking of food cravings, I remember that with Arwin, I was really into salt-and-vinegar crisps, but I had no special cravings when it came to the triplets. By the way, how are your parents?

Lucie: They've been sending me texts every couple of days, but the interval between texts is shortening. Don't worry, I've got a plan.

Weina: You're going to avoid them until the baby comes, aren't you?

Lucie: Yup.

Weina: Genius.

Lucie was about to reply to Suzie's prior question when she got a push notification. A text from Mark, whom she had also been ignoring.

Are you free for lunch next Tuesday? We can go to our place at Robertson Quay.

Our place. She knew the restaurant he was talking about, tucked in an unassuming side street away from the bustle of Robertson Quay, with its cozy black booths upholstered in actual leather, which had prompted her to joke that it felt almost barbaric, enjoying the meat while sitting on the skin of the same animal. Mark had pointed out that she was clearly not letting this ethical quandary prevent her from ordering seconds, and she had said well, this was her journey of mindful eating and she was going to refrain from eating red meat for the rest of the week (applying her System of Offsetting), and Mark had laughed and agreed to join her. And then he had given her that look, a half smile with his left eye squinted, that said, *Wow, you're weird—but you're* my *weirdo.* He had squeezed her hand and brought it to his lips for the quickest kiss. Her heart ached at that memory.

Come on, Lucie. It's just lunch. In broad daylight.

It was never just lunch, she knew that. But she said yes anyway.

Chapter 20

W ow. You look nice," Collin said, looking up from the waffle machine. He usually made breakfast for them before they headed out for work, although the last two days he'd left early to go hiking at a nearby reservoir. Things had been a little strained since the ob-gyn visit the day before. He quickly added, "I mean, nicer than usual."

Lucie, who was wearing a long-sleeved black silk jersey wrap dress with a loose blazer, patterned hosiery, and electric-blue kitten heels, her hair done in a loose chignon, smiled. "Thanks. I have a lunch date, later." She had been unsure of how to classify it, but "lunch date" sounded better than "potentially disastrous catch-up with my former fiancé, and also it's premium yakiniku, so."

Collin did a double take. "A date?"

"Yes, a *date*." It came out snippy instead of breezy. "Don't look so shocked. You make it sound like I'm a swamp creature."

"Oh, you're very eligible. I just . . . I just didn't know you were already looking."

"I'm not *not* looking. And aren't we all?"

Collin pursed his lips. "I guess."

The waffle machine—a novelty Star Wars one that Collin had recently acquired—beeped, and Collin busied himself filling two plates with waffles until she touched his arm and shook her head, indicating that she had to run. "Meeting with the bosses," she said, regretfully eyeing the sourdough waffles.

Collin nodded and bent his head to eat standing at the opposite end of the kitchen island to her. With his head down, he said, "That was a fun day, wasn't it?"

"What was?"

"Our not-date. Barring the ER part."

Lucie chuckled. "It was the best not-date I've ever been on, barring the ER part."

"It might even be the best *date* I've ever been on," Collin said, "even with the ER part."

He looked up and they locked eyes; Lucie's stomach fluttered at the expression in his eyes. *He felt something too, didn't he?*

But in a flash it was gone, and she wondered if it had even been there in the first place.

He put his fork down with a sudden clatter, jaw set, expression determined. His pronouncement face. "Look, Lucie, I've been thinking, after yesterday's thing at the ob-gyn . . ."

Lucie realized she was holding her breath and let it out with a *whoosh.* "Yes?"

"I thought, maybe things are getting a little . . . tense between us because we're too entangled and focused on the baby, so if you're not, ah, well . . ." He cleared his throat. "What I meant to say is, if you're not against the idea of dating, if *you're* dating, maybe we should, uh, date—"

Each other?

"Other people, openly."

Lucie blinked. *What?*

"I mean, we did talk about it, or do you want to do the public breakup for your parents' benefit first?"

"What? No! I mean, we don't have to wait for *that*. I'll just—of course!" Lucie said, almost shouting to emphasize how certain she was. "I mean, I'll just text my parents and say we've broken up. But yeah, what I mean is, I don't see a reason why not." After all, she was going on pre-dates with Mark, wasn't she?

"OK, well, that's good," Collin said, turning away to pour new batter into the machine. "Good to know you're OK with that. Although maybe we should wait as long as we can before we faux break up in front of your parents. You shouldn't do it over text."

"Sure, I'll wait as long as I can before I announce that we're done to my parents. As for dating, good to know how you feel."

Collin busied himself with the waffle tongs. "I'm not in a rush, but yeah. Good to know how you feel about it, too."

Isn't it wonderful when everyone is in agreement, Lucie thought sardonically.

"Anyway, I thought you should know . . . I'm going to see my dad later. We're going to have dinner."

She was surprised. "Oh wow, that's really great, Collin. A big step!"

"It's . . . a step."

"In the right direction," she said encouragingly.

He bent a little closer to her belly, and said, "Hey, li'l one, I'm going to see your granddad today. Your mom talked some sense into me."

Lucie laughed. Collin tipped her a nod. "Sure I can't tempt you to take some waffles to work? For a snack?"

"Why not," she said, rubbing her belly and smiling. She looked up and they chorused, "The baby demands it!"

Collin grinned. "I'm putting that on a T-shirt. For both of us. When the baby comes."

"Then please make sure your T-shirt is at least as large as mine."

"I can't guarantee that," Collin said, mock serious as he made a show of sucking in his stomach. Lucie covered her mouth to smother a giggle and something in her belly fluttered. Twice.

Her eyes widened. "Oh my gosh, Collin! The baby just moved. Come!"

"What? Already? Isn't it early?" He rounded the table in a flash. Then, as though she was a giant Fabergé egg, he gently placed his hand on her belly, running it up and down in slow circles.

It was the most prolonged contact they'd had since the tryst. He was looking at his hand, murmuring "Hey, baby" repeatedly, oblivious to her physical reaction to his proximity. Her heart was beating so hard she was worried for the baby's eardrums, and her nipples could take someone's eye out. And she might be salivating—more than usual, that is.

"Collin," she said, with great difficulty. "It's over. It's stopped now."

"Has it?" he said, massaging her bump as though by doing so he'd be able to coax another movement.

It took all her willpower to gently push his hand away before she did the opposite. "It's stopped, completely."

"Right," he said. "Oh, hey, wait." He reached out and tucked a strand of loose hair back, a finger grazing the top of her ear and sending a delicious tingle down her spine. "There. Now you look all professional."

She bit her lip and avoided his eyes. "Thank you."

"No problem, Lucie," he said, clearing his throat and jamming his hands into his pockets.

They both stood there quietly, not moving, too close to each other for a couple of beats before she snapped herself out of whatever lunacy had possessed her and stepped away, muttering that she'd see him the next day.

She had trouble concentrating at work that morning. Was it just a reaction to sensual deprivation, or had she developed a crush on Collin? Or maybe Mark was reawakening old passions, tickling dormant neural pathways? Or all of the above, supercharged by all the hormones? Pregnancy libido was real, although one had to wonder what the evolutionary point of this was. She was already knocked up. Someone upstairs was having a laugh at her expense, surely.

AT THE YAKINIKU place, Mark was early. He'd chosen not to face the entrance as she entered, fifteen minutes late (a work call with Diana). He was fidgety—drumming the table, his posture hunched, unlike his usual self. Old Mark would have faced the door, waiting with his best smile, every movement calibrated. That would have been her move, too. So to see him in this state of unease—it loosened something in her as she walked up to him, her heart pounding.

"Mark," she said. At her voice, he turned around. "Hi. Sorry I'm late."

"No worries." He hugged her. "I'm so glad you came. I was . . . worried you wouldn't turn up. Not that I would blame you."

She nodded, sat down.

He called the server over and was starting to order for them, before he stopped and said, "Shit. I forgot to ask you what you wanted to eat. I just thought . . . What would you like?"

"It's OK, you've already ordered all my favorites."

They chatted easily—work, the economy—the questions she needed to ask not surfacing. She studied his face when he was occupied with the business of grilling meat: how fine he looked, his skin healthy and barely lined, his body fit under the tailored shirt, his thick black hair spliced with a few silver strands.

He gave her odd looks when she cooked her meat cuts for longer than she used to. He was having a glass of wine with lunch, and he seemed surprised that she had refrained from the same. Finally, he asked the question she'd been dreading. "You're not really eating. I've even ordered your favorite wine. Is everything okay?"

At first, she thought she would lie and say she was not feeling well. Or that she was extending her yearly Dry January run. Then she thought, *Fuck it*. Maybe there was an element of revenge or malice in her wanting him to know. Regardless, she took a beat. "Mark, I'm pregnant."

He blanched and put his cutlery down. The cube of meat he'd been grilling made loud sputtering noises as it blackened. "What? Since . . . I don't . . . How far along?"

"Over three months." She grabbed the hissing meat with her chopsticks and dunked it into a sauce bowl.

"Wow," he said. "Wow." He slumped back on his side of the booth and just stared at her for a while, his mouth slack; it was as though he'd forgotten how to arrange his face. "I mean, congratulations?"

"Thank you. I'll take it."

"Who's the father? Are you with someone? I didn't know. . . ." He glanced down at her ring finger.

She could have laughed. "I'm not seeing anyone, Mark. I don't need to be."

He did a double take. "Good God. I'm so sorry. Did the asshole . . . ?"

"Not an asshole. This was planned. And the father and I are raising the child together here in Singapore."

"I don't know what to say," Mark admitted, his expression pained. "I-I'm flabbergasted. I, well, I was hoping to fix things between us."

"I'm not with him," she said, too quickly. "He's just the co-parent."

She hated the way she'd said that. It diminished the role that Collin played in her life. And fix what, exactly? What was he proposing?

In one of the emails Mark had sent a couple of months after she'd left for New York, he'd evoked the Japanese art of *kintsugi*, of repairing broken pottery pieces with gold, to come together after breaking apart in a beautiful way. Lucie had had to prevent herself from hurling her laptop out of the window or burning something. The rage she'd felt seemed unsurmountable. But now, when she looked at Mark, who was a picture of genuine remorse, who was *doing the work*, she couldn't summon up the old rage. She had meant it when she'd forgiven him on the lawn.

"What do you want, Mark?"

"Just time," he said simply, reaching out to hold her hand. "Your time. I don't want anything else for now. And I accept that your circumstances might have changed, but how I feel about you, what I want from you, hasn't."

"I don't . . . I don't understand."

He took a deep breath. "Lucie, I want you back."

LUCIE REMEMBERED LITTLE of what came after this declaration of intent. It had not come as a complete surprise, because she knew, from her own careful due diligence (mutual friends who could be trusted to shut their traps) that he had not been seeing anyone in the last two years, and how he'd looked at her when she slid into the booth. The twinned flames of hope and pain.

"I want you to know that I will do anything necessary to win you back," he'd said, when the meal was over and they stood outside, waiting for their taxis. He'd paid for their meal before she could ask to split it, having given his card to reception even before the lunch had begun. He held her hands in his. "I want to be with you. There's no doubt in my mind." His eyes dropped to her belly. "And this . . . pregnancy doesn't change a thing."

But it changes everything, Lucie thought. A man offering to care for the child of another—that had consequences beyond the both of them.

And did she even want Mark? It was all happening so fast.

"This is all too much, too soon." Her thoughts-to-speech filter had been eroded by pregnancy, clearly.

"I didn't mean to throw it out like this, on our first dat— meeting. But I couldn't let you think all I wanted was friendship. I'd be lying, and I don't want to hide anything from you anymore." He gave a shaky laugh and regarded her. "You seem different after New York, Lucie." The taxi arrived. He opened the door for her. "Volatile," he said, as though it were a bad word.

"Maybe you've just forgotten how to read me."

"Then give me time to remember," he said softly, before she pulled the door shut behind her.

As she lay in bed that night, she saw all her favorite Mark-Lucie moments in a slow, wistful reel, all the "first times" that had meant something to her. The first time they went on a real "date": sushi and sake in a hole-in-the-wall in Causeway Bay, after the firm's casual Friday drinks. The first time he held her hand in public after months of subterfuge. The first time they watched a horror movie together and she heard him yelp. The first time he told her that he loved her, in bed, soft rain underscoring the confession, "Gymnopédie No. 1" by Erik Satie low in the background.

The good played, and then that one bad, but how lovely was the good, like the ground coming up after winter, the ice melting to reveal all—the green stirrings of spring, of life, and the bodies under the thaw.

◆ ◆ ◆

Lucie: Let's go for a jog tomorrow. I haven't seen you in ages!

Suzie: OK. Twofer meetups. I dig it.

On Thursday, Lucie left work earlier than usual despite the pressing workload, needing the release of a good run, her first since she fell pregnant. Now that the pregnancy was more established, she was itching to get back to it.

She rubbed her bump with a gentle hand. *Hey, baby, I don't know what happens in there when I run, but if you hate it, just knock, OK?*

She came home and ran into Collin, who she'd missed that morning on account of an early-morning conference call. He was stretching in the living room, ready for yoga. "How was dinner with your dad?" she asked, as she absentmindedly removed her blazer and started unbuttoning her blouse in front of him. Her body was overheating, as it was apt to do these days.

Collin averted his eyes, but not before she caught his eyes lingering on the deep V of her camisole. Her skin goosebumped. She stopped and went to get a glass of water. "It was . . . fine," he said, uncharacteristically unforthcoming. Lucie picked up on the hesitation and bit back her next question. In spite of his very American frankness, he was secretive when it came to matters of the heart. Access to the real him had to be earned, in trickles. "You're more oniony than you think, mister," she said under her breath.

Collin swiveled around in Warrior Pose. "I'm sorry, what?"

"Never mind," she said. Her phone beeped a reminder and she got up to go to her room to get changed. "I'm going to the Botanic Gardens for a jog with Suzie."

"Want me to come with?" he asked.

"No, it's fine."

"OK," Collin said. "Is everything all right? You look a little . . . flustered."

I'm blushing because I caught you watching me, and you don't want to know what filthy, filthy things I'm thinking. "I've been running alone way before I met you, honey."

"But you're not alone anymore," he said, gesturing at her belly, then himself. He smiled his crooked grin. "Let me be your water boy."

"No thanks," she said, laughing and wrinkling her nose. "You'll just cramp my style."

"I'll have you know I am a triathlete. Anyway, text me in an hour so I know everything's fine?"

"You can track me on the app," she said, wagging her phone. She didn't mention that this was what she and Mark used to do as a practice—which was how she found him and his boss. Ironically, Mark had been the one to suggest they make each other mutually traceable in the first place.

"I'd rather not," Collin said. "Where's the mystery in that?"

She blew him a kiss, which he caught with an exaggerated swoon. "I'll be fine."

He grabbed her around the waist without warning, lifting her with a whoop and twirling her around in the air as she giggled. "We should go dancing, if you feel good enough to jog. I've joined this wonderful Lindy Hop community and been waiting for your nausea to pass."

"Dancing?" Lucie said, swatting his arm so he would put her down. "I don't know, Collin. I'm so busy."

"Just once, please?" He put her down gently.

Lucie rested her brow against his cheek. "Oh Collin." Still dizzy, breathless, and laughing, she said, "I'll think about it." Then she caught her breath and headed upstairs to her room.

Dancing! She shook her head. Sometimes she found herself forgetting who she was when she was with Collin.

RUNNING OUTDOORS HAD always been her favorite exercise. She liked varied terrain, liked the feel of the sun and wind on her skin, even the humidity and smog in this part of the world. She ran without distractions, phone silenced. It was how she disconnected from the pressures of her world. Running always clarified her thoughts, and she needed clarity.

I meant every word I said, Mark had texted that afternoon. I will fight for you.

I don't even know if there's anything left to fight for, she said.

I know there is. I felt it between us on Tuesday.

She ran harder.

"You look like you have demons on your back," Suzie shouted, appearing by her side in what could only be described as "not enough running gear."

"Are those . . . are those . . . leather trainers? And . . . and are you wearing a bralette?" Lucie said, between pants. "Your boobs!" Suzie was wearing an oversized white T-shirt and a pair of leggings that could have been tights.

"Oh, my clothes? I forgot to switch gym bags, and my used running gear from last week was *literally* growing mold, so I had to improvise with what I had on hand." Suzie smiled and waved at a staring woman walking a butter-blond Pomeranian by the track. "Don't worry, I'm only running with you for half an hour before I bail, and as for my boobs, they can handle it," Suzie said breezily. She gave Lucie a sidelong look. "I wouldn't worry about me jogging with my perky Bs when you're flapping about with Cs that are becoming double Ds!"

"I'm not worried about your boobs outlasting mine," Lucie said wryly. She thumbed her chin at an oncoming runner, who, while staring at Suzie's chest, nearly ran over the Pomeranian. "I'm worried for the collateral damage. You are going to cause an accident."

"Well, cry me a river if a couple of pervs pass out," Suzie said.

"Thanks for the laugh," Lucie said. "It's been a crazy week." She filled Suzie in on the Mark and Collin situation.

Suzie sighed, her pace slowing. "Why are you even thinking of getting back together with Mark?"

"You used to love Mark."

"I used to love *Dawson's Creek*, but people outgrow things." Suzie gritted her teeth. "Just . . . just be cautious around Mark, that's all."

"I will be," Lucie said, then, innocently, "Don't you still watch reruns of *Dawson's?*"

"Oh, is that a cockapoo?" Suzie said, pointedly ignoring her. Suzie knew all the dog breeds. She had always wanted to have a dog growing up, but her family preferred not to have dogs as pets, and now she was too busy to have one. But it was her dream to one day have a lawn full of chow chows, or a "soon-to-come breed that's aggressive but deceptively cute, like me."

"Anyway," Suzie said, easily outpacing Lucie despite not being a regular runner or even fit (she went to the gym to network). These days, Lucie found herself easily winded, so she was jogging at a much slower pace. "I must say I can't sympathize. It's difficult being single at our age, and more difficult as a divorced Muslim woman." She threw a glance at Lucie. "Also, I feel like every time we chat these days, all we talk about anymore is Weina and babies, or you and babies, or you being wooed by Mark and Collin."

"Hmm?" Lucie said, distracted by a man walking a rat-dog hybrid. "Wooed by Collin? He doesn't like me *that* way. Why, do *you* think he's into me?"

"Forget it," Suzie muttered. "Anyway, you really need to avoid Mark until you have a clearer idea of what you want."

A sensible suggestion, Lucie thought.

But after that, every time she saw Mark's name on her phone, she knew that sooner or later her restraint would crack, especially when he sent her a picture of her engagement ring.

The caption read, It's still yours.

Chapter 21

AFTER ONLY FOUR hours of fitful sleep, Lucie barely had time to bolt down a bowl of sludgy oatmeal at her desk and now she was due to speak in front of all twenty-three partners and principals. Today was her debriefing of her secondment in New York, and she had a feeling that after it the partners would be announcing this year's candidates for partner. *Please be cool, baby*, she willed her baby. *We're in this together, OK?* Her stomach churned.

"Are you OK?" Vanessa said under her breath, with a sidelong look of concern; Lucie's face had turned green when someone had placed an espresso in front of the principal seated next to her.

Lucie tried not to breathe in too deeply. "I'm good," she said, trying not to think about throwing up. Lucie was determined to present a strong front, mentally and physically. There'd already been rumors circulating that she'd been leaving work early and looking a bit peaky. If she didn't have to, she wasn't going to reveal she was pregnant till she was at least six months along. She was carrying small, so that helped. Her plan was to work on all projects right up till the time the baby busted out of her. There was no way she was giving the partners any excuses to remove her from hot projects or the elusive list of equity partnership. After all, it had been a bumper year for the firm, and they had to reward the hungry. And was Lucie hungry, metaphorically and literally.

"Gentlemen, ladies," Samuel said, nodding toward Diana and Lucie. She and Diana gave each other the once-over that women in high-powered positions did, subtly assessing each other's clothes and accessories, but in a nonthreatening way since they were not in direct competition. Lucie valued Diana's approval of her sartorial style, and she could tell that her outfit—a gray, boxy long-sleeved top accessorized with a turquoise Hermès silk scarf, maternity wool slacks, and low kitten heels—was not impressing the older woman, who was immaculate in a sharp midnight-blue trouser suit, tailored white shirt, a discreet gold chain, and three-inch nude patent YSL pumps.

"The first order of business is a presentation from Lucie, who spent two years in New York cultivating leads while consulting on tax structuring for us, as you might remember. Lucie, if you please."

She'd been sweating over her presentation for weeks, worrying over every word and figure, but she needn't have—at the end of it, the management team, including Samuel, applauded her and told her that she had done well in New York. "Almost as though you barely had fun over there," Samuel said.

"Well, Samuel, I can confirm that I hardly did," she replied in jest.

"That's what I like about sending single women your age for such secondments," he said. He clapped his hands, and everyone else joined in the applause with more vigor, Lucie's face burning.

"Great work, Lucie. Next up, the latest project from COR-PEXA, a global corporate services firm that wants a review of its business model in view of new, more-tech-savvy start-ups in the sector coming in . . ."

Lucie let her mind drift. It happened often these days. Her brain wanted to think about *Ways to communicate with your unborn child through music* and *How much masturbation is normal when you're in your second trimester?*

". . . and Lucie will be leading the CORPEXA project."

Shit! She snapped to attention upon hearing her name. There was polite applause and a congratulatory nod from Diana. Her first project as lead principal. "I'm honored," she said. "Thank you for the mandate."

"Of course," Samuel said. "Congratulations. If this goes well, I think we're looking at a promotion for you this year."

Lucie tried to look simultaneously modest and competent. "Thank you, Samuel, for your trust."

"The first female partner since Diana!" Samuel chuckled. "Well, it had to happen one day, eh?"

Diana gave Samuel an icy nod and said nothing. Lucie plastered a nonthreatening smile on her face. *I'll try not to let my lack of a cock get in the way*, she thought. *Asshole.*

She left the office at 6:30 p.m., earlier than she should have, wanting to go home and unpack all that had happened that morning with Collin. He was usually home before her, and they had standing dinner arrangements for when neither of them had "outside" plans. Her heart lifted at the thought of celebrating her win with him, asking him how his day went, and sharing the horrifying fact that a novel she'd been wanting to read, which was set in 1980, was listed online as historical fiction.

She was humming her favorite tune from *Folklore* as she

reached the apartment, a bounce in her step, when she saw some-one standing by the door, shifting his weight uncomfortably. "Excuse me?" she said, reaching a hand into her pocket for her keys. When the man turned around, she breathed a sigh of relief. It was Collin's dad. "Uncle Peter," she said, recalling his name just in time.

"Hi, Lucie," he said, shaking her hand. She invited him inside. "Something to drink?"

"Ah, no thank you. I'm not staying for long. Don't want to bother you."

"No bother. Are you waiting for Collin?" she said. She was glad they were seeing each other again, so soon after their big dinner. While she didn't think the dysfunction in her family could be remedied, she was glad she could help with other fami-lies. "Did you have something planned?"

"No," Peter said. "I just . . . came by to drop off a gift for you both." He passed her the paper bag he was carrying. "I had planned to give it to him at our dinner, but he didn't come."

What? Lucie schooled her features into a polite mask, even though her thoughts were racing in dizzying circles. Why had he lied to her? "I'm sorry he didn't show. Has he"—she hesitated, feeling like she was betraying Collin, but she needed to know the truth—"has he done this before?"

Peter sighed. "It's complicated. It's been a long time since it happened. I travel a lot for my work—I help restaurateurs fran-chise and expand—and I have tried to mend our relationship over the years. I'm guilty of . . . many things, not being present is one of them. But I'm really *trying.*" He rubbed his palm across his eyes in a tired gesture. "And I thought I was making a break-through. *At least he meets up with me,* I thought. He doesn't say much, and we end up talking about nothing but surface-level things, but he still turns up. And when he told me about you two and the pregnancy, about the move, I thought, it's great he's moving here, right? We'll be closer. This is our chance. But now that he's actually here, he's doesn't show for the first home-cooked meal I've ever invited him to." He shook his head. Lucie ached at the defeated expression on his face.

"I'm so, so sorry to hear that."

Peter gestured to the paper bag. "Open it later. It's for you, anyway."

"Thank you."

"I'm happy he has you. He doesn't . . . he doesn't open himself up to people much. Especially after his mom died."

"I always thought he was the popular one." She thought about the way Collin was with her: always bouncy, full of laughter, light. Always joking around.

"Well, I don't know about you, but I know my son, even if he doesn't want me to. He's a closed book. Pretends to be otherwise, but you'll see. He doesn't let people in."

After he bade her goodbye, Lucie opened the gift (a six-pack of onesies), sat down, and thought about what Peter had said, and all the things Collin had preached, about being open with her family, back when they were talking about the plan. It was laughable now. Because even if Lucie didn't tell her parents everything, she didn't withhold affection from them. Whereas Collin . . .

Your dad was here, with a gift, she texted Collin. He would draw his own conclusions from that.

He didn't reply for over an hour. Then—I'm staying out late. Don't wait up.

No acknowledgment of the subtext of her message. *You lied.*

She felt wrong-footed, unsure. Who was this man? And why

did she think he could co-parent with her? He owed her nothing. They were held together by the flimsiest of agreements. Maybe she had made a mistake.

But she was immediately remorseful. Collin had moved for her and the baby. He was committed. *Give it two seconds, will you?* she chastised herself. *How incredibly faithless of you to jump to extreme conclusions.* This arrangement was only going to work out if she believed in, and respected, her decisions in this arena, too. *She* had chosen him; *she* had done the homework. And she had to believe he would honor their arrangement, no matter what.

She ate, watched a couple of episodes of a Netflix drama, starting every time she thought she heard footsteps in the corridor. She fell asleep on the couch halfway during the third episode and woke up around midnight, cold, the patter of rain and hail on the window loud as a drumbeat. She looked up from the living room to the second floor and saw his bedroom door wide open. He hadn't come home.

Chapter 22

~~~~~

LUCIE WOKE UP on the couch, disoriented, the next day when her alarm buzzed at 6:45 a.m. Collin had covered her with a throw and left a note on the table. *You were snoring*, the note said. *Cute.*

He'd come back after all. She could see that his bedroom door was closed from her vantage point. It made her inordinately glad, until she was hit by guilt that she had, indeed, expected him to run at the first hint of conflict.

She found a second note under the first: *I went over to Dave's for a work-related chat then a really long walk to clear my head. I'll explain about my dad later.*

Give him a chance to give his side of the story, Inner Weina piped up.

She was getting ready for work when she discovered her first pregnancy-related stretch mark—on her boobs.

She stared at her chest—spectacular, albeit with nipples now the size of continents—in the mirror. While she had never really obsessed about the size of her breasts, she'd always understood that their modest size hadn't exactly "helped" her out in life. *Where were you when I needed to get backstage at that Jay Chou concert fifteen years ago?* she thought wryly, prodding them. She would need to get new bras. What she'd seen of maternity bras was not fun: grandma straps and thick padding designed to rein in, not titillate. Pregnancy was not only *tons of fun*—who wouldn't enjoy hurling without warning or realizing they needed to pee in the middle of a Bible-sized PowerPoint presentation, twice—it was also a nonstop thrill ride to Expenditure Town. She was grateful for her pregnancy, of course, but—hold on—she squinted in the mirror at two tiny, pale beige nubs parallel to her armpits that had appeared seemingly overnight. What in the fresh hell were those?

She took a photo, captioned it ??? Just found these???, and sent it to Weina, who immediately video-called her.

"Yikes!" her friend said. "What's going on?"

"What do you mean, 'yikes'? WTF are those? Don't *you* know?"

"*Ch-ch-ch-ch-changes, turn and face the stra-ange.*" Her supposed friend started singing Bowie as she googled something on her laptop. With a flourish, Weina read out the results, "I'm no expert, but from my Google search, it appears you have a case of su-per-nu-me-rary nipples. Yeah."

"Speak nonmedical, woman!"

Weina read out, "Supernumerary nipples . . . blah, blah, blah, accessory nipples or in some cases *boobs* that grow as a rare pregnancy side effect." She clicked on a couple of images and let out a screech of horror and delight. "So cool!"

Lucie fought back nausea. "Cool? Fuck off! This is not 'cool.' This is horrifying. When does it revert? You told me the nipples go back to their pre-preggo state, you *told* me! Who, aside from the baby, will want to see my boobs now?"

It struck her then: for all the playful banter about her and

Collin dating other people, who would date her now? She was a thirty-seven-year-old single mom-to-be, with *four nipples*. Collin would have no problem finding someone with a flip of his sun-streaked hair—whereas she was facing the odds of a three-legged horse in the Kentucky Derby. *Of course* she was glad to be a mother, God, yes, and again, she didn't understand why she had to justify this to an invisible audience of judgy women, but she hadn't planned for the identity to be her entire life. No shade to those who did (again, the invisible audience in mind). What she wanted was to meet someone, ultimately. But she'd foolishly glossed over the real-world difficulties of dating as a woman in her late thirties. With a baby. And with no alimony-paying ex-husband to boot. And *four fucking nipples*.

A cold toad hopped into her stomach and settled itself there.

"Yes, your nipples should *technically* revert," Weina hedged, "but as for these *accessories*"—she giggled—"I'm not sure; the websites don't say. You might have to trawl Reddit or some such place." On screen, Weina could be seen scrolling down and clicking merrily away at more images. "Man, am I glad I didn't get these at all. Wow, this woman's case gives new meaning to the phrase 'side boob.' Hers are ginor—"

Lucie hung up and screamed.

◆ ◆ ◆

Mom DO NOT PICK UP: Are you seriously going to ignore us forever?

◆ ◆ ◆

Mark: Hey there.

Lucie: Hi.

Mark: We should have dinner.

Lucie: I don't know if that's wise . . .

Mark: Just a friendly dinner, Lucie. I managed to bribe my colleague for the contact details of Singapore's top 10 confinement nannies. It's a restricted list, as you know. Word of mouth recommendations only.

Lucie: Wow.

Mark: I have to pass it to you in person, though. So, dinner next Thursday? Friday?

Lucie: I'll let you know.

THAT NIGHT THEY were to have dinner with Collin's friends, a couple from Baltimore. The man, Aaron, had spent several years in Singapore as a child. He and his wife, Kay, worked in catering and ran their own business. They were in town for a trade conference and had reached out to Collin over Facebook.

Lucie came home early and found Collin waiting for her in the living room, already dressed for their night out. His expression was somber. He gestured for her to join him on the couch.

"Listen, about yesterday, I'm sorry. I didn't mean to lie about meeting my dad. It's just . . . I just couldn't bring myself to enter his home. Like it was a threshold that I couldn't cross, symbolically. Like a vampire." His tone was amused, trying to make light of the situation, but Lucie wouldn't let him.

"You told me we should be open with each other. Foster a spirit of transparency in our soon-to-be family. This makes me wonder about everything you told me."

"I swear, there's nothing else I'm hiding," Collin said emphatically. He saw her raised eyebrow. "I'm serious."

"Your father says you are a closed book, and I'm now wondering if I've been missing something."

"Lucie, I want to be open with you." He put a hand on hers, clasped it. "Please, believe me. I have been truthful in everything else. Your trust in me matters more than anyone else's. Please."

They stared at each other, almost eye to eye, for a few charged moments. "OK," Lucie said finally. "Don't lie to me again."

"I won't. And I promise I'll see my dad, *properly*, before the baby comes," he said.

Once again, Lucie flashed on the scene at the table with Famous Cajun Fried Chicken, only this time the child was asking, in a querulous, tearful voice, "Why don't I have grandparents? Even Tom, the kid in my class who eats boogers, has grandparents," and all she and Collin could do was stare, mutely, at each other, despair mirrored on each other's aged faces.

It was so real that Lucie shuddered and crossed herself.

For dinner, Lucie had chosen a rooftop bar in the city overlooking the Singapore River, her go-to spot for out-of-town visitors. The city state spread before them, a kaleidoscopic carpet of light and sound, its mirror image stippling the skin of the slow river.

"These cocktails are so expensive," Kay murmured, looking over the menu. "Almost the price of half a day of childcare, wow."

Lucie stared. "You two have children?"

Aaron nodded, a smile creasing his face. "Two, actually. Nine and seven."

"Oh, I didn't know." She slid Collin an accusatory look, and he shrugged. "Who's watching them now?"

"They are with their godparents."

"Godparents!" Lucie said. "Nice godparents to watch your children while you attend this conference."

"Definitely. We do the same for them when they hike in the Appalachian Mountains. A fair six-week exchange, really."

"Six weeks!" Lucie exclaimed.

"Yup. We're going to Bali later, after the conference ends," Kay said. "And then Hanoi and maybe Chiang Mai this time. We love traveling in this part of the world, and the kids are older now."

Aaron stretched on the tiny barstool. "We do this exchange every other year, in summer. Our friends send their kids over to stay with us, vice versa the next year, then we send them all to camp. It's the only way we can have some time to ourselves. We don't have family who can help with the kids."

Lucie shook her head. She couldn't imagine leaving her children for over a *day* with any of her relatives, much less friends. "What kind of camps are these?"

"Oh, sports camps, drama camps, religious camps, etc. They usually last anywhere from one to eight weeks; the kids stay on-site."

"With no supervision?"

"They have camp counselors."

"And you trust them to take care of your kids? You trust your kids not to do anything stupid?"

Kay and Aaron traded looks. "We want them to be independent, for sure."

"We definitely want our freedom. Just because we're parents doesn't mean our world should revolve around our kids."

Collin was nodding. "Thank you, I keep telling her that. We don't stop being who we were before parenthood. Like when I mentioned wanting to hike in Nepal after the kid came, maybe once he was two, and Lucie nearly had an aneurysm. She said I should focus on the child and not endanger my life."

Aaron cocked his head, regarding them both. "But you're an experienced—*oof!*"

Lucie had stepped on Aaron's foot by mistake. "I'm so, so sorry," she apologized.

"She meant to step on my f—*oof!*" Collin winced as heel connected with toe.

Lucie tried to pretend she hadn't just purposely trod on Collin by speaking loudly, "YOLO is not a mantra to live wild, but to live cautiously. You *literally* only live once. I think we have a duty to put our kid's safety and, by extension our safety, above all. To the detriment of *some* hobbies."

"That's one way of approaching parenthood," Kay said tactfully, "but we don't have the same approach to life. Anyway, risk is subjective, isn't it?"

Not according to insurance companies, Lucie thought.

"Would you do that?" she asked Collin later, when they were home.

"Do what?"

"Drop our kid off and travel, nary a care. Let them run wild without supervision."

Collin chuckled. "I think summer camp hardly qualifies as no supervision. And Aaron and Kay's friends are the point people for emergencies while the kids are at summer camp. It's a great arrangement, really."

"Let's agree to disagree."

Collin's eyes were mirthful. "Live a little, Lucie. Didn't your younger self once dream of spending time away from your parents?"

"Yes—and thank God they didn't indulge me. Lord knows what I would have become." *Constant supervision!* was the mantra in the Yi household, and weren't all the Yi siblings materially successful? Divorces and marriage-less states aside.

Collin squeezed her shoulder. "Darling, I think you would have turned out the same—just as lovably hard-boiled, driven, and obstinate as you are right now."

Lucie wanted to smack him and kiss him, for being so observant, for picking the very qualities about her that she admired yet worried that others found off-putting. "Once again, let's agree to disagree," she said.

"I look forward to many years of interesting conversations," Collin said with a grin.

What else will we disagree on? Lucie wondered, as she bid Collin good night. *What kind of parent will he be? And what kind of parent will I be?* She didn't have the answers she was hoping for. When it came to parenthood, all she had was theory, and every time she thought she had something figured out, she was confronted with alternatives, sometimes a whole spectrum of them; the fear of making the wrong choice crept up on her, stunning her with its ferocity. It would be nice, she thought, to have someone who would make those decisions for her.

◆ ◆ ◆

Hannah: The parents are so annoyed that you haven't set a date that they are texting me for advice! A nice development?

◆ ◆ ◆

Weina: Supernumerary nipples. I thought triplet stretch marks were bad. Aha. Ahahahaha.

◆ ◆ ◆

Mark: Hey.

Lucie: You again.

Mark: 😀. The band that we almost hired for our almost wedding is in town, want to go? And I have the list *dangles it*

Lucie: You had me at "list." Can we have congee first? I'm going through a congee phase.

Mark: I know just the place.

AFTER WORK, MARK and Lucie headed to Maxwell Food Center for their friendly dinner date—she liked the century egg and chicken congee there. He ordered a large bowl for her and added all the garnishes she liked—a mountain of chopped scallions, fried anchovies, and crisp garlic chips, laced with soy sauce.

Just before they started eating, he handed her a printout with a small smile. "Here's the reason why you agreed to see me."

"Thanks," she said awkwardly, throwing the list a cursory glance. She hadn't really been serious about needing the so-called secret list of confinement nannies and their contact details to meet him, but she was happy to have it—these numbers were rarely advertised, since top confinement nannies relied on word-of-mouth referrals.

They spent a few moments eating in silence.

"How's the pregnancy?" he said, startling her. Mark wasn't one for much talking during meals. He might play music in the background, usually jazz or classical music (he loved Liszt and Chopin); he might indulge in light, sporadic chatter if his mood was bright, but he didn't banter. That was one of the biggest contrasts with living with Collin: the chatter and movement. Collin was energy personified and loved engagement; Mark had a stoic, calm presence.

"It's been quite . . . fun," Lucie said hesitantly, treading carefully because of their own past and his condition.

"That's good to know." He reddened slightly and did something unexpected, bending close to Lucie's belly. "Hi," he said. "I'm Mark." He didn't say "uncle." "I hope you don't mind me spending time with your mom."

The baby *leaped* at the sound of Mark's voice. Lucie gasped. "Oh my gosh, the baby is moving!" she said. She grabbed Mark's hand and brought it to her belly. "Feel it!"

He laid his hands on her and a look of wonder flashed across his dark eyes. "I feel it," he said, his eyes widening. "Wow, friend, you're strong!" Lucie tried to ignore the pang in her heart when she saw a slight wobble in his smile.

"The baby likes you," she said. Mark brought a fork of fried carrot cake to his lips with a small smile.

At the jazz bar they sat down on a leather couch in an alcove facing the stage. Midway through the evening, Mark reached across the couch and held her hand, cupping it between both his hands like he used to. She didn't pull away.

"I had a great time tonight," he said later. They were lingering by the lobby of her condo, unsure of how to end the night.

"Me, too," she said, her eyes meeting his with a question.

He put an arm around her and kissed her. It was tender, sweet, wistful. Lucie let herself be kissed, her eyelids fluttering. *Yes.*

He pulled back and just looked at her, saying nothing. Raking his eyes over her like she was something precious and noble. "Well," he said, gently tracing a finger over the curve of her cheek, "that was worth two and a half years of waiting."

Then he bade her good night and left.

Stay, Mark. It was all she could do to stand there and watch him walk away when she wanted to crush herself against him. *Don't go.* When they'd started planning for their future, they'd always envisaged having children as a given, until it wasn't. And now she was doing this with Collin, and Mark's absence threw the flaws of her plan into sharp relief. Maybe embarking on something this life-changing without someone like Mark was bound to go wrong.

SHE LET HERSELF in quietly, not wanting to wake Collin up. It was almost eleven. Thinking she'd get a yogurt, she stepped into the kitchen—and promptly crashed into someone.

Shit!" she shrieked, springing back upon contact.

Hi," Collin said mildly. Lucie blinked, her eyes adjusting to the dark, and realized that Collin was wearing what looked like a loincloth . . . no, he was wearing what looked to be a tea towel around his waist. Oh God, it *was* a tea towel—well, two, twisted together hastily. She could see the words "Good Morning" stitched on it. He'd *literally* just grabbed the towels off the oven door, probably as soon as he heard her come in the front door. And now she had lost all power of speech. Not since Dobby had a tea-towel outfit produced such an effect on her. "I didn't even know you were out. I thought you were asleep."

Think! Speak! Don't stare! "I . . . I'm not," she said, reaching around him for the filtered water jug and pouring herself a glass, careful not to brush his skin, which was everywhere. He had either a tattoo or a birthmark on his lower abdomen. Oh God. She wrenched her eyes away from his ridged stomach and fixed her eyes on his head, pinching her inner wrist so the pain would overwhelm her other senses. Why was he walking around naked in their house and using their *kitchen towels* as modesty rags? She was going to have a chat with him when he was more dressed. "What were you doing before I got in?"

"Well, I was doing yoga upstairs and got thirsty, so I came down to grab a drink."

"Naked."

"Yes, naked. You should try it. It's freeing." He was standing very straight, possibly to compensate for the fact that he got caught without his pants, one hand on his hip while the other gripped the end of a towel, trying to look stern. Tough work in a crotch hanky. "What were you doing, working late again?"

"I wasn't working the whole time," she said. Just the thought of her workload summoned her thoughts back from the dirty hinterlands. "Besides, I was with a friend." Collin wouldn't have approved of her meeting Mark, based on what she'd told him about the other man. But didn't people deserve second chances?

"Well. OK," he said. He cleared his throat. "You might want to, ah, leave the kitchen first, since the towel doesn't entirely cover the, erm, back of me."

How . . . juvenile. The word cut cleanly into her thoughts. "Right. So, in that case, good night," she said. Eye to eye, she backed away from the naked man she was supposed to raise a child with.

Mark would never put himself in a situation where he had to wear "Good Morning" kitchen towels.

Maybe, just maybe, it was high time she appreciated just how much of a gift that was.

Chapter 23

〜〜〜

IT WAS NIGHT *in Narnia. There was a sexy knock on the door. Queen Lucie threw open the door to find her sexy acolyte, General Mark, at the door.*

Your Highness, he said. The Western Coalition is seeking an audience with us. They want to form an alliance. A sexy alliance.

"No way," Queen Lucie said. "We told them that their last proposal was just . . . whelming. If they want face time, they need to send me a real stud."

"Like me?" A silky voice said from the shadows. A centaur stepped out into the light of her dwelling. It was Lord Collin, and he was wearing nothing but a white tea towel on the horse end of his—

Ringggggggg!

Lucie woke up, her heart pounding. Her dreams were getting out of hand. Months of not getting any action, in addition to a cocktail of ridiculous hormones, did things to a person.

She plodded to the mirror, morosely getting ready for work. Pretending she hadn't seen Collin half naked (or replayed the image in her mind) in their kitchen, Lucie went for Resting Pregnant

Face when she ran into him making breakfast the next morning—thankfully dressed.

"Slept well?" he asked lightly.

"Wonderfully," Lucie said. "I had . . . a lot on my mind. Work!" She practically spat the last word out.

"Right." An amused flicker in his eyes. "You work late pretty often, don't you?" he said, whisking a bowl of egg mixture.

"Depends on what you call late," she said. "But yes, whether I was in New York or in Singapore, I would typically stay in the office until eight even on a light day."

He poured the egg mixture over some vegetables in a sizzling pan before turning and contemplating her. "Why do you work so hard? What do you enjoy about your job?"

She glanced at him, startled by the question. It was unusual for someone to ask about work in such a blunt manner. Usually it was always couched in terms like, "So you like what you do?" Almost as though it was rhetorical. People were afraid of hearing the truth, and telling the truth, about vocations. So much time was spent working that the default assumption was, by God, you'd better like what you do, or at least like what your job brings you, enough to be spending your time like this.

"Every day, every client is different. I like the intellectual challenge of the job."

He nodded. They were silent for a while, the frittata cooking in fragrant sputters.

"What about you?" Lucie asked, when the eggs were done and he began plating them.

"Well, I definitely didn't dream of working as a software engineer, although I like designing systems, coding. I thought I was going to be a nature reserve guide or something outdoorsy, but then you know—reality check. But I treat my job as a means to an end. I work to live, then take time off to travel and hike."

"So what do you like about your job, then?"

"It's not always fun, of course. And it doesn't always pay well, if you're not working for the right company. But it's like your System of Offsetting, right? Balancing out the bad in a job with the good, finding the sweet spot with what you can bear. I like that I can work remotely. That's freedom."

She shrugged and bit into the frittata. "A job is ultimately just a job." She twisted her lips into her father's sardonic smile. "We work, and then we die." Work was about bettering one's life, one's family's fortunes, that's what her parents had always said. Sacrifice was integral in the setting up of one's family altar.

"So how long have you been with Discovery?"

"Hmm. Six years or so? I don't know. But I've only ever worked for two companies. You?"

He gave a self-conscious laugh. "Well, it's not going to impress you, but . . . nine."

"Holy crap."

He started cleaning up the stove top in brisk movements. "I guess I've always been less patient with jobs than you."

"You don't say," Lucie said.

"I don't regret my job-hopping. Look, I just wanted to understand why you find it important to invest so much of your time on earth in your job. As long as you are content, then I'm not going to try to tempt you to come home earlier, so you can rest and eat more of my tacos."

Trust him to make tacos sound sexy.

Whatever his intentions, his questions had a destabilizing effect. She'd never really questioned herself on this front. Sure, she liked many aspects of her job—the veneer of prestige and respectability her job offered her, the intellectual satisfaction especially—but she had no good answer for why she thought spending so much time at work was worth it.

"I guess the money helps, too, if I'm being honest. And I think as a future parent, earning as much as I can makes the most sense." She had to admit that if she wasn't getting the kind of money she got as a management consultant, she would've long bailed on her job—or throttled her bosses, some of whom were definitely human cockroaches.

He nodded. "Fair enough," he said diplomatically.

"You can be the fun parent," she said, and winced when she heard the slight disparagement implied in her categorization, although Collin chose to let it go.

"How's your work going?" she asked to change the topic.

"Not great," he admitted, taking a seat facing her, drinking his morning detox tea. "A couple of Dave's biggest corporate clients just dropped us, and there's a bug in the platform that's flummoxing everyone. We've had a couple of disagreements. There's a real chance I might be out of a job. Last in, first out, you know."

"I'm sorry to hear that."

He raked his fingers through his hair and pulled on an unruly tangle. "I wouldn't be too disappointed, to be honest, if not for the fact I need the visa. The corporate culture isn't what I'd hope it'd be. It's chaotic. Dave's not a great boss." He winced at some private memory. "I've already tentatively put out feelers to see if I can find a better position elsewhere."

"There are so many tech companies in Singapore. You'll find something that pays better, easily."

"Well, for me, 'better' doesn't automatically mean more money. I am looking for job satisfaction. Anyway, a big reason why I was happy to work with Dave is because I would have been able to spend a lot of time with the baby, but now it seems he wants to triple my workload and time spent in the office. For a pay raise, sure, but if I agree to that, who's going to take care of the child if we're both working full-time jobs?"

"Well," Lucie said, clearing her throat, "I kind of thought maybe a combination of live-in help and my parents . . ."

".What's the point of having a child if someone else is going to raise it? Handle the day-to-day stuff?"

Lucie crossed her arms and raised her eyebrow. "Sure, it's important to spend time with your child, but a big part of parenting is about providing financially for the child and securing their future."

"We'll agree to disagree, and let's see who the child grows up being close with," he said lightly.

The unintentional barb stung, but Lucie wasn't swayed. Raising a child costs money, lots of it, and Lucie wasn't going to apologize for prioritizing her career in one of the most expensive countries in the world. She wanted her child to have everything they wanted, to be comfortable from the moment they were born.

But all Collin was focused on was the small details. "Speaking of money, I noticed you aren't tabulating all our expenses for splitting, and I don't mean the utilities."

"What do you mean?"

"I'm taking about all the items you pay for, off the books," he said, eyebrow raised.

For the past month or so, whenever they'd needed groceries, Lucie had used a local app to get their necessities delivered online and put it on her tab. She had also been buying what Collin called "luxury items" (organic fruits, granola, chocolates, vegan ice cream—essentials, really) on an ad hoc basis, squirreling them into the cupboards and fridge, which she then insisted that Collin help himself to. The house had enough food and supplies to last through an emergency two-month lockdown. And she had migrated some of the recurring household expenses to apps she was using her Singaporean credit cards to pay off.

"Don't think I don't know what you're doing," he said. "I'm going to start leaving money on the table for you."

"Don't be silly." For some reason, the suggestion made her angry. Also, even seated at the kitchen table, her swollen feet were bothering her more than usual, which made her heels uncomfortable. "Why is everything so cut-and-dried for you? Are you calculating everything?"

Collin held his hands up in a placatory gesture. "I'm just trying to do my part."

"You are being a jerk, is what you're doing," she said. Then she burst into tears.

"Whoa!" he said. He came over and tried to hug her, but she moved away. "What's going on?"

"You're too nice."

"I'm a jerk—and I'm too nice?"

"Yes, it's a thing! You're being a too-nice jerk. You're always doing the right thing, even if it's something that I wouldn't necessarily enjoy. Do you know how tiring that is? I'm sick of it! And most of all, I just—I just hate that you think everything is so fucking transactional between us." And that was what it was. It was tiring, this push and pull. What were they? She was tired of the gray area they lived in.

At least he had the good grace to look appalled. "I'm sorry I'm coming off that way. I am genuinely trying to do what I think is right."

"I'm sorry, too," she said, perplexed at how raw her emotions were. She was usually so in control; now the smallest things set her off. And she didn't understand why things were getting so complicated. It had been simple and now it wasn't. With every day that passed, the lines that they had drawn between them were blurring for her, and she couldn't tell what he was to her anymore, but the same didn't seem to be happening to him. And that was the problem, wasn't it? She wanted more when she shouldn't, and he wasn't even aware of the change—or worse, he didn't want any of that and was pretending that all was status quo between them.

Dammit, Lucie, she thought, digging her fingers into her thighs. *You should have known better than to develop feelings for Collin.* She was going to have to work harder at keeping herself in check.

Chapter 24

Lucie: Girl's lunch this Saturday is on, right?

Suzie: Yup. It's been a while. I've got some news of my own, too.

Lucie: Oh really, what news?

Weina: Yes to lunch! I've got a business idea I need help on, and I could use a break. The triplets are going through a regression again!

Suzie: What is that?

Weina: Something you'll never experience, lucky you.

Weina: Oh wait, that didn't come out right. I mean, because you chose to be child-free, you won't, you know. Have sleepless nights.

Weina: At least as the result of screaming babies. I'm jealous of your undisturbed sleep, really.

Weina: Erm, Lucie, help me out here.

Lucie: I think we got that you're sleep-deprived and that didn't come out as tactful or finely worded as you'd like. Halal dim sum this Sat?

Weina: Yes, please. Suzie?

Lucie: Suzie?

As IT HAD been a bumper year for babies—Lucie enjoyed thinking of them as a crop, a hardy, pest-resilient, super crop that withstood acts of God—Dr. Joyce advised them to book their prenatal class of choice as soon as possible or risk being waitlisted.

Fucking kiasu *parents*, Lucie groused, as she found herself waitlisted on all ten of the highest-rated prenatal courses.

Why was parenting so hard? Or rather, why was life on this planet, with its abundant resources so unevenly distributed and oftentimes wasted, so artificially tough? Why couldn't she get into a bloody prenatal course? This wasn't the Ivy League—

And speaking of Ivy League . . .

"We could just read a book," Collin suggested when he came home to find that she'd been refreshing the registration page for her second-choice course every few minutes for the last hour, hoping to clinch a couples' spot on one of the new dates announced.

Lucie turned her frightful, bloodshot eyes at him. "What did you say?"

"We don't need a prenatal course. We can read some books, talk to friends . . ."

"You didn't even read the books I bought us," Lucie said. "Anyway. This class is taught by a PhD and has great reviews."

Collin sighed. "OK, but don't forget, back in our parents' day, there was no such thing as prenatal class and everyone got on fine."

"Yes, friend, but don't forget, back in the day"—Lucie's voice was scathing—"people didn't wash their hands with soap after making bricks out of cow dung and had five kids in their twenties, and radiation and nanoplastics weren't a thing so everyone had gung-ho sperm and eggs, so they could *afford* to chance it, because backups."

Collin and Lucie stared at each other. A cosmic battle of wills played out without a single word being uttered. Finally, he shook his head, breaking the tension, and walked away.

Lucie went back to refreshing the page and was rewarded, forty minutes later, with a slot, which she seized, gratified by her persistence. As her own upbringing had proven, nothing should be left to chance.

THE COURSE STARTED with great promise. Quiz sheets were handed out to every participant on their way in, and the instructor, Dr. Mae Sim, a smartly dressed woman in her forties with a PhD in childhood nutrition, hurrying to assure everyone that nothing would be graded; they just wanted to have an idea what the general level of understanding was, to be able to correct any common misconceptions.

It was a multiple-choice questionnaire with twenty questions. They had fifteen minutes. Lucie was uncapping her pen before the others had taken their seats.

"I've never seen you so excited about anything before. Not even food," Collin noted under his breath.

"I love exams," she said, spinning her pen around her thumb like she was a student again.

"You mean, you love showing off," Collin said.

"Stop mansplaining."

"How is this mansplaining?"

"I'm not sure, but I say so." Lucie gritted her teeth. "Anyway, it's important to be well prepared, as you would be if you had read the pregnancy and childcare prep books I had bought you. Nothing should be left to chance."

"You bought fourteen books, Lucie. I mean, I understand reading one or two—and I am getting to it this weekend, but fourteen?"

"I read them all and I have a full-time job, too."

"Lucie," Collin said. "I understand that you want to cover all your bases. I do, too. But I want you to know something."

If he tells me to relax I will shank him with my pen, Lucie thought.

He put his hand on her hers, stilling the pen mid-spin. "You're good enough. And you're going to be an excellent mom. Whatever your score."

He squeezed her hand. She cleared her throat, confused by the sudden emotion welling up in her. "Thanks, pal. But you're still not getting out of reading those books."

He sighed. "Sure, I'll read . . . two." They smiled at each other, and he gently cupped her bump. The tenderness of his touch radiated through her. She was absurdly moved. And—her breath hitched a little—turned-on. Fucking traitorous nipples (the normal ones) were tunneling through her bra *to* him. It was a fleeting thought, but something must have changed in the atmosphere because their eyes met, and he dropped his hand, flushing, a guarded look stealing over his features.

Why did he do that every time it felt like they were getting close?

Because he's trying to be a professional. Unlike you, you perv.

"I'm *not* a perv," she said hotly, drawing a surprised look from the couple beside her.

"That's good to know," Collin said under his breath, grinning at her, friendly again, making her wonder if she had been imagining things.

After Mae had asked the couples to exchange their sheets, she gave them the correct answers. Lucie was gratified that she had gotten fifteen out of fifteen questions right. Unnervingly, so had Collin.

"That's amazing. I guess you have been studying after all?"

"No, I cheated, actually. From you." He chuckled, pleased with himself.

Mae brought up a beautiful PowerPoint presentation, beginning with an overview about pregnancy and the generic changes pregnant women could expect: weight gain, hair loss, swollen ankles, etc. There was no mention of what Lucie was beginning to term the Unmentionables. While she wasn't historically inclined to question authority figures, it was as if pregnancy had unleashed a new side of her, and that side had no filter.

She raised her hand. "Pardon me, Mae?"

Mae smiled at her. "Yes?"

"Why doesn't anyone talk about flatulence, chronic wet crotch, and nasty big-veined nipples?"

Titters. Collin was staring at his hands.

Mae said, her face reddening, "Oh, that, you can find out online."

"I really feel like you're not giving a full picture without delving into the gross stuff."

Several women nodded. Mae said, curtly, "I'll be happy to talk about what's not covered in the slides *in private, after class* with anyone who asks. Next!"

Lucie fell silent, flushing.

After the class was done, Lucie marched out without a second look. Collin rushed after her with the course materials. "Wait, aren't you staying back to ask her questions?"

"Nope. I'm never going back. I'm going to find us another class, one where we're free to ask the questions we want and get the answers we need." If there was anything she learned from Collin, it was an appreciation for plain-speaking. Outside of work and when she was with her parents, of course.

"I agree," Collin said. "If you can't talk about the bad along with the good, you have no business teaching others about motherhood and babies."

"We're merging," Lucie said with a teasing grin. They got into a waiting taxi and were headed home. Collin reached across the seat and clasped her hand, and Lucie gave it a quick squeeze before retracting her hand in as offhand a manner as she could. What he saw as casual physical contact between them was becoming too much for her to bear, for what it wasn't and what it couldn't become.

At a lull in the traffic, she said, "Sometimes, I wonder . . . if we'd met in person without the platform, how it would have been."

"You and I would never have met in real life," he replied, an inscrutable look stealing across his features. "We run in such different circles." He chuckled in an attempt at levity. "Not to mention, countries."

She dropped her gaze at her lap. "But let's say we did. Hypothetically speaking, let's say we ran into each other in a park or whatever, and I asked you out, or you did. Do you . . . do you ever think about or wonder . . ." She cleared her throat. "You know, if we would have—"

Made it this far. Farther.

Next to her, Collin appeared to be weighing his words carefully. "I do."

"And?" Her heart was loud and had migrated to her throat. And it seemed to have sprouted tentacles.

"It would have been special," he said in a gruff voice. "It would have been something."

Their eyes met and held. If she kissed him now, nosy wide-eyed taxi driver be damned, would he say no? "Collin—"

He looked away first. "Hypotheticals aside, there's something you need to know."

Lucie braced herself. Judging from his posture and expression, it wasn't life-threatening, but it didn't sound promising, either. "What is it?"

"I'm, uh, well, I'm seeing someone."

Turns out the gulf between not-promising and life-threatening was relatively small. *What?* Her heart screamed as it was stabbed. *Since when? Who?*

"That's *great*," she said, lying even as her motionless heart slid down her chest cavity. "When did this happen? What's her name?"

"Justine. Justine Maya. I met her while night-hiking a week ago."

LUCIE HAD BEEN looking forward to seeing both her friends over lunch that Saturday, so she couldn't pretend that she wasn't disappointed when she arrived, almost fifteen minutes late, to see Weina alone at a table at the bustling halal dim sum restaurant.

"Where's Suzie?" Lucie had to ask when another ten minutes had lapsed and Suzie had not made an appearance or texted.

"Probably caught up at work, you know how obsessed she is," Weina said. The waitstaff were giving them the evil eye: they'd been nursing cups of pu-erh for half an hour.

After sending a quick text to Suzie, Lucie ordered chee cheong fun and more tea. They tucked in with relish.

"So what's the business idea you wanted help on?"

Weina put down her chopsticks. "I'm thinking of getting back into the game. Start my own one-person consultancy."

"That's amazing!" Lucie said. She'd heard this before, after Arwin, but this time Weina seemed serious. "You should do it. You keep saying you miss work."

"I do. I have been. I just feel so much mom guilt, you know? I've always wanted to be a hands-on mom, and I do enjoy being home with the kids. But I think it's time to get back out there."

They exchanged a few ideas on how to proceed with client acquisition and marketing, only breaking when another waiter walked past and gave a pointed stare as she pushed the dim sum cart past them, which the two of them ignored.

"I'm excited for you," Lucie said, when they were done with the business plan.

"Thank you. I'm excited, too! Anyway, how's the second trimester treating you?"

"All right, I suppose," Lucie said, crossing herself. "I have another scan tomorrow."

"Oh good," Weina said. "I love scans. At this stage you can see the baby's face and everything," she said, wriggling her eyebrows. "You can even hazard a guess if you want, about the sex."

"It's fine." Lucie smiled fondly at her belly. "I don't need to know. I just care that the baby is healthy in there. By the way . . ." She leaned forward, whispering, "I need to ask you about my—"

"Speak up, it's loud in here."

Lucie spoke up. "About my belly button. Is it always going to be poking out like a giant third nipple?"

A passing waiter gave her a startled glance.

Weina sighed and waved the waiter over, saying, "Let's order first."

Before they knew it, Weina had led Lucie down an extremely graphic rabbit hole of the prenatal and postpartum bodily changes to expect.

"It's going to rain hair, everywhere. And your vagina . . ." Weina shook her head, sadly, stretching her hands apart like an expanded rubber band that would never snap back again.

"Didn't you deliver the triplets via C-section?"

Weina made a face. "Yes, but with Arwin, it was natural *allllll*"—she leaned in close and bulged her eyes—"the fucking way. My labia—"

"Yes, yes, I know, curtains," Lucie finished as quickly as she could.

Weina nodded grimly. "And C-sections aren't fun either, trust me."

"You're so selling childbirth to me."

"I haven't even told you about the Hulk-like swelling of all your extremities and your soon-to-be flappy mom boobs." Then blithely, as though they'd just been discussing cricket or something equally tame, with zero segue—"Is Collin still coming with you to the doctor's?"

"Of course."

Weina gave her a shrewd look. "How are things with you two?"

Lucie pretended to have missed her question by fishing out her phone and intently scrolling through the notifications. The truth was, she didn't know. Ever since they'd had that exchange in the taxi, it felt like Collin was pulling away. As for Mark, he'd been sending her messages that were variations on "Missing you" and "Let's meet again." "Wow, it's been almost an hour, and our dear friend Suze is still AWOL, with not a word."

"She's so late," Weina said with glee.

"But she's never late." Come to think of it, she hadn't spoken to Suzie since their group text on Monday. It was the longest they'd ever gone without chatting, either in person or over the phone. The only thing she'd received the last few days was a BTS meme that she was pretty sure Suzie had mass-forwarded to most of her contacts.

If she didn't know better, Suzie was avoiding her.

"Oh, wait, I got an email from her. How odd," Weina said, squinting. "She says she's sorry, but she can't make it today. No explanation. Huh."

"She has been acting weird," Lucie muttered.

"I hope you two sort it out before my dinner party next weekend." Weina loved hosting dinner parties, and now that she was finally free from the triplets' "tyrannical monopoly of her mammaries," she was planning a splashy return to form. She was inviting a few of their mutual friends for a party of eight.

"Me, too," Lucie said, distracted by a new message notification from her mother. She wanted to meet at Lucie and Collin's on Sunday evening—somehow, unsurprisingly, she had gotten their address. "Anyway"—she lifted her glass of tea, gesturing for Weina to do the same—"here's to new beginnings. For you and your new venture, which I'm so proud of you for launching, and to me figuring out motherhood."

"Hear hear." They clinked glasses. "Shall we order real food now?"

Lucie sighed and nodded. She ordered double portions of har gows, lo mai kai, and egg tarts. She would need the extra calories if she was going to face her mother.

IVY CHEN WAS scheduled to drop by the condo the next evening around nine o'clock. She claimed she wanted to see where "her favorite daughter lived." Once again, Collin was out—not that Lucie was keeping tabs, of course. She'd seen the photos he had posted of his latest outing with the woman he said he was dating (multiple appearances in his IG over two weeks), this Justine Maya, with deep bronze skin, glossy black hair, and generous curves. They looked perfect together.

Urgh. Justine Maya. What a try-hard name.

She was hate-scrolling through Justine Maya's IG when her mother arrived, ten minutes early.

"I can't believe you live here," Ivy Chen said, after she'd surveyed every single room, "when you could be living with us in a house with a garden, with proper furniture. And your parents."

Oh God, no. "It's close to work," Lucie said neutrally.

"It's very messy. So much junk. The energy cannot circulate."

Like many Chinese of her generation, Ivy Chen still adhered to principles of feng shui. Lucie looked around the room, seeing it through fresh eyes, noting the overabundance of fluffy throw pillows (that had proved useful during horror movie marathons); the many, many framed photos of Collin's family and friends (she had just two, one with Weina and Suzie on their graduation day from university, and one of the Yi family, everyone unsmiling); the rugs and artwork that he'd insisted they buy; the decorative pieces that he'd brought in from his New York apartment. True, the home *was* cluttered—but in a cheerful, lived-in way. It felt like a home. "I like it," she said defensively.

Ivy cleared her throat. "You're now, what, almost six months pregnant?"

"Just over five months."

"Not that it matters, now that you'll definitely show, even if we get the biggest tent dress." Her mother sighed. "So—when's the wedding? Your Ba and I have been waiting for you to lock down the date."

And there it was. The real reason for her mother's visit.

Lucie shrugged. "I don't know."

"You don't know?" Ivy said, surprised. "But it's been ages since the dinner, and we left you so many messages . . ." Her eyes narrowed. "Wait, are you—are you even getting married?"

Lucie kept mum.

"I see." Ivy shook her head. "That's not a good idea. Not just because your father is going to explode when he finds out. This Collin guy—what's his problem? Why is he hesitating?"

"There's no problem." A frisson of annoyance shot through her. "And what makes you think *he's* the one hesitating?"

"You're right; he's not that big a catch." Her mother said this as though it were a fact and not an opinion. "If there is no hesitation on either side, then problem solved. Get married. At least on paper. Of course, you should get a prenup if there's a big disparity in your assets but get married otherwise."

She started rattling off reasons why it was a bad idea to be a single mother in Singapore. "Single moms don't get special handouts in Singapore; if you pass away and you don't have a valid will, all your assets go to, well, us, not your child, by default. And Lucie—you're going to face a lot of judgmental folks. Folks worse than us."

Lucie gave a short, hollow laugh. "Worse than you and Ba?"

Her mother sighed. "Again with the hyperbole. Dear, trust me on this. If you're unwed you're going to come up against so much gossip and social stigma—yes, even in this day and age. Ma and Ba are just trying to protect you. We're like a vaccine."

Lucie's laugh was genuine this time. "A vaccine?"

"Yes. We're bad to you, but we're never going to be as bad as what the world can be. Case in point: your sister. She's not the one who cheated, but she's got the rotten end of the stick. Custody battle. Alimony battle. And it's been tough mentally and emotionally. People talk, and even when you tell yourself to tune them out, it takes a toll. Ask her."

Lucie fought to keep her face impassive—her mother was conveniently glossing over the fact that a lot of the unpleasantness her sister had faced had come from their parents. That had hurt Hannah more than the tasteless comments from their relatives or acquaintances.

"As for being a single mom—it's hard, Lucie. You'd want the support a partner can provide, be it physical, financial, or emotional. Now, I'm not *saying* Collin is the kind of man who would leave you in the lurch without paying child support or whatever"—although now that she said it, Lucie couldn't help but see it unfolding—"but having that marriage certificate does make things easier for you, because it makes dissolution harder."

Her mother was the OG glass-half-empty person.

"After Hannah and Gerald divorced, it was fine for him to go and marry another woman without any baggage. The women are always the damaged goods. We bear the brunt of any kind of failed relationship, especially when children are involved, and I would hate for you to experience even half of what Hannah faced after . . . after the bastard left." Her mother didn't swear often, so Lucie knew Ivy Chen detested Gerald with the strength of a thousand suns. "So, if nothing else, make it hard for Collin to leave."

Lucie shook her head. "That's such a bad reason to get married. I'm not trying to trap Collin. Also, I . . . I'm not *in love* with him, Ma."

"I'm not talking about a 'trap,' Lucie—I'm talking about security. And all this 'love' talk is so . . . so *basic*, like the young people say. Do you think your father and I are still married to each other because we're in love? That we have butterflies in our stomachs whenever we see each other?"

"Er . . ." Lucie had a hard time imagining her father having butterflies in his stomach, unless it was the stomach flu. "If I had to hazard a guess, the answer would be . . . not anymore?"

"Wrong!" her mother said. "I mean, correct! We never did."

Excuse me?

"You kids know we met at university and that we got married. What you don't know is—neither of us were each other's original love matches. I had another boy, very handsome—yes, don't make a face like that, Lucie; I was young once, and my figure was sick, as the young people say—and Ba had another girlfriend, who wasn't so sick, but never mind. Our parents were friends, and they thought we would make a good match. So they urged us to date and get married, and after considering the pros and cons, we did. And it has been a brilliant partnership for over forty years."

Lucie couldn't argue with her mother on that front. Her parents were a formidable team.

"Your father and I have many similarities that worked to our advantage. When I see him, I see my equal, someone I can rely on to always take my back."

"'Have.' It's 'have' my back."

"Yes, like you say. Now, you are friends with this Collin, yes?"

"Yes."

"And he is a good man? He will ta—have your back?"

"Yes. Very much so."

"Now, what is marriage, after the physical passion is poof, dead, gone, but friendship, companionship, partnership?"

She had a point, but so did Lucie. "I want a love marriage, if I ever get married."

"Hannah and Suzie had love marriages, too, and did those work out? Love marriages are the ideal, for some folks, but the truth is, Lucie, marriage—in any form—*is* the ideal you should be aiming for. I was rooting for Mark, as you know, but if we can't have Mark, then let's have Collin. In the end, you'll have the security of marriage. Then the rest is hard work, compromise, and dedication. Something your generation doesn't really excel in. And that's the real reason marriages are failing."

Lucie bit back a retort—while she did want to defend her generation against her mother's flippant generalizations, she was also really tired, and her mother never listened once she made up her mind, anyway.

Ivy Chen fluffed her immaculate curls with a ring-laden hand. "Do you know why neither your father nor I play mah-jongg or cards? Even when a whole bunch of us went to Macao for Auntie Ling's second daughter's marriage to that real estate tycoon's third son and the boy had a whole private room booked for us in the casino?"

"Urm, it's against your religion?"

"Wrong! Because we are smart and good at math."

"OH MY GOD, *please* don't humblebrag at a time like this, Ma."

Ivy Chen swatted the air impatiently. "Don't tell me how to act, Lucie. I'm too old to change my ways. But I've lived long enough to know this: No matter what the movies or books tell you, love is a gamble, and the house always wins." She patted Lucie's arm before turning to leave. "Take the path that grants you the most security and forget trying to win at love. Life is hard enough as it is. Make things easy for yourself. We just want you to be happy."

Settle, her mother was saying.

What Ivy Chen didn't know was Mark was indeed back in play. And that her spiel had been convincing enough for Lucie to think that, maybe, if there was anyone she ought to marry, it should be Mark.

Chapter 25

~~~~~~

Lucie: Hey, what's going on?

Suzie: What do you mean?

Lucie: You flaked out on our girly brunch.

Suzie: I'm sure you had plenty to talk about, between you both.

Lucie: We did, but we still missed you. You've been so quiet. Wanna have mocktails this week?

Suzie: We could do coffee instead. I know a cool place where we can have *handcrafted* lattes.

Lucie: Coffee? Ah crap. Maybe not coffee, the smell can get overwhelming. Who knew being pregnant would mean giving up the joe. How about a juice bar?

Suzie: I guess. Btw you forgot to ask me what my news was.

Lucie: Oh shit, yes. What is it?

Suzie: I got a cat.

Lucie: Wow that's awesome. Show me pictures?

Suzie: Lucie, you know I hate cats after the Great Feline Scare of 1993. I can't believe you forgot! Are you even listening to me?

Lucie: I'm so sorry!!! I was distracted. And sleep deprived. What's your REAL news, tell me!!!

Suzie: You're always distracted these days. Anything that isn't baby-related doesn't interest you. Whatever, I'm out.

Lucie: I'm really sorry, Suzie. There's just so much going on right now. I promise I'll make it up to you.

Lucie: Suzie?

Lucie: Suzie?

IT STARTED TO rain just as Lucie was getting ready to head home, her back aching after two sedentary hours focused on a complicated note she was drafting for a client. She made her way to the ground-floor lobby, distracted with thoughts of work she still had waiting for her. Judging by the long queue for taxis, it was going to be a long wait for a private-hire car, and expensive to boot, what with the peak-hour and rain surcharges. She sighed, her stomach growling despondently. There was no chance for a home-cooked meal since Collin was out tonight, presumably with Justine bloody Maya.

She was about to book a private car when someone called her, and she looked up from her phone to see Mark, idling in his Range Rover, at the covered pickup and drop-off point for private cars and taxis.

"Hi, good-looking," he said, grinning when he saw her. He strode over and offered an arm to her. "Hold on to me, the floor is slippery," he said.

"Hey." She, took his arm and carefully approached the passenger door he held open, aware of the envious eyes of some of the people waiting for their rides. "How long have you been waiting here?" she asked him when he slid in the driver's seat beside her. It was 8:50 p.m., late by even their standards.

"A while," he said, a boyish grin on his face as they started driving away. "Well—I tipped one of your building's security guards to let me know when you were leaving, and I waited in one of the side roads till I got his text and drove over."

"Th-that's sweet?" And maybe a little—creepy? But in a romantic way?

He gave her an appreciative look. "Pregnancy suits you," he said softly, putting a hand on hers.

She did feel good. Her belly was still barely showing under her slick wardrobe choices, she was curvy for the first time in her life, and the color was back in her cheeks now that she wasn't wan from nausea. Her skin, though blotchy and prone to sudden flushes, was clear, smooth. Her hair shone with health. "Thanks."

Mark lifted her palm and pressed it to his lips, and a tingle skated down her spine. "You're welcome."

She thought he was bringing her home, but instead he pulled up at his.

"What are we doing here?" Looking at the warmly lit building, she felt the the sour, metallic tang of nostalgia tinged with sadness flood her mouth.

"Come up," he said softly.

She didn't want to budge. It was safer to stay seated. "What are we doing here?" she repeated.

"There's something you need to see."

Curiosity got the better of her. She followed him, wanting to see what used to be her home.

"Welcome back," he said, opening the door and leading her into the house.

It had barely changed. The accent wall had the same dramatic floral wallpaper in teal- and gold-accented hand-painted silk that they had picked out on impulse in Brussels while on holiday, even before they had moved into this condo; the same large wrought-iron mirror in the dining room reflecting the retro crystal-and-brass chandelier Mark had ordered from an artisan in Japan; the faux fireplace with its cast-iron surround; the seal-brown three-seater leather couch where they had watched thousands of movies and made love, which had followed them home from their place in Hong Kong. And their photos, still in the same sterling silver Tiffany frames that she'd gifted him their last Christmas together dotting the rooms. The only changes were a wooden chest used as a side table and the ceiling fans, which had been swapped for dark, bronze-bladed ones.

It was as though she'd never left.

"I ordered in dinner from that zi char place you like," he said, leading her to the dining table, where a feast suited for a party of five was laid out in plastic takeaway containers. "I'll have to reheat the food; it's been about an hour or so."

She laughed. "Some things have not changed." Mark didn't cook, unless you counted instant noodles and reheating.

When he had placed everything back on the table, they sat down. He commanded Alexa to play some Jay Chou—the Alexa was new—and soon they were biting into cereal butter prawn, cashew nut chicken, Chinese spinach with three types of egg, sticky coffee pork ribs, and black pepper Sri Lankan crabs. And for dessert, a special order from their favorite café: blondies in salted caramel and Earl Grey tea. All the things she enjoyed.

By the time they had finished their meal, it was easy to remember why they'd lasted as long as they had.

"I should leave," she murmured, when she saw that it was almost eleven.

"I have one final surprise," he said, a serious inflection entering his voice. "In the guest room."

"As long as it's not attached to you," she said in an attempt at levity.

"It is avowedly not," he assured her, gesturing for her hand, which she put in his with the tiniest hesitation.

"Surprise," he said, turning on the lights to show a completely redone room painted in soothing pastel blue, with a single bed and a chest of drawers in eggshell white, and an off-white Stokke cot, sleek and oval, overgrown with brand-new plush toys.

"I bought it a couple of weeks ago," he said, not really looking at her, a flush creeping up his neck. "You can use it for the baby, if you move back. If you want to, of course."

He must have thought he'd done well, but it made her flash back to the cot they'd had. That one had been in blond wood, with a fairy-tale white canopy draped over it.

And just like that, the illusion that time had not passed shattered. She turned on her heel and walked out, sick to her stomach.

"What's wrong?" he said, grabbing her hand.

She shook his hand off. "You bought the same cot," she choked out.

At first, she could tell he wasn't sure what she meant, then understanding flickered in his dark eyes. A stricken expression seized him, but only for a moment. Then his Mark-in-Control face righted itself.

"It's a Stokke cot, Lucie. *Everyone* has a Stokke."

"Not everyone," she said, blinking in surprise at his presumption, his privilege—that was a cot that cost close to fifteen hundred dollars new. Collin would never have bought a Stokke cot, for one. He found them offensively expensive—his words. She loved their green IKEA cot.

"It's not even—it's not even in the same color as the previous one. I'm really trying here," he said, his voice shaking.

"I know, Mark."

Suddenly his mouth was on hers, hungry, and she was reciprocating despite the tears that poured down her face, with a ferocity fueled by confusion and pain. She was tired of being pulled in all directions. Mark loved her. And God, this at least hadn't changed—he still felt insanely good. She wanted him. She pressed her body against his, the need raw. He lifted her up and carried her to the single bed, whispering her name as he trailed slow kisses over her lips, her neck, and down to her collarbone, and her breath quickened. *Hurry*, she willed. *Make me forget.*

His hands traveled down the front of her blouse to the first button before they stopped.

"Is this OK?" he asked, uncertain, and it was this question, this pause, that jolted her back to reality. She pulled away, wiping her tears, conflicted. Wanting more, not wanting more; wanting less, then wanting him.

Finally, she drew away. "Not like this," she whispered.

"I'm sorry." He was contrite, helping her up. "I don't—I wasn't trying to take advantage or anything."

"I know."

"I told you, I want to do everything right this time."

"Me, too."

Her eyes flicked to his and he held her gaze. He still had one arm around her waist, and if she didn't get out of there, there was no telling what would happen. Her self-control was very, very tenuous. She bit her lip. "I should head back to mine, then." *Shit, shit!* Her eyes cut to Mark's, and she saw from his face that he'd heard it, too, and she steeled herself, heart thudding, for his reaction.

A couple of seconds passed before Mark spoke.

"Let's go," he said, his voice emotionless. He turned away from her and headed for the door. "You're the boss."

Chapter 26

~~~~~~

Today's the day! Party of ten! Weina ended her text with a row of smiling emojis. They had broken Weina. The original party of eight had somehow morphed into a party of ten at the last minute: Suzie, Weina, Lucie, Mark, Collin, Simon, Justine, Zul, Yu Ling, and Dinesh. Collin, not knowing that Weina's parties were meticulously planned, had asked a few days ago if he could bring "a friend" (Justine Maya), so Lucie, rather litigiously, felt she had the right to ask Mark, so Weina, discombobulated by these changes, decided she couldn't, in principle, say no to plus-ones, and so Dinesh was allowed to bring Yu Ling, his wife. Then she had to tell Zul and Suzie that they could each bring a plus-one, and when Suzie and Zul both (thankfully) declined, Weina decided to ask Simon, who was notoriously low profile and preferred not to join his wife's social events, to even out the numbers, so now they were ten.

Zul was a good friend of Lucie's from Hong Kong who had just moved back to Singapore a month after she and Collin arrived, while she and Dinesh had been close when they worked together at Discovery for two years before her secondment in New York. So it was nice to have everyone gathered in the same place, to be able to say to Collin, "This is my tribe." Although she wondered how she would introduce Collin to them. The concept of elective co-parenting was so new. And some people—she was thinking specifically of Yu Ling and Dinesh, who were both religious—would definitely have Things to Say about having children out of wedlock.

When Lucie arrived, Weina advised her to say Collin was her "partner"—"But what about Mark? How should I introduce him to the others, since they know we're broken up, but he's my plus-one?" Lucie wondered, to which Weina muttered, not quite under her breath "'My lesser half'—and leave it at that, and if you wanted to hide that you are pregnant that's fine, too. You can get away with it, especially since we can seat you first," she said, eyeballing Lucie's bump under the loose, sleeveless midnight-blue empire-line dress she was wearing.

"I don't really want to," Lucie replied. There was only so long you could hide a pregnancy, and she was done pretending—at least outside the office.

"You're probably right," Weina said. "What time is Mark coming over?" She said his name with curled-lip disdain.

"He should be arriving with everyone else at seven for cocktails. I sent him on an errand for extra cake."

"All right." Weina's eyes were beady. "Are you guys a thing again?"

With some reluctance, Lucie brought Weina up to speed. She didn't mention the cot, or Mark's long-term promises, just that he was eager to restore their relationship.

"So, not a thing yet—but you see a future with him?"

"Maybe," Lucie said cautiously. "I've seen real change in his behavior, and I think he's working hard at therapy. You're a big proponent of therapy, aren't you?"

"Yes," Weina said. She sighed. "I'll give him a chance."

"Suzie's definitely coming, right?" Lucie asked wistfully.

"She said she was when I asked her ages ago, but she didn't officially RSVP." Weina often lamented the dying art of RSVPing, which Lucie agreed with to a certain extent—a text, email, or phone call to confirm you're coming was just common courtesy, although if Weina had her way, they'd be responding officially with handwritten RSVPs for all her events (Weina had a little stock of her own personalized social stationery, which she deployed with delight). She dragged her palm over her face; she looked exhausted. "Let me send out a chaser text."

"Are you OK?"

"Yeah, I'm just trying to get the start-up launched while the triplets go through yet another sleep regression."

"Weina, you need to get some rest. Can you get a night nanny? It's OK to ask for help."

Weina sagged and something in her surrendered. "I will consider it. And what about you? Have you thought about going for counseling longer term? One grief dinner party isn't going to help your anxiety."

"I'm planning to," she said. "When the baby is here."

"Great."

There was a loud ping. Weina picked up her phone and grimaced. "Urgh, Suzie's not coming."

"She's not?"

"How rude to cancel so last minute. She didn't even bother coming up with an excuse!"

Lucie was quiet. She hated that Suzie couldn't even just come out and say she was over being friends with her, just because

Lucie was going to be a mom. She never thought this would be the reason their friendship started cooling off. Was she not fun enough for her oldest friend anymore?

"I'm going to start drinking," Weina announced. She left and returned with a bottle of champagne and two flutes, one filled with orange juice for Lucie.

Two flutes of champagne later, Weina received another text, which made her swear extravagantly.

"What now?" Lucie said warily.

"Simon canceled! Says he managed to score face time with someone important working in the local financial services regulator and he can only meet tonight."

It only made sense for Weina to finish the bottle of champagne.

FRESH OUT OF the office, Zul, Dinesh, and Yu Ling arrived in a whirr of chatter (they'd met in the lobby on the way up) and were handed their drinks of choice by the waitstaff hired for the evening. Lucie introduced Collin when he arrived last, Yu Ling and Zul giving him very lingering looks of appreciation.

"Sorry about Justine's last-minute cancelation, Weina," Collin said. "Something happened last night and, uh, she's not feeling well. She sends her apologies."

Lucie tried to arrange her face in suitable commiseration and barely succeeded.

"At least you're here," Weina said. "You darling boy." Despite Lucie's attempts to water down Weina's blood alcohol level, she was tipsy by the time dinner was due to start. "And I'm sorry Justina couldn't make it." She did not sound sincere at all.

"Justine," Collin said. When Weina had left them to speak

with the others, Lucie signaled to Collin that she needed to speak with him in private. They hung back from the group.

"My ex-fiancé, Mark, is coming tonight," she said in a low voice. "I thought I should give you a heads-up, because he's very interested in meeting you. I would have told you earlier, but it's been really hard to catch you at home the past few days." No thanks to her avoidance of him, she didn't say.

"Oh," Collin said. She couldn't read the look in his eyes. "I didn't know he was back in your life."

"He's . . . we're . . . we're working on things. We might . . . we might get back together." She shrugged.

"No," Collin blurted, his eyes blazing with a rare intensity that caught Lucie off guard.

"I'm sorry?"

"We need to talk—" Collin started to say when the doorbell rang.

"I'm here!" It was Mark, lugging a crate of bottles and a cake box. He greeted Weina with a big hug, murmuring his appreciation at being invited, to which Weina gave a stilted "You're welcome." To everyone else, he said: "Sorry I'm so late, but I had to pick up this cake from some 'atelier' all the way in the boondocks. I don't get why we had to get this cake when any of the five-star hotels would have been able to supply a suitably atas one." He nodded as the other invitees were quickly introduced, having never met the others except for Zul, who nodded back and gave a little wave.

"It's from a place that only produces nut-free cakes," Lucie said, gesturing to Collin. "Collin's allergic."

"I see," Mark said, smiling, his eyes fixed on Collin. "So you're Collin, the nutless guy."

"I think you meant 'nut-free,'" Collin said, not smiling. "And you're Mark, the ex."

Mark's jovial face slipped for a split second. "Thankfully, in my case, it's reversible."

"OK, OK, party people, now that all the *adults* are here— thanks, Mark, for the vintage Bollinger—let's grab some drinks and have a seat." Weina said, Host Beast Mode on, determined to defuse the tension.

Both Mark and Collin attempted to sit next to Lucie before they realized that all the seats had handwritten name cards in little dishes of porcelain pebbles, drafting them to opposing ends of the table, on the same side, so that they didn't even have to see each other. And Lucie was placed in the middle on the other side. Platters of sashimi and sushi were laid out in a wave of gorgeous color in the middle of the table, with torched tuna steak for Lucie.

Lucie and Weina gamely tried to get the conversation at the table flowing, but Mark was having none of it, preferring to respond in monosyllables. In the end, the others stopped trying to involve him and chatted among themselves.

"So what's the deal here?" Yu Ling piped up, looking from Lucie next to her to Collin. "I didn't get the whole story except you're back from New York and living with Collin?"

Lucie was aware, from the corner of her eye, how intently Mark was observing her. "The reason I'm back in Singapore is because . . . well . . . I'm pregnant," Lucie said slowly.

A burst of congratulatory noise erupted around the table. Yu Ling reached over and hugged Lucie. Zul promised to acquaint Lucie with his aunt, the premier postnatal jamu masseuse in Singapore, "who can shrink ladies back to their prebirth size."

Weina, who'd been chasing the ikura in her bowl with an unsteady spoon, perked up visibly.

"How many months?" Yu Ling asked. "We'll have to do a baby shower, won't we, Weina?"

"Hmm?" Weina said, mind clearly still on the woman shrinker.

"I'll chat with you later about it," Yu Ling said wisely.

"I'm almost six months," Lucie said.

"You look fabulous," Yu Ling said.

"She certainly does," Zul said, winking at Collin. "Absolutely glowing. By the way, my auntie Rosmah also does prenatal massages, if you're interested."

"OK, Zul, cool it with the hard sell," Weina said. "But just to clarify, is your aunt able to shrink *everything* to its original state, even *down below?*"

"And Collin's the baby daddy?" Dinesh asked, almost throwing himself at the conversation.

"Yes," Lucie said, looking down the table at Collin. "He's the dad."

"I'm the dad," Collin said softly, holding her gaze.

Mark dropped his fork down with a clatter. "It's interesting that we're talking about fatherhood. When I think about the father of a child, what's most important, I think, is someone who is not afraid to stick around to take care of a child. Take full responsibility from the get-go. Not talking specifically about your situation, of course."

"I agree," Collin said pleasantly. "That's why I plan to be there for all of it."

"Unless a better arrangement presents itself," Mark said.

"And what would that be?" Collin said, still pleasant.

"Maybe she gets married," Mark said forcefully.

The table fell silent. Zul looked at Mark nervously and said, "Isn't Collin with her?"

"No, he's not," Mark said. "They have an"—a lip curl—"arrangement."

Yu Ling glanced at Mark, then Collin, then back at Mark. "What do you—"

Lucie stood up before she even knew what she was doing. She wasn't ready to discuss their unusual circumstances, to open up their arrangement to judgment. She had to put a stop to it. "I'm right here," Lucie said quietly. "And I don't want to talk about this. It's between me and Collin."

A hush fell over the table, broken when Weina said morosely, "My first dinner party of the year is panning out well."

After a few minutes of tense eating, during which Lucie regretted ever asking Mark to the dinner, he decided to excuse himself. "Listen, I'm sorry to take my leave so early in the evening. I've got a work call with New York. Good to see you all again." Then, pointedly, he walked over and kissed Lucie on her cheek. "Thank you again, Weina, for the invite."

"I didn't invite you," Weina told him frankly. "She did." She pointed at Lucie.

"Bye, everyone," Mark said again, deciding not to follow up. "I'll see myself out."

"I guess he doesn't want cake," Collin said, under his breath.

Chapter 27

~~~~~~

COLLIN AND LUCIE were home by eleven o'clock, Zul having dropped them off.

"Nightcap? Rooibos?" Collin asked, clearing his throat.

"No thanks," she said.

They entered the dark, moonlit living room and, without exchanging a word, flopped down on the couch.

"That went well," Collin said. "At least, no one died."

"Har, har, har," Lucie said.

"You laugh! But it's not a given when someone like me comes to dinner! All we need is a gust of peanut dust, faulty EpiPens, and no close hospitals. Bye-bye, Collin!"

Lucie had to choke back her nervous laughter. "I don't know why I'm laughing. I really don't. It's not funny."

He chuckled. "It's good to hear you laugh. Things have been a little tense, haven't they?"

"I . . ." She hesitated. "I missed you, Collin. I miss talking to you. I don't know how, but I'd like us to go back to how we were when we first got here."

His face was inscrutable. "Sure, we can go back to how we were before."

The baby was moving, as though they wanted to chime in. Without a word, she took his hand and placed it over her stomach. She watched a look of wonderment creep over his features, and her heart clenched.

"Anyway, speaking of tense, I resigned from Dave's a few days ago."

Already? "Oh," Lucie said. "What happened?"

"I guess working for a friend is ill-advised. Let's just say he took advantage of my being in Singapore, hostage to the employment visa, and started asking for favors."

Lucie immediately thought of the kind of favors Weina's uncle did. "Illegal stuff?"

"No, nothing so cut-and-dried like that. He was just making me . . . do certain things I wasn't comfortable with. Anyway, don't worry, I have feelers out for something else, and I've got money saved up for expenses for a few months, so, y'know, don't worry."

He was worried. She could read him well now. Lucie struggled to keep her face impassive as she digested his announcement. There was a chance he wouldn't find something—what would that mean for them, for the baby?

I told you, this is a house of cards. Her doubts always took on her father's voice.

"Anyway, I've been thinking about what you said about jobs," he said, breaking the silence. "I don't know why I am working for Dave, earning very little, when I could be using that time to work in a job with more security. So that's what I'm going to do: look for a job that gives us more security, even if it means less 'fun.'" His lips thinned into a smile. "For us."

Lucie bit her lip. "Please, Collin. You don't have to do anything like that on my account. You have your philosophy regarding life and work balance, and I respect that. Let me be the main breadwinner—or the only one, until you find something suitable." He'd moved to Singapore for them. What was this if not a relationship of compromise?

"You would be all right with that?" he asked, his eyes boring into hers.

"Yes. I mean, I think." She tried to keep her tone unconcerned, but she could feel her shoulders bunching up around her neck.

"You're tense," he observed. "I'm sorry I did that. Can I give you a backrub?"

She nodded. He shifted behind her and leaned close.

As soon as he touched her, even through the fabric of her dress, she knew that things had changed irrevocably between them, at least from her perspective. He was kneading her with small, deep, circular movements in a perfectly respectable, platonic way, never straying from her neck and shoulders, yet each movement elicited prickles of electricity down her spine. She wanted more from him.

"Go lower," she said, her voice husky.

He moved his hands down. Down her spine. Digging his knuckles a little harder when he reached her lower back. She groaned and pushed herself against his hands.

"Where does it hurt?" he asked.

"It hurts everywhere without you," she said, without thinking, half-jokingly.

His hands stilled. "You don't mean that."

She turned around and said, "Collin."

He slid his hand up and gently moved her face closer. "Lucie," he said, like it was the first time he'd ever spoken it.

And then he pressed his lips on hers.

The first few seconds of the kiss weren't magical. Real-life isn't a fairy tale. Instead, it was a cocktail of confusion, shock, and nerves, and some teeth bashing.

And then they started really kissing. Hungrily. He gently lowered himself over her to deepen the kiss, parting her lips and dipping his tongue into her mouth with a sigh of something close to desperation, like he'd been holding himself back. This time his eyes met hers and stayed. *Yes.* She skated her hands over his chest, under his shirt, committing skin and muscle to memory. And it wasn't enough. This wasn't enough by far.

More. I need more. More of his kisses, more of his touch, all of him. *I want him,* she thought. She hadn't felt this way about someone for a long time, not since . . . Mark.

A switch flipped. She broke apart from him. "W-wait. Hold on a sec. I c-can't."

"You can't what?" he whispered, leaning forward again before she put a palm on his chest to stop him.

"This. Us."

He drew back. They were breathing heavily. "OK, what's wrong?"

"What just happened . . . I can't. Not to Justine," she said. "I won't be that person."

"Huh?" he said, confused.

"Justine, your girlfriend. I'm not going to be the reason why you're cheating on your girlfriend. After Mark . . ."

The mention of Mark's name brought an immediate chill to the proceedings. Collin straightened up and a shadow stole across his face. "I'm sorry you thought that," he said in a flat voice. "I tried to tell you at Weina's: Justine and I broke up this morning."

Lucie cringed. Was that why he looked like someone had gut-punched him? "I didn't know . . . I mean, I'm sorry."

Collin rubbed a palm over his face. "It's fine. It wasn't working out anyway."

"It wasn't? Why? What happened?" *Did she hurt you?* was what she really wanted to know. She balled her fists. She was usually a pacifist, but for Collin, she'd bend the rules.

"No." He hesitated, flushing, not looking at her. "To be honest, I'd been dating her while pining for someone else."

Great, now there was someone else? Lucie was *jealous*; the blood roared in her ears. "Who is it?" she asked, trying to keep her voice casual.

He gave a short, shivery laugh, almost as though he couldn't believe he was about to tell her. "Oh my God, Lucie, don't you see? It's you."

If she hadn't been seated, she would have fallen out of the chair. "Me?"

"Yes, you," he said, reaching out to brush a finger over her lips. "I have developed feelings for you. In spite of everything."

His confession of his true feelings toward her should have been welcome, but its phrasing, that caveat, stung her. "Gee, thanks," Lucie said, puffing out her cheeks and letting out a breath. "I didn't know I was so unlikeable."

"Lucie, in all seriousness, this was not supposed to happen. I wanted us to stay friends for a reason."

She bit her lip. "Because of how we met?"

"No, of course not." He sighed. He was wringing his hands in his lap now. "If you want the truth, it's because I've never had a romantic relationship I couldn't see the end of, couldn't see how it would end, and I didn't want us to meet the same fate, especially with a child involved."

Damn, who hurt you, Collin? Lucie searched his face, needing to understand. "Have you ever asked yourself why that is?"

He furrowed his brow and looked down. He looked so vulnerable that Lucie had to stop herself from reaching out for him and crushing him to her. "I know that's fucked up, that it's some kind of defense mechanism. I guess I kind of grew up thinking I was a liability, y'know, with my health being what it is. I've always wondered if my condition hastened the breakup of my parents' marriage." He saw her expression. "Look, I know better now, but I genuinely thought that for ages growing up. It ate at me. I guess . . . I-I was always pushing people away before they could get close. Not just girlfriends, I keep friends and family at arm's length, too."

She thought about the fact that he had been with a person for three years, someone he thought he could father a child with, yet they had never even moved in together. She recalled him setting up the reunion with his father, but only at the airport. And how he'd been unable to meet with his father alone after that.

"That's no way to live," she said.

He let out a breath. "I know. Believe me, I know . . . but things are different when it comes to you."

"What makes you think, our baby aside, that this is any different? If I open my heart to you, how can I trust that this isn't some . . . some passing fancy for you?"

"I don't think there's any way I can guarantee you forever. But what I do know is, we have something here, something special." He stroked her face, the intensity of feeling in his eyes making her breath catch. "Somehow I think it will last. Because when I'm with you, I don't think about how it'll end. I can't see our end, Lucie. That has to mean something for us. What if we have a chance at being right, together?"

A *"chance"* at being right? Collin, who was diametrically opposite to her. *It's just the novelty factor*, she told herself. *Humans like shiny new things.* That had to be it, the fever that had gripped her. But the cold harsh light of day shone on the gaps of his confession.

The shiny new thing drew close again and began dropping gentle, burning kisses on her right temple, her cheek, the corner of her lips, and soon she would not be able to say no. And that would be a mistake. When he slid his hand down her back, she pulled away from him. "Stop," she said, quietly.

"Why? Since Justine's no longer in the picture, nothing's stopping us from taking this further," he said huskily, drawing close again.

She put a hand on his chest. "Except there is. On my side there still is."

Mark.

He heard it, even if she didn't say it. "I see." The softness in his eyes vanished.

"No, no, you don't. This isn't a game, Collin." She took a deep breath. "I can't risk being your flavor of the month. It would jeopardize everything."

He reacted as though she had slapped him. "Do you really think so little of me?" Hurt and anger flashed in his eyes. He raised and lowered his fists, his breaths coming fast and shallow.

She looked away. "I-I don't know *what* to think about you, at least . . . at least not when it comes to this."

"All these months, everything we've talked about, living together, isn't enough to show you who I am? Who I can be?"

"It's not about who you are alone. It's about who we are together." She inhaled and exhaled quickly, before she lost her nerve. Collin hadn't started out wanting her or a traditional family—he'd never believed in marriage. He'd only wanted a baby. Whereas she'd always wanted to start a family with someone, not just have a kid. The latter was a last resort. And now Collin wanted more, true, but even his confession felt like a warning, so pitted with red flags that she wondered if he wanted her to pick it apart. At this stage, a relationship with her baby's father wasn't something she wanted to leave to chance—if she chose Collin and they broke up, nothing would be left, not even the original arrangement. She had to shut it down, for both their sakes. "We're meant to be co-parents, nothing more."

Then a dark silence that rang for the longest time.

"Wow, Lucie. Just . . . wow."

They stared at each other. Then without another word, he left, taking the stairs to his room. A door slammed.

She looked up at the ceiling above, where his room was— where he was. She saw him in her mind's eye, flesh and blood. She could go to him now. She could open herself to the possibilities he was offering. But—she shut her eyes, trying to stop her imagination—it wasn't just about him. Not anymore.

Any wrong step taken in the name of passion could ruin something sure, something good. Something right, finally.

Should I risk a solid, tangible relationship built on years of history for a budding, undefined thing? Or was the unknown worth sacrificing the known for, worth the risks?

Except risk wasn't an unknown quality. You could calculate risk. It had real-world, tangible implications. *Remember—love is a gamble, and the house always wins*, her mother had said.

On the one hand was Mark, who she had loved. Who she still loved. Who she knew intimately. Who she had seen at his best and his worst.

On the other hand was Collin, who was all risk without clear reward. A gamble in which they could lose everything.

They weren't playing house—they were having a baby. And

her baby needed a proper family. Mark was the one who could offer her what she and her baby wanted. Needed.

She took her phone out and typed a question. When she got the reply she wanted, she started packing an overnight bag for Mark's. It was time to think about the larger picture.

Chapter 28

~~~~~~

SHE ARRIVED JUST after midnight and knocked on his door, aware that a door was closing behind her even as this one opened, a block of amber light and a silhouette of a rumpled figure in the doorway, stretching out a hand to take her overnight bag before she'd even needed to ask.

"I just need some space from everything," she said, a little embarrassed. "Could I crash here, for a couple of nights while I figure out what to do next?"

"What happened?" Mark said, his jaw twitching. His eyes searched her face, dipped down to her belly. "Are you both OK?"

"Of course," Lucie said, not wanting Mark to get the wrong idea.

"This is your place as much as it's mine," Mark said, putting a hand on her waist and gently leading her in. "Sit down; you're pregnant."

Lucie let herself be guided into the living room. He left and came back with a cup of water. "Careful, it's hot," he cautioned.

Lucie took a sip and winced. "Could I have some ice in this, please? I'm so sweaty."

Mark shook his head. "Wait a while. You shouldn't be drinking cold water in your state. Wind." He was referring to a TCM concept of pathogenic wind, which was bad for the system. "I'm pressure-cooking some red date tea, so we'll have some in half an hour, before you turn in for the night."

Lucie blinked, unsure if she'd heard right. "Red date tea?"

"Yes, I have a couple of bags of dried red dates lying around and I make myself a tea whenever I get tired and need a boost."

He understands. Lucie sagged into the couch. She'd forgotten that Mark had his own herbalist. There would be no need to press Mark to respect TCM.

They chatted softly, sipping hot water, then red date tea, till Lucie, drowsy from the events of the day, fell asleep on the chaise end of the sectional. Mark was carrying her to his room before she could stop him. Just as he dropped her off, she reached out and wordlessly pulled him down, and he wrapped himself around her, planting soft kisses on her temples. She let herself drift off, comforted by his familiar warmth.

The next morning she woke up next to Mark, in the same bed they used to share, disorientated by how nothing, and everything, had changed, by what she'd set in motion by coming over. Sure, he smelled the same, and his arms wound around her felt the same, comforting and right, but so much had happened between them that she couldn't pretend it didn't feel strange to be lying there next to him.

"Hey," she said, when she saw that he was awake, too.

"Hey yourself," he said, his breath warm against her temples, the perfect gentleman despite what could only be described as epic morning wood pressing against her lower back. "I've never been as glad as I am right now to wake up next to you."

She nodded, feigning morning breath, unwilling to make the same declarations yet.

Her phone beeped. I made breakfast. Come down please?

Lucie put the phone away, her heart squeezing. She pictured Collin bustling around in their kitchen, preparing breakfast; dependable, reliable Collin, who, no matter what was happening between them, put her needs ahead of his feelings. Making one of his impressive Sunday brunches: french toast to start, then smoked salmon, poached eggs, grilled sausages, mushrooms, tomatoes, homemade yogurt, and a smoothie.

He'd be quieter than usual, watchful, waiting for her to speak first, maybe hoping to clear the air about yesterday. So she wondered how he would feel when he called up to her, knocking on her door, hopeful, until he realized she wasn't home.

He had opened his heart to her, wanted to build a relationship with her. And she had left anyway. Because unlike Collin, she *could* see how this would end, all of it broken, all of it wasted. And a baby with parents who couldn't stand each other.

I'm so, so sorry, Collin. Now, let me put our needs ahead of our feelings.

SHE AND MARK got breakfast at their favorite brunch place in Dempsey Hill, an affluent enclave of eateries and specialty shops where you could get anything from oysters to Kobe beef to dessert decorated with twenty-three-karat gold leaf. After dim sum, they went to a café with floor-to-ceiling windows overlooking a park, where Lucie ate an apricot cake with almonds and Nutella ice cream with an almost indecent relish.

Mark smiled at her as he drank his coffee. "A penny for your thoughts?"

"This is sparking all kinds of memories, us having brunch here."

"Good ones?"

She paused. "Yes," she said, truthfully.

Under the table, their fingers met. She laced hers through his, and he squeezed her hand gently before bringing it to his lips, sending a jolt of electricity through her. Why couldn't this all work out, still? Having this baby and having Mark? Collin didn't have to come with the baby. They had always accounted for the possibility that either or both of them would date and maybe get serious with a third party. So what if her choice happened to be Mark? Collin would continue to have equal access to the child, of course. Nothing would change there. All she was doing was removing herself from the dangerous slide into physical attraction. Moving the needle back to where it had to be.

She imagined telling her parents that she was back with Mark. And then one day, maybe even marrying Mark for real. While it wouldn't be the wedding they'd envisaged, it would at least make it seem right to the rest of the world. Just announcing their engagement would definitely reduce the friction in their interactions with her. Maybe she could finally return her parents' texts with something more substantial than one-worded replies. Maybe she could even start joining them for Yi family dinners again—with Mark. Just the fact that Mark was back in her life would minimize any friction, if not cancel out their disappointment, surely.

"Would you like anything else?" a server's voice broke her reverie.

"An iced almond milk hazelnut latte, please," she said. Across the table from her, Mark smiled at the server, and said, "Make that two."

When he took her hand between his and kissed it, she closed her eyes and didn't think about Collin, which is to say she thought about him in the oblique way one thinks about an achingly gooey chocolate-chip cookie when one is biting into a rice cracker.

Not that Mark was a rice cracker, of course.

No, Mark was . . . Mark was . . .

Carrot cake, yes. The most perfect, healthful of all desserts, combining all the important food groups and fulfilling Lucie's System of Offsetting. And it wasn't nut-free.

Chapter 29

~~~~~

Lucie: Hey, we missed you at Weina's.

Suzie: I wasn't well. How are you?

Lucie: Good, you?

Suzie: Not too bad.

Lucie: I missed you.

Suzie: I've been missing you for a while . . .

Lucie: Would you like to meet up?

Suzie: I would, but not right now. I just need some space.

Lucie: Why? Did I do something wrong?

Suzie: Oh Lucie.

LUCIE CLOSED HER eyes, fighting the fatigue and low-level anxiety she'd been feeling since she moved in with Mark. It hadn't been easy adjusting to a new place—even one she once lived in—and the resulting insomnia was taking a toll on her. Worse still, she'd given herself a week to figure out her next steps, figuring the physical space would lead to mental clarity, but she was no closer to resolving her conflicting emotions than she was to solving Goldbach's conjecture. There were too many variables at stake.

You don't have to move out if you need space, I can, Collin had offered.

No, don't worry. Staying at Mark's wasn't another cost to them, but if Collin moved out, he'd be incurring more expenses when she was the one who needed the distance.

And now she was going to add another variable to the mix: work. More specifically, the firm had announced via email that it was going to promote a principal, the selection process would begin in a month, and the evaluation would take over a quarter. She'd already gotten another email from Samuel saying she was one of the principals in the running for partnership. Her stomach fluttered with dread. Perfect timing to announce her pregnancy, of course.

It's going to be OK. You have nothing to be worried about.

It was time to quash the rumors that she and Vanessa had heard about her "condition." She'd seen the looks. With a little less than four months to go, despite everything she did to make her bump less visible—ruffles, layers, scarves, chunky jewelry, and boxy blazers—it was no longer possible to realistically disguise the evidence, so to speak.

She'd done all she could humanly do. Lucie closed her eyes and decided to pull the lever.

First she told Vanessa, who let out a whoop and impulsively gave her a hug. "I knew it," Vanessa crowed. "I knew you were pregnant. The caffeine strike. And your wardrobe change and the fact that you were always so early to meetings, so you'd be seated first. You can't fool your PA."

Lucie smiled. "I'm sorry I couldn't tell you earlier."

Vanessa waved the apology away. "It's fine. We all know there's a *pantang* period for Asian folks. Anyway, is this official news yet?"

"It's about to be," Lucie said grimly. "I hope it doesn't impact the partnership interviews. Wish me luck."

"Oh, Lucie, I don't think you have anything to worry about," Vanessa said, smiling, although her eyes said otherwise. She was probably thinking of Ana Becker, pregnant German casualty of Discovery Asia Consulting.

Then Lucie drafted an email to the partners, cc'ing the human resources department.

Dear partners,

I am writing to notify you that I am approximately six months pregnant.

In the meantime, I heard about the equity partner position that has become available and wanted to assure everyone that I am still very much interested in being considered for it. I am prepared to work through my maternity leave, albeit in a reduced capacity, to ensure the clients have access to me at all times.

Last year, I brought in the largest share of business among all the principals and project leaders, and indeed for the past three years, even while I was in New York.

I am the most often requested consultant in this firm.

I am sure the firm, with its excellent reputation and forward-thinking equal opportunity hiring practices, will accord my candidacy with due consideration.

Thank you.

Lucie Yi

She hit "send" with more confidence than she actually felt. Her hands were shaking: she was about to find out how valued she really was at the firm.

CONGRATULATIONS! KWOK YIPERN wrote back. You're joining the Parent Club at last! I didn't know you were married.

I'm not, she replied.

Oh, how brave of you. I guess you'll have your hands full as a single parent. Hope the work will still matter to you. LOL.

We are so pleased for you, said another colleague. Family is very important here at Discovery Asia Consulting. Lucie was pretty sure the partner who sent that, Fred Chong, did not know what year his three children attended, offhand. He was traveling 80 percent of the time, and his PA was legendary for writing up summary reports on their progress at school.

The other partners and principals wrote back to congratulate her, effusively. Samuel simply replied with Splendid news.

Two hours later, Samuel called. He'd asked that Gordon Liu, another up-and-coming principal, replace Lucie as lead on the CORPEXA project. "Just until you're back from maternity leave, of course. And I heard you're doing this on your own."

"I'm not on my own . . . I have a partner."

"Right. That's good to know! I'm sure he or she—I'm progressive, you know—and you will be very busy in the months ahead . . . We're legally obliged to give you four months off, after all, won't want any trouble with the authorities, would we." He chuckled darkly. "We want you to enjoy motherhood, though you are welcome—but in no way obliged or encouraged—to continue working on your files, understand? Then once you're all rested up, you can come back, full-steam ahead."

"But that's . . . that's ages away." Even if she forwent her four months of maternity leave, took just a month, even two, off and spent the rest working from home, it would still be almost half a year away.

Six months was a long time.

"CORPEXA is *my* project. I got the client onboard in New York."

"Yes," Samuel said, sounding distracted. "Don't worry, we'll still keep you on the project as a tax consultant, of course. They'll understand once they hear you're pregnant. You'll still be working on it."

It wasn't the same thing. It wasn't even in the same ballpark. Lucie knew it, Samuel knew it. It would probably mean she couldn't pull in the numbers needed to be considered for partnership this year, even though Samuel hadn't said her candidacy was withdrawn.

She thanked him and hung up the phone.

The girls were wrong—about her trying elective co-parenting, about her trying to break the glass ceiling as a single mother. The more things changed, the more they stayed the same.

AND THEN IT was official: she found out from a formally worded email that she was definitely not being considered for partner this year. But better luck next round!

I'm OK. I'm OK.

She swiped her tears away angrily in the taxi as she headed to childbirth class. After the first disastrous trial class, they'd found a course run by doulas—a little more alternative and not on the top-ten lists, but at least they were immediately given a spot. She hated the fact that work had made her cry, especially when shedding a tear wouldn't change a thing. And she couldn't let Collin, or the fourteen other pairs of parents at their childbirth education class, see her like this.

Crying in public in front of strangers—that's how she got into this mess.

By the time she arrived, composure back in check, Collin was already out front. She ducked her head and pretended to fix something on her sleeve, needing to take a beat to wrestle her pulse back to normal. Seeing him again was a giant kick in the groin— and she should know about kicks, since their baby was amping those up, too. On top of the heartburn, the hiccups, the vagina farts, the general flatulence, and of course, the supernumerary nipples.

She wasn't complaining, of course. But still, she had gotten the short end of the stick when they were handing out symptoms.

She and Collin approached each other as though they were dueling fencers.

"Yi."

"Read."

Collin's mouth quirked, and Lucie felt an immediate rush of secret affection. All the things she'd been wanting to say, the big and small, the minutiae, bubbled to her lips. *How are you? What did you have for lunch? Did you know the baby flutters around in there like a goldfish most days?* She missed him.

He indicated with a jerk of his head that they should head in. They found a space and settled down quietly.

"When are you coming back?" he asked.

"Three more days, maybe."

"I told you, I could move out."

"Please don't."

At the labor and breathing techniques segment of their class, the instructor wanted the pregnant women to simulate going into labor and practice various breathing techniques with their partner. When she saw that her partner was supposed to hold her while she huffed—the couples around them giggling and generally having a laugh—she immediately volunteered to be part of the demonstration, so that the instructor would hold her instead.

"Do you even want me here?" Collin said in a low voice, after the class had emptied, and they were alone in the hallway.

"There's just a couple more classes on labor and breathing techniques, and I just think because we're platonic, I should be up in front with the teacher."

"You're afraid of me touching you?" Loaded question, loaded glance.

She hesitated before answering, "I'm not *afraid*."

"Sure doesn't look that way," he said. He stepped closer to her and Lucie felt her body respond to his proximity, the tiny hairs on her arms standing, like he was a magnet. She wanted to touch him, to be touched by him, and—meeting his hooded gaze—he knew it. That quirk in his lip told her as much.

"I told you"—she swallowed hard—"it's not about that."

He gave a short laugh. "Don't worry, even if there are other hands-on segments in the future, we can keep it strictly hands-free, if it eases *your* mind. I won't *touch* you. See you next class." Whistling, he started walking away.

My Ex Would Never walk away from me.

She turned to walk in the other direction before she realized the futility of that act of defiance: there was only one exit. Life was irritating like that.

AT THE END of the second week of camping out at Mark's, she came home after work to find him sitting in the living room with an air of anticipation.

"Good, you're home."

"You must have waited long," she replied. It was close to nine o'clock. He'd offered to pick her up, but she'd declined. She liked zoning out in the taxi after work. Mark had a way of requiring her attention.

"No issue." He got up and led her wordlessly to the nursery, a room she'd avoided since the night he'd shown it to her.

"Surprise," he said quietly, when the lights came on.

He had returned the oval Stokke cot and installed a pale-gray, solid beechwood rectangular model from an upmarket Spanish brand that had LED lights embedded in the transparent sides to light up softly at night.

"I could paint it hot pink, if you'd like," he murmured in her ear.

"Thank you, Mark," she said, surveying the nursery, her eyes prickling with unshed tears.

He kissed her forehead and started to move away when she reached out and pulled him to her. More, not less. She'd been denying herself for so long, feasting on scraps. She parted his lips, stroked and licked him with her tongue till she ached for him and she felt him press into her in desperation, stumbling till they bounced up against the wall. More. More.

"Take your clothes off, Mark," she said thickly.

At the sound of her voice, he gently placed a hand on her shoulder and disengaged, his breath fast and erratic. "We were going to take the physical side of things slow, remember?" he said in a thready whisper.

She tried to pull him back. "Maybe I don't want that anymore." She was so tired of thinking for everyone.

"We have to," he said. He glanced at her belly. "For all our sakes. I can't . . . I can't jeopardize . . . this, even if . . ." He didn't finish the sentence. He didn't need to. "Let's wait a little. I want to make sure you're really ready before anything physical happens. I have to take care of you. Would you let me do that?"

It sounded so nice to be loved. To be cared for. She nestled against him, nodding. He nuzzled her. "Is it too soon to ask if you'll move back in, finally?"

"It's not too soon," she said. "I want to. I want this life."

He tipped her chin up and brushed her lips with his, a smile creasing his eyes. "Then welcome home, Lucie."

Chapter 30

〜〜〜〜

HOME. *SHE WAS home.*

Lucie opened her eyes early Saturday morning to the smell of her home going up in flames. Bacon-scented flames.

Shit! she thought, snapping to attention and fumbling out of bed. She poked her head into the other bedroom, panicked, calling, "Mark! Mark! Get up! The house is on fire!"

"I'm in the kitchen," Mark called out. Sure enough, when Lucie entered the kitchen, she saw him standing by the sink sheepishly, rinsing a sizzling and smoking pan in the sink, wearing his trademark weekend morning casual attire of choice: a white polo shirt, beige chinos, and a spotless denim apron.

"Cooking?" Lucie inquired mildly.

"Guilty," Mark said, pointing at the crisping black mass in the pan. "I was trying to make you roasted pork belly."

"Mark," she said, trying to suppress her laughter, "I think you need to start with baby steps. Make a scrambled egg first or even french toast?"

He came over and kissed her nose. "But I like to go big."

"Hmm," Lucie said. "Sometimes, in life, you need to start with the small things before you go for the big leagues."

"Like this?" He put an arm around her and pulled her in for a chaste kiss.

"Yeah."

A loud *pop* interrupted them just as Lucie was thinking she really didn't need breakfast, which was very unusual for her.

"Told you not to eat so many beans," she teased, as he disengaged himself to check on the still smoldering, crackling charred mass.

He nodded distractedly, not getting the joke. "I paid a lot for that pan," he said ruefully, poking at the blackened mass with a wooden spatula. "You're going to have to teach me how to cook. If you still don't know, it's high time you learned how, especially now that you're going to be a mom."

Lucie stiffened.

"Surely you didn't survive on takeout in New York," Mark said, an eyebrow raised. "But if you did, we'll have to work on systemic lifestyle changes, once you move in. Home-cooked, organic everything."

The smallest current of irritation coursed through Lucie. *Has he always been this pushy?* She was immediately contrite. *He just wants what's best for you.* Maybe this was just the way he came off, in typical alpha-Mark fashion, but he had always had—with only one exception—her best interests at heart. And he wasn't holding her hostage. She had a choice.

"I can cook," she said evenly. "But I'm not sure how much time *we*'ll have for cooking once I return to work after maternity leave."

"Right, we'll have to get live-in help, of course," Mark said. "Also, I love that you're still as ambitious as ever, but now that

you're going to be a mom, maybe . . . maybe you'll like to reconsider your hours. I mean, I am earning enough for all of us to be
more than comfortable. Just putting it out there."

Lucie's stomach lurched.

"Anyway, we'll have to get movers to bring all your stuff here."

"Ah." Lucie had anticipated this. She tried for nonchalance.
"There's no need to do that just yet. I'll just move some more of
my everyday stuff here, like clothes and toiletries, as we go along."

"Oh," Mark said, his face clouding over. "I see."

Lucie rushed to explain herself. "It's not that I don't want to
move in. . . . I just need to move in on my own terms. It's not just
about what I want to do, I have to consider my arrangement with
Collin, and I wa—should maintain a shared residence with Collin, for when the baby comes. So that he has equal access to the
baby when we co-parent."

He nodded, but his expression was cold as he turned away
and began scouring the pan with hard, abrupt movements. Lucie
faltered in her resolve. Whether it could be attributed to authori-
tarian parenting or an innate quality of her nature, there was a
part of her that responded to a withdrawal of approval with an
almost Pavlovian desire to rectify the situation—to restore favor.
She had to remind herself that she couldn't give in, it wouldn't be
fair to Collin. Still, she said, meekly, "I just need some time,
Mark. Please."

His posture softened. He gave her a tight smile. "I understand. Take as long as you need."

Relief flooded her. She relaxed. "Since I'm moving in, could
you promise me one thing?"

"Name it."

"You and Collin will have to learn to get along. If this whole
three-way is going to work out."

"This is the worst three-way I could possibly be having," Mark muttered. "But, yes, I suppose it would be prudent to have him over and hash out, man-to-man, how we're going to handle you and the whole baby business."

"You mean, 'work out how we're going to share parenting responsibilities,'" Lucie said, a little disconcerted by his choice of words.

"Yes, of course," Mark said. "I'm sorry, this is new territory for me. You've had some time to figure out this whole arrangement, but it's still something I have to wrap my head around, conceptually." He regarded her with an inscrutable expression. "To be honest, Lucie, I never would have expected someone like you to do something so . . . left field."

"What do you mean?"

"You always wanted to do things the right way."

She bristled a little at what he was implying. *Remember, you had the same reservations too. He just needs to be educated.* "Just keep an open mind and give this . . . *him* a chance."

Mark turned away, giving the ruined Le Creuset one last disdainful look before throwing the pan and its contents into the bin. "All right. I'll be the bigger man. For you."

SHE WENT BACK to Collin and hers after work that Monday, rehearsing what she would tell Collin. *I'm moving to Mark's. We're getting back together.*

Mark had therapy on Mondays; he had given her access to his calendars, in case she wanted to check in on where he was (he even told her she could trace him on the app), but she told him that if she couldn't trust him then there was no point in them even trying.

Also, he'd fucked his boss at work, so an app that would trace where he was at all times was moot. If a man like Mark wanted to cheat, he would find a way to hide it. She didn't tell him that, of course. But no one ever said that you had to tell your partner everything on your mind.

When it came to Collin, however, she was nervous.

The one thing your Arrangement hadn't covered was the possibility of you two catching feelings for each other, the knowing voice in her head whispered. *And it seems like that has happened, hasn't it?*

She shut down that thought with a violent shake of her head. *No. Not today.* She was in control, or she would regain control of the situation. All she had to do was proceed as planned. Give her most promising relationship a chance to flourish, secure the best possible outcome for her child: being in a stable, loving relationship versus one that had begun so transactionally.

Surely Collin would understand.

Why am I so nervous? If she was honest, from the way she was sweating and the light-headedness, she felt like she was betraying them.

She tried to make it sound positive when she met him that evening at theirs. All their conversations were at the kitchen table these days. Utilitarian wooden chairs were not conducive to romantic interludes, unless you were descended from alpine folk or had a very numb butt (she was neither).

"You'll have access to everything, of course—all the ob-gyn appointments, our birth classes, when the baby comes, etc. Nothing changes in that respect. We'll just . . . see each other less. And the burden of keeping me sane until the baby comes will be shared between you and Mark."

"It's not a burden. It never was," he said quietly, a muscle twitching in his jaw.

Why does he always say such perfect things? she thought. She gave herself a mental shake. "I'll continue to pay my share for this apartment, of course. I mean, I'm still handling the payment to the landlord."

"We don't have to keep this place. I did some budgeting, reviewed my finances . . ." He laughed when he saw her do a double take. "Yes, I know, it's something I should have done much earlier in my life, but no time like the present, right?"

People can change, Inner Weina whispered.

Well, then, remember that Mark has, too, she countered, and Inner Weina slunk away.

In all the important ways? Inner Suzie piped up.

"I can find a cheaper, smaller place, especially if the baby is going to live with you. Forty-six hundred for an apartment that only one of us will be using is a heck of a lot of money."

"Fifty-five hundred," she corrected him without thinking.

He blinked rapidly. "I'm sorry, how much is our rent?"

"Fifty-five hundred dollars," she repeated. *Oh shit,* she thought, when she saw the way his face changed. She'd completely forgotten her private arrangement with the landlord. She tried to backpedal with her best poker face on. "Oh, what? I meant forty-six hundred. You know, whatever was in the rental agreement. Pregnancy brain, you know."

Silence. He was angry. She could tell by how loudly he was clenching his jaw, how still he held himself. "No. Not pregnancy brain. You were sure. I can't believe it, Lucie, you've been lying to me this whole time!"

"I wasn't lying," she mumbled, flushing. "Forty-six hundred is our official rent. It's in our contract."

"I can't believe this. How much do I owe you?"

"It's no big deal."

It was not the right thing to say—she knew it as soon as she heard herself say it. His nostrils flared. "But it *is* a big deal. My feelings about this are just as valid as yours. I want to contribute equally, you know that. But I'm already so stretched financially, especially now that I'm leaving BofBofGo. I can't believe you would lie to me about this. We're supposed to be a team."

She gaped at him. Why did he make it sound as though she'd set his great-aunt Michelle on fire? She was doing him a favor. "Have you found a new job yet?" *So much for initiative and drive*, she thought.

"I'm looking. But there's nothing out there I really want to do."

"So man up and compromise," she blurted.

The silence between them was loaded and unpleasant. She saw him grinding his molars.

"Thanks for making your feelings about me perfectly clear," he said coldly. "In the meantime, I want screenshots of all our utilities and food expenses. The real amounts. I'll wire half the money to you by the end of the week."

"Good. By the way—" she started to say, meaning to ask him about his plans on Thursday, to see if he was free to come to hash things out with Mark.

"Splendid," he said, already standing up and walking away from her, his jaw set.

AT HER NEW home with Mark, armed with a superfood smoothie loaded with pre- and probiotics, Lucie sat down and tackled the division of the expenses that she had hitherto taken upon herself to cover. She'd been paying for a lot more than she realized, not just groceries and basic utilities, but many of their little luxuries:

streaming services, takeouts and food deliveries, taxis they took together. It was hard not to feel just a little bit vindictive after spending four hours compiling a list of expenses on a spreadsheet and taking screenshots of all the receipts and bills. At the end of that exercise, Lucie was irritable, mostly with herself. The sum was close to six thousand dollars.

She was left with a sinking feeling that he was right: money was power in a relationship. There were expectations behind it, no matter what was said out loud. Collin had been right to insist on equal financial contribution and not let her bankroll their lifestyle; he always stood up for himself and what he believed in, even if it didn't sit well with others. As she attached the Excel doc of all their expenses to an email of apology, she found herself wondering why, even when Collin challenged her worldview, she didn't shy away from the confrontation.

Chapter 31

～～～

THIS IS DEFINITELY not *going to end well.*

Collin finally agreed to what Mark called the Parenthood Parley, until Lucie pointed out they were hardly in disagreement to begin with, so Mark changed it to the Parenthood Peace Talks. The three of them gathered for late drinks. Mark couldn't even bring himself to invite Collin for dinner. Now Mark, Collin, and she were standing in the living room, the men making small talk with daggers in their eyes. Mark, Lucie noticed with some discomfort, was smiling hard and drinking water. He only drank water when in company for one reason, and Collin was not going to like it.

Now they were discussing beer, but really—

"I'm not a fan of IPA," Collin was saying. "I like a light, refreshing drink."

"Course you do," Mark said, masquerading his distaste with more teeth in his smile. "Lucie told me which brand of lite lager you drink, and I have a whole case of it chilling in the fridge."

"Thank you, you are too kind," Collin said. "You can keep the beer, though. I'm staying away from beers." He patted his perfect abdomen. "Bloat."

—they were being assholes.

Mark's face twitched, almost imperceptibly. "What would you like to drink, then?"

Collin's eyes flitted over Mark's bar. "I'll have a single-malt whiskey, please." Collin never drank whiskey, usually. "Whatever you have that's open."

"You're welcome to any."

"Any?"

"Any."

"Then I'll have the twenty-one-year-old Oban." Collin smiled.

Lucie saw Mark flinch. It was his favorite. And expensive.

"Great. Neat?" Mark was smiling again just as he turned around and reached for a glass tumbler and the Oban.

"On the rocks."

Mark's back stiffened. "How many ice cubes?"

Collin pondered this. "A tumbler full," he said decisively.

Lucie could tell, from the stillness of his back, that Mark was in pain. Mark didn't believe in single malts with ice—it was almost sacrilegious.

Mark recovered and served the drinks—Lucie's, a glass of sparkling water with a shot of wild berry cordial, no ice—and the talk turned to exercise regimens and supplements. Both men worked out; Mark was much taller, wiry; he had been genetically blessed with the kind of lean physique that needed little upkeep but trended less on the muscular scale, unlike Collin. Mark admitted that he was less "sculpted" than he would like, because, as he told Collin and Lucie, laughingly, he had a career.

"You must have a lot of time to work out, now that you're unemployed."

"I do enjoy the gym, but I'm not exactly unemployed. I do freelance for a couple of tech firms. There's money coming in, no worries," Collin said. "Maybe not flatten-a-rainforest-for-profit kind of money." He looked straight at Mark. Lucie sighed. Mark's firm in the United States had recently been in the news for accepting a mining company's mandate. She didn't like it either, but it wasn't the kind of thing Mark had much say in, even as a partner.

Mark's teeth grinding was not audible above the orchestral music, but Lucie, seated next to him, could feel it.

Lucie cleared her throat. "Maybe we should get to the heart of the matter."

"Yes," Collin said, looking at Mark. "Let's talk about how we're going to raise my and Lucie's child together."

With Mark in the mix, the biggest issue was, unsurprisingly, money. Mark was adamant that he wanted to contribute to the child's care while the child was under his—their—roof, although he wasn't going to butt in with opinions on the issues they had already hammered out solutions to. He phrased this as deference to Collin, but Lucie knew it was because for Mark, money was the only meaningful battleground.

Day-to-day child-related expenses, Collin insisted, had to be split three ways, always, except for the "big-ticket" items under the original co-parenting arrangement, such as education, health-care, and childcare. Receipts kept. Unless they amounted to less than fifty dollars. Anything that cost more than one hundred dollars had to be cleared with the other parent. Mark rolled his eyes and said that it would be aggravatingly administrative. "What's a hundred dollars?" he said. "I can't be calling you up every time I need to buy the child a jumper or a rattle."

"We can run a preapproved list of big, recurring expenses, like bulk orders of diapers, but new items need to be cleared with both of us. And please don't be buying hundred-dollar jumpers or rattles."

"This is such a pain," Mark muttered.

"I love how we're all coming together, working as one," Lucie said.

It went on in the same barbed vein for a whole hour and a half; both men bandying veiled insults at each other while Lucie, resigned, ate haw flakes and snuck the occasional Instagram scroll, sometimes giving her feedback, which was then picked over for hidden favoritism.

Y'know, unlike what I'd always imagined, having two men squabble over me, crossing swords like some medieval fantasy, is kind of the *opposite* of fun, she told her friends later over group chat—it hadn't escaped her notice how inactive the chat had been; most times, she conversed directly with Weina, and all her texts to Suzie were read but not responded to. Each "read" notification that Suzie left hanging stung Lucie.

I don't know, it sounds kind of hot, Weina wrote back. Even if one of them is Mark. So what happened?

Lucie gave them a quick summary of the events.

Ouch, Weina said.

Is Simon as much a caveman as these knuckleheads?

Not at all. Simon is really relaxed. And patient. Nothing fazes him. That's why he's great at crypto. And in bed.

WEINA! GROSS!

Lucie waited for Suzie to chime in. She did not.

A FEW DAYS later, it was Collin's turn to summon her for a meeting after work. When she offered to drop by their place, he rebuffed her, suggesting a local vegan café instead. He claimed that it was easier for her, but Lucie wondered if he didn't want to be alone with her at theirs anymore, if the memory of their kiss made him eager to put physical distance between them. *Or maybe I'm the only one obsessing over it*, she thought wryly. He had probably moved on with another Justine Maya type. She was fine with that—the jolt of nausea after this thought was definitely *not* caused by Collin and *entirely* the result of her baby's newfound dance moves.

And why the need for a face-to-face reveal? Lucie wondered what he wanted to tell her. She'd detected some tension in his voice, and Collin wasn't one to be fazed easily.

She walked into that café gingerly, her steps halting. Her back had been killing her lately, what with the long hours at work and just the way bodies got when pregnant. When Collin looked up from his phone and saw her mincing walk, he leaped out of his chair and hurried to her side, asking if he could take her tote. He looked pained by her discomfort, but she laughed off his questions about her health.

"Tell me," she said, once they had placed their orders with the waiter.

"I've been offered a job."

"That's great," she said, surprised. "What's the job about?"

"A series-A tech company, which my NDA forbids me to name. I'll be a chief software architect." His lips twisted sardonically.

"Collin, that's wonderful." She wanted to hug him, but something in his demeanor told her it wouldn't be welcome, so she remained in her seat.

"It is. The role is interesting, it's well paying, with equity. You won't have to worry about my contributing anymore. I'm planning to accept." His laugh was short and humorless.

"That's not what this was, at all. Anyway, congrats on the offer, but why haven't you accepted yet?"

"Because . . . because the job will require me to be based in Seoul, at least for the next six months."

"Seoul!" she said, shocked. She forced herself to speak calmly. "But I thought the whole point of being a co-parent is that we'll actually be in the same . . . neighborhood. The same country."

"It's only temporary. They would rotate me back in Singapore after that. And I don't want to get in the way of your happiness with Mark. I think he doesn't like me very much. And if you're living with him, then what's the point of me being here, full-time? Any visitation rights I have will be shared anyway, so I can work around it with you when the baby is older."

Lucie said nothing.

"I'm still going to be involved. I'm just trying to work out the best compromise for me, to be responsible financially for the child as much as I can."

Her heart gave a strange lurch. "It's not about money," she insisted again.

He sighed. "It *has* to be about the money, at this stage. You've always known it was important to me to contribute fifty-fifty, like we'd always planned. Look, in the early days, the baby will have you both, and I'll just be getting in the way."

"But as soon as the baby comes, should I . . . don't you—don't you want fifty-fifty access?"

"With Mark in the picture, do you think it's even feasible, possible, for us to keep to the fifty-fifty plan? What is best for the baby?"

She shook her head. "I don't want to deprive you of anything, especially time with the child."

"You're not. I'm putting the baby, and your welfare, first. I'm here for you both, and if I have to, I'll just resign and move back to Singapore, get some lesser job." He gave a short laugh. "But this is a great opportunity, and at this stage, it's the only one that will allow me to be in Asia, with the right benefits. I do want to be an equal contributor in terms of finances, even if I can't *physically* be with you both all the time." He shrugged. "And there are many ways to be a parent. Just because someone is physically present with the child all the time doesn't mean they are spending quality time with them. And so many parents are forced to live apart from their children anyway, what's the difference if I do the same?"

"You told me that your father's absence damaged you."

"I didn't say 'damaged.' Look, I turned out just fine. And our baby will have a father figure. Mark will also be a father, another parent. Who's to say a two-parent model is the best?"

Lucie sucked in her bottom lip, unsure.

"Hey." He tipped her chin up and met her gaze. "We'll get through this," he assured her.

"I'll miss you."

"Me, too," he said. He paused, then said, in a rush, "Should things change, I mean, if you change your mind, about wanting to be with Mark"—he cleared his throat—"just move back in. I'll sort something out with the company."

"I can't ask that of you. Even if things don't work out between me and Mark."

"Are things going well? Between you and him?"

She hesitated before nodding. The light in his eyes dimmed.

"Can I touch your belly?" he said at last. She nodded, and he placed his hands on her. She bit her lip as he bent his head and whispered to the baby, or maybe to her, "I'll miss you, my love." Tears sprang to her eyes. Lucie wanted her face to be impassive, but his gentle, loving touch was almost too much to bear.

He looked up and their eyes locked in an unguarded moment, too late for her to mask her emotions. The want was written in her eyes for him to see, as his was. She trembled. If he kissed her now the charade would be over. She turned away, eager to restore order, when he grasped her hand under the coffee table and clasped it tight. Her thoughts telescoped to another afternoon, in a hotel room, where he'd done the same, and her breath hitched.

"You have feelings for me," he said, urgency in his voice. "I know you do. That night after Weina's . . ."

"Of course I feel something for you," Lucie said quietly. "But life is not just about feelings." Feelings tarnished, attraction eroded.

"Why won't you give me a chance?"

"It's not that. It's just . . . I can't see how we'll work out. We're just so different. But Mark and I make sense." She tried to shake his hand off, even though every part of her wanted to do the opposite, wanted to bring it to her lips instead. She steeled herself to meet his gaze. "You remember that when we first chatted, I warned you about me. I'm cold; I live my life by numbers." *Look away. Please.*

He was quiet for a while. When he finally spoke it was in a whisper. "You're not cold. You just want to think of yourself that way, because it's easier to live like that," he said, releasing her hands and standing up. "Running away from your true feelings, living a lie, pretending you don't have a choice." He shook his head. "You're not living, Lucie—you're just existing."

She reeled back as though slapped. She wanted to defend herself but had no words to offer. He was wrong; he was right. Maybe she was a coward; maybe she was being brave enough to do the smart thing for both of them. Whatever it was, this was the path she had chosen, and she was sticking to it. Not that it mattered: he was leaving. He was already gone.

Chapter 32

~~~~~~

A MONTH AFTER SHE moved into Mark's spare room, Mark
suggested they go on a babymoon.

Mark being Mark, she soon found herself—after being told
to pack for a weekend by the pool—in one of the five-star resorts
in Jimbaran Bay, Bali.

"You deserve a babymoon, and Bali has great medical facili-
ties." The "just in case" hung in the air. "And we don't have to
stay in the same room if anything about this arrangement makes
you feel uncomfortable," he'd said. "I mean, I hope we will, but
you know, no pressure. We can just—swim." He'd opened his
eyes wide to convey the innocence of his sentiments.

Still, he had taken an ocean-view two-bedroom villa at a resort
known for its beauty and romantic swankiness, so that was quite
a lot to be spending if they were just there to "hang by the pool."

She bit her lip. A lifetime ago, Bali had been one of the hon-
eymoon destinations they had considered. He clearly wanted to
romance her.

She smiled at him and said, "Let's just see how it goes," when
really what she was inclined to do was throw him over the cre-

denza and sit on him like furniture. Truth be told, she very much wanted this vacation to end with the rekindling of old passions.

"Your stomach is growling," he said, grinning. "I'll get them to send over some lunch. What would you like?"

"Oh, I can hold off till dinner. I'll just have some fresh fruit and bread for now and maybe get a massage. And if you don't mind, for dinner, maybe instead of eating at the restaurant we can order room service instead . . . You know, just in case the food smells trigger . . ." She trailed off, unwilling to sully the romantic atmosphere with the words "bouts of projectile vomit," which was a distinct possibility whenever fish, coffee, or sweaty feet were in the vicinity.

Mark got it. "Why don't I book us a private dining experience by the pool?"

"I'd love that." There was no way romance was off the cards after *that*.

THEY SPENT THE day lazing in one of the obscenely large pools and had a one-hour couple's massage in their villa, although Lucie requested that the masseurs perform the massages in their own rooms (late-stage pregnancy made her flatulent).

Mark was sound asleep when she crept into his room, peaceful as a baby. Lucie admired his form and decided to eat while she waited for his reanimation. Mark did not like being woken up from sleep, even for sex.

So she rang for more cake.

As she chomped into a selection of patisserie, carefully noting her favorites—a cloud-colored, pandan-laced coconut cream concoction was so divine tears sprang to her eyes—so that she could get more sent, she pictured Collin making a face when she first told him about her diet. She chuckled, then quickly forced herself to think about sea cucumbers, which were easily the grossest creatures around. No way was Collin Read inserting himself into this experience!

A yawning Mark walked into the room, dressed in a white bathrobe and glowing with relaxation, just as she was about to ring for more cake.

"Nice massage?" she teased.

"Brilliant. She loosened knots that I didn't know I had. She really worked me." He chuckled.

Lucie froze. For the briefest second, she flashed back on the moment she walked into the room and caught Mark with his boss, and her smile slipped just a little. Would she never be able to suppress that memory and move on? She hugged herself and turned away.

He had seen it, the shadow. He came over and put his arms around her. "We have to move past that," he said, a pained look in his eyes.

"I have, but I can't always police my memories, Mark," she retorted, her tone more biting than she had intended.

"That's fine, but please don't let it hold any more power over us. We have a bright future together. You, me, and baby. A real family." He smiled and stroked her belly. An ache, different from the one elicited by Collin's touch, seized her.

Their villa's butler rang and led them to a private table surrounded by water on a pontoon at a pond, dotted with flowering water lilies and floating candles on handmade banana-leaf holders. It was transportive, until the waiter brought their menus and told them that lobster was the night's special, and once again, her thoughts telescoped to Collin.

Lobsters are nautical horndogs, Collin's voice teased.

So she didn't order the lobster special, because she was not thinking about Collin at all.

She turned her attention to Mark, who glowed with a sexy tan offset by his crisp white linen shirt. White shirts stayed white till the end of the night when it came to Mark—it was one of his skills. That, and crafting a perfect romantic experience for two. The five-course Balinese-inspired menu he had picked, along with the mocktails, was perfect, fragrant and delicate. She ate everything. She smiled at everything. He stroked her hand across the table, and it felt right. She wasn't drunk but something close to it.

Later, they walked hand in hand back to their villa, the susurration of wind ruffling the dense dark-blue vegetation, the burbling of water features, the strange call of insects, all coalesced into a kind of magic that could wipe clean the past, forgive anything.

It was time to move forward in their relationship. It was time to jump his bones.

"So . . . here we are," he said, when they were alone at last in the living room.

"Here we are," she said, very aware of his body, the gap between them. He was still hesitant around her, not wanting to make the wrong move, so she took the smallest step toward him.

He drew her close, bump and all, and nuzzled her hair. "I'm so glad you're here. It doesn't feel like anything's changed between us, does it?"

Lucie pasted a smile on her face and did not reply. Some things had changed—her body, for one. And some of her feelings about him. But what relationship didn't evolve?

"I want us to be together for as long as we both shall live," he said, dipping his head to kiss her. He started nipping at her earlobe, sending shivers down her spine. Every nerve in her was awake, rejoicing at the contact. She was dimly aware that he was unbuckling his belt.

Unbidden, a memory of another room, in another city, with Collin, his wavy hair falling across his face as he trailed kisses up her thigh, surfaced. "Stop," she blurted.

Mark fumbled the buckle. "Excuse me?"

"Not you." She cleared her throat and banished all thoughts of Collin to the junk mail of her memories with a hard shake of her head. "Sorry, I'm a little . . . rusty." She couldn't be as candid with Mark as she was with Collin—they didn't have that kind of relationship. She leaned wholeheartedly into the kiss, determined to focus on the present, while her hand focused on Mark's present, which soon made itself known.

Mark was trying to be gallant about his hard-on. "I've been waiting to kiss you since I saw you again at the dinner party," he said breathily.

"Stop talking," she whispered, pulling him to her as they groped their way through darkness into the bedroom and fell, Lucie on top, onto the waiting bed, Mark wincing as she landed squarely on his stomach, elbow first. "Oof," he said, when she barely missed his crotch with a knee.

"Sorry," she said, between determined kisses.

"It's OK," Mark said, sliding a hand down the back of her floaty peasant top to unhook her strapless bra, before pulling down the sleeves of her top to expose her shoulders, her chest. Thank God for moonlight, which was definitely not high definition enough to pick up any accessory body parts. Mark made little groans of appreciation as he cupped her breasts. "You're so beautiful," he growled. It almost made her forget she was wearing pants with an elastic waistband.

Almost.

Elastic waistband pants were not as easy to slip off, apparently. There was a lot of tugging and pulling, but at last the wretched pants were off, along with her maternity undies, which were, of course, extraordinarily sexy. "Utilitarian" was not a design style, underwear-wise, that elicited gasps of cross-eyed passion. But Mark did not seem deterred.

He lowered his face to her thighs and began kissing them, working his agonizingly slow way up, up, up, until—

"Ow!"

"What!" Mark reared back. "Is something wrong? Did I hurt you?"

"Oof!" Lucie stared at her stomach, from which the baby was attempting to claw its way. "The baby!"

Right on cue, a bumplike protrusion mushroomed on Lucie's belly, possibly a fist or a knee. But very, very Third-Party Real. It happened again and again. Maybe Balinese food had stimulating properties, because the baby was performing judo kicks to some EDM beat.

Many emotions flashed across Mark's face, most of them hard to read, but Anything But Horny was a good shorthand. "Wow, the baby is really . . . active."

"Yes," she said, trying to get *him* to be active again.

"It's just . . . so . . . present," he said. His enthusiasm down below was fading away. She could feel its departure even as she tried, valiantly, all hands on deck, to bring it back.

"Let me distract you," she said, giving him a sexy nibble on his neck, then his collarbone, and was just about to unfasten the second button on his shirt when the baby delivered a chop to her pitiful bladder. She bit, and Mark yelped.

"I'm so sorry," she wheezed, clutching her lower abdomen as he massaged his bite mark ruefully.

"The baby kicks even . . . down below?" Mark's face was pale.

"Well, not really. It's like the baby is kicking the roof of . . . hey, where're you going?"

He had gently withdrawn and sat at the foot of the bed, belting up. "I'm sorry. This is—this is too weird for me. I think I just need to digest this information and maybe come back to it?"

"Sure," Lucie said, trying not to sound too sad.

He kissed her cheek, the death knell for passion that night. "I just don't feel comfortable doing anything when the baby is so . . . present. Look, I, ah, just need some time to, ah, wrap my head around the logistics."

Lucie closed her eyes and let Mark leave in a murmur of mea culpas to take a cold shower. Since it was unlikely that their romantic evening was salvageable from this logistics curveball, she unbuckled her pregnancy belt that covered half of her belly and moaned softly as all of it sagged comfortably into place. Somehow, even in the most romantic of settings, with the most amazing man, her best-laid plans had not gotten her laid—and pun aside, she couldn't help feeling dejected.

Chapter 33

~~~~~~~~

LUCIE WAS BEGINNING to feel like the living embodiment of the "It's been eighty-four years . . ." Rose Dawson meme—way too much time had passed since she'd seen any action down below. After Bali, Mark had explained he was uneasy about having sex with her, and she had respected his decision and his offer to "help out"—when he phrased it that way her libido shriveled up and died like a slug on a hot plate. She tried to make her peace with her situation. After all, there were only another eighty-four days left. Or thereabouts, until the baby came. And maybe another eighty-four days after that for her to heal completely, although Weina had helpfully and horrifyingly detailed how she and Simon managed barely two weeks after Arwin, with the help of—

Lucie shuddered and vowed never to buy coconut oil again.

Now she and Collin were on the way in a taxi to see Dr. Joyce for possibly the last time before he flew to Seoul in less than two weeks. For some reason, they both looked like they'd lost a childhood pet.

"You and I have got to figure out what names we'll use for our baby," she said, wanting to lighten the mood.

"Yup, I have my top-ten names for boys and girls, and a couple of gender-neutral ones in case we want to go that way. You come up with yours, we'll discuss, pick our mutual top threes, and when the time comes, we can just pick one at random if we don't agree."

"You don't 'pick names at random,'" Lucie said, horrified. "You're not serious?" she sputtered, until she realized he was grinning. "You should *never* joke about names. Names are important!" She drew a deep breath—

"Uh-oh, I sense a speech coming."

And she exhaled. "Damn right! Names, nouns, they mean something. For example, the word 'cookies,' cynically plundered from its sweet origins for nefarious, misleading use in tech. It's such a benign word, 'cookies,' right? So instead of 'trackies' or 'cache junk' or something malicious-sounding, you're asked 'Will you accept cookies?' And you think, 'Aww, that's yummy,' and maybe you actually eat some cookies, then five websites later you have downloaded the equivalent of spyware onto your laptop and they know everything about you including what kind of underwear you *really* buy online."

Collin's mouth twitched. "I'll give this more thought."

"You'd better!"

"I have been, you know. I'd like a name that could be Japanese and Chinese, and easily transliterated into English," Collin said.

"Well, that's easy, then," Lucie said sarcastically.

"I'll find it, you wait," he said. "I've been googling."

Lucie sighed. "We're doomed."

"Choi!" he said, crossing himself and making her laugh. "Thanks for rearranging this appointment so I could come with you."

For her last three appointments, she'd gone alone during her lunch breaks so she could grab a bite to eat while waiting for her turn—in spite of the partners taking away her biggest files, some of her previously dormant clients had contacted her for new work, and she was busier than before, although lately she found herself wondering if it was worth it, especially now that she wasn't sure she'd ever make partner.

"Yes, yes, of course," she said. "It's the very least I can do before . . . before you go."

"You know I love seeing our little one."

Our little one. She liked the sound of that.

OUR GIANT ONE, more like.

Dr. Joyce didn't mince her words. "Your baby is in the ninety-fifth percentile, weight-wise, for their age group."

"Looks like it's going to be a big one," Collin said cheerfully. "I was over nine pounds at birth. My mother always said my size made her want only one kid."

Lucie spun around and glared at Collin. "This is important information that you should have shared when we were parent-dating."

Dr. Joyce played peacemaker. "Well, there's a high chance the baby is going to approximate that weight, given the projected growth rate, but I need to stress that this is just an estimate, of course. Sometimes it's less."

"So the opposite could also be true?" Collin wanted to know.

"You mean . . . you mean the baby could be even larger?" Lucie nearly shouted.

"Possibly," Dr. Joyce said, kindly.

"I hate you," Lucie told Collin.

"I know that already," he said. "But why are you assuming that it's my genes that are making a big baby here? Your family is very tall. You are what, five eight? You might want to ask your parents what your birth weight was."

"I'm not speaking with my parents, I don't think. They've stopped texting me. And that means they have now entered into the Cold War stage." Lucie laughed wryly. "Just a couple of stages left before they kidnap me in the middle of the night and ship me off to a place without internet so I can have the baby. Then they'll pretend I adopted it. I do carry small, after all."

Dr. Joyce's eyes were very wide.

"I think she's joking. But her parents hate that she isn't married," Collin told Dr. Joyce.

"That's unfortunate," Dr. Joyce said. She hastened to add, "I mean, it shouldn't matter if you're married or not. What matters is you love each other."

"Oh, we don't," Lucie said. "We're just friends."

"T-that's fine, too."

Lucie took a deep breath. Collin, hands braced on his knees, muttered, "Here it comes."

"I don't get why you need to be married before you procreate. Like, if someone in a loveless marriage had kids, it was fine, because at least they had that piece of paper. Are you married, Dr. Joyce, if that's not too forward a question?"

"Well, ah . . ."

"You don't have to answer. I would consider it too forward a question," Collin told Dr. Joyce.

"Mmm . . . ," Dr. Joyce said. Her gaze slid to the framed photograph of her family on her desktop. "I'm married, yes."

"For how long, if you don't mind?"

"Twenty-three years," Dr. Joyce said, scrunching her face after doing the calculations. "Wow. Time flies."

"Nice," Collin said.

Lucie got more animated. "But let's say you fell out of love with your husband. You guys are at the end of your divorce proceedings, but one hot, sultry night, celebrating the end of an acrimonious tussle with a bottle of red wine, you have a final fling, and then you get pregnant and give birth *after* everything's been finalized. The child would be considered illegitimate, did you know that? How does that differ from Collin's and my arrangement?"

"Ah . . ." Dr. Joyce's eyes darted around the room. "I think . . . I suppose . . . no different?"

"She's full of hypotheticals, this one," Collin told Dr. Joyce.

"But you chose each other for a reason, right?" Dr. Joyce said, almost pleadingly.

Lucie and Collin regarded each other.

"I guess," Collin hedged, his corners of his eyes crinkling.

"I really didn't have much choice," Lucie said. "The other guys I matched with were much, *much* worse. One couldn't tell the difference between waterboarding and wakeboarding, but claimed he went to HARVARD BUSINESS SCHOOL, all caps. Another had the audacity to ask me if male pattern baldness ran in my family."

"And it doesn't, right?" Collin said. "I mean, it's a little too late now."

"Way too late," Lucie agreed, reaching over to clasp his hand. "The infusion of DNA is done."

"No take-backsies."

"Nope."

They grinned at each other; meanwhile Dr. Joyce was staring very hard at the clock. It was possible that she didn't have many couples joking around like this in her examination room, but then again, how many pairs of Lucie-and-Collins were there in this part of the world, really?

Chapter 34

A ND THEN IT was July. In a tropical country like Singapore, without marked seasons, time had a way of slipping by unnoticed. But Lucie noticed, even as she closeted herself at work, trying to fill her days, her mind, with the noise of it. The baby was coming soon. Anticipation and fear that had rested like a stone in the pit of her stomach resurfaced. She began to have what she called "sweat dreams," the kind one woke up from drenched in sweat but with little recollection of what transpired therein.

There were ten days left till Collin's departure. Then six. Then two.

He'd booked his flight for a Sunday afternoon. The days slipped by, quickly, and the day before he was due to fly to Seoul, he asked her over the phone for a favor. One Saturday night with him, no Mark.

"We spend it at our home, a last hurrah. One entire evening and night. You stay over tonight. Then I fly out tomorrow, two o'clock. I'll leave the house at noon."

"It's really happening," she said, almost in disbelief. "You're moving to Seoul." She shook her head.

"Yes."

She tried to sound upbeat. "What are we doing?"

"A taco-and-movie night, and a surprise."

She told Mark about it, not asking for permission but needing him to understand. It was, after all, going to be the night before her baby shower, where they were going to make their first official appearance as a couple again to a circle of her closest friends and family, including her sister. She expected some pushback, but aside from a lip curl of distaste at the sound of Collin's name, he wished her a good night out. He was magnanimous. He had won, after all.

"It's probably safer if you let me drop you off at Collin's instead of taking public transport," Mark said, although Lucie knew it wasn't really an offer but a done deal.

She nodded. "Sure."

"And I'll pick you up for the shower?"

"I'll be up bright and early at ten."

"That's not bright and early."

"It is, for a Sunday. Especially when you're about eight months pregnant."

Mark gave a wan smile. "Who are you? You used to be up at seven, even on Sundays, just to work."

That wasn't her anymore, though. And it might be a good thing.

As soon as she arrived, Collin herded her and her overnight bag upstairs. "Get rested. Take a nap if needed. We're going out tonight."

"I'll nap. But where we going? What are we doing?"

"It's a surprise."

"My ankles are so swollen," she protested.

"I'm bringing you out," he insisted, taking her by her hand. "I've already got a car booked and tickets have been bought."

"Tickets?" she echoed.

"Yeah, tickets." He shooed her upstairs. "Go nap! We'll have dinner at six and be out of the house by seven."

"I'm not going to be able to sleep now."

But she did, of course. Her body had been made simple by all the hormones.

At 5:30 p.m., she woke up, slapped on some makeup and a sleeveless, knee-length, black wrap dress. Sure her ankles were the size of lemons, but, boy, did the V-shape neckline showcase her eye-popping cleavage.

She wore ballerina flats and gingerly made her way down the stairs to be greeted by Collin, who was not wearing athleisure—Dockers! A white linen Nehru-collared shirt! Dress shoes!—and thus, breathtaking. Or maybe it was the fact that the baby was pushing up against her lungs, who knew.

"You look lovely," he said earnestly.

"Save it, knocker-upper."

"Honestly, you do. You're—"

"If you say 'glowing' I will punch you in the bladder and give you a taste of what our child is doing to me sixty times a day."

"Right," he said, grinning. "Anyway, we're going dancing."

"Dancing," she echoed, as though he'd spoken Klingon (which he did speak, by the way)—or was it Elvish? One of those.

"Yes. Lindy Hop."

She sighed. "Collin, I am eight months preg—"

"Yes, and?"

"There are sacs of fluids that are jostling for supremacy in me. And I must keep them all tucked, unburst, inside me at all times."

He cocked his head at her. "You do hear yourself when you speak?"

"Sure. It brings me much pleasure listening to myself babble."

He shook his head, grinning. "OK, well, we'll go at our own pace, and when you're done, you're done. We can sit at one of the tables by the dance floor and just watch the others."

She snort-laughed. "I must warn you, I haven't danced since . . . since . . . I stopped clubbing . . . like in 2014."

"How is this even possible?" he cried, aghast. "One should never stop dancing."

That's how Collin differed from Mark. For Mark, dance was something you grew out of, the way you graduated from fluorescent cocktails. You just moved on to "age-appropriate hobbies," like going for wine-tasting sessions and acquiring watches with complicated movements, probably to compensate for the fact that your body was gradually losing its ability to perform complicated movements.

"I want you to feel like a bird," he said, holding out his hand. "For just one night, I want you to forget you're pregnant. I want you to feel like you're on a real date, with me."

He had her at "forget you're pregnant." God, what she wouldn't give to forget that for just a night.

So she took his hand and said, deadpan, "Let's go boogie. One last hurrah for the Dream Team."

AT THE LARGE rooftop bar hosting the Lindy Hop dance event, people gathered and greeted each other warmly, including Collin. It turned out that Collin was a regular at their biweekly dances.

Lucie took in the crowd. Around ten couples of all ages, a

handful of singles, and two instructors, a man and woman in their late twenties. Most people were dressed in vintage-inspired clothing, the style ranging from pants or jeans with suspenders and shirts, to casual suits, to folks in full skirts or swingy dresses. A few hats and some fascinators. Red lipsticks galore.

The first half hour, the instructor taught the basic footwork so that absolute beginners like Lucie could get into the groove.

Only Lucie wasn't really a true beginner, not in dance.

When Lucie was six, she'd started ballet classes under a famous Singaporean teacher who had danced as a principal ballerina in *The Nutcracker*. Weekends were dedicated to co-curriculum classes: art, drama, ballet, Kumon, and tennis, although Lucie cared only for ballet. She liked that it allowed for precision and grace, a marriage of both. The best dancers needed both the technical and the alchemical sensibilities, the ability to bind music to movement, and vice versa.

By the time she was eleven, having passed the sixth grade Royal Academy of Dance ballet exam, her teacher told her she should seriously consider applying herself to it and encouraged the Yis to consider enrolling her in the Singapore Dance Theatre.

"She has immense potential," the teacher said.

The words immediately galvanized Ivy Chen to do the exact opposite. She reduced the frequency of the classes. She changed ballet schools, swapping the teacher with a less dedicated, less experienced, less *interested* one. The class size was bigger, too, with less individualized focus. Ivy Chen didn't stop the classes abruptly, which she knew would cause a rebellion—she turned ballet into just another class that Lucie had to attend.

She took away the magic.

With an uninterested teacher, Lucie became just another student. And slowly but surely, whatever had made her exceptional dulled. Dance became routine. Her movements became matter-of-fact.

She stuck with it till she was fourteen, then gave up in eighth grade, the practice now just a decorative footnote in her college applications.

It was only years later, as an adult, that she understood what her mother had done. Excised the pleasure from her young life. And only recently, watching Collin jiggle, upper limbs joyously uncoordinated with his lower on the dance floor, did Lucie understand that that deception had changed the course of her life.

"You're good," Collin said, comically surprised when she executed the basic footwork with ease and started the passes with him.

"Try not to look so surprised," she said wryly.

"She's a natural," one of the instructors said with approval.

After the half-hour lesson was up, the music started, and the couples began dancing in earnest.

"You glad we didn't stay home?" he said as he shimmied around her.

"Yes!" she said. "This is amazing! I'm so glad I wore my pregnancy belt for this!"

She must have shouted the last bit because a few couples turned to stare at her belly. She waved and bopped around to Christina Aguilera's "Candyman." At first, she and Collin stuck to the footwork taught by the instructors, but he started improvising and she went along with his more outrageous passes, game face on.

He didn't care who watched him. He went for all his moves without reservation, so that when he completed one he called the Jellyfish Shinbuster, some couples stopped to stare at the spectacle. He was also half a beat off or more—not that he cared.

Not one to be outdone, Lucie incorporated a couple of (very clumsy) pirouettes in their next pass.

"*Magnifique! Magnifique!*" he shouted in an exaggerated French accent. Nobody clapped.

"We suck," she said. "*You* suck." Well, maybe he didn't suck, but he was mediocre.

He laughed. "You sound surprised."

She flailed her arms. "You just talked about it so much."

"Must you be good at something in order to enjoy it?" he replied.

He had a point.

"There's something incredibly freeing about being bad at something you love, isn't there?" he said.

"Yes," she said. *Yes.*

They resumed dancing, completely oblivious to the beat now, making up moves as they went. She knew she looked like one of those wacky waving inflatable tube guys, one that had swallowed a refrigerator.

And still—she danced.

"Switch partners!" the instructor yelled.

Sweaty, dizzy, she mock bowed to Collin and shimmied over to her next partner, a very tall, thin, and much older man in a linen suit, who regarded her as though he could break her, which— after she put her hands in his and he squeezed—she realized he probably could.

"You're very pregnant," he said with a look of concern.

"Don't be afraid," she told him, breathless. "The baby is held in by very restrictive undergarments."

"She's tough," Collin shouted over the music, twirling by with a dazzling woman vibrant in a sleeveless scarlet dress. The old man grinned and took them at their word, and soon she was whirling like a dervish again.

The hour flew by. They switched partners again and again, and when the circuit was done, she was back in Collin's arms, sweaty, laughing, hair totally undone, enjoying herself so much she couldn't stop smiling. She was finally in the groove, even if she was one of the least experienced Lindy Hoppers out there.

As they jiggled haphazardly, Lucie thought, *I look like a fool.* And then, *But I'm having so much fun that I don't care.*

Almost as though he had read her mind, he asked, "When was the last time you didn't care about how you looked because of how much fun you were having?"

She said she didn't know, but that wasn't true. She thought of taco night, hiding behind pillows, shrieking and shoveling chips into her mouth as homemade guac stained her fingers. She thought of them cooking together, stinking of grease. She recalled long conversations about nothing and sometimes everything, laughing too loud in cafés or bars or at home. She had been herself each time. The only common denominator was Collin.

She would miss him so much.

At this, her heart squeezed painfully and threw her balance off; one of her flats disengaged and flew into the path of another couple. Collin retrieved it and she put it back on.

"Are you sure you were a promising ballerina when you were nine?" he teased in a low voice.

"Yes, I was," she said, composing herself, trying to sound light-hearted. "I was very good. I just haven't danced for a long time. Plus, I'm almost eight months pregnant. I'm allowed to be a little uncoordinated."

"Hmm," he said, a half smile on his lips. "If you say so."

"You don't believe me? My parents took videos. I have them saved somewhere."

He grabbed her and twirled her. "Lucie, *I don't care.* Just be in the moment with me, won't you?"

He dipped her, and she squealed on the way up.

"I always have fun with you," she told him, tears of laughter in her eyes.

His amber eyes crinkled at the corners. "You're such a doofus," he said, wiping a stray tear and making her breath catch. And that's when she knew it was over, the charade that they could just be friends. Somewhere along the line, they had crossed the Rubicon into new territory. They did it dancing.

Then the lights dimmed and a slow song came on to wolf whistles and cheers. All around them, couples drew close, or broke away from the shuffling crowd for a breather.

Collin's eyes held a question and she nodded, after a brief hesitation. It was just one more song. It was just a song.

He pressed his cheek against her forehead and held her close, and her breath caught in her throat.

"Lucie," he said, each syllable a caress. In the middle of the crowded dance floor, they stood in a little noiseless cocoon, the tension between what they wanted and what they were entitled to informing the way they pressed against each other, never fully closing in. They weren't dancing so much as they were discussing their future. Yes, no. No, yes. Round and round they circled, tighter and tighter together. Yes. No. Yes. Yes. Yes.

Then the song ended and she broke the spell, pulling away from him at last, because she couldn't keep him when he wasn't hers. This night was a goodbye, not a reunion. The time for yesses had passed.

You chose Mark, she reminded herself.

When the dance was over, Lucie told him she needed to go back to Mark's. If she stayed over, she would be giving Collin—and herself—false hope.

He walked with her to the door of Mark's condo, which felt like the longest walk they'd ever taken together. "Lucie—"

"I have to go," she said, the effort in trying to keep her voice steady hardening it. "Have a safe flight."

"Have a safe flight"—surely the most generic of goodbye phrases. But the alternative was ruining the serenity of their farewell by saying the most outrageous of things, like *This feels wrong; don't go.* Or *I don't know what I want, but it sure as hell isn't you leaving.*

"Have a safe flight," indeed.

But he understood. Some things were indeed better left unsaid, if saying them changed nothing.

Chapter 35

⌇

THE NEXT DAY, Mark found her curled up on the bed in the spare room and woke her up. If he was surprised, he didn't show it. He just drove her to the baby shower as though they'd always planned it that way.

Weina had invited ten of their closest friends and colleagues to gather in the private room at a swanky café. Lucie walked under a balloon arch into a roomful of women who cheered when they saw her, including Suzie, elegant in dark denims and a white top under a bronze-and-peacock-blue kimono-style jacket. Lucie's heart leaped with hope that the last two months of frostiness was thawing. She missed Suzie fiercely. She'd opened her mouth to call out her friend's name when Suzie looked in her direction. Their gazes met. Suzie nodded at her coolly but made no move to speak to her. Disappointment flooded Lucie. She wanted to go to her best friend, but a stubborn self-righteousness kept her rooted to the spot. She feigned impassivity and broke off her gaze, made herself walk toward another cluster of friends. But even in her hurt, Lucie noted with discomfort that aside from Vanessa, Suzie, and Yu Ling, all the women were pregnant or already mothers. And everyone except for Suzie, Hannah, (and possibly Vanessa) was married or in some kind of long-term relationship. Vanessa, she knew, didn't care; coincidentally or not, she was the only one who was in her twenties, and Hannah was not interested in pursuing a relationship. Whereas she knew that Suzie, though child-free by choice, didn't want to be single.

Weina seemed to also have picked up on how alienating it could be for a single woman in a roomful of women who were in another stage of their lives, because she buzzed over to Suzie with Vanessa in tow.

Suzie and Vanessa chatted for a bit, then Suzie excused herself and slipped out the front door before Lucie could corner and confront her. The baby shower passed in a blur of activities and chatter, and with her as the center of attention, Lucie didn't have a moment to herself—and a dull headache soon left her short-tempered and on edge. She barely noticed when an hour had passed and one of the servers let her know that she had someone named Mark waiting for her at the reception.

"Hey, hon," Mark said when she went to get him; he handed her a lush bunch of blush-pink peonies and roses. "For you!"

"You're not supposed to be here," Lucie said, a flash of irritation clouding her pleasure at the stunning bouquet. Weina had said that partners were not invited, and Mark knew that.

He grinned and shrugged. "Yes, but I wanted to surprise everyone with special goody bags," he said, gesturing behind him to a couple of waitstaff struggling with armfuls of gold gift bags. "You remember Claire, my PA. She recommended I pick these up for the ladies. Cookies, spa coupons, hand cream, etc."

"That's nice," Lucie said in a small voice. Weina was going to flip when she saw the gift bags (she had prepared her own for the attendees). She cocked her head so he could kiss the one cheek that didn't have a boob drawn on it in lipstick. "Would you please place them with the other shower gifts in the private room?"

"Sure. Where are you off to?"

"The bathroom," she said. The bathroom was located in an annex, next to the garden. "You can join the ladies in the private room, if you want some food and drink."

"Sure, would you like a drink? I'm parched."

"A Boobini, extra milk please," Lucie said.

"Gotcha." He kissed her nose and headed toward the room. As he walked in, a furtive-looking Yu Ling darted out to join her.

"What's up?" Lucie said, giggling at her shifty expression.

"We didn't want to alarm you, but"—she dragged Lucie over to the windows overlooking the gardens and pointed—"isn't that Collin by the bench?"

It was. She glanced at her phone and saw his message to her: I'm outside, if you can spare a moment. While Mark had strode into the room with the confidence of a popstar headlining a concert, Collin was bouncing on his heels in the café's private garden, letting her decide if she wanted to see him. And want to see him she did. She was already brisk walking to him before she could think.

Because in spite of her best efforts that day, at joking, laughing, singing, to occupy her mind, time and again her thoughts had circled back to his departure. And how she hated the way she'd left things with him.

"Collin," she said, her voice coming out an octave higher. "What are you doing here?" *I'm so happy to see you.*

He looked up at her. In the sunlight, his eyes were amber gold, ringed with green. "I had to see you before I leave."

They grinned at each other shyly until Lucie became aware that anyone could see them through the glass doors from the café—and some people were watching. "Come here," she said, dragging him around the corner to a secluded part of the garden. "No gawkers here."

They found a bench and sat down in the shade. Her heart was speeding up, her skin hot and flushed; she was light-headed. All the classic signs of an allergy—or, in Lucie's case, a major case of the falling-for-yous.

No. No. No. He's not who I'm supposed to be feeling this way about.

As if to underscore a point, her baby drop-kicked her in the gut.

She tried to focus on his least attractive feature: his knuckles. They were knobbly and hairy, a little veiny when he clenched his fists.

Oh God, even his knuckles were beautiful to her now. She couldn't help how she felt around him. Happy. Giddy. Silly. Drunk.

She swallowed and stared at the ground for as long as she could, fighting the urge to look at him. Might as well blindfold herself. She was hopeless.

"Lucie."

"Yes?" she croaked, not looking at him.

He tipped her chin to meet his gaze.

"Lucie, I want more."

She was not expecting that.

"I have feelings for you. Big feelings. Crazy feelings. I'm nuts about you."

"Did you . . . did you just . . ."

"Yeah, yeah, I did. I punned."

She clapped her hand over her mouth to stop the giggle threatening to ruin the moment. "Sorry, go on."

"Lucie, I want to be with you." He traced the lines of her face with a finger, leaving prickles of heat in its wake. "I hesitate to call it love . . . but if this isn't love, what is?"

Love. Her thoughts caught on that word, and she sobered up quickly at the seriousness of what he was confessing. She could still stop them from jumping off the ledge into the void. She shook her head. "No. It can't be. It's the hormones. Our apartment is spiked with hormones. Like VOCs, they are messing with our equilibrium. You don't want me that way."

He threw his hands up. "Lucie. Stop."

"I'm with Mark."

"Mark is your past, Lucie," he said. "I'm your future."

"Why should I trust that you know what you want now?"

He glanced at his hands and mumbled the next part, as though embarrassed. "Spending time with you, I let my guard down the way I've never done in any of my relationships. And I found myself falling for you. I *know* this isn't like anything I've ever experienced before. I know."

He fell silent. Lucie looked down at her belly.

"It's just because I'm the mother of your child," she said, determined not to give in. "You're conflating—"

"Lucie, stop it," he said. "I swear to you, even if we weren't having this child . . ."

"*Choi,*" she said, crossing herself.

"Yes, *choi,*" he echoed, a weak grin on his face, "but what I'm saying is whether or not you were the mother of my child, it wouldn't change a thing." He gripped her hand, his eyes boring deep into hers. "I have a hunch that you could be my One and I'm not running away anymore. I'm here to let you know that I'm prepared to stay here, to drop my plans of moving to Seoul, if you choose me."

"Collin, I don't want you to compromise on your dreams."

"My career has never been my dream, you know that. I have bigger, better dreams now. Let me stay." He tightened his grip on her hand. "Let me fight for you."

"Fight for her?" A voice sneered. Lucie slid her hand out of Collin's as Mark strode across the garden with her mocktail of choice, the Boobini, presented in a large yellow bowl with a jaunty paper nipple stuck in it. "Fight for her? Mr. Flighty Pants? Now that's rich."

Collin's face blanched. "You."

"Yes, me, her rock while you were busy sampling the local delights. Typical."

Collin's eyes met hers, and she saw the hardness enter when he watched her standing by, shell-shocked by Mark's insinuation and aggression, not knowing what to say. "What do you mean by that?" he said, balling his fists.

"You know exactly what I mean," Mark said softly, setting the drink down by their bench before stepping too close to Collin. "I don't have to spell it out for you." Mark gave him a withering look of contempt. "Lucie may be too wrapped up with the pregnancy to see through your good-time-boy facade, but *I* do. You're not the kind to stick around when shit hits the fan." Mark pointed at Collin but directed this statement at Lucie. "You should see the kind of women he dates."

How many Justine Mayas had been—were still—in Collin's life? Their dating was the one area they had never discussed in depth. Every insecurity Lucie had was amplified. She and Collin were very different—he'd said as much that they would never have met under "normal circumstances." What was the type of person he usually dated? She had no idea. And similarly, how could she be sure of her feelings for him if *he* wasn't her usual type? There was no margin for mistakes here—the stakes were too high.

"Were you following me?" Collin said, anger written all over his face, his fists still balled.

"Yes, yes, I was. I have no qualms admitting it. I wanted to make sure Lucie knew what kind of man she was letting into her life—our lives." Mark shrugged. "I wanted to *protect* you, Lucie."

Collin cut his eyes at her. "Wow."

Lucie's face reddened and she said hoarsely, "Mark, that's . . . that's an invasion of Collin's privacy."

"Trust me, I'm doing it to protect you. He's a good-time boy." Mark was caustic. "Just here for the conquest. At the first hint of difficulties, men like him run for the hills. When it comes to commitment, to family, you don't just need someone who makes the right decisions; you need someone who you can count on, period. You need a real man."

"Says the bully and cheater," Collin retorted.

The baby decided to join in the fun by delivering a swift kick to Lucie's bladder to show her who was the ultimate boss.

"Lucie," Mark and Collin said at the same time.

Growing up on soapy telenovelas, Lucie had, like many before her, fantasized about having two men—two handsome men, to boot—duke it out for her affections. But now that this was happening, it was as desirable as a pair of accessory nipples. She wanted none of it.

"Enough. Both of you need to sit down and sort your shit out somewhere else, far, far away from me," she said to the both of them. "I don't have the energy for all this chest-thumping *crap*. All I ever wanted was a family, but this—this is a fucking circus. I'm out."

Then, with a very ungainly heel turn, Lucie left her own baby shower.

Chapter 36

～～～～

LUCIE CHECKED HERSELF into one of her favorite hotels in the city to give herself some much-needed space, hoping the change of scenery would clarify her feelings. She needed to think without either one of the men crowding her. Also, this hotel was noted for its spa treatments and massages. After another week of working late, disrupted sleep, the upheaval with Collin leaving, and her violently sexless state, she figured she deserved a relaxing massage.

She texted Weina to let her know what was going on, a little worried how she would take the mother-to-be walking out on the event she had carefully curated, but Weina's reply was immediate and calming: You take care of yourself and don't worry about the girls. They are all pretty much high on sugar, and a couple are actually drunk. Me included. LOL.

Before she could reply to Weina's flurry of champagne bottle emojis, Collin sent her a text. Look, the whole drama today with Mark was messed up, and you not even sticking up for me was not right. This limbo isn't healthy for any of us, and I think it's best for everyone's sakes that I leave for Korea and we both take some time to reflect on our next steps. I'm always a call away if you need to talk or want my input or assistance, OK?

She read and reread the text until her eyes blurred, anger, embarrassment, and guilt rising bile-like in her throat, choking her. She'd been caught off guard when Mark had castigated Collin and hadn't stood up for him the way she should have. With deepening unease, she wondered if there was maybe a part of her that *believed* Mark's accusations, that didn't trust that Collin would stay—how much of it was tangled in her own insecurities, she didn't know.

I just wish everything was clear-cut and spelled out for me, so I don't have to second-guess everything.

No matter, though. In the end, Collin had chosen to leave. Just as Mark had predicted.

Mark's texts were conciliatory, caring, in contrast:

Are you okay? Where are you? Do you need anything from Collin's apartment or our place?

No, she texted. But thank you. I just need to be on my own for a little while.

Don't forget this Saturday is my parents' 45th wedding anniversary. They are so excited to see you again.

I won't forget.

So, I know you need space but I think for safety's sake, you should just text me with your address and I'll drop off extra prenatal vitamins and all the TCM herbs you should be taking. Gotta follow doctor's orders.

Mark thought of everything. The guilt that stemmed from having feelings for Collin rose in her throat before sliding back down into the pit of her stomach, hot and bilious.

Eyes on the prize, Lucie Yi, she told herself. Mark was the goal. Whatever Mark's faults were, he always looked out for her. The way a good partner should. Qualities a good father should have.

A family was about stability. She flashed on Hannah, whose co-parenting arrangement seemed to consist of struggle upon struggle. She thought about Collin, whose insecurities had left him emotionally guarded. Could he ever really be trusted to be a stable romantic partner? Could they, as a unit, endure?

A good parent always puts the needs of her child first. Even if . . .

Lucie closed her eyes. *Even if it means denying yourself.*

If you need me, I'm here.

I know, she wrote back to Mark. I know.

"I'm excited for today," Mark said, when he picked her up. "My parents are going to be so pleased about . . . everything."

Lucie looked out of the window, unsure of what to say. After five days apart, Mark was acting as though the confrontation with Collin had never happened. Like everything was great. Classic fake-it-till-you-make-it-ism. Except today, there was something brittle in the quality of his optimism.

People say that when you marry a person, you marry their family, and Mark's family had always been a draw for Lucie. They were unlike most people of their generation she'd encountered—

hyper in tune with their emotions, prizing communication, open to new ideas and trends. After her reconciliation with Mark, he had filled her in with more details: in their past lives, before Mark's sister's death, Mark's father, who had been a high-ranking naval officer, and his mother a noted historian, had never had much time for each other or him, and in the tumultuous years after his sister's death when they had been rebuilding their lives, he'd left the navy while she switched to a part-time position. Spending that time together, exploring guided meditation, and speaking with their spiritual leaders had helped them heal, as much as they could. They were proof that you could move on together, even after your world had been shattered.

It was supposed to be a small, casual lunch with his parents. But the table set in the dining room with a view of the landscaped garden groaned under a mini buffet—satay, roasted pork belly, Peking duck, a garden salad with yuzu, longevity noodles with mushrooms—with a beautiful centerpiece of lilies.

"This is too much, Mrs. Thum," Lucie said, taking perfunctory bites; her appetite was shot. Next to her, Mark was eating with slow, wary precision. "Are we expecting others?"

"Well." Felicia Thum shot a look at Mark. "You know us Chinese. Our wedding anniversary is as good as any to overindulge, food-wise."

"Food is all we have in our old age," Mark's father, Thum Choon Hong, intoned drolly. "Let us be gluttons."

"Also, it is a special occasion, dear, you joining us again."

"Yes, it certainly is," Choon Hong said.

"And we are so excited about the baby," Felicia said, smiling warmly.

"We're excited, too," Lucie said.

"Well, to be honest"—Felicia exchanged a look with her

husband—"it's not ideal that you and Mark aren't married yet, but we heard that it's on the table."

"It is," Mark said, looking down at his lap.

"No pressure at all," Choon Hong said. "We're just glad to see you two back together. And the baby is just the cherry on the cake, really."

"We can't wait to meet our grandchild!" Felicia said, her eyes shining.

A sinking realization dawned on Lucie. Mark's parents believed that the child was his. Did he not think about how the lie wouldn't hold if the child came two whole months too early, given her return to Singapore? Or was he planning to lie about that, when the time came, and say that the baby was premature? Was it so unthinkable, even for his relaxed, worldly parents, that their son might care for another man's child? There was nothing shameful about wanting a child, nothing shameful about how she and Collin had gone about it, as unconventional as their method might have been. Why should she care, if she was just trying to bring more love, more joy, into her life?

To be a parent, to have a child—surely these were worthy goals that justified the means?

She shouldn't be ashamed anymore. Otherwise, what was the alternative, to lie to everyone aside from her closest confidantes forever, or stand by and allow Mark to do it for her, which was just as cowardly . . . if not more?

She thought about what Hannah, her mother, even the nurse at the clinic had said about children from nontraditional households. Remembered the comments from the partners in her firm.

Now her appetite disappeared for good. "Yes, well . . ." The words dried up. She reached for the tray of satay and busied herself with the task of choosing a few skewers.

"There's no great pressure to get married, of course," Choon Hong prodded gently.

"Well, Mr. Thum, nothing has been decided yet, regarding . . . everything."

Mark scooped a bite of longevity noodles into his mouth. "We just want to take things slow."

Felicia and Choon Hong held hands across the table. "Well, we just want you kids to know that we're supportive of your journey, with all its ups and downs," Felicia said.

His father nodded. "As Mark might have told you or not, we've been through some challenges of our own these forty-five years. We, ah, separated for a while after Lily's death. But we found our way back together."

Felicia rested an elbow on the table and cupped her chin in her palm. "Every step back to each other was a deliberate choice. It wasn't easy. We wanted to quit, so many times."

"Many times," Choon Hong affirmed.

"Underneath it all, though, was the love. That was always there."

"And now, here you are," Mark said hollowly.

"Yes. Here we are. I'd like to think all our struggles made us stronger as a unit." Felicia reached out and held Lucie's hand in hers. "I know you have both been through so much, and you've had a time apart—yet here you are, back where you left off. Because you know there is something here to be treasured."

"Let's toast," Choon Hong said, raising his glass of wine. Mark raised his, as did Lucie her glass of sparkling water. "To second chances."

"To second chances," the table echoed. Lucie watched with a pang as Mark's parents kissed.

"Second chances can work out," Felicia said, directing her

comment at Lucie. "It won't be easy, but if you both believe in it, go all in, and put in the work, it's possible."

She's right, Lucie thought. *I need to be all in.*

IN THE CAR ride back, Lucie vowed to course correct. She loved Mark, and she and Mark had always made sense; her dalliance with Collin was just that—an aberration in a series of careful choices, but nothing that careful offsetting couldn't help. Take a leaf out of the manual on the Lucie Diet.

As they were pulling into the car park, she put her hand on Mark's thigh and said, "I've made a decision."

He turned to her, his dark eyes ablaze. "And?"

"I'm ready to commit to us," she whispered.

His face broke into a bright smile. He drew her close. "Wow. You have no idea how happy that makes me to hear. You know I want us to get married, once things . . . *settle down*, of course. I'll do right by you . . . I'll legitimize the baby and treat the baby as though it's mine." He nuzzled her hair. "No one besides us, and the girls, need to know otherwise. It'll be better for all our sakes that way; we'll be shielding the baby and us from gossip. We'll be a real family. It's almost like a do-over for you and me."

A do-over. Lucie swallowed and forced herself to sound upbeat. "That's . . . that's so generous of you," she said.

"I love you, Lucie." He pressed his lips against hers briefly. "Always."

Lucie sank against him, eyes closed, listening to the hum of his steady breaths and telling herself this was where she belonged. That she was doing what was best for all of them.

Chapter 37

~~~~~

SHE TRIED TO forget about Collin, to go on with her life with Mark, who, in sensing a certain reserve in her actions, dialed up the care and attention, lavished her with gifts. She wanted for nothing. And yet.

She wrote Collin and Suzie texts she didn't send. She missed them both a lot, although she tried not to admit it to anyone, even herself. She tried to distract herself, to occupy her last carefree days before the baby's arrival with the goodness of her friendship with Weina, watching her and Simon with the kids, practicing on the triplets all the skills she had picked up at class, and gaining confidence as Weina, encouragingly, said things like, "Don't worry, there's three of them, haha," while Lucie whispered choi's under her breath, even as she laughed.

And still, there was a part of her that kept saying, *It's not enough.*

SUNDAY MORNING AT Hannah's home, the sisters discussed Mark and Collin. Hannah wanted to know if Collin was really out of the picture. "I thought something good was brewing between you both. There's respect and a solid friendship. Whereas with Mark . . ."

"He has done the work, seen the professionals," Lucie said. "He wants to change." Then, haltingly, "I'll be happy with him."

"Interesting choice of tense," Hannah noted.

"I do believe all three of us will have a good life together," she said, with much more conviction than she felt.

The sisters were silent. "Which of us can claim to know what goes on in another's relationship," Hannah said. She hesitated, then hugged Lucie. "If you are sure, then I'm rooting for you both."

"Thank you," Lucie said. She gathered her courage to ask Hannah the next question, something she had recently begun to wonder about. "Hannah, I never did ask you—what was the worst part about leaving Gerald?"

Hannah twisted her fingers in her lap. "That's an oddly specific and peculiarly phrased question to ask out of the blue, after so long."

"I know you wanted it, of course. It's just . . . it's just I saw how everyone treated you after the divorce. Still are treating you, in fact. It couldn't have been easy."

"It wasn't," Hannah said slowly. "I guess the worst was how I was *made* to feel about it, even though I knew it was right." She pressed her lips together till the blood left them, silent for a while. "It sucked to be seen as a failure, an embarrassment to the family name, even though no one ever came right out and said it." She laughed bitterly. "No wait, that's not true. Some did."

"You know I don't feel that way."

"Yes, I know. But it would have been nice to have more vocal support. Look, I'm grateful for your help with the kids when I needed someone to look after them, but what I really, really needed, back then, was for someone to say, 'You didn't make a mistake.'" She glanced down at her hands, motionless in her lap. "However I felt seemed irrelevant. Everyone else's opinion seemed to hold more weight than mine and it was beginning to affect me, although I tried really hard to put on a happy face. Sometimes I still feel like that."

Lucie flinched. "I'm so sorry, Hannah. I didn't know. I guess I was a little too wrapped up in myself back then."

Hannah attempted a smile. "I know, you and Mark were sickeningly perfect. I can understand why my presence must have been radioactive. On some subconscious level, I guess you didn't want my energy invading your bubble. As it were, some of you were walking around on tiptoes around me, afraid of hurting me. That was the most exhausting, me pretending not to notice how you were censoring yourselves—even harder than the criticism. I hated the disconnect between how I felt about *my* divorce and what others were making me think I should feel."

"My God . . . I-I'm sorry. You're right. I should have been more supportive."

"Thanks," Hannah said. "I accept your apology. And to answer your unasked question: I don't regret it. He cheated, sure, and that was terrible. But he also wanted something from me that I couldn't give. When I was with Gerald, I felt like I was performing a role, and now that it's over, I'm finally able to live my life openly the way I want." After the divorce, Hannah began openly identifying as aromantic, even to their parents, but they had dismissed it as a "phase," a reaction to the divorce.

"What do you tell the parents when they tell you that you just haven't found the right man?"

"I just let it be. Sometimes you just have to pick your battles.

Silence doesn't mean you're weak. And I've come to realize that if someone doesn't want to make the effort to understand who I am, then I guess we'll never be truly close. Of course, you have to do the work and know what you are in the first place. Do you?"

"Yes, I do," Lucie said, again with more conviction than she felt. She shook her head in admiration. "You know, I've always thought that you were the grittiest one of all three of us. Anthony and I had the fight wrung out of us early on, I guess."

Hannah shook her head. "No, I don't believe that. Too many people get away with saying the choices in life have been made for them. You always have a choice when it comes to fighting for what you want. You only stop having a choice when you stop fighting."

"I just want to do right by my child, be a good parent," Lucie said.

"Then fight for what you want, what you believe in. That's how you should parent—by showing them that you take care of yourself, your needs, just as you do theirs. How can someone who is unhappy or unwell do the best for their child?" Hannah stood up. Outside, rain was starting to fall. "I think if you choose to live authentically, that's an example of a life well lived. That's what being a good parent is about."

AFTER THE RAIN had subsided, Lucie went for an evening walk in the Botanic Gardens. The Japanese regarded forest bathing—being immersed in and connecting with nature without distraction—as a form of therapy for the mind, body, and soul. The Botanic Gardens were a good, close second to a proper forest, eighty-two hectares of flora and fauna smack-dab in the middle of an urban jungle.

Immersion was good, especially since movement was getting progressively more difficult. She entered the park, found a bench, and sipped on the very nature-inspired bubble tea (Earl Grey honey latte, extra boba) she had purchased on the way there, the ice tinkling melodically in her metal tumbler.

She wondered, as she always did after a while, what Suzie was up to. Her chat with Hannah made her realize how often she hid behind inaction to avoid conflict. That ended now. She took a deep breath and called Suzie.

"Hey," Suzie said on the second ring.

"You picked up!" Lucie said, surprised.

A curt laugh. "Yeah, why wouldn't I?" Suzie said. "You're not trying to sell me diet pills or a time-share in Bali, so we're good."

"Are we? You took off about ten minutes after the baby shower started."

"Well, try looking at it from my point of view. Twelve women, nine of them moms; five, including you, pregnant. Five! There was barely any room to move without knocking into a swollen belly. I was, no joke, holding my arms to my sides. And it's not like I didn't try to mingle." A sour note entered her tone. "A bunch of women next to me that I tried to talk to about new cinema releases, *literally* the most banal thing to talk about after the weather and food, iced me out and started comparing the absorbency of different diaper brands. I had to get out of there."

"You could have come earlier just to hang with me . . ."

"I could have," Suzie agreed, without adding more.

The silence between them was so loaded that Lucie could hear the blood pounding in her ears.

"Look, I don't know what's going on. Why are you avoiding me?" Lucie had promised herself she wouldn't raise her voice, but she was tetchy from a lack of REM sleep exacerbated by her indecision, her whole body was bloated and gaseous, and she was emotionally drained. "And don't say you're not. I know you are."

Suzie was quiet for a long time. And she was not eating. "I'm sorry, I know I haven't been the best friend—"

"You've been a fucking ghost," Lucie said.

Suzie swallowed hard. When she spoke next, her voice was so soft Lucie had to strain to hear it. "It's so juvenile, I know it. Staying away, instead of just telling the person how you feel."

"Did I do something wrong?"

"You want the truth? I just . . . I just can't be around you right now. And this will sound trite, but it's not you; it's me."

"What the hell does that even mean?" Lucie exclaimed.

"It hurts, all right?" Suzie blurted. "It fucking hurts."

"What?"

"God, I didn't want to talk about this because it's so stupid. Don't get me wrong, I'm so, so happy for you, Luce, I really am. I am so, *so* happy for you. But I am also so, so fucking sad. Because I've lost you."

"What do you mean?" Lucie said, surprised.

"Look, I've done the empirical studies, OK? Our friendship will never be the same—if it even survives. I've seen it happen to so many of my close friends. It starts off with all the scans, and then all the baby milestones that I can't chip in about. Then the childcare . . . and preschool, after-school enrichment classes to make your kid the next genius on the block, bitching about *kiasu* parents while you become one. Your kid's first kiss. Their first everything." Her voice broke. "And I won't have anything to say about that. I'll just be nodding along, with this fake smile slapped on my face. And that's not me. I'm not a bullshitter. I want to participate, I want to contribute so, so much, but I'm going to be that loser kid at the edge of a play circle, watching the cool kids build snot castles or whatever."

"That has never been cool," Lucie said.

"See, that's what I mean. I miss this. I haven't joked with you in ages." Her voice trembled. "I feel like such a jerk for staying away. But I'm afraid we're already drifting apart and I'm afraid of getting hurt."

Very gently, she began to cry. And then Lucie started to cry. They didn't speak for some time.

"I'm sorry," Lucie managed at last. "I've been so wrapped up with what's going on I totally forgot to ask how you're doing." She wiped her eyes with the back of her hands. "Why didn't you tell me you were afraid of losing me? That would never happen. We're too good of friends for that to happen. I mean, look at you and Weina. She has kids and you two are still close, right?"

"Well"—Suzie sniffled—"not really. I love Weina; she's an old friend, but nowadays we don't really have much to say outside of casual texts or chats without you in common. We're friends because of our history, but I wonder if we'd be chatting as much without, well, you as the glue. Even when we were all single and child-free, you and I were always more kindred spirits. Within the Fab Trio and without, you're who I feel more connected with. We're Bill and Ted, Weina's the spare."

"Ouch," Lucie said, grinning despite the tears.

"I don't mean it meanly. I told you, I love Weina. But I won't be dissecting pop culture or crushing on BTS with her the way I do with you. We're Meredith Grey and Cristina Yang. *You're* my person."

"A-am I at least Cristina in the equation?"

"No, I'm Cristina, obviously." She took a deep breath. "And if

I can be totally honest, there's something else. Look, I don't want what you have, no offense"—that was Suzie, direct and honest—"you guys know I don't want children. I'll happily corrupt yours and Weina's, of course. I'll be their cool aunt Suzie, but at the end of the day, they are yours. But the love part? I can't pretend, as happy as I am for you, that seeing you in love, seeing you loved by Collin and Mark, isn't hard on me. You know I've been putting myself out there with little success. I've been single for close to three years, Lucie, and it's great on the good days, but really rough on the bad days. I'm lonely, Lucie."

I'm lonely. Even though they'd been friends for decades, Suzie was rarely so vulnerable and frank about her emotions, and it broke Lucie's heart how much she'd failed her friend when it mattered.

"Is there . . . is there anything I can do? To make you understand that I love you and will always want to hang, to talk about non-kid stuff?"

"No, no, silly. Just work on being a walking incubator and figure out what to do with Mark and Collin. You've got enough on your plate. I told you, it's not you; it's me."

"So, what does that mean?"

"I'm good, truly . . . I just need some time and space to process my feelings, to work on maybe getting myself some of that sweet, sweet adoration, but I'll be fine. I'll come back. I-if you need me by then, of course."

"Suzie," Lucie said suddenly, her voice low, "you will always be my Cristina. My Ted. I know things are strange between us now, but how I feel about you will never change. I will never stop BTS-meme-texting you. I will never stop sending you clips of me screeching bits of Taylor Swift. And I'll never stop loving you. Kids or no kids, guy or no guy."

Suzie's voice hitched. "Stop. Don't make promises you can't keep."

"Cross my heart, you will never be relegated from the Premier League of my affections. You were here first, Suzie. No matter how much things change"—Lucie's voice broke—"I want to go through it all and grow old with you."

"Words are cheap, Luce," Suzie said laconically. But the smile in her voice was back.

They spent a few moments in companionable snuffling. "Have you decided what you're going to do, about Mark and Collin?"

"I don't know."

"I think you do. You're Lucie Yi. The second smartest person I know, after me, but this isn't about smarts. What does your heart want? You just have to stop and listen to yourself. No matter how much the answer scares you, be brave."

Suzie was right: Lucie did know what she wanted. She wanted Collin. She'd wanted Collin for a long, long time, and she couldn't replace him with Mark, no matter how much sense Mark made. She just had to be honest with herself and stop running away from it. Because in the end, happiness was both a journey and a destination paved with risk, and despite not knowing the odds, she thought she'd like to bet against the house this time, in joyful wide-eyed folly, if it meant she could start something with Collin. After all, she thought wryly, she was nuts about him.

Chapter 38

〜〜〜

LUCIE WAS HUMMING with nerves as she waited for Mark to come home after work to his for the last time, even though looking at her, thirty-seven weeks pregnant and stretched out on the sofa with a pillow under her legs, a casual observer would be hard-pressed to detect her agitation. Yet she was fairly crawling out of her skin. Details of the home that she had loved before now irked her to no end. The twisting vines in the silk wallpaper; the faux fireplace and its affectation of sophistication; the silver Tiffany frames that she'd never liked but he'd always wanted—the decor was all Mark. She tapped her fingers on her lap and tried to distract herself by finding all the prime numbers under one hundred, losing her train of thought often whenever the baby kicked, and then she got bored and made herself a cup of instant noodles (Mark's one food vice) and set about eating it, so that when she finally heard his keys in the door she had calmed down somewhat, and when he entered, sternly handsome in a suit, she was able to ask him, in a clear voice: "Tell me what you think about the death penalty."

"What?" Mark said, caught off guard. He dropped the keys on a side table and busied himself with putting away his things.

"Tell me what you think about the death penalty," she insisted, sitting straighter on the couch.

"It's not my problem?" he said, shrugging.

"I want a position," she said. "I want *your* position."

"I really don't care, as I'm not planning to commit a crime, honey," he said, reaching for his Lagavulin 16 and pouring a generous measure into a glass.

She took a deep breath. "What about euthanasia?"

Mark put his glass down. "Are you dying?" he said slowly.

"No, I'm not. I just want to know what you think about issues."

"Issues that don't concern us?"

"They concern all of us, even if we aren't directly involved," she said.

Mark shrugged and said indulgently, "I'll start recycling, if that makes you feel better." Recycling had been an issue they diverged on in the beginning of their courtship, but he had laughed at her "naive idealism," so she'd never discussed any other important issues with him, to avoid further confrontation.

As for his lackadaisical attitude toward environmental issues, Mark didn't believe that he should be personally inconvenienced, when he donated a generous sum to World Wide Fund for Nature every year. What was the need for a holistic lifestyle change when he could pay people to handle the problem? Having outsourced his guilt, he could do what he wanted in his private life. For him, the System of Offsetting worked—whereas this was the one area it never had for her.

Mark was watching her with an expression that said that she

was the one with a problem. *Apathy*, she thought, *toward important issues is not attractive. If you don't have a strong opinion, if you can't take a stand and stick to it, who are you, really? What will you be like as a husband, a parent, a father?* How had she never understood this about Mark before?

Maybe because I didn't really understand it myself.

He cared for her, that was clear. She didn't doubt that he meant it when he said he would do anything (except recycle) for her. He loved her. But even in the way he loved her, everything was self-focused. He wanted the best for her—from his standpoint. He believed, rightly or wrongly, that getting married to him would solve her and her child's future problems, that he was saving them. He treated her as precious because he believed she belonged *to* him. When had he ever asked her what she thought was best?

It was possible to love someone in a selfish way. Here he was, doing it so well it took her years to see it for what it was, and what it wasn't.

"You should sit down."

He sat down on the sofa warily, his eyes on her. "What's up?"

"We need to break up," she said in a rush, not wanting to lose her nerve.

He drew a hand over his face, as though she was a child throwing a tantrum. "Lucie, not now. I'm tired."

"I'm serious. I don't want this life with you." She had rehearsed this, made sure that she left him no room to maneuver. No filler words. No ambiguity.

He stood up. His tone was sharp. "Wha—what? I don't understand. Where's this coming from? I've done so much for us, for you. Even therapy. I've put in the work to fix things."

She heard the sincerity behind his words and bit her lip. "And

I appreciate that, of course. It's great that you've been going to therapy. But it should be for and about you, and no one else. It shouldn't be so we can be together again."

He looked at her blankly. "Lucie, you and I *belong* together," he said, still trying.

You and Mark are perfect for each other. She'd heard variations of that phrase ever since they'd been together, and she had subscribed to it wholeheartedly. But it was no longer the truth. "You know what, for the longest time, I thought so, too. But I don't think we share the same values, Mark. I don't even think you know what you stand for."

"Just because I don't *recycle*?" he said.

"That's one aspect of it."

"Mr. Fucking Enlightened Soft Boi put all kinds of ideas in your head, hasn't he?" he said, his voice harsh and low. He shrugged her hand off, got up, and began pacing the room, as far away from her as he could. "Heal the world through yoga and truth circles bullshit."

She flushed. "Don't talk about Collin like that. You don't even know him."

The pacing slowed as comprehension dawned on him. "Oh my God. Are you . . . are you *in love* with him?"

Yes . . . yes, I am. The answer came to her, clear as day. Collin made her entire being take flight. She knew it now. But, in front of Mark, she censored herself, even now. "I-I don't know exactly what I feel for him. But I'd like to find out."

He stopped pacing completely. When he met her eyes, she was startled to find that he was crying. He never cried. "I d-don't . . . I don't understand," he said, swiping at a trail of tears with jerky motions. "You were ready to commit to me just a couple of days ago, Lucie. What happened?"

I woke up from a dream. She shook her head wordlessly.

"I love you so, so much. Don't you love me, too?" His voice was pleading. She could see how hard this was hitting him and she almost lost her courage. She hated hurting him. Hated disappointing him.

Enough. She gave herself a mental shake. If she was to be any kind of parent, she was going to have to get used to disappointing other people, so long as she believed in her choices. She steeled herself for what she had to say next.

"Yes, Mark, I do love you, but it's not enough." She blinked back tears. "We have grown as much as we can together, and I think"—she tried to soften the blow—"I think deep inside, you know it, too. We end here."

For a moment, she thought she had gotten through to him. That they could finally be open with each other, speak without artifice. Instead, he dragged his eyes from her and resumed pacing, muttering. "OK, you know what? You're confused. It's the pregnancy hormones. There's just no other explanation for the way you're acting. You were so sure. Now you're vacillating. Let's just take a step back, and maybe you'll change your mind again, come to your senses."

She cringed at his words, like she couldn't be trusted to make the right decision. She had thought she was doing the right thing, getting back together with him. Once, she could have easily lived the rest of her life with him. But the baby, and Collin, had changed the prism through which she viewed life and its priorities. It was no longer enough for her to live her entire life correctly for all the wrong reasons, not when she had had a taste of what a life of unfettered joy with the right person could be.

Joy. She chose joy.

She shook her head. "Mark, please. I know what I'm doing."

He stood still and faced her. "Haven't you punished me enough?" he said quietly.

His words were like a slap in the face. Lucie felt as though she'd been split wide open. This was the real Mark. Seven years with him, and this was what he thought of her. That she was trying to hurt him on purpose. Now she had confirmation that he never knew her at all. "Is this what you think of me?" she said, barely able to say it. Seven years. Oh, the wastefulness of it.

Mark pressed his lips together and closed his eyes for a brief moment. When he opened them, he had regained his composure. A hard smile twisted his lips. "What else would you call this?" he said.

"I need to go," Lucie said in a trembling voice, turning to leave. She would not break down in front of him. But before she could take a step, though, a wave of light-headedness broke over her. She groaned, feeling something give, then a wetness. She hobbled to the couch and keeled over it. In a flash Mark was by her side, holding her. "Lucie, don't panic"—he was clearly panicking—"but I think your water just broke."

"What?" Lucie said, confused. She looked down at the liquid pooling between her legs. *That's not water.*

"I'm not due for another three weeks," she said, fear shooting through her. *My baby.*

Mark bent and held out his arms. "S-sit," he said. "I'll carry you."

Lucie hesitated before acquiescing. Their eyes met as she wound her arms around his neck, and the hurt in his eyes made Lucie look away. "I'm sorry, Mark."

He gave an imperceptible nod before lifting her up.

"Let's go," Mark said at last, his face taut, but back in control. Lucie saw a flash of who she could have been if she had stayed with Mark, and despite the pain and anguish they were feeling, she knew without a doubt she had made the right decision.

Chapter 39

〜〜〜

THE CAR RIDE to the private maternity hospital was the longest twenty minutes of her life. Mark fell silent for the rest of the way (his backseat, Lucie realized with a pang, was outfitted with an infant car seat in bold teal) except for the moments when Lucie gasped at a contraction. Those were still irregular, so she knew she had time before the baby was theoretically supposed to come, but she texted Collin to let him know it had begun.

It's happening! Well, it just started, but I assume I'll be giving birth within the day.

I'm taking the next flight out, Collin texted back. Wait for me—unless you can't.

Collin, she texted, finger trembling, get here safely. I—*I can't tell him this over text*—we need to talk. Urgh, ignore the cliché. We need to talk, but in a good way!

Clearly she needed to work on her written communication skills.

She dropped a text to the girls on their group chat to let them know she was at the hospital with Mark, and separately to Hannah so she could tell their family that her labor had started, but that they didn't need to come to the hospital yet.

Even though it was 8:00 p.m., the registration area was bustling, so they had to wait for their turn. When her ticket was called, Mark helped her to the registration counter, where a nurse, a petite woman in her late twenties with a bright, friendly face and sporting an olive short-sleeved uniform, took down the details of her labor. "How often are the contractions spaced apart now?" she asked.

"I've only had about two or three, in the last twenty minutes," Lucie said, grimacing, "but my water broke an hour ago." She bit back a cry as a contraction came. "And I'm about three weeks early."

The nurse nodded, tucking a stray lock of black hair back into her neat bob as she made some notes in her device. She asked a couple of questions that Lucie answered, then said, "I don't think you need to check in yet."

"I want her in the care of medical professionals," Mark said authoritatively. "It's not safe for her to be at home."

The nurse regarded him. "I don't mean to contradict you, sir, but it's not standard procedure to admit when the contractions are this irregular and far apart."

"I'll pay," he said, coolly, "if that's an issue."

"I would really prefer that you didn't," Lucie said.

"May I ask what is his relation to you?" the nurse asked her, sensing the tension.

"He's my friend," Lucie said, while Mark said "partner" at the same time.

"Friend," Lucie said firmly. "Mark, you're overstepping. I can make my own decisions as to whether to get admitted or not, and beyond that." She grimaced as another contraction racked her.

"Oh, don't be ridiculous, Lucie," Mark said. "No one knows you like I do. If anything happens, you'll need to assign me authority to make sound decisions on your behalf." To the nurse, "My partner is estranged from her family and should anything happen to the baby, I will need to be granted power of attorney to make decisions on her behalf. Where are the forms?"

"We're not together anymore, Mark," she said through gritted teeth. "And I'm not estranged from my family—well, yet. We just aren't that close. And I've already assigned a lasting power of attorney to someone else. It should be in the admission records." Lucie directed her response to the nurse, who was now looking nervously between Mark and Lucie.

Mark regarded her in surprise, again choosing to ignore her comment about them having already broken up. "What?"

"The father of this child is the man I have entrusted with a lasting power of attorney on all medical emergencies related to my pregnancy, Collin Read. His contact details are in the admission form."

"Oh, for fuck's sake, that loose cannon in Korea?" Mark exclaimed. "That's ridiculous! He's not even in the same country! He could be stuck on a plane at a critical moment. You need someone trustworthy here, now!"

"Then Sushila Mahmood will decide," Suzie said, appearing beside them at the reception, out-of-breath and flustered. "I got here as soon as you texted. I can't miss the birth of my best friend's firstborn. Maybe the second one, but not the first. Anyway, I'm up for the tough medical decisions, that is"—she slid a look Lucie's way—"if Lucie still wants me to be the one deciding her fate. I think I'm on the list as the second choice after Collin, and I've also signed some forms."

"Of course you're next in line, and of course I still want you to have that power," Lucie said, a weak grin on her face. She hugged her best friend. "Welcome back."

"OK, great. Anyone but Mark then," he said bitterly.

"Well, excuse me, Sourpuss McLoser," Suzie muttered.

Lucie took a deep, shuddery breath and said, "I'm so, so sorry, Mark. I really am. But if you choose to stay, it's going to have to be as a friend."

He looked at her, his face ashen. "You and I can never just be friends." They looked at each other for the longest time, the air thick with unspoken tension.

"No, I suppose not," she conceded at last. "I'm sorry, Mark."

He made a small sound at the back of his throat that tore through her. When Lucie reached out to comfort him, he brushed her hand away. "Don't. Please."

He turned and hurriedly walked away, but not before Lucie glimpsed the stricken expression on his face.

And that was part of the problem, wasn't it? Lucie thought, watching him leave, a piece of her heart breaking. They had never learned to be friends.

"What do you want to do now?" Suzie said, linking arms with Lucie.

"I want to have a slice of cake at the café and catch up." Lucie grimaced as a contraction seized her. "Though I don't know how much time I can give you."

"I'll take anything you can give," Suzie said. "Your last few moments as a single, carefree being before a lifetime of servitude. Ha ha."

"Let's go," Lucie said firmly, leading Suzie to the coffee shop she had just spied around the corner. "I think I'm going to have a very expensive, very handcrafted latte to help get this baby out at last!"

THE COFFEE WORKED. Or at least nature kicked in. Hard. In the uterus.

Since her contractions were more regular and spaced less than six minutes apart, they admitted her to the labor ward. She rested in her private delivery room with Suzie. Dr. Joyce occasionally popping in from her rounds, while the nurse on duty monitored Lucie and the fetus's vitals from time to time.

"Remember, Big Vagina Energy," Weina counseled, guiding Lucie on how to breathe through video call while she arranged for last-minute sitters for her children. She was even scheduling them in four-hour shifts, in case this was a long one and she had to duck in and out of the hospital. "You are a warrior!"

"You really don't have to be here, physically," Lucie protested. "I totally under—*STAND!*" She screeched the last syllable as she felt a contraction rip through her extremities. "MMMW-WAARGGHHHHHHH facker duck!" The contractions were painful and regular now.

"What was that?" Suzie asked.

Weina shrugged. "I think when you're in that much pain, normal expletives don't cover it."

The nurse on duty, Florence, gave her a quick physical examination and murmured that she would summon Dr. Joyce.

"Give me *all the drugs*!" Lucie shrieked to Dr. Joyce, who had just arrived. "Mainline the epidural into me right now!"

Dr. Joyce activated her Professional Soother voice. "Yes, I

will give you the epidural when it's time, but not yet. You're only two centimeters dilated, plus the anesthesiologist isn't here yet. However, you may have the laughing gas we talked about, if you—"

"Give it *now*," Lucie snarled.

Everything became a little fuzzier and funnier after that.

BUT TEN HOURS later, after a harrowing night with nurses and the midwife routinely stopping by to check on her, and more huffs from what Lucie called the Joker mask than anticipated, she was still not more than three centimeters dilated.

"We're going to have to schedule an emergency C-section," Dr. Joyce said the next morning when she came in to check on Lucie at 8:00 a.m., her brow creasing as she looked at the fetal heart monitor.

"What? You mean after all those stupid truckloads of pain, I *still* have to have surgery?" Lucie said in a voice barely above a whisper. She was spent. The laughing gas was no longer helping.

"Yes," Dr. Joyce said, giving her right shoulder a rueful squeeze. "I'm sorry, I really am." She explained that the baby's heart rate was concerning. "We should get you prepped for surgery over the next hour."

"OK, let's get the baby out safely."

Lucie waited in her room while they prepared to admit her to the operating theater. She texted Hannah and the group chat to update them. Hannah texted back to let her know that she, Anthony, and their parents were waiting in the café to see her now that visiting hours had started. They had expected the baby to have arrived by now.

"We can only let four persons in your room at any one time," the nurse on duty said when he dropped by to inform her that her family was waiting in the hallway.

"Send them in, please."

I wish Collin was here. He had to be close—last she heard from Suzie and Weina, who had been texting Collin with updates while Lucie had been busy being in labor, he had landed and was making his way to the hospital. And then a new wave of anxiety threatened to overwhelm her. Even in her state of exhaustion, she worried about what her family would say when they saw Collin by her side and understood that she was forsaking stability and guaranteed matrimony for a man they perceived as a wild card.

The Yis arrived in pairs. Yi Wei Liang and Ivy Chen, followed by Hannah and Anthony. Su Mei was at home with the children.

Hannah's face was drawn tight. "Oh, Lucie," she said, her eyes welling with tears. "Are you OK?"

Lucie gave a weak laugh. "Do I look that bad?" she tried to joke.

"You're the color of blanched tofu," Suzie said from the corridor just outside Lucie's room, where she and Weina were loitering, not technically breaking the maximum visitor capacity rule. "But then that's how she looks most days. Everybody be calm and stay positive! Big Vagi—I mean, big energy!"

Lucie laughed weakly. "Thanks a lot, Suzie."

"You have about twenty minutes," Dr. Joyce said. "We're about to prep her for the C-section."

"Any news from Collin?" Lucie directed the question to Suzie.

"He's on his way."

"Collin?" Ivy Chen said, confused. "What do you mean? Isn't he in Korea? Where's Mark?"

Her father's gaze landed like a ton of bricks on Lucie, scrutinizing her. This was a look she knew well, the look that forewarned: anything she said had better be worth his time.

"I broke up with Mark, and he left."

"Haiyah!" Ivy exclaimed. "What nonsense is this? Why are you fighting at this eleventh hour? Can you fix it? This is not the time to be making impulsive decisions."

So many questions, and not one of them was about how she was feeling.

"I think I've known for a while that Mark and I have grown apart," Lucie said quietly. "We broke up just before I was admitted."

"Which means it was the wrong decision, clearly," Wei Liang said. "But it's not too late to remedy the—"

Just then a knock sounded on the door and Collin, looking flustered, burst in wearing dark-wash jeans, a rumpled white-collared shirt, and an olive-green sweater, breathing hard. "Lucie! I'm so, so sorry for the delay. There was a holdup at immigration, I couldn't find my boarding card, and then I couldn't find my luggage, can you believe it? So much for the perfect streak. Oh, I hope . . . did I miss any—"

"Nothing. Just . . . perfect timing for the shitstorm," Lucie said, smiling weakly, holding out her arms, into which Collin folded with relief. He kissed her on her forehead and then stepped back, dazed, suddenly aware and overwhelmed by the number of people in the room, some of whom were openly hostile at his appearance.

Suzie poked her head in the room and asked Collin, "Did anyone stop you from coming up to the room?"

"Er, no, I just asked for the room number and came straight up."

"Great, no one's monitoring," Suzie said, pulling Weina into the room with her. "Hi, Auntie and Uncle, Anthony, Hannah." Weina murmured the same.

"Why is Collin here?" Ivy asked Lucie.

"He's here because he's the father," Lucie said, as though her mother had just blanked on the past five months.

"That I am," Collin said.

"I *know* you are the father, Collin," Ivy said in an icy voice. "What I'm confused about is, how did it get from you and my daughter talking about marriage, to her getting back together with the love of her life, who she has seemingly just dropped for no good reason, to you reentering her life? What is this—this conveyor-belt-fiancé situation?"

If it weren't for the fact that she was being insulted by her own mother, Lucie thought that *Conveyor Belt Fiancé Situation* sounded like the name of a pop song or the title of a rom-com she would enjoy.

"This whole mess could have been easily avoided if better choices had been made," her father said, not looking at Collin or her, but at the spot on the wall behind her, where a wood carving of a lotus flower bloomed.

The careful tapestry of half-truths and omissions was unraveling. Lucie knew there was no point in fabricating another story. She had destroyed her safety nets; Plan Mark was gone. There was only the truth.

So she began, at last. "Well, Collin and I never thought we'd be getting married, if I'm being honest. We were just thinking of having a baby and sorting out the rest later, since neither of us was getting younger. It seemed unfair that just because we had awful luck in love, we should miss out on having children. Life is short."

She could see, from the corner of her eye, Weina, Suzie, and Hannah nodding in hard agreement, each for different reasons.

"So I did my research and went on a site for matching partners interested in having a child together in a platonic, co-parenting arrangement. I met Collin, parent-dated him, went ahead and had sex"—her mother flinched—"and lo and behold, we got lucky. It happened. We decided to move back to Singapore, where things got complicated, fast. Because of Mark, because of other factors. And now you have the full story."

For a long time, no one spoke. Her parents wore identical, shocked looks on their faces. It was novel—her parents were not easily rattled.

"I'm not sure I understand," Ivy said weakly, sitting down on the bed. "You *chose* to put yourself in this ridiculous situation? Did I not raise you with morals and values?"

"It's the shortcut mentality that this generation has," Wei Liang raged. Lucie hunched her shoulders, instantly flashing back to her childhood, when she would make herself smaller almost as if, by doing so, she would absorb less of his anger. "They think that without the hard work, the sacrifices of commitment, they can just get what they want."

"What makes you think I'm less committed, just because I didn't fall in love with her in the beginning?" Collin said.

"The marriage component is a key part of the equation," Wei Liang said. "You're shirking the responsibility of marriage."

"That's right. You have to take responsibility . . . for . . . for . . . for your dick job!" Ivy said.

Out of the corner of her eye, Lucie saw Suzie dig her fingers into her arm to stave off the laugh-shakes. It would have been funny if she weren't still having contractions.

Collin took a deep breath before replying, "I'm not shirking anything, Mrs. Yi. I have an arrangement with your daughter to take care of our child, together, and I am prepared to honor it. It goes beyond some legal framework. I don't need that to bind myself to your daughter by obligation—I have love."

"Love," her father said bitterly, "runs out. And then Lucie is going to be like Hannah, except worse off. Cast aside. No rights whatsoever if you decide you've had enough of this casual arrangement." He turned to her and pointed to Collin. "You understand that this man is a flight risk."

"I'll risk it, then," Lucie said, meeting her father's gaze squarely. "You're right. I did make an impulsive decision, but nothing in life is sure, despite all our work to make it so. Except for the fact that I get a child out of this."

"And not that it should be a deciding vote, but I made Lucie the beneficiary of my life insurance policy very early on in our time in Singapore," Collin muttered. "It's worth a heck of a lot—well, not buy-a-yacht money, but helps-with-a-down-payment money."

"That's so sweet!" Lucie said, surprised. "You didn't have to do"—she winced as a contraction gripped her—"that."

"Well, my mom and dad were the original beneficiaries, and with my mom gone and Peter in agreement—"

"Who's Peter?" Wei Liang interrupted.

"His dad," Lucie said.

Yi Wei Liang's expression upon realizing that Collin referred to his father, in public, by the latter's first name was disapproval of biblical proportions.

"Anyway, as I was saying, Pe—*Dad* was happy to hear that I added Lucie as a beneficiary, so that's that. The policy's worth a tidy sum if I die, so . . ." Collin ran his hands through his hair with a rueful smile.

"You met up with your dad?" Lucie exclaimed.

"Yes, a couple of times before I left for Korea. It was really good."

"Collin, that's wonderful," Lucie said, reaching out for his hand and clasping it. "You dope." Lucie teared up. "I've never been made a beneficiary of any insurance life plan before. That's so—"

"Romantic?" Collin offered.

"Practical and responsible," Lucie said at the same time. Their eyes met, and Lucie grinned weakly. "And romantic, OK."

"OK, OK, enough bullshit, this isn't a K-drama, see?" Ivy interjected, waving her hand in their faces to get their attention. "So what happens now? What does this *mean*? You two getting married or what? Or same kind of limbo nonsense again?" The angrier Ivy Chen got, the stronger her Singlish became.

Lucie took a deep breath. "We don't know yet, but we need to work at being a family first before anything else. We'll figure the rest out once the baby comes. Though I won't lie"—she chuckled—"administrative hurdles aren't exactly top of my concerns right now."

"This is disappointing," Wei Liang said.

"Why?" Hannah spoke up suddenly. "Why are you disappointed when they are clearly committed to raising the child together?"

"Because that means the child will be a bast—illegitimate when it's born. It'll be on all the official records, and it will impact the child's entire life in Singapore . . . until and if *someone*"—he spat out the word like it was a barb—"takes responsibility to rectify the situation and legitimize him." He turned to address Collin, pale with anger. "She should have been married by now, to Mark, or to you. Then this unfortunate situation wouldn't have happened. The shame."

"Stop it!" Hannah said. Her eyes glimmered with anger. "Why can't you guys just be supportive of your children for once?"

"Hannah," their father said, "I don't need to hear from you right now, after all you put us through."

"I'm not shutting up," Hannah snapped. "Lucie shouldn't need to marry Collin or Mark just so you all look good," Hannah said, pointing at their parents and Anthony. "No one should have to make such personal sacrifices for the sake of saving face."

Affronted, Anthony, who'd been unusually silent the whole time and standing unnoticed at the foot of the bed, raised his hands, and said, "Hey, I'm not part of this press-gang. I want Lucie to be happy."

"By not standing up to our parents, you are condoning their behavior," Hannah said with feeling.

Anthony turned to their parents and said, quietly, "I don't want my political career to have collateral damage, especially when it comes to my own sister. I don't think Lucie wants to marry either one of these men."

"Well," Lucie said. "I wouldn't say I'm *opposed* to marrying Collin one day," but of course nobody heard her. Except Collin. He leaned down and gave her forehead a kiss.

"Likewise," he said.

"And I fully intend to take care of her, in the manner she—*we* think best."

"Then marry her," Wei Liang challenged.

An unknown swell of bravado, possibly borne of hormones and drugs, made Lucie say, "Ma, Ba, I respect your opinions, but this is my life. Our life. We're not getting married just so people won't be offended. If we did so, wouldn't you say that cheapens the whole institution of marriage?"

Wei Liang said quietly, "It cheapens you, as a woman, to be with an illegitimate child."

That sucked the Big Vagina Energy out of the performance she'd been putting on for her parents' sake. Suddenly she felt very small and foolish again. But only for a split second. She knew that their decision to have the baby this way, without marrying for show, was right for the both of them.

Lucie caught Hannah's little shake of a head. *You tried. It's OK to not win this battle*, her expression said.

Hannah was right, but Lucie needed to stand up for her decision and for what Collin meant to her. Forcing herself to meet her father's gaze, she said, her voice level, "I know you don't agree with our choice, and that's your right, but all I'm asking from you, as my parents, is compassion. If you can't support this . . . then please leave." Half-hoping that they wouldn't actually take her at her word.

Wei Liang said, "Let's go."

"Ba," Lucie said, tearing up.

"Let's go," Wei Liang said, his face closed. "Anthony, come."

"We just need some time to process this," Ivy said, glancing from Lucie to her father. "I'll see you after your surgery, all right? You'll be fine."

"Anthony," Wei Liang said, again.

"No, I'll stay," Anthony said firmly. "With my sisters."

His face dark with anger, Yi Wei Liang left, followed by his wife, who gave Lucie a quick hug before she, too, bent to his will.

"That's nice," Suzie muttered.

Lucie said nothing. It took everything for her to even breathe. She wanted them so much to be in her life for her child's sake.

"They'll come around; parents always do when grandchildren are involved," Weina said gently. Hannah nodded and smoothed Lucie's hair back as she grimaced at another contraction.

Anthony and Hannah hugged her and told her they would wait in the cafeteria. "We need to catch up, too," he said meaningfully to Hannah, to which Hannah gave a watery smile. "I have full faith in the medical team and will keep abreast of all developments with *much* interest," he said at the doorway, in what Lucie assumed was his politician voice, which was meant to inspire and subtly intimidate.

Collin's phone vibrated. "Peter's here," he said, squeezing Lucie's heaving shoulders. "Can he come in to say a quick good luck?"

"Of course," Lucie said quickly.

Peter Read came by and hugged her, wishing her a safe surgery. He said all the right things and made her and Collin smile, but she couldn't help wishing it had been her own parents telling her that they supported her decision. But that was what growing up meant, sometimes: choosing our own happiness at the cost of disappointing the ones we love most.

Dr. Joyce and a nurse entered, checked her vitals, and told her that the surgery should proceed ASAP.

"We'll need to prep you," the nurse said.

"What can I do to help?" Collin said.

Inner Weina chimed up, *Remember, if you have an unplanned C-section, it's better if . . .*

"Actually, yes," Lucie said, perking up a little. "There is something you can do."

"What is it?"

Lucie locked eyes with Dr. Joyce and the nurse and smiled. "Oh, you'll see."

THEY WERE TAKEN up to another floor and shown into a small annex attached to an empty operating theater, where her surgery was scheduled.

The nurse, whose name tag read "Ella," came back with a disposable razor and a can of shaving cream before leaving the door to the room ajar. "Usually we do this for you, are you sure?"

"I'm sure," Lucie said.

"Call me if you need help," she said, looking at Collin dubiously. "And be careful."

"Ah, what do I do?" Collin asked the nurse.

"She'll tell you," Ella said, before giving them a goodbye wave. "You have five minutes, all right?"

Lucie waited till they were alone before turning to Collin and handing him the razor and shaving cream. "You wanted to help? Shave me for my C-section."

Collin raised his eyebrows and said, visibly shaken, "What?"

"I need to get it done anyway, and I'd much prefer you to do it," she said. "Dr. Joyce needs a clean entry point to make the C-section incision. So—chop-chop!"

Collin took the razor. "Well, this is . . . a surprise." He gazed, she presumed (it was hard to gauge sightline when your belly was bigger than a watermelon), at her crotch, with much less enthusiasm than he had the first time he encountered it. "To think I beat Mark to this," he joked weakly.

"Honey, I would not have let Mark touch this task with a ten-foot pole. I would have sooner let the nurse shave me dry." Lucie held his chin. "You are the only man I think I would want doing something so intimate."

He smiled wryly at her. "My darling, that makes me the

happiest man, I think." He held the razor and said, "So. Where do I start? How?"

"You've shaved your face before, right? Just"—Lucie bit her lip, shrugging—"dispense some shaving cream and mush it into the bush."

He mushed it into the bush. Not that she could tell from her vantage point (or the drugs in her system). Her belly was so large he could have been building a Lego Death Star under there and she wouldn't have known.

"All right," he said, miming pitching forward with his eyes shut. She smacked him on the head and he opened them. "Now is not the time to joke!"

"OK! OK! I'll be seriously confident."

He took the razor firmly in hand and shaved her, carefully, cleanly, without incident or complaints.

As THEY WERE wheeling her into the operating theater, Lucie's heart galloped in her chest. She'd never had any surgery before, and she was afraid of needles.

"I'm scared," she said.

He squeezed her hand. "I know. But you're also the bravest person I know. Aside from maybe my great-aunt Michelle in Florida, who once grabbed a trespassing juvenile alligator by its tail and hauled it over a fence. You can do anything you want, Lucie."

She reached for his hand and squeezed it, and he squeezed back. The nurse indicated that he needed to scrub in, but that Lucie would go in first to get sedated.

"Collin, wait." She shot a glance at the nurse. "Before we go in, can I tell my partner something in confidence please?"

"Can," the nurse said in Singlish, stepping back. "
to get you in soon."

"I'll be fast."

He held her hand. "You're going to be fine," he said.

"We hope," she said. "But in case things go awry . . ." She was very specifically thinking about the horror stories. The ones that Weina wouldn't tell her about, which she'd had to excavate from the deep dark bowels of postpartum threads, the worst of the worst-case scenarios. The kind that make you look at mothers who choose to go through birth after birth, and think, *Oh, you brave, foolhardy souls.*

"Choooooi," he said, adopting her favorite interjection with passion. "I won't allow it."

"It isn't up to you."

"I know. But from all the articles, *and* the books you made me read, C-sections are quite safe."

"I'm a glass-half-empty kind of person."

He laughed tenderly. "Could have fooled me."

Then he kissed her as though she wasn't lying on a bed in the hallway of one of the busiest hospitals in the country.

When she was younger, she naively believed that one *fell* in love, by chance, by fate's mysterious orchestration and machinations. That it was just something that happened to you. A bone that, if you were lucky, the universe threw your way once in a lifetime to balance out the awful, and more than once if you were extraordinarily blessed. But that wasn't true—not entirely. Sure, there was an element of luck in it, but the way she now saw it, love was intention; love was hard work, an overgrown destination you had to clear your way to, chainsaws blazing. If you waited around to have your finger pricked à la Sleeping Beauty—the most basic of all of Disney's princesses, in Lucie's opinion—then you were asking to spend your entire life asleep.

Most of all, love was a series of choices you made daily with another person—and she wanted to make those choices with Collin.

"Collin Read, whatever happens in there, I want you to know that I choose you. I choose all of you. Even the parts of you that you think aren't good enough—to be clear, I am talking about your very janky dance moves—I choose you." She narrowed her eyes. "So if things go wrong, you better take good care of our kid or I will *haunt* you."

"Got it," he said, laughing. Then, turning serious, he cupped her face and kissed her tenderly. "I choose you, too, Lucie. All of you." A pause. "Even the punny side of you that surfaces *way* too often."

She socked him weakly on the arm. "Don't make me cry. Or laugh. I'm too exhausted from labor."

He caught her hand and squeezed it. "I can't promise you I won't make you laugh, but I'll try my best not to make you cry."

She squeezed back. "I look forward to that."

And so, Lucie Yi and Collin Read proceeded to the operating theater together to welcome to the world the first good decision they'd made together.

Chapter 40

~~~~~~

THE BABY WAS a miracle.

Lucie couldn't stop looking at him. His perfect, smushed, velvety face that was more mouth than anything.

"He looks just like you," she told Collin.

"I don't think you mean that as a compliment, somehow," he said lightly, but he was grinning.

"We have to give him a name soon," Lucie said. It had been four days since the baby's birth, after three days spent in the NICU for monitoring, and they'd gone over their favorite names on both their lists without coming to a consensus so far. "Did you google something that fits your parameters? Because I have to say—the best I came up with was Takeshi. Takeshi Kaneshiro Yi-Read."

She was half joking, but also not. Takeshi Kaneshiro was Lucie's favorite actor growing up, though she was hard-pressed to recall exactly what films he'd been in.

"Ren. Ren Marie Yi-Read." Marie had been his mother's name.

"Ren?"

"Ren."

"I like it."

Lucie handed him to Collin so she could eat the papaya and fish soup and congee that the nurse had brought. She watched him circle the room with the baby, his features serene.

"I hope you're not allergic to tree nuts or lactose intolerant," she heard him say at one point.

"I hope you don't end up being a criminal or a male chauvinist," she added. "That's more important, in the grand scheme of things."

"And I hope you don't pun," he added, his back turned.

"I heard that!" she said.

He sat down on the couch facing her, the baby sleeping in his arms. They smiled at each other. "You're staring."

"I'm not." She was. She was afraid that this was a dream.

"Don't worry, I'm not going to drop him."

"Choi," she said sleepily.

"Yes, choi," he said, gazing ceiling-ward, in a mock God-help-us manner.

She rolled over, smiling, listening to him coo at Ren. A couple of minutes later, she was asleep.

SUZIE AND WEINA visited, along with Zul, Dinesh, Yu Ling, and a few of her colleagues—including Diana, who brought her a much too expensive pram and actually hugged her.

Suzie handed her a gift and asked her to open it. She obliged and laughed when she saw what it was: a bundle of animal onesies for older babies—"Custom-made!" Suzie crowed—that were, well, unusual, to say the least. Lucie pulled out the first one, deep iridescent golden-emerald, and showed Suzie, Weina, and Collin.

Collin, notably, flinched. "A scarab, really?" It had wild red eyes.

"Dung beetle," Suzie corrected cheerfully. "*Dung beetle.* Call it what it is."

"Oh-kay." Lucie waggled another one that looked as though it had jumped into an electrocuted bath, its Popsicle-orange eyes bugging. "And this is . . . an angry squirrel?"

"Wrong. It's an aye-aye!"

The rest of the onesies were a snail, a hairless cat, and an anteater.

"I want photos of Ren in all of them," Suzie said.

"Urm . . . sure?"

"I want to see the photos in the wedding banquet slideshow," Suzie said, folding her arms over her chest. "If I'm going to be forced to attend your kids' weddings—and this goes for you too, Weina—I want some color and texture in the proceedings. I want some *interest.*"

"Who says you'll be invited?" Lucie said, poker-faced.

"I'm the cool aunt; I have to be. They will scream for your blood if you don't. I will have raised them to be allegiant to me, above blood relatives."

"I'm looking forward to lots of cool aunt playdates," Lucie said, smiling at Suzie.

"OK, enough fawning," Weina said. She was grinning when she leaned over and whispered, sotto voce, "You're going to love what I bought you!"

Lucie opened Weina's impeccably wrapped gift box with Collin's help (it had a huge satin bow over the box and more tape than necessary). She laughed when she saw the contents: it was, of course, a MamaOneWrap. *Two* MamaOneWraps.

"Version 3.0," Weina informed her. "It's now static-proof."

One was safflower yellow and the other a limited-edition cloud print by a Japanese manga artist.

"Wow," Lucie said, pretending to wipe tears from her eyes. "Ren's life is now complete."

"Oh, there's more," Suzie said, throwing Weina a wink. With a flourish, she handed her a poster of the three of them as Charlie's Angels, with Collin in the background as Bosley. Collin, predictably, and true to life, was shirtless.

"This," Suzie said, with deep satisfaction, "will go in the kid's nursery, right over his bed."

Wryly, Collin asked, "Should I even ask how you got a picture of me without a shirt?"

"My uncle," Weina said, while Suzie said, simultaneously, "The internet."

Really, it had been Lucie.

DURING ONE OF Weina's postnatal visits at chez Read/Yi, Lucie brought up the possibility of her working with Weina as soon as her maternity leave was over. After she'd been rejected for partnership, she had been toying with the idea of leaving the firm for a while—and now she couldn't see what else was holding her back from doing just that and taking things easier. She had been pursuing partnership for the wrong reasons; this much was clear to her. Being with her child brought home how little she cared about the work, and though the money was important, Collin's new job was paying enough that she could consider alternatives, including working for Weina's start-up. They'd also been generous enough to let him work from Singapore till the baby turned two months old, after which he'd complete his six months in

Seoul, and thereafter spend three weeks in Singapore and one week in Seoul per month until the baby was two.

Lucie hadn't known if Weina wanted to work with a friend—there were many ways it could all go south, she knew—but when she proposed it, Weina's reaction was so effusive, so enthusiastic, she was relieved. Weina even suggested that Lucie come on board as an equity partner as soon as she could, but Lucie declined.

"I have to work my way up."

"Don't be ridiculous. We're all friends here. Plus, you have way more current experience and reputation than I do. I'd be tapping your networks!"

"That's the thing, I *am* being a friend and looking out for your interests. I'll start as a senior consultant, until I hit a target. You've done all the hard work, setting this up. Don't sell yourself short, and don't let me take advantage of you."

Weina laughed. "All right, all right, you're on a super-expedited partnership track then. You'll be a senior consultant to start with, with a one-month probation period in case we suck as work partners. As for your salary, I know you'll have to take a huge pay cut, but I'd be happy to revise it as we go and give you some options. I mean, my start-up is not a big, fancy firm like yours was—"

Lucie shook her head. "Don't worry about it. Let's take it slow, do a good job, and expand with prudence."

"Prudence. I like that," Weina said. "Dammit, I should have used that as the company name."

"What did you decide to name your company?"

"I called the company Liv-Ling Legends Advisory. Get it? Liv-dash-Ling." She smiled, proud of that Frankenstein pun/portmanteau. Liv had been Weina's English name, before she had quit the investment banking world.

Lucie cringed. "I got it in the first instance. I'm not printing that on a letterhead."

"You want to work with me or not!" Weina snapped, irritated. That's when Lucie knew she had already ordered the (very expensive) office stationery.

"OK, Liv-Ling Legends, Liv-Ling Legends," Lucie said soothingly. God, it was like a tongue twister, and not in a fun, sexual way.

Weina was huffy. "I get that you're a pun snob. So bring in your first million USD of business, then we'll talk about changing the name of the company."

Lucie promised herself that she would get the name changed in a year's time.

BABY REN DID not turn out to be lactose intolerant, but he was stupendously colicky, or so it seemed to the exhausted parents. Even with the help of the night nanny Peter Read insisted on paying for ("My gift to the new parents!"), they barely slept in the first four weeks, and Lucie felt like she had only the faintest grasp on the fundamentals of living aside from feeding him, eating, and falling asleep—sometimes doing two or all three of these things together.

"Are you glad you did this with me?" she asked Collin, when the nanny had taken the baby for a bottle feed and they were lying on the couch, looking like someone paintballed the front of their clothes with milk and spit-up.

He cocked an eyebrow. "A leading question, I see."

"Answer at your own peril. I've had a grand total of three and a half hours of sleep last night."

"Then, yes," he said, grinning, tucking a stray lock of her hair behind her ears. His face grew thoughtful. "It was the best decision of my life. And you, what are your thoughts on the Arrangement?"

Lucie thought about it. Her parents still hadn't called, even after her repeated attempts to reach out, although someone had dropped an unmarked *ang pow* in their mailbox thick with cash. Mark's absence in her life would always hurt. She didn't know if she would be successful as a business owner. Everything in her life was a gamble right now. And yet, even with her clothes smelling like sweat and milk, the dishes towering in the sink, and less than four hours of sleep per night for the fourth day in a row, Lucie realized that she was happy. "It's everything," she said.

As for romance . . .

Six weeks after Ren's birth, after Ren had mercifully fallen asleep, she cornered Collin outside the nursery.

"Pants off," she said.

"What?"

"Just do it."

He fluttered his obscenely long eyelashes at her. "Aren't you supposed to get cleared by your ob-gyn before any kind of physical activi—?"

"I think I'm good," she said, already out of her clothes (a black sleeveless tank with nursing access, patterned with milk stains, and the leggings that she hadn't changed in two days—the perfect attire for seduction).

"Well, I'm not sure I can actually perform," he said conversationally, his eyes twinkling, as he let her pull his gym clothes off. "I mean, I want to do it; I do. But physically I might be . . . impeded. I haven't slept in days."

But he did. It wasn't a problem.

They were both a little stunned by how good it was, almost eleven months after the first time.

He held her after, her breasts and face leaking gently onto his chest. "Well, that was efficient," he said, kissing her neck.

"Totally utilitarian," she concurred. And then she burst into loud, noisy tears, because that's what she did these days, cry when she was happy. And sad. And when they ran out of pistachio ice cream and nipple cream. "I feel so good now."

He wiped a tear off her cheek. "Clearly."

"Hush, duckie." She cupped his face between her hands and kissed him, long and slow. They laced their fingers and closed their eyes: for now, between the second and third feeds of the day, they had all the time in the world for romance—and possibly a nap.

Acknowledgments

～～～

THE FOLLOWING PEOPLE made this book happen: My agent, Katelyn Detweiler: my gratitude for all your enthusiasm, support, and good cheer. Truly, you are the best. Also Sam Farkas and Denise Page at JGLM.

My thoughtful, meticulous book whisperer of a US editor, Kate Dresser, Tarini Sipahimalani, Elora Weil, Nishtha Patel, Samantha Bryant, Jennifer Eck, and everyone who worked so hard on this at Putnam.

My generous and amazing UK editor, Ore Agbaje-Williams, and the wonderful team at HarperCollins UK, as always.

Elaine and the Trehaus team: there's no better place in Singapore to write and get things done if you're a parent.

The people who spoke with me about a difficult topic, especially S.

Sangwany, your daughter V made an amazing donation in your name to an important cause, and I hope you liked the inclusion.

Many people contributed expertise during the creation of this book: Dr. Jasmine Mohd, Dr. Hua Zen Ling, Dr. Sharon Foo,

Dr. Lynn Koh, Dr. Ying Wei Lum, Ying Ling Lum, Allen Tan, Leong Chuo Ming, Kirsten H (for that incredible donut joke), Helen Rozario, Chris Thong, and Ivan Fatovic. Thank you for your time; any mistakes I made in this book are mine.

My 2020 cohort of author friends and other kind authors who made this journey fun. Special shout-out to the one I had the pleasure of meeting up most with: Balli, my long-lost book twin.

In the past two years, I was lucky to have had acts of kindness from the following people: Kevin Kwan, who was generous with his time and advice; authors Jesse Sutanto, Jayci Lee, Sajni Patel, Madi Sinha, Beth O'Leary, and Ali Hazelwood; Lindsey Kelk, who is so funny and lovely; Malaysians Tengku Zatashah, Carmen Soo, Daphne Iking, Yen@stilettoediva, and Serena C, who championed my book online for a then-unknown Malaysian debut author; Sam See and Wayne Cheong, my comedy friends; Rowan Lawton, who is the kind of agent you'd want in your corner!

SP Katong, especially Chelsea and Nancy.

The booksellers, bookstagrammers/booktokkers, librarians, book critics, and many, many lovely folks who talked up *Last Tang Standing* (even when ARCs were hard to come by), and other reviewers who have been gracious with their time and their support.

The National Arts Council of Singapore, National Library Board, and the Arts House Limited for your support to a resident writer.

My loyal readers, my cheerleaders, thank you for sticking with me; read on!

The Schneider-Wohls and other Hos, as always, thank you for the love and care.

To my closest, oldest friends, Serena and Laura, for listening and taking care of me these last two years.

My parents and my kids: you're still stuck with me, so let's make the best of it—as we do, haha.

Olivier, for your grace, patience, and love for me and the kids, even when we are unlovely.

LUCIE YI
IS *Not*
A ROMANTIC

~~~

Lauren Ho

———

Discussion Guide
Excerpt from *Last Tang Standing*

———

BOOK
ENDS

PUTNAM
—EST. 1838—

Discussion Guide

~~~~~~

1. Lucie and Collin meet on an inventive platform for singles who want to get pregnant. How would you approach such a platform to find your perfect co-parent?
2. What did you think of Lucie and Collin's relationship contract? Do you think rules can lend themselves to great friendships, or impassioned romances? Why or why not?
3. In what ways do you think Lucie's and Collin's varied lifestyles and mismatched upbringings set the tone for their relationship?
4. At what point did you sense something more than platonic blossoming between Lucie and Collin?
5. How do you think Lucie changes over the course of her pregnancy?
6. To what extent is Lucie a romantic? What does it mean to be a romantic?
7. Based on Lucie's descriptions of Singapore, how would you describe the "Singapore experience"?
8. How do you think Lucie's cultural surroundings contribute to her indecision about Mark and Collin?

9. What did you think of Mark's reaction to meeting Lucie again? Do you think he expected to be reunited with Lucie in the near future?

10. What do you think was the main reason Lucie gave Mark a second chance?

11. Suzie admits she's afraid of losing Lucie as a friend once Lucie has a child to focus on. How do you think Suzie and Lucie will navigate their relationship from here?

12. At the end, Lucie decides to leave her job and join Weina's start-up. Do you think it can be risky to work with friends?

13. What kind of parents do you think Lucie and Collin will be?

14. How do you think Collin and his father's relationship will develop over the years? Especially now that Collin will have a family of his own?

15. In this story, friendships, family, and romance are all intricately intermingled. How closely interrelated are these areas in your own life?

Keep reading for an exciting excerpt from
Last Tang Standing, *by Lauren Ho.*

Chapter 1

~~~~~~

Tuesday 9 February

Hope. That's what the Spring Festival, the most important celebration in the traditional Chinese calendar, is supposed to commemorate, aside from signalling, well, the coming of spring. Renewal. A time for new beginnings, fresh starts. Green stuff grows out of the ground. Politicians fulfill their campaign promises, concert tickets for A-list pop stars never get scalped, babies get born and nobody gets urinary incontinence after. And Chinese families all over the world come together in honor of love, peace, and togetherness.

But this is not that kind of story. This is a story where bad things happen to good people. Especially single people. Because here's the deal: for folks like me who find themselves single by February, Spring Festival is not a joyous occasion. It's a time for conjuring up imaginary boyfriends with names like Pete Yang or Anderson Lin, hiring male escorts who look smart instead of hot, marrying the next warm body you find, and if all else fails, having plastic surgery and changing your name so your family can never find you. For desperate times call for desperate measures, and there is no period of time more desperate for single Chinese females over the age of thirty everywhere than the Annual Spinster-Shaming Festival, a.k.a. Chinese New Year.

God help us persecuted singletons; God help us all—spring is coming.

IT WAS NOON. Linda Mei Reyes and I were sitting in a car in front of our aunt's house in matching updos, smoking *kreteks* and hunched over our smartphones as we crammed for the toughest interview that we would face this year, the "Why Are You Still Single in Your Thirties, You Disappointment to Your Ancestors" inquisition. Our interrogators lay in wait, and they were legion. The Tangs, our family, were very prolific breeders.

Each year, as was customary on the second day of Chinese New Year, Auntie Wei Wei would host a lavish luncheon for all the Singapore-based Tangs. These luncheons were mandatory Family Time: everyone had to show their faces if they were in town; the only acceptable escape clauses being death, disability, a job-related trip, or the loss of one's job (in which case you might as well be dead). If you're wondering why Auntie Wei Wei commanded such power, aside from the fact that she was housing our clan's living deity (Grandma Tang), it's because she was our clan's Godfather, minus the snazzy horse head deliveries. Many of the older Tangs were in her debt: not only did she act as the family's unofficial private bank for the favored few, she'd basically raised the lot of them after my grandfather passed away in the 1950s and left my grandmother destitute. As the eldest of a brood of nine siblings, Auntie Wei Wei had dropped out of secondary school and worked two jobs to help defray household expenses.

That's how her siblings all managed to finish their secondary schooling, and for some of the higher achievers, university, even as it came at her own expense.

At least karma had rewarded her sacrifice. After migrating to Singapore in her late twenties, she had married well, against the odds, to a successful businessman; when he died soon after (of entirely natural causes), she'd inherited several tracts of land, the sale of which had made her, and her only daughter, Helen, eye-wateringly wealthy. Hence her unassailable position as de facto matriarch of the Tang clan, since there is nothing that the Chinese respect more than wealth, especially the kind that might potentially trickle downstream. Posthumously.

Ever since I moved to Singapore from London about six years ago, as the sole representative of my father's side of the family in Singapore I'd been obliged by my very persuasive mother to attend Auntie Wei Wei's gatherings. Since my father was her favorite sibling, Auntie Wei Wei had paid off a lot of his debts when he passed and now she basically owns us, emotionally, which is how real power works. I used to enjoy these gatherings, but since Ivan, my long-term partner, and I broke up nine months and twenty-three days ago, way too late for me to find another schmuck to tote to this horror show, there was ample reason to dread today's festivities. Why, you ask? Because Chinese New Year is the worst time to be unattached, bar none. Forget Valentine's Day. I mean, what's the worst that can happen then? Some man-child you've been obsessing over doesn't send you chocolates? Boo-hoo. A frenemy humblebrags about the size of her ugly, overpriced bouquet (that she probably sent herself)? Please. Your fun blind date turns out to be the Zodiac Killer? Tough. Just wait till you have to deal with Older Chinese Relatives. These people understand mental and emotional torture. They will corner you and ask you questions designed to make you want to chug a bottle of anti-freeze right after. Popular ones include: "Why are you still single?"; "How old are you again?"; "What's more important than marriage?"; "Do you know you can't wait forever to have babies, otherwise you are pretty much playing Russian roulette with whatever makes it out of your collapsing birth canal?"; "How much money do you make, after taxes?"

As we've been programmed since birth to kowtow to our elders, we force ourselves to Show (our Best) Face at these events, no matter how damaging they can be to our ego and psyche. So that is why, dear Diary, two successful women in their thirties, dressed in orange floral cheongsams they panic-bought the night before, were trying so hard to get their stories about each other's imaginary boyfriend straight to placate an audience that they will not see again for another year.

"It's easy for mine," Linda was saying. My cousin and best friend, Linda is only half-Chinese (the other half being Spanish-Filipino), so she had some wiggle room with the family, but even the normally cold-blooded litigator was sweating in the air-conditioned car. "Just remember that Alvin Chan, whom you've met before by the way, is not just my boss but my boyfriend, and just, you know, extrapolate from there. Make up the details."

"What do you think I am, an amateur?" I snapped, holding up my iPhone to show her a photo of her and her "boyfriend" at a recent gala. I pulled up a screenshot of Korean actor and national treasure Won Bin—unlike Linda, I did not have a hot boss. "Now *you* remember that my boyfriend's name is Henry Chong, he's a Singaporean Chinese in his late thirties, he's the only child of a real estate mogul and a brilliant brain surgeon, and he looks like this." I held the phone in front of her face so she could be inspired by the perfection that is Won Bin.

"Too many details," Linda said, not even looking at the screen. "It's always the details that trip liars up. Keep it simple."

"Not if you're prepared, like I am. You, however, look wasted."

"I'm prepared. And I'm dead sober," she said emphatically before burping gin fumes in my face. Yet somehow her softly braided updo looked fresh while mine was already unspooling, like my life.

I muttered the Lord's Prayer, or what I could recall of it, under my breath. It was going to be a long day. "Remember, Henry's a partner in a midsize Singaporean law firm. He is currently meeting with a client in Dubai, and that's why he can't be here with us today. Oh, and he's tall. And hot."

"Got it," Linda said, rolling her eyes. She took a deep drag from her third "cigarette" of the morning. "Anything else I should casually drop during the convo? Maybe the fact that he has a massive cock?"

"If you're speaking to one of the older aunties, then yes. Go for it, with my blessings."

Linda sighed, stubbing out her "cigarette" in an ashtray. "Got it. And if anyone asks, Alvin's skiing in Val-d'Isère."

"Val-de-Whut?"

"Val-dee-Zehr. It's in the French Alps, you peasant." She grinned. "Here's another tip: peppering a convo with unpronounceable place names usually deters further lines of questioning. Most people don't like looking unsophisticated."

"Good point," I said. "OK, in that case nix Dubai, make it Ashgabat."

She flashed a thumbs-up. "Ashgabat it is. Anyway, there's a chance that none of the relatives will remember who I am since I've not been back in Asia for over a decade, so I might be safe from attack." Linda's family was somewhat estranged from the clan, one of the reasons being that her mother had married an "outsider," i.e., a non-Chinese; plus, having spent most of her formative years attending boarding school in England meant she was less involved, and less inclined to be so, in clan affairs. That was why she kept a low profile with the Tangs since her move to Singapore last Feburary as part of her firm's new market expansion plan. "I could have skipped this whole do and just stayed home, so remind me why I'm putting myself through this shitshow again?"

"Because you love me?" I said brightly.

She snorted.

I narrowed my eyes. "You owe me, woman. Without the help of my excellent notes and last-minute tutorials you would have failed your final year of law school, since you hardly attended any of the lectures."

"Keep telling yourself that. Anyway, I seem to recall being promised a champagne brunch at the St. Regis if I did well today."

"Yes," I grumbled. "I just hope you put as much effort into Henry's history and character development as I did for Alvin's."

"Don't worry. I didn't graduate top of the class—"

"Second. I was first."

"—*top* of the class for nothing. I've got the whole story down pat. Relax." She punched me in the back. "Straighten your shoulders and try not to look so browbeaten. It's no wonder you haven't been made partner."

It took all my self-control not to stab her in the eye with my cigarette.

Perhaps sensing she was in mortal danger if she didn't change the subject, Linda took out a bottle of Febreze and proceeded to baptize us with it. "Anyway, I have one last piece of advice before we go in."

"What?" I said, between coughs.

She pinched my arm, hard. "Whatever happens in there, do not cry in front of them. Don't give those jerks the satisfaction."

"*You* are hurting me," I yelped, eyes welling with tears.

"I really hope no one gives us *ang paos*," Linda said darkly, oblivious to the suffering of others as usual. "They get extra bitchy when they do. I'd rather they just insult us without feeling like they earned it." She was referring to the red envelopes containing cash that married people traditionally give out to children and other unmarried kin regardless of age or sex during Chinese New Year. For kids it's a great way to get extra pocket money, but getting *ang paos* as an adult in your thirties was a special kind of festive embarrassment, akin to getting caught making out with your first cousin by your grandmother. At least the adult recipient can comfort himself imagining the internal weeping and gnashing of teeth the married *ang pao* giver must undergo as he is forced to hand over his hard-earned cash to another able-bodied adult. In our experience, the intrusive questions and snide put-downs were definitely the giver's way of alleviating the mental agony of this reluctant act.

"Let's not be too hasty," I said, crossing myself in case she had jinxed us. "Last year I made almost six hundred bucks easy, three hundred from Auntie Wei Wei alone."

Two breath mints and liberal spritzes of Annick Goutal later, we were red-eyed and ready to face all the orcs that our family tree could throw at us. Auntie Wei Wei lived in an imposing double-storied bungalow in a quiet, leafy neighborhood in Bukit Timah. The gate and double doors of her home were thrown

wide open with no security guards stationed at the gate, no salivating rabid dogs on patrol, and no military booby traps set up
on the grounds. You could literally just stroll in. Which we did.

In all honesty, the casual indifference of wealthy Singapor-
eans to what I would deem basic precautionary measures and,
quite frankly, the sheer lack of initiative shown by local burglars
never failed to amaze me as a Malaysian. Even *I* could have
picked this place clean with no trouble or special training whatsoever. All I would need is a couple of duffel bags, maybe a sexy
black leotard, a pair of sunglasses, Chanel thigh-high boots, a
French accent . . .

"Are you daydreaming again?" Linda's voice broke my reverie,
in which I was back-flipping over a field of laser beams à la Cat-
woman (circa Michelle Pfeiffer).

"No. Why?"

"You're just standing there, drooling. Get in." She pushed
open the front door, which had been left ajar.

I stifled a sigh of envy as we made our way to the reception
room. Despite it being the umpteenth time I'd stepped into her
home over the years, I was impressed. The mansion, with its
black marble floors, high ceilings, and bespoke wallpaper, whispered of entitlement and the power to buy politicians. Auntie
Wei Wei had had the place decorated in chinoiserie of the high-
est order. It was hard not to gawk at the fine detailing on the
antique porcelain vases and lacquerware, the elegant scrolls of
Chinese calligraphy and ink paintings, or to refrain from touching the dancer–shaped blooms of the rare slipper orchids flowering in their china bowls and the stuffed white peacock, with its
diamond white train of tail feathers, perched on its ivory base in
one corner of the room. All that was missing were some casually
scattered gold bars.

It was apparent that every (official) member of our clan had made the effort to Show Face: man, woman, legitimate children, and domestic help; although it was almost 1:00 p.m., three hours after the gathering had officially begun, the place was still packed with close to fifty people. As per usual with such gatherings, everyone was dressed to the nines with their most impressive bling. You could hardly look around without a Rolex, Omega, or Panerai, real or fake, nearly putting your eye out. Key fobs of luxury cars faux-casually dangled or peeked out from pockets. Most donned red, an auspicious color for the Lunar New Year. Many Tangs were also red in the face from the premium wine and whiskey they were knocking back like there was no tomorrow, courtesy of their host. A free-flow bar can bring out the reluctant alcoholic in any Chinese, Asian flush and stomach ulcers be damned. But for me and Linda, boozing Tangs are not usually the problem: it's the sober ones we had to be wary of, the ones drinking tea as black as their stony hearts, their beady eyes looking for fresh prey. I had vivid memories of being forced to recite the times table or some classical Chinese poem in front of these raptors, their breath bated as they waited for me to make a mistake so they could run and get my parents—that way, we could all be shamed *together*. That's how they get off.

At least the food looked amazing; I would have expected nothing less from Auntie Wei Wei. In one corner of the hall was a long buffet table laden with drool-inducing Chinese New Year delicacies such as whole roasted suckling pig; at least four different types of cold noodles; steamed sea bass; beautifully crispy Peking duck; fried spring rolls; pomelo and plum chicken salad; and *niangao*. On a separate table, the desserts: a huge rose-and-lychee cake flanked by two different types of chocolate cake; assorted glazed mini-cupcakes; macarons the perfect red of cherries;

trays of golden, buttery pineapple tarts; bowls of pistachios, cashew nuts, and peanuts; platters of cut tropical fruit; and bright pyramids of mandarin oranges and peaches. It was too much food, but by the end of the evening everything would be gone. Gluttony, after all, is a Chinese art form and we've had millennia to perfect it.

Over the din of Chinese New Year songs blaring from sleek Bang & Olufsen speakers and drunken chatter, Linda and I looked for Grandma Tang so we could pay our quick respects before joining our single, pariah peers. Linda, being a head taller than my five foot three, scanned the room and found a queue waiting to greet Grandma Tang, who was wearing a crimson batik cheongsam and all the imperial jade in the world. Someone had seated her in a thronelike high-backed chair in one corner of the hall on a makeshift pedestal, where she could peer imperiously (but blindly) down at the crowd. She was so old and wizened that when we got to her and wished her the standard Chinese New Year greeting of a long, prosperous (*never* forget the "prosperous"), and happy life, she grunted in derision, which is the old lady equivalent of "hah!"

I get my sense of humor from her, of course.

After wishing her thus, we waited for a few uncomfortable seconds before realizing, to our growing horror, that she had no intention of giving us elder singletons *ang paos*. And so, to the chorus of jeering children, we made our shamefaced way to the other end of the room, where a herd of our similarly luckless-in-love cousins were huddled together for safety. The swiftest path to them, however, brought us by some sober aunts who were stationed by the bar, simultaneously haranguing and groping a terrified waiter. There was no way we would be able to avoid them.

"Walk fast," I hissed, gripping Linda's right palm in mine so that she wouldn't canter off in the direction of the bottles of Johnnie Walker Black lined up on the bar's countertop. "And don't look around." We pretended to be deep in a discussion, laughing maniacally as we scurried by the aunts, but to no avail. One of the women, deep in her seventies and dressed in an ill-fitting burgundy cheongsam, detached herself from the gaggle of vultures, I mean, aunts, and lurched over, grinning at me. It took me a while to recognize her as she had slathered on a Beijing opera mask of makeup, and by then it was too late. Leering at me was none other than Auntie Kim, the tyrant who used to make me recite the times table in front of all the Tangs when I was a wee preschooler. I say "auntie," but to be honest, even though I see her at every single Tang gathering, I have no idea if she's really my aunt or if she is even related to me. In many parts of Asia, it is perfectly acceptable to call anyone above the age of forty, be they relative or not, "auntie" or "uncle" in lieu of ever learning their actual names—the grocer, the taxi driver, the retired accountant who does your taxes, the local pedophile—anyone. Unless, of course, you are about the same age or older. Then you're just asking for a good old slap in the face.

I scanned the room, looking for an open window, a friendly face, or a hatchet, but there was none. I tried to catch the attention of my unmarried cousins, clustered a few steps away. Two of them waved before averting their eyes. Cowards.

"Andrea Tang Wei Ling,* why so late?" Auntie Kim shouted in Singlish to all and sundry as she scanned me from top to toe,

---

*In Asia, Chinese naming conventions dictate that family name comes first, followed by the given name (consisting of one or two characters), as befitting our collectivist culture. Here, baptismal or English names are written before the Chinese surname + given name, and not as part of the given name. If a Chinese person is calling another Chinese by their full name, you can be sure their intentions are not cuddly.

ignoring Linda (Linda was right: she had effectively been forgotten by our family). "Why you here alone? No one want you issit?" She chuckled. "Aiyah, I just joke only, but maybe also true hor, hahaha!"

Everyone within earshot was smirking. Someone's loser kid chimed in in a singsong voice, "Auntie Andrea doesn't want to get married because she doesn't want to give us *ang pao* because she's stingy!" This outburst was greeted with laughter. The loudest laughs came from my feckless single cousins.

Normally Linda would have left me to die in the proverbial gutter by then, but Linda had KPIs* and she was not one to disappoint. Without hesitation, she shoved me aside and clasped the woman's papery hands in her own. "Auntie Kim, don't you worry about ol' Wei Ling here. She's doing very well. It took some time, but she's finally found herself a man!"

I wished she wouldn't say it with such gusto.

"Really, ah? Who?" Auntie Kim was incredulous.

"Henry Chong. Oh, he's *such* a darling, way too good for Wei Ling, really. Very smart. Very handsome. Very big, er, shoulders."

"Hen-Ree?" Auntie Kim mused, sucking on the vowels like they were her missing teeth. "Hen-Ree where right now?"

"Not here," I said petulantly, my arms crossed to hide my sweating pits.

"Oh, he's always flying here and there, that busy bee," Linda said. "Henry's a partner in a *big* law firm. Very *big*. Two, *three* hundred employees." She leaned close to Auntie Kim and stage-whispered, "He's very, very rich."

"A lawyer?" Auntie Kim exclaimed. "Rich some more . . . good, good. And he is Chinese, right?"

*Key Performance Indicator. Self-explanatory, really.

"He can trace his Chinaman lineage all the way to the first caveman Chong to have carnal knowledge of a woman, Auntie," Linda said, poker-faced.

"Wah?" Auntie Kim's grasp of English was as strong as Britney Spears's vocal range.

Linda tried again. "Henry is one hundred percent Chinese, pure as rice flour."

"Oh, like that, ah, good lor. Make sure you keep this one, Wei Ling, don't let him fly away, can!" said Auntie Kim, mollified. Having received all the information she needed, she handed us each an *ang pao* and lurched away, her ropes of gold chains clanking, this time heading in the direction of my terrified twenty-nine-year-old cousin, Alison Tang, who'd just arrived and was about to slink into a corner. The trooper had worn pink lip gloss and styled her hair in pigtails to appear younger. Alas, Auntie Kim, despite her decrepit condition, was not so easily fooled. "Alee-son! Alee-son! Where are you going? Why nobody with you again? Why—"

"Let's go," I said, dragging Linda past a trio of red-faced men exchanging loud and drunken reminiscences till we reached the singles posse. Our presence was acknowledged, barely; nobody wanted or dared to break eye contact for too long with their phones. Most were legitimately working (*Not even the most important holiday for the Chinese can stop me from slaving for you!* was the subtext they were channeling to their bosses), while some were Facebooking or surfing mindlessly. The most brazen one of all, Gordon, was browsing Grindr profiles. I watched him text-flirt with one guy after another and wished I could do the same and put myself out there in all my mediocre glory.

To my horror I realized, when Gordon started laughing, that I had spoken out loud without meaning to, which tended to happen when I was under stress. "Andrea darling, just do it! It's really easy. Want me to set up a profile for you? On Tinder, of course. Or that hot new location-based app everyone's talking about, which is like Grindr but for straight people. You know the one: Sponk!"

I demurred; Tinder and Sponk heralded the death of romance to me. As if you could reduce the search for the all-important Someone Who Won't Kill You in Your Sleep to a thumb-swiping exercise based (mostly) on photos. And since I had no Photoshop skills to speak of, I didn't stand a chance—everyone knows that you had to have a hot profile photo or at least one where you looked like you hadn't given up in order to get any matches. These days I resembled a slightly melted, sun-bleached garden gnome, no thanks to my punishing schedule at work. Maybe if—

"Why, look who it is, my favorite niece, Andrea!"

I turned and saw Auntie Wei Wei, resplendent in a sunset-orange silk *baju kurung* and dripping in diamonds, striding toward us. My stomach clenched; I knew why Auntie Wei Wei was coming over and it certainly wasn't to praise my sartorial choices or make small talk. She always had an agenda when it came to members of the clan; she stuck her nose in everyone's affairs and gave unsolicited advice or orders, but nobody dared to contradict or stop her.

"I'll pay you five hundred bucks if you come out to Auntie Wei Wei right now," I whispered in desperation to Gordon. When I didn't receive a response, I swiveled my head and saw that Gordon and the gang of smartphone-wielding cravens had somehow migrated to the far side of the drawing room and were all texting as if their lives depended on it.

I turned back around and found myself face-to-face with the

matriarch of the family. Behind me, I heard, rather than saw, Linda sidling away like the traitorous lowlife she was, but alas for her, the gin from earlier in the car was already working its dulling magic.

"Linda Mei Reyes!" Auntie Wei Wei said in her loud, commanding voice. "The prodigal niece herself. Now isn't this a lovely surprise to have you grace us with your presence at long last." She gave Linda a dismissive once-over. "Huh. Still as hipless as a snake. Where have you been hiding all this time? Did your father finally decide to cut the purse strings?"

Linda froze. This was the only chink in her armor—her financial dependence on her father, despite what she proclaimed to the world. "I'm the partner of a law firm and my boyfriend skis in Val-d'Isère," she said weakly to no one.

"Well, good for you, working with Daddy's pals. I'll say this for José—he always took care of his children, which is more than I can say about my sister." She shook her head and tsk-tsked. "As for you, Andrea"—Auntie Wei Wei turned her attention to me; the blood in my veins ran cold—"are you sick? You've lost a lot of weight. I can see right through you." She waggled a finger at me. "You need to fatten up or you'll lose what's left of your figure. Men don't want to marry scrawny women, you know."

I gave her a rictus grin to match my loser, non-childbearing hips. Last year I was too fat, this year I was too thin: Auntie Wei Wei could give Goldilocks a lesson or two. "*Gong xi fa cai*, Auntie Wei Wei. You look well," I said, lying. Auntie Wei Wei looked like she had crossed the Botox Rubicon in the dark.

"It's the exercise and regular facials, you should try some—I can park a Bentley in one of your pores. Anyway, did you come with Linda? What happened to Ivan?"

"I have a *new* boyfriend," I said, after I'd successfully fought the impulse to pluck out Auntie Wei Wei's eyeballs. "His name is, ah, is—"

Auntie Wei Wei cut me off. "If he's a no-show, he's not serious. You youngsters these days." She sighed. "You know you're wasting your best years being a career woman, right? The Tang women tend not to age well, I must say, speaking from a personal standpoint only, of course." She gave me a pointed look.

Don't cry! Distract her! Distract her! "What about Helen, then?" I blurted before I could stop myself. I felt kind of low bringing up her still-single daughter, who was turning thirty-eight this year.

"Oh, haven't you heard?" Auntie Wei Wei's frozen eyebrows gave a heroic spasm of joy. "That's our big announcement this Chinese New Year: Helen's engaged! She's marrying a banker, Magnus Svendsen—isn't that a lovely name? Mag-nus! *So* regal!"

"What?" I squeaked, most eloquently. Helen Tang-Chen, who I knew for a fact to be openly gay to all her contemporaries, was getting married—to a *man*? What sorcery was this?

Auntie Wei Wei couldn't have looked more self-satisfied. "It's a little bit of a whirlwind romance, I must admit, but who am I to stand in the path of true love? We're having the Singaporean reception at Capella in May of next year, just after my big sixtieth birthday bash. That's more than enough time for you, and Linda, to find a date, I'm sure. And maybe"—she gave me another pointed look—"both of you could get a more flattering outfit this time, something less . . . off-the-rack?"

I tried to find my voice but my throat was closing up.

Auntie Wei Wei's tone conveyed the pity her eyes couldn't. "You know, I always thought my daughter would be the last to marry among all the Tang women of your generation, but it looks like that's no longer the case."

A wave of nausea overwhelmed me as the realization broke: for the first time in my life, I would indeed be last at something.

"You TRAITOR," I said for the umpteenth time.

We were sprawled on the couch in Linda's penthouse apartment in River Valley, performing the postmortem on Auntie Wei Wei's party with a little help from a bottle of tequila and a bag of Doritos.

"I had to, Andrea, I had to. You saw what she was like!"

"You *betrayed* me. Just left me alone in hostile territory!"

Linda yawned and stretched. "Oh, quit your histrionics. You would have done the same. Besides, she got her claws in me anyway. I'm still smarting."

"Can you believe she only gave us fifty dollars each as *ang pao*," I said feelingly, "when she was way, way more vicious this time?"

Linda shrugged. Money talk bored her—what excited her was winning. At everything and anything. And status. And designer bags. "I don't get it. When I saw Helen in Mambo last December, she swore to me that she was never, ever getting married until gay marriage was legalized in Singapore. And now she's marrying a man? What gives?"

I was stalking Magnus Svendsen on my smartphone. "Have you seen how hot this Magnus looks in his photo? And it's, like, a photo from an annual report. Nobody is supposed to look hot in those—you can't even openly use filters on LinkedIn." I squinted at the photo. "Look at that face! He's so . . . so . . . *symmetrical*."

Linda glanced at the offensive photo in question and made a face. "Urgh! How unfair. The very least she could have done was take one of the wonky-looking ones off the market. Maybe he's also gay?"

"Does Auntie Wei Wei know that *Helen* is gay?" I asked hopefully. Not that I was planning to throw her under the bus, of course.

Linda rolled her large hazel eyes. "Of course she knows. Don't you know that she once caught Helen messing around with her tutor in their house? But Auntie Wei Wei just pretended like it never happened."

My stomach growled; I had barely eaten at the gathering from all the pretend-texting and one bag of crisps was not enough. "I'm hungry. Pass me the Doritos?"

"We're out of Doritos."

I fell to my knees in mock despair. "Dear God! Can anything else go wrong today?"

"My Netflix is down," Linda added. She checked the bottle. "And we're finally out of tequila."

I curled into a fetal position on the carpet. Clearly this day could get worse.

"Wait." She disappeared and came back with an opened bottle in her hand and a glass. "Here. Have some of this cooking wine. Not sure if it's still good, it's been sitting in the fridge for about three days since Susan made spag bog for me"—Susan was Linda's part-time help—"but you have plebian taste, so."

"Wine is wine." I sat up, ignored the proffered glass, and took a giant swig from the bottle before passing it to Linda, who guzzled half of it after a sniff and a wince. That's what I liked about her: she might look like Harrods on the outside, but on the inside Linda was straight-up T.J. Maxx—hobo without the chic.

She sat cross-legged on the floor next to me. "You know, I heard what that witch said to you. I'm sorry."

"No biggie," I said. "It didn't hurt at all."

She hugged me. "Shh. It's just me here. You don't have to lie."

My lower lip trembled. "It should have been Helen," I said. "She was supposed to be my fail-safe, the Last Tang Standing." Now there would be no one else (older) to share the burden of deflecting criticism on being single from my relatives.

"There, there." She kissed me and let go. "I really don't know why you still go to these things just because they're hosted by family. I wouldn't have."

I had often debated this, too. Linda didn't understand because culturally she was more Westernized than I was. And she really wasn't part of the clan and never had been; having lived most of her life in the Philippines, she had never grown up within this support system. Auntie Wei Wei and the rest had seen my mother and me through when everything had come crashing down on our family, when we found out about my father's cancer and the bills, and when my mother had her own health issues. They were interfering, they were nasty, but they were still family. For all that they had done for me, I had a duty to show up and humor them, at the very least.

You don't run away from family.

"Anyway, you let your family dictate what you should or should not do *way* too often. Is this how you want to live your life? What about what *you* want?"

"What are you talking about? I make my own choices."

"So you say. You've been incepted so hard you can't even tell, or rather you don't want to, what's your decision and what's theirs anymore." Linda began ticking off a laundry list of items. "Let's talk about how you live in Singapore instead of London, like you've always wanted to, just so you can be close to your family."

"It's called sacrificial love, thank you very much."

"Sure, but you don't see your mother more often than when you were living in London, do you? And let's not forget how you're an M&A lawyer when you never gravitated to that during law school. Or how every man you've dated since you moved back home has been the male version of your Ideal Self According to Ma."

"I don't have a type," I protested weakly.

"Whatever you say." Linda yawned and began doing yoga stretches. "Anyway, I'm playing devil's advocate here, but since they're harassing you to settle down and you have no willpower to defy them, why don't you start dating again?"

I glared at her. "I make my own decisions, not my family. Anyhow, the way things are going at work, I don't have time to date, not if I'm going to be the youngest equity partner of Singh, Lowe & Davidson."

"An admirable quest! Hear, hear!" Linda said. She swigged from the bottle of wine. "Here's to us, sexy, independent working women!"

"Well, you're independent until your salary runs out. Then you go running to Daddy."

"Shut up."

I gave her a big kiss on her right cheek. "You know I love you. Thanks for coming today, really. It meant a lot to me."

She shrugged. "You're welcome. Oh, and FYI, I booked us our table at St. Regis for the champagne brunch you owe me." She laughed at my sour expression. "What, did you think La Linda would forget?"

I stared glumly at my lap and shook my head. When it came to collecting debt, the Chinese never forget.

About the Author

© Marvin Kho

Lauren Ho is a reformed legal counsel who now prefers to write for pleasure. Hailing from Malaysia, she is currently based in Singapore, where she's ostensibly working on her next novel while attempting to parent. She is also the author of *Last Tang Standing*.

CONNECT ONLINE

hellolaurenho.com
🐦 hellolaurenho
📷 hellolaurenho
🅕 hellolaurenho